"I don't know why I should frighten you . . ."

A lock of his hair fell across his forehead as he gazed down at her. Dappled in the shadows, he sensed her continued scrutiny. More than he wanted to see was revealed in her velvet dark eyes. "It's not me you're afraid of, is it? It's you. Do I," he asked in a soft, sensual voice, "threaten your narrow, safe little world?"

"Yes!" Denials came too late. Shaking her head in disbelief of her admission, Dara pressed her body tight against the massive pine tree. He stood poised, like a night-summoned predator, dark, sleek, and far too powerful. She felt boneless and lost under his caress. There was an enticing wickedness to his expert touch and voice, and every one of her nerves were alive to them as her breathing became labored . . .

Praise for Theresa DiBenedetto's *Wildflower*:

"A story to treasure."—*Romantic Times*

Silver Mist

Theresa DiBenedetto

CHARTER/DIAMOND BOOKS, NEW YORK

For Joan Hammond, a friend to walk with on life's paths, and for my father, in loving memory.

SILVER MIST

A Charter/Diamond Book / published by arrangement with the author

PRINTING HISTORY
Charter/Diamond edition / December 1990

ISBN: 1-55773-420-8

Charter/Diamond Books are published by The Berkley Publishing Group, 200 Madison Avenue, New York, New York 10016.
The name "CHARTER/DIAMOND" and its logo are trademarks belonging to Charter Communications, Inc.

PRINTED IN THE UNITED STATES OF AMERICA

10 9 8 7 6 5 4 3 2 1

Acknowledgments

I wish to thank Stuart McIver, a Florida historian who makes the past come alive; and Barbara Coulson of the Ocala Public Library and the librarians of the Hallandale Public Library for their help.

Chapter One

"STAY THERE! Not another move or I'll use this on you!"

The breathy feminine order made Eden McQuade pause on the threshold of Rainly's only general store. In reflex, the rifle he held at his side had been cocked and aimed even before the last words were spoken. Tension rode the tall man, backlit by Florida's hot July sun as he stood framed in the doorway.

Predatory instincts alerted, Eden swept his gaze over the shadowed interior of the store. There was no one in sight. Hearing no further sound, he eased his finger from the trigger but held the rifle barrel at thigh level. Eden hadn't expected a welcome in Rainly, but he hadn't thought to be threatened, either.

Furious mutterings reached him from the back of the store. Curious now, he stepped forward, skirting the dry-goods table.

"It's just like Matt not to be around when I need him. Thinks he fooled me, going off to Kelsey's ferry to unload sweet potatoes when I know he went to gossip. The boy's eighteen years old, and I can't get a lick of work out of him."

This last was followed by a screech, sounds of stamping, and then several solid *thwacks*. Eden grinned.

He'd come into town to buy supplies and end six weeks of enforced celibacy; it seemed both his needs might be met at one stop. Southern ladies in distress were well known for their most charming and very warm displays of gratitude. He made his way down the wide off-centered aisle, ducked to avoid the low hung coal-oil fixtures, and smiled upon hearing the rising inflection of the intriguing feminine voice.

"Wait! I see you, you little critter. Oh, no! Not in there. Come out, you fool thing. You'll get hurt if those boxes fall. I should call Reverend Speck to give you his sermon about God's creatures not harming each other. Hah! Provoking . . . varmint! Do you know"—*thwack, thwack*—"what my papa will do when he sees this ruined flour? Blame me, that's what!"

Eden stopped at the open doorway of the storeroom. A quick scan showed the room held a sole occupant, and he set his rifle aside, a rueful smile tugging his lips. At least he hadn't made a fool of himself rushing to aid the slowly straightening figure of a young woman, surrounded by slanting shafts of morning sunlight that poured in through the uncovered back windows. Dust motes danced in the light, and he leaned against the wooden doorjamb with no thought of being discovered, since she appeared deeply vexed by whatever distressed her. He had a partial view of her face, smooth skin, the creamy satin of citrus blooms, a tip-tilted nose on whose bridge perched gilt-rimmed spectacles.

His smile deepened; her clothes were too proper to be true. Schoolmarm variety: pristine white high-necked shirtwaist and a deep blue skirt whose hem was flour-dusted where it brushed the floor. Prim, starched, and proper. It was rather enticing the way the tiny buttons marched up her stiff spine to a slim column of neck above which mink dark hair was neatly braided and thickly coiled. *Charming* was the word that came to his mind as he thought of opening each of those buttons.

She appeared slender. One delicately boned hand, two fingers ink-stained, clutched the broom handle. The other rested on her barely curved hip. She wasn't wearing a bustle. Unconventional, he decided. Hearing her mutter once again about varmints, he scanned the room seeking the cause.

He took a thin black cigar from his pocket, clamped it between his teeth, and struck a match against the doorframe.

Dara Owens gave a startled cry as she spun around with her hand pressed to her throat.

"Oh, gracious! You frightened me. But thank goodness you're here, sir. I need you," she announced to the stranger. Her voice was breathy soft, her eyes dark, wide, and thick-fringed behind her glasses.

And I need you, darlin'. His eyes ranged lazily down to her chest, and the rapid rise and fall of soft lushness revised his first thought. She wasn't too slender at all. His gaze lifted to engage hers as he lit the cigar.

"Will you help me?" Her rounded chin lifted, and she swallowed before meeting the warm pewter eyes framed by thick black lashes.

He glanced around at the cluttered stacks of boxes and piled burlap bags. "I heard you yelling and stomping. What's the problem?"

"I do not yell. Well, maybe a bit. But I was provoked, you see. No one's here to help." The smoke from his cigar spiraled upward as he used his thumb to tilt back the brim of his black, flat-crowned hat. Dara gave herself a mental shake. Why was she staring at him? But then, he was just as guilty of staring at her. "If you'll help me, why, then I'll be ready for you."

"Will you?" Speculation brightened his eyes. *Ah, that charming Southern gratitude*. She tilted her head to one side, peering owlishly up at him, the delicate curve of her brows slightly arched. Yes, indeed. It seemed he was about to have all his needs met with one stop in Rainly. But a scratching noise in the far corner distracted him. "What's that?"

Dara turned around, holding the broom with both hands. "A varmint." She hadn't heard him move, but he repeated his question so close behind her, the words shivered over the back of her neck. "A possum."

His lips hovered over the faint feathering of soft hairs edging her upswept braids. "Well, you won't chase it out with a broom." His liquid, gritty voice was rich with humor. Dara's head shot up and the top slammed his chin.

"Sonofabitchin', jack-witted pea goose!"

Her words of apology died aborning. Dara paled, then spun around, staring at him, abashed that he would dare forget himself so far in the presence of a lady.

"I should take that hard head of yours and tailtuck it permanently," he muttered.

Even her two younger brothers under the influence of Abner Colly's home brew had never made such a colorful and seemingly impossible suggestion of what could be done with her body. Seeing the fury lighting his eyes, she stifled the temptation to use the broom on him.

He rubbed his chin and glared at her. "You made me bite my tongue."

"I was going to apologize. After what you just said, sir, your mouth will benefit from a thorough washing with Cobb's laundry soap. We have a special on the purchase of sixty bars and it's said to be a dirt killer. As for your injured tongue, sir, you know what you can do with it!"

His grin slowly became tantalizing. "Oh, darlin', *I* know, but I wonder if *you* do."

Dara swallowed. She wouldn't look anywhere but at his mouth. She tried to ignore his words, but his lips beckoned with their sensuous fullness. How could a man's mouth be so finely molded and promise so much? When had she ever noticed such a shameful thing before? Heat climbed from her toes, curled up in high-buttoned shoes, to the top of her flushed face. Gathering her courage, she launched her own attack.

"Sir, whatever are you doing sneaking around back here? Whatever it is that you wanted, please come back later. I find your patronage most unwelcome now. If you'll excuse me, I have work to do."

"I thought you needed my help with the little varmint. As for what I wanted, that would depend on what you're offering." He leaned his hip against the stacked boxes, blocking her into the corner.

She didn't want to notice his smile or the neatly clipped sideburns bracketing freshly shaved cheeks that gave way to black hair curling softly against the collar of his gray faded work shirt. Her gaze strayed unwillingly down the lean length of his body. The slightly bent leg holding her prisoner was covered in worn denim. She inhaled to ease the sudden restriction of her lace-edged collar. Slowly shaking her head, bemused and annoyed by her reaction to him, Dara clutched the broom handle tighter.

"Are you always this fearful?" he asked.

"We don't have many strangers coming into Rainly."

"You soon will." His words were a promise, but elicited no response from her.

A slight scuffing noise brought Dara's attention back to the opossum. She was determined to rid herself of this little varmint first and then the larger one softly chuckling behind her amused by her obviously flustered state. Dara elbowed the man aside. She peered down between the stacked boxes but couldn't see where the creature was hidden.

"If you get me an empty burlap sack," he said, "I think we can manage to get it out unharmed."

She wanted to refuse his offer, but she'd lost so much time already. A token protest seemed called for.

"You really shouldn't be back here."

"That's a failing of mine, doing what I shouldn't be." His light gray eyes were amused, his deep voice soft, hinting of unhurried days, as she glanced over her shoulder at him.

"The sack?"

In a huff Dara crossed the room, still holding on to the broom. "Are you sure," she asked, returning with the burlap bag, "that you can get it out unharmed?"

"I've been known to be gentle when the occasion calls for it, darlin'."

"Don't call me that. And do be careful," she warned as he nudged her aside with a gentle push. With both hands folded across the top of the broom handle, she watched the taut play of his shirt as he began stacking the boxes anew. She wasn't standing that far behind him and surprised herself by staring at the leanly curved buttocks brushing her skirt as he bent down to lift aside the last box.

"Get ready," he whispered with the sack in one hand

as he slowly reached down to grab the small gray-furred animal with the other.

"Easy, now . . . Got 'im!"

But the sharp-clawed little animal who played dead while trapped now darted forward, and Eden yelled for Dara to catch it. When she swung the broom in reflex, it landed with a solid *thwack* across Eden's buttocks, thrusting him forward into the hastily stacked boxes.

"Damn fool woman! What the hell are you doing?"

Dara turned scarlet. Her ears felt blistered as his swearing continued.

Eden moved so fast, she lost her breath. Coming up and around, he grabbed the broom and Dara along with it to jerk her hard against him. Her reading glasses slipped down the bridge of her nose, blurring the sight of his face for a moment before she pushed them back into place. The glasses were not necessary for her to see him, she only wore them in the dimly lit store, but now she felt they offered some protection from his glowering look.

Eden was vaguely aware of the scampering sounds of the opossum scooting out the door. His head throbbed from hitting the box, but his arms were filled with lush femininity, warm, sweetly scented, and as rigid as the corset confining her. He lowered his head, one hand blindly reaching out to ease her deathgrip on the broom handle. Dara released her hold the same moment he did. It fell to the floorboards with a clatter, raising flour dust to choke them. She pushed against his chest, coughing, and from the front of the store heard her name being called.

With a shove, Dara was free, gone in a swirling flutter of skirt and lace-edged petticoats, leaving Eden to combat additional clouds of dust. Eden's coughing turned to chuckles. He had certainly underestimated the lady. Either she was a natural disaster waiting to happen upon some unwary soul, or he'd lost the charm that never left his bed empty. With a most rueful shake of his head, he began brushing off the light coating of flour clinging to his clothes.

Dara was doing the same to her skirt as she hurried down the aisle, her warm smile faltering when she realized who had called her. "Jake, I thought you would be at the train station."

"Luther said Anne's train won't be in for at least an hour." He turned around to face her and frowned. "What happened to you?"

"Oh, nothing. I ran into a varmint in the storeroom. Matt forgot to latch the back door last night, and we lost a one-hundred-pound sack of flour. Thank goodness Papa didn't see it when he left this morning." Standing beside him, Dara smiled brightly, wondering why she didn't tell him about the man back there. But then, Jake could be overprotective at times, since she was his wife Anne's best friend. And she certainly didn't want him to confront the stranger in her store and give anyone food for gossip. Reassuring him with a pat of her hand, she said, "Don't worry so. I managed quite nicely to prove there's no easy pickings here."

"You're sure you're all right?"

"Quite. Don't fuss. Now, what can I get for you?"

"I thought I'd surprise Anne with one of those fancy tins of tea you were unpacking yesterday."

There wasn't anything unusual in his request, but then Dara stepped back and noticed what he was wearing. "A gun, Jake? Why? Were you thinking a gift would bribe Anne into dismissing the fact of you wearing it?"

Knowing Dara's aversion to guns, he tried to brush off

her questions with one of his own. "Whose wagon's outside? I don't recall ever seeing it before."

"Most likely someone came in while I was in back and didn't find what they were looking for and left. Maybe they went to the bank."

"Where's Matt?"

"Down at Kelsey's. You know everyone is talking about the news."

Jake's expression became grim. Running his large-boned hand through a thick stock of lightly silvered brown hair, Jake leaned over the counter. "Now you understand why I'm wearing a gun, Dara. And you shouldn't be alone in the store. No telling who might start drifting into town. I saw your pa this morning heading out to your brother Pierce's farm with a load of supplies and warned him, but he was sure Matt would stay with you."

"Jake, what are you worried about? This is the same town it's always been. Nothing happens here. Nothing that would cause you to wear a gun. Goodness, Jake, when was the last time you arrested anyone? And if you had to, there's no jail to put them in. I thought as justice of the peace, your job was to *avoid* trouble, not to encourage it. And Anne will be upset seeing you wear a gun again. In her . . . well, her delicate condition . . ." Blushing, Dara paused and lowered her head. It was unseemly for an unmarried woman to mention such matters to a man.

"Dara. I know all that, but I can't forget what I was," he stated with the cool authority that marked every move of his sinewy body. "I'm aware of how my wife and most of the townsfolk try to forget my reputation, but I can't be caught unprepared. I won't run."

"Are you so sure there will be violence if these men

come here?" Dara shivered, glancing back down the aisle, knowing she hadn't heard the stranger leave the store. Was he standing back there, listening to them? And if he was, could he be the type of man Jake feared would be causing trouble?

"You've never seen what a mining boomtown's like. I wish to God I didn't know, but I do. I don't want to see Rainly destroyed, but since the *Gazetteer* blasted the news of Albertus Vogt's discovery of phosphate in Florida, I'd bet before the week is out there'll be men swamping this town till they outnumber us. You just don't understand," he finished in a bleak voice. Stepping aside, he reached for a tin of tea from beside the coffee grinder. "Put this on my account, Dara, and understand that I'm not going looking for trouble, but folks 'round here made me welcome, they respected me, and I married one of their own. Rainly isn't going to be one of those wide-open Western towns. We have law here, and I'll just be doing my job to see it stays that way."

"And you need a gun to do it?"

"Dara, you're as innocent as Anne about what—"

"Stop talking to me as if I were a child. I resent it."

"I didn't mean to insult you." His sigh bespoke his impatience. "What I should do is talk to my thick-headed brother-in-law about marrying you. I know," he said, holding both hands aloft, "Clay's got his reasons and you've got yours. I ain't prying, but you two should be married and soon. Failing that, I'll make sure Matt understands that he is to stay in the store with you."

"If you're trying to frighten me, you're succeeding."

"Good." His narrow-eyed stare was directed toward the back of the store. "If you're warned, Dara, you'll be careful. Varmints come in all shapes and sizes."

"Gracious! You're making all this sound like those

dime novels Matt reads. People in Rainly have more than a six-shooter mentality. The most exciting thing that's happened in the last year was when Elvira Dinn forbade Miss Loretta from attending the ladies' box lunch social for shooting the drummer when he climbed into the window of her private parlor. Poor Miss Loretta," she said, trying not to smile. "She was absolutely mortified that the man was intoxicated and tore her new lace curtains. But then, too, Elvira had no right to say Miss Loretta shot that man to keep him inside. Anyway, everyone knows she's sweet on Luther."

"Sweet she may be, but Luther's worried about who she'll be letting into her boarding house. We all know there hadn't been enough business here to keep body and soul together for her. But Luther'll watch out for Miss Loretta. You watch out for yourself."

By the time Jake left, Dara had quite forgotten the stranger in her storeroom. She was shocked by what Jake implied. Rainly had no crime. Men didn't wear guns. They had no violence here.

"You should heed Jake's warnings."

Startled, Dara looked up. The stranger was standing right inside the counter, bold as the brass spittoon by his scuffed boots.

"You know Jake Vario?" She paled at the thought.

"No man ever really knows another."

"That's not an answer." With a wrinkled nose, she stared pointedly at the lit cigar he raised to his mouth. "You shouldn't be smoking in here," she primly informed him, backing away from him until she was able to sit on the high stool. Gracious, but he was certainly tall!

"I told you, it's a failing of mine"—he met her inquiring gaze with a grin—"doing what I shouldn't."

"I agree. It is a failing. You should see Reverend Speck about it. I'm sure he could help you. The church is one mile out of town, past the train station. You won't be able to miss it."

"Are you always this rude to customers? Seems a mighty poor way of doing business, and there doesn't seem to be much to the town." He leaned against the counter, blocking her exit, taking a drag of his cigar.

His critical tone brought a cool note to hers. "We have everything we need."

"Do you, now?"

"Yes." Her chin jutted forward as if daring him to dispute it.

"Somehow, darlin', I doubt that *you* do."

Hectic color spread across her cheekbones. Dara firmly settled her glasses in place.

"Do you need to wear those?"

"Pardon?"

"The spectacles. Must you wear them?"

"In the store I do," Dara replied. "The light isn't the best to read the tiny catalog print and sometimes the labels . . . oh, gracious, why should I bother to explain to you."

"You were being polite," he suggested helpfully.

"If you continue, you will make that act difficult for me."

He didn't answer, merely nodded, satisfied that she was becoming flustered.

While it wasn't unusual for her to be alone in the store her family owned, she wished she had let Jake know this man was here. She wasn't frightened of him harming her, but he was certainly testing her will to remain unruffled in the face of his provocative sparring. Besides, there was a solidness to his lean build as he stood blocking the only way out from behind the counter that she refused to challenge.

"I have work to do," she announced in dismissal, pulling the J. L. Mott plumbing catalog toward her and opening it blindly.

"A porcelain-lined French bath?" he read over her shoulder. "Why, darlin', we share an inclination toward anything French." Over her spate of furious sputtering, he read, "Comes with 'Supply Fittings and Unique Waste and Overflow, and the Cocks are of the Improved Pattern with Ebony Handles.' My goodness," he continued, " 'the Supply Valves are the best-known form of compression, durable and easy in movement. To empty: the Stand Pipe is raised and turned slightly to the right or left; a still further turn will permit the Stand Pipe . . .' " He stopped suddenly, covered the page with one spread hand, and inquired, "Does anyone know what you read when you're alone?"

Mortified, Dara could only stare at him. She didn't want to understand the direction his thoughts had taken, but his tantalizing grin plus the laughter in his eyes refused to let her deny it.

"Oh, dear Lord," she whispered as he straightened to return to his imprisoning post. Her unwilling gaze strayed down his body and remained there.

"Now, as to what I want." The pause was deliberate. He wanted her to look up at his face. She provoked him with her curious and innocent gaze lingering on the jut of his narrow flanked hip and the uncomfortable tightening fit of his buttoned fly. There was no way he could hide the semihard state of his arousal. But then, he never had to. Eden knew himself to be a man finely attuned to his senses, and right now they were filled with warm, sweetly scented woman. He hadn't denied himself anything he desired for more years than he sometimes cared to remember. He wasn't about to start now.

"I'd be glad to shuck down so you could satisfy both our risin' curiosities, darlin', but first," he drawled, "I'd suggest you lock the doors. I'm not in a mood to be rushed."

Gasping, Dara blinked, her spectacles slipping down her nose. She couldn't have heard him correctly. "I beg your pardon?"

"You have my pardon." His glance held her in predatory thrall. "And anything else of mine you'd like."

Affronted by his words and manner, Dara clenched her teeth. "If you have come here to buy something, I'd suggest you go . . . go find it."

"And if I already found what I want?" he asked with a voice rich in humor.

"Everything we have for sale is clearly marked. Leave your money on the counter."

He withdrew the cigar from between his lips and gazed thoughtfully at it for a moment before beginning an insolent but thorough inspection from her slightly mussed braids down to the tips of her shoes peeking out from beneath her skirt. "No," he stated with a rueful shake of his head, "not everything is clearly priced. And telling strangers to leave their money on the counter makes you a trusting little thing."

"No. I'm not a trusting little thing." Her eyes targeted to his. It was the sinful promise that held her. Black feathered brows arched arrogantly above those eyes framed by thickly curled lashes. The stormy gray irises were mates for the clouds preceding a wild windstorm. Dangerous eyes, teasing her to know if the hints of lightning and thunder were the sources of heat she felt touch her.

"Reconsider, darlin'? I know you could satisfy me without too much trouble."

"I doubt that." Dara straightened her spine. She had never faced such bold candor in all her twenty-two years. "I think you'd better leave. I find your manner contemptible."

"Darlin', I'm all for accommodatin' a lady, but it isn't my manner you're staring at." Ignoring the choking noise she made, he pulled a piece of paper from his breast pocket. "Here's a list of supplies I need."

Dara grabbed it from his hand. "The shovels, picks, and steel rods are all hanging on the right front wall inside the doorway. If you load them first, you can bring your wagon—I assume that's your wagon out front—around to the back door to load your foodstuffs. I'll total your purchases. And that, Mr.—"

"Silver'll do, and my pardon for the oversight of not introducing myself." He fixed his hat on his head with the brim slanted forward and stepped out from behind the counter.

Dara couldn't help herself. She called out to his retreating figure, "What kind of a name is that?"

"Just a handle folks hang on a man."

The floorboards creaked as he reached the front of the store. Dara found a rich curiosity urged her to ask, "Didn't you have parents to give you a good Christian name?"

"Sure. Didn't yours?"

"Of course they did." But she wasn't about to volunteer it. The man had taken enough liberties as it was. She glanced back to his list, checking off the items and tallying them as he set the tools in the open doorway. "We don't stock chocolate candy," she called out to him. "The heat would spoil it. We do have a fine selection of hard candies." He had been walking back toward her and stopped. Looking from her mouth to the colorful assortment of glass jars lining a shelf behind where she primly sat and watched him, he frowned.

"That's all?" He moved to the counter, leaning over it. "Cravings," he informed her with a serious note, "can be the undoing of a man if he doesn't make an effort to satisfy them."

"Has anyone ever informed you that you can be the devil's own provoking—"

"I've been told and stopped apologizing for it a long time ago. I guess I'll settle for some rock candy."

Dara stood up, nudging the stool aside with her hip. "How much did you want?"

"More'n a mouthful," he answered with perfect seriousness.

Her hands shook as she filled a large paper square with the crystal hard candy. After twisting it closed with a vicious yank, she weighed it on the scale using the smallest of the brass counterweights.

"I've already stacked two sacks of flour, one of cornmeal, and one of coffee by the back door. I'll take a barrel of pickled beef for now, but I couldn't find the sugar loafs."

She merely nodded, setting the candy down in front of him. Reaching beneath the counter, she tore off a piece of brown wrapping paper and lifted a ball of twine. From the lowest shelf she opened a tin and removed two sugarloafs. "Will that be enough?" she asked, looking into his face. He was no stranger to the sun, but a farmer he was not. With the amount of supplies he was buying, she couldn't dismiss him as a drifter. That left him to be one of those men the newspaper reporters had called "adventurers" coming here to look for the newly discovered "white gold."

"I'll need to open an account. I don't know how often I'll get into town for supplies. Would—"

"See my father." She busied herself with itemizing his purchases.

"Owens? Like the name on the sign outside?"

"That's right."

"As in Miss or Mrs.?"

Dara looked up. "I consider that a personal question." All the starch she normally used in her linens went into her voice. "I charged one dollar a piece for the shovels," she began, shoving the totaled list in front of him. "And sixty cents—"

"Just tell me the total. I trust you not to cheat me, darlin'."

"Stop calling me that!"

"Sure enough, but I'll caution you to charge more for the tools. Your stock will be gone before you know it. Wouldn't surprise me none to hear that some enterprising vulture bought it up to resell at a higher profit."

"That would be unfair and cheating!"

"Jake was right. You are an innocent. And you didn't believe him, did you? Well, that's only one of the changes about to happen to Rainly. And that, Miss Owens," he stated with a studied look at her ringless fingers, "you can take to bed with you as gospel."

"What I take to bed or not isn't any of your business!" Horrified to hear herself yelling, Dara backed down. Anyone could come into the store and overhear them. Gossip spread faster than butter on hot corn pone, and she had been the object of it once too often. Chastising herself didn't help the itch in her palm to feel itself meet his cheek. "Stop staring at me."

"Guilty as charged, but hasn't any man ever had the sense to tell you you've only yourself to blame?"

She refused to answer. "Please pay your bill and leave." Her hand was small, palm and slender fingers cupped to receive the gold coins he counted out and then dropped one by one into her hand.

He gathered up the paper twist of candy and put it in his pocket, his steady gaze never leaving her face. "Are you going to run?"

Clutching the money, Dara glanced back at him. "I never gave it a thought."

"Didn't you?" He had to give the lady her due; she had pride, even if he was tempted to goad her further. "What's the best time to meet your father?"

"Meet my father?"

"To open my account, darlin'. I assure you my intentions are not honorable."

"Unfortunately, I cannot doubt that. He'll be here on Thursday."

"I'll be back. I promise."

Dara sank onto the stool as he flipped the brim of his hat with a jaunty wave and headed toward the back door. Shaken, she rested her head against her folded arms on the counter. Whatever had possessed her to engage in verbal sparring with a perfect stranger! Resentment swelled inside her. This was Clay Wescott's fault for waiting to marry her. He had more excuses than J. L. Mott had plumbing fixtures in his catalog. But that only reminded her of what had just happened.

"French bathtub, indeed! Why, that man made everything sound positively indecent." Her head snapped up. "Jake was right," she whispered. "Varmints certainly do come in all shapes and sizes. Good riddance to both of them."

Her thought was almost echoed by Eden McQuade as he loaded his wagon. He had the supplies he'd come for, but the problem of his celibacy remained. Rainly didn't boast a saloon, which meant there was a decided lack of available females. It wouldn't last long, but . . . the sudden remembrance of the overheard conversation the prim Miss Owens had with Jake Vario made his eyes bright. There was a boardinghouse in town, and he was sure to find a hot bath, maybe a little decent brandy, and a willing female to scrub his back. The Miss Loretta they discussed certainly sounded like she wasn't adverse to men.

He rolled the barrel of beef onto the flatbed of the wagon, straining to lift its heavy weight, and glanced back toward the store. Lord help him. When had he been so enthralled by a woman's mouth? He tied the barrel into place, venting some of his frustration on securing the rope to the low-sided wagon. Then he paused and pulled the candy out of his pocket, twisting open the paper. His thumb edged the rough sweets, thinking how soft her lips would be if he rubbed them just so, and her eyes . . . such sweet provoking innocence.

Ruefully he shook his head. He'd just been too long without a woman. He settled a small piece of candy between his lips. His mouth was filled with coolness, then a burst of sugared sweetness. He climbed onto the seat, urging his team of horses around. Did that fool woman know she whispered with her eyes to touch? More'n likely she was as straitlaced as her corset. She probably deserved the man Jake claimed was his brother-in-law. Jake married? He didn't want to think about Jake at all. Finding him here did not fit in with his plans. Five years could be a long time in some men's memories, but then, he and Jake hadn't parted on the best of terms.

Guiding the horses to enter the main street, Eden looked over the empty platted lots.

Rainly seemed to hold a few surprises, maybe a challenge or two. The blasting whistle of the incoming train split the air as he headed toward the livery. He thought about the men who would swarm into the town, men hungry and greedy to grab the claims that promised riches. Eden knew better. He'd mined silver from Mexico to Nevada before he had discovered phosphate on land he owned far south of Rainly. He knew mining to be hard, dirty work few men had the courage or drive to stick with until mining paid off. It was the violence that went hand in hand with greed that he hated, even if he wasn't a stranger to it. Jake had the right of it; trouble was coming. But then neither he nor Jake was a stranger to trouble. They'd handled their share, except when there was a woman involved.

Eden passed the two-story clapboard house surrounded by a neat white picket fence. A small elegantly lettered sign proclaimed that boarders were welcome. Built on the corner of Illinois Street, the house was shaded by towering oaks festooned with Spanish moss that dappled wicker furniture on the wide wraparound veranda. Not a breeze stirred the air, and not one person was abroad as he urged his team at a walk down the main Charleston Street. He could see the weathered roof of the livery now.

It was a shame, he mused, what would happen to this farm town. But then, phosphate was as valuable to the expanding nation as gold. Industrialization spurred a migration to the cities that caused farmers to deplete the mineral resources of their land in an effort to meet the increasing demand for food. Chemical fertilizers including phosphate were desperately needed. The reporters had the right of it to call the mineral "white gold." He wished for more time before the news leaked out, but Albertus Vogt and his partners had kept their discovery hidden as long as they could while they bought up twelve thousand acres of farmland in and around Rainly for pittance money.

With the railroads slicing the distance between the oceans, and the telegraph opening communications, many of the cities were growing at too rapid a rate. Some of the cities boasted the newly invented telephone and electric lights, although he knew they kept the old gas jets on standby. Progress wasn't about to be stopped, and Eden would be a fool to think it could. And who was he to blame any man for thinking he'd join ranks with the likes of Jim Fisk, Jay Gould, or Commodore Vanderbilt? They were only a few of the proclaimed self-made millionaires some called "robber barons."

Power and money were the laws in the new age of the land. And for a man better known in Western mining circles as Silver, his smile was deeply satisfied. His place was richly secured in the coming scheme of things.

He might have amended that thought if he'd been at the train station.

Chapter Two

JAKE VARIO KEPT pace with the slowing passenger cars of the train. He searched each dust-glazed window for a sign of his wife, then smiled when he saw her waving to him. The train agent was already swinging down a set of steps as Jake came to a sudden stop before them. But then Jake's smile faded and his eyes narrowed. Tension gripped him when he met the amused gaze of the man who alighted first. He backed away, not in fear, but to give himself room. Jake's right hand unconsciously released the rawhide thong of his gun holster.

With a smooth gesture, the man spread open his jacket. "There is no need, *amigo*," he stated with quiet emphasis. "As you see, I am not armed." He paused, then added after an exaggerated smile, "Many of us wondered where you had disappeared to."

"Did you, *amigo*?" There was a sarcastic harshness to Jake's words, a deadly coldness in his eyes. His hand remained hovering over his gun. "Did you come to pick a few bones clean, Lucio?"

"The years have not changed you, I see. But you are unfair to accuse me of this." Slowly, so that there was no mistaking his intent, he removed his square-crowned hat to fan himself. "This place has the heat of my country. It is good to be where it is warm again."

Jake didn't answer. He studied Lucio's face. The deep-tanned skin owed its color to heritage rather than the sun, as did ebony hair, slicked back and away from strongly molded features. Jake's eyes tracked the flash of a large diamond pinkie ring as Lucio's hand first smoothed the narrow slash of his mustache, then flicked a bit of lint from the silk and worsted suit lapel.

"Still wearing the ring?"

"Always." Lucio's smile never reached his dark eyes. He replaced the hat on his head. "And you are still too wary, *hombre*. But there is no need for this hostility between us," he assured Jake, pulling a large diamond-encrusted watchcase from his heavily embroidered vest pocket. He didn't open the case, but tilted it so Jake could see what else he held.

It wasn't the watch Jake was meant to see; it was the three silver nuggets attached to the chain, and he refused to react to the deliberate goad.

"You're blocking the way for the other passengers, Lucio."

"It was not my intent." Lucio stepped aside, his gaze level with Jake's. "You come to meet someone?"

Once more Jake didn't answer. He studied each passenger stepping down. Some he nodded to. A few of the men he noted were strangers, and these he scrutinized closely, including two he decided he would keep an eye on. When the petite blue-suited figure of his young wife descended the steps, he had to force himself forward, unable to smile or match the joy of her sparkling blue eyes as she hurried to his side. Jake returned her quick hug, but over her shoulder, his gaze remained fixed upon Lucio.

"Your luck still holds, *amigo*. I had the pleasure of

meeting the lovely *señorita* when she boarded the train at Ocala."

Anne lifted her head from Jake's chest, gazing up at him. Her husband wasn't paying attention to her. He was glaring at the other man.

"The *lady* is my wife. Take a good look, Lucio, so you never mistake her for someone else, or this time I'll kill you." He ignored Anne's cry. The promise he made was in a flat, hard voice that threatened the same violence as did his taut stance. No emotion flickered in his eyes, and for a moment he thought Lucio would refuse his order. But the man turned, his look thoughtful upon Anne's oval face. There was both delicacy and strength in the features framed by upswept blond hair and a simply styled feathered and veiled hat.

Anne was bewildered by the tension between the two men. Her gloved hands tightened around Jake's waist, ignoring the gun he wore. She saw nothing violent about the hawk-faced man her husband just threatened. Anne gazed at Jake's face. She knew his past, and now, now she confronted all her unspoken fears. Despite Jake's reassurances that it would never happen, it appeared his past had caught up with him. His gentle strength, his loving ways, had convinced her to set fear aside and marry him over her brother's objections. Until now she hadn't once regretted her decision. She felt chilled despite the heat, her hand falling between their bodies to touch the full drape of her bustled skirt. She wanted to withdraw from Jake's arms, to withdraw from the stranger he had become in these last minutes, a stranger capable of violence. But Anne had been schooled to be a lady. The lessons served to hide her feelings.

With his arm protectively hugging Anne's shoulders, Jake asked, "Any more questions, Lucio?"

"*Nada*," came his cold response.

"That's good. See you remember that, *amigo*, if you decide to stay in *my* town."

Lucio made a leisurely but mocking inspection of Jake's double-breasted work shirt, worn brown cord pants, and boots. "*Your* town?"

"Mine."

"The years have not been good enough for you to make such a claim, Jake."

Jake threw back his head and laughed. The chilling rippled sounds made several men milling about the platform turn to stare at him. "I'm the law here, *amigo*. All there is. And the years have been very good to me, Lucio. I can walk here without watching my back among these friends." Without another look he urged Anne to walk away.

Lucio Suarez thoughtfully stared after their retreating figures. His fine sole-leather trunk was set down beside him on the wooden platform along with two matching smaller bags. A ready and generous tip was handed over to the conductor. Lucio could afford to be generous. He had plans for Rainly.

"*Señor*, there is a place to store my luggage until I have need of it?"

"I'll put 'em right inside the ticket agent's office for you, sir."

"And where may I find good lodgings and a decent piece of horseflesh?"

"Cross the street. Boardinghouse's on Illinois. Can't miss it. Only place that takes in borders. And Early Yarwood over at the corner livery is the man to see for a prime-blooded bit of stock. Early's from Virginie."

"Can you direct me also to the land office?"

"Ain't got one." The agent glanced up to see if the

train's water tank was filled, then looked back at Lucio.

"I have need of information," Lucio prompted, another gold coin appearing between two smooth long fingers.

"Ain't my town, but I'll oblige with what I can." He pocketed the coin quickly. "'Course, if you really wanted to know things, you should be talking to Luther Marlow. He's the ticket agent and postmaster here. Knows everyone."

"I am most interested in a man who comes here as I do, a stranger." Lucio smiled. "You would not forget him, I assure you, if you saw him or heard his name."

"Got a passel of strangers coming here in the last few weeks. Suppose there'll be more." He wiped his brow with a crumpled bandanna he pulled from his pocket. "What's the fella done?"

"A matter of a debt owed, nothing more. He is tall and lean, his hair as dark as my own, but his eyes are light, the same as his name—Silver."

"And that's all I heard, Dara. Jake was ready to take him on right there."

"Was Anne all right?" Dara glanced at her younger brother, Matt, as she finished drying their supper dishes. His affirmative nod prompted a sigh of relief before she asked, "Did this man stay in town?"

"He took a room over at Miss Loretta's and rented a horse from Early. Rode out along the Rainbow, west toward Amos's farm."

"I wonder what he'd want with Amos?" Dara folded the damp linen cloth and set it down on the counter. "Matt, do you think Jake is right, that there'll be trouble because of these men coming here to mine?"

"Kelsey thinks so. I don't know yet. Say, Dara, will

you be all right alone if I go out for a while?" His lanky frame was halfway out the back door when she looked up. "C'mon, Dara."

"Where are you planning to go, Matt? You know Papa doesn't like you down at Kelsey's at night."

"Can't you answer me without a lecture? I'm not a boy anymore. And who said I was going to Kelsey's?"

"Well, pardon me!" She smoothed down the sleeves of her shirtwaist, already sorry for her outburst. Lately they had been at each other like a pair of alligator turtles. And everyone knew how vicious those creatures could be with their evil beaks ready to make mincemeat out of the hands of the unwary, even if some folks hereabouts thought they were good eating. Matt's restlessness added to her own hidden discontent. She'd spent the last ten years raising him; he couldn't expect her to stop worrying about him because he thought himself a man.

"Dara?" he softly coaxed.

She went to his side, resting one hand on his finely muscled arm. "Matt, I'm sorry. I know it's hard for you with Papa and Pierce not understanding what plagues you. I don't understand you myself at times. You act like you have the green-apple nasties, but I'll try to curb my worrying over you."

He grinned with no trace of his former animosity reflected in his amber-colored eyes. "What you need," he said, tapping the tip of her nose with one finger," is a husband and children to mother."

"Would you like to tell that to Clay? Oh, forget I said that. It's not all his fault." She sighed, leaning her head against his shoulder at his urging. "I guess I have a little of the same restlessness plaguing me. I'm worried about Anne and Jake, too. She married him believing his past would never follow him here. And while no one could ever doubt his gentleness, even I was frightened to see him wearing a gun today. Now you tell me there's a man in town that Jake threatened to kill. If Clay finds out, he'll be furious." Dara felt a bit guilty not telling Matt about the man she had met called Silver, who also seemed to know Jake.

"We can't worry about it. Clay won't like you interfering again." He gave her shoulders a gentle squeeze. "Besides, Jake can take care of himself. Now can I leave?"

Searching his face, so much like their father's, Dara decided to back down. "Are you going sparking?" she teased. "Is that what has you so distracted these last few weeks?"

"Maybe," he answered, without committing himself.

"I've seen the way you look at Roselee Kinnel at service, Matt, and so has half the town. Well, never let it be said that I stood in the way of love." Dara held his hand before he moved away. "Just be careful. I'm sure more than one stranger came into town today, and the Kinnel farm is nearly a mile out. You . . ." She stopped herself from saying more. Matt's face had that closed look that meant he wasn't listening. "Go on, but not too late. We have boxes to unpack tomorrow."

Matt nodded and Dara watched him cross the back wooded lot of their land which sloped down toward the Withlacoochee River. She turned and looked with satisfaction around the kitchen of the clapboard house she had been born in. All was as neatly ordered as her life. She took a moment to lower the flame in the coal-oil fixture hanging over the large square oak table, and then she, too, left the house.

A walk by the river would fill the lonely hours until it was time for bed. And perhaps, she thought, the night's tranquility would help her forget the disquiet of remembering the stranger whose eyes would not let her forget his name. She resolved not to encourage him should he come into the store again, but Dara had a feeling his boldness would make this vow difficult to keep. It didn't help to remind herself that she shouldn't be thinking about any man. She was promised to marry Clay Wescott. But instead of bringing comfort, the thought stirred a bitter discontent within her. And it was only now, when she was alone, that Dara would cry for all the wasted years of waiting.

Dara was annoyed by the way Matt disappeared right after breakfast the next morning. She washed clothes, hung them out in the already white heat of the sun, and, fuming, returned to the house. Wednesday was her weekly baking day, and now she had to open the store.

Carrying a large pottery bowl filled with the fresh eggs Matt must have picked up from Varina Kinnel, she propped open the back door, hoping a cool breeze would come up from the river. After setting the bowl on the counter, she hurried to open the front doors, using a matching set of cast-iron bulldogs to keep them in place.

Glancing up, she was surprised to see Jesse Halput, owner of the sawmill, bringing a loaded wagon of cut lumber down Williams Street. He bypassed the bank and continued toward her, pulling into the empty lot next to the store. Curious, Dara stepped out onto the wooden porch and walked down its shaded length.

"Mawnin', Miz Dara," Jesse said.

"Jesse." She nodded. Indicating the wagon, she asked, "We didn't order any lumber. Or is someone planning to build here? I didn't know the lot had been sold."

" 'Pears so. This one an' a few more. Recall 'bout two years ago that Withlacoochee and Wekiwa Lan' Company was toutin' Rainly bein' paradise?"

"Certainly. But Jesse, everyone knows nothing came of it. They had all those fancy brochures made up and rented land offices up north, but only a few people bought farms around here, and poor Miss Loretta lost her money."

"So most folks figured."

She watched him wrap the thick leather reins around the pole break. But the way Jesse sat, fingering his gray scrub beard, she could tell he was thinking about what he wanted to say. She followed his thoughtful gaze down the center of Charleston Street. Since it was the town's main avenue, it was one of the two widened and timber-cleared ones. Williams was the second, where Jesse's sawmill and home were situated. The rest of the town's platted streets were really wagon-wide lanes leading to the few other homes and businesses in town. It crossed Dara's mind that the man called Silver had been right in his callous assessment of Rainly. There wasn't much to the town. The admission rankled.

Gesturing with one raw-boned, scarred hand, Jesse finally said, "Man come by yesterday, ordered enough cut boards to burn my blades and build on the empty lots from heah to the cornah."

Dara's eyes widened behind her glasses. "Why, he could have five, maybe even six stores clear down to Illinois Street, depending on what he intended to build."

"That's 'bout what I figure. He asked 'bout hirin' mah three boys to do the buildin'."

Hiding her annoyance with Jesse's way of dragging out whatever he knew, Dara moved to the very edge of the porch. Jesse leaped down from the wagon seat and began unloading the lumber. Tall and straight, he was as strong as the lumber he milled. He and his wife, Sophy, had come to Rainly with her parents. Jesse had worked for her father at his mill on the Ashley River, but that was before the war, before her parents had lost everything. She could remember her mother telling the story of a frightened Sophy, new bride that she was, coming to the South Carolina countryside and how they had become fast friends that first day. Sophy had proved that friendship in the days following her mother's death. But Dara did not want to think of the past.

"Do you know exactly what he's planning to build here, Jesse?"

"Didn't say."

"Well, did you find out who our new neighbor will be?"

"Might be the man what ordered this, and then again, might not."

"Jesse! What kind of an answer is that?"

"Only kind I got. Too hot to get yoreself frazzled, Miz Dara," he calmly informed her. Taking four twelve-foot lengths of lumber from the wagon bed, he set them on the slow growing pile. Stopping to wipe the sweat from his brow with the back of his hand, he glanced toward her. " 'Iffen you met the man, you'd be understandin' he weren't one to be botherin' with questions." Grinning, he added, "You and mah missus be askin' the wrong man. Seen him over with Mr. Dinn at the bank. Try talkin' to Elvira if you can get to her afore mah Sophy does."

"But I trust you to tell me, Jesse," she insisted softly, holding his narrowed gaze with her own.

For a moment Jesse was taken back in time. Dara looked so much like her mother, but the picture forming in his mind of Malva Owens and his own graceful Sophy wasn't here in Rainly. Stately whitewashed columns replaced the rough-timbered roof support where Dara now leaned. Two gaily dressed young wives stood side by side, bell hoops swaying, throwing kisses, then waving. They thought the hands they clasped in fear went unnoticed by himself and Cyrus Owens as they rode off to war. Jesse blinked, realized Dara was softly calling him, and abruptly turned to finish unloading his lumber.

"You alone in the store, Miz Dara?"

"Matt's around town somewhere," she answered, wondering what he had been thinking of to frown so. "Papa and Pierce should be back sometime tomorrow. Did you need their help with something?"

The last boards were set down carefully, and with his long legs Jesse stepped easily onto the porch. "Since yore trustin' me, you listen. We all know strangers be comin' heah, lookin' for white gold, but you nevah take any chances bein' alone with one of 'em, Miz Dara. Their ways ain't ours. Menfolk 'round heah are right 'spectful of their womenfolk. You'll be extry cautious if yore alone in the store without yore brothah. And doan' be wanderin' down by the rivah like you do at night."

"I'm not a child anymore, Jesse. If you know something, please just tell me. I heard what happened to Jake. Anne was so upset that she didn't stay more than a minute yesterday. I know that men came in on the train, and some left town soon afterward." She silently reminded herself of the one man she had met, and if truth be told, she hadn't really stopped thinking about him.

Jesse tugged his beard. "Yore pa doan' like talkin' much 'bout what happened aftah the war afore we come down heah. Reminds me of it. Saw worse destruction when strangers come to pick our bones clean. I doan' know nuthin' for sure," he stressed, "but I warned mah Caroline, her being so young, and ah'm warnin' you. Folks heah might be stirred up and raise more he—'scuse me, I mean more heck than a 'gator in a dry lake 'bout this heah minin' of phosafat and then again, might not. These heah men'll be bringin' money into Rainly and that's good. But they'll be bringin' othah things, too. Things a lady doan' need to know. So jus' be careful," he warned again, stepping off the porch.

Dara didn't have more than a few minutes to wonder why fear timbered Jesse's voice. She had waved him off and turned, only to find the very man she couldn't chase from her memory right before her eyes. He was mounted on a barrel-chested bay horse before the store's hitching rail. Had she thought to dismiss his smile so easily? Yes, she reminded herself, and with good reason.

His gaze flickered lazily over her. This morning her starched white, full-sleeved shirtwaist had a pert black bow at its neck, the veed lace trim calling attention to the lush fullness her corset pushed upward from below. Her long skirt was dour black, but he couldn't ignore the way it wrapped around her slender form. She appeared cool and crisp in the heat of the morning.

"Good morning, *Miss* Dara Owens," he greeted her, touching the brim of his hat. "Mighty pretty piece of land your house sits upon backing all the way to the river. Your father chose well. Prime town land will be at a premium shortly."

"My, you have been busy since yesterday, haven't you?" she returned coolly, noting how he stressed her unmarried title. Watching his fluid dismount, which tautened his black cord pants, she felt a sense of alarming anticipation. The pale blue double-breasted shirt accentuated his tanned skin, and Dara had to look away. "Best tie your reins or your horse is liable to walk off or be stolen. Haven't you heard Rainly won't—"

"Old Sinner won't run off," he assured her.

"Sinner?" She couldn't help but smile. "Why?" With the flash of his charming and ingratiating smile, she thought the name would fit the man as well.

"He ran off once from a herd of horses I was trailing and followed me. Couldn't shake him. Reminded me of an old proverb my daddy was fond of quoting: 'The sinner isn't cast out, but casts himself out.' "

"Gracious, what sins could a horse be guilty of?"

"Stealing."

"Horses do not steal."

"Happens all the time. A wild herd is composed of mares, colts, and fillies. Can't have but one stallion as leader. Sinner here probably took a notion to cull a few mares for his own, lost the ensuing fight, and ran off."

"To follow you?"

"To follow me."

She tried to stifle her laughter, but his smile, then his chuckle, enticed her to join him. Eden felt the tiny claws of desire sink deep to hear her laugh. Her eyes were merry, her cheeks sun-blushed, and her lips . . . he looked away just as Dara recalled all her good intentions not to encourage this man and stopped.

"I see," he said with a pleased look at the stacked lumber, "that Jesse started to deliver my order."

He stepped up onto the porch, and Dara stepped back, glancing up at him. She took in the full import of what he said, but this time refused to be drawn in to conversation with him. The mere thought of his being a neighbor, of seeing him every day, unsettled her in ways she didn't dare comprehend.

"Not even a bit of curiosity, Miss Owens? It's a refreshing but most unusual trait to find in a woman."

His mockery brought forth her annoyance. "I'm as curious as anyone else, I suspect, but I was taught it is considered rude to question strangers."

"Feel free to ask me anything that will change my status," he urged with a spark of humor.

Dara shook her head, feeling the heat of her cheeks reach her earlobes. The man was simply impossible!

"Are you angry because I found out some answers to the questions I had?" He smiled, cupped his square jaw with one hand, and held her gaze with his own. "I admit, I was surprised to find out—"

"As I said, you've been busy with the gossips, but you wasted your time if you discussed me." If her deliberate interruption didn't stop him, the move she made to walk past him with a sweep of her skirt should have.

"Edward Dinn and his wife, Elvira, over at the bank give more than receipts for money deposited."

Spine rigid, hands clutched around the folds of her black serge skirt, Dara forced herself to look at his face. She knew exactly what he had learned about her. She should have felt pleased that he knew she was promised to marry Clay Wescott, but Elvira wouldn't leave go without telling him all the juicy details of why they weren't married yet.

His widening smile, too charming, too confident, revealed white teeth bracketed by creased bronzed skin. She had, in her musings yesterday, determined his age to be in the thirties. There was a lean hardness to him that showed the years had not all been easy ones. But Dara suspected that was by his own choice.

"Did you come here to buy more supplies? If not, I'm

sure Elvira would be happy to gossip the day away with you. Excuse me."

He'd angered her and thought about following her into the store, but he saw Miss Loretta, the owner of the boardinghouse, walking rapidly toward him. She resembled a stuffed partridge today, and while he had found her company charming enough last evening, he abruptly decided to forgo it now. Dara could wait. He tipped his hat politely as the woman stopped a moment to greet him, then quickly mounted Sinner.

Dara had paused just inside the doorway. She wondered where he was going, then chastised herself for the thought. Why did he deliberately seek to provoke her? Continuing on until she slipped behind the counter, she left off musing about him as the slightly panting Miss Loretta Parkville entered the store.

"Gracious, Dara," she called out, "he's simply charmin'. Ah believe he's as handsome as one of mah beaus. Turned blockade runner durin' the war, and Ah lost track of him. 'Course, yore heart's been settled for a time on Clay and you've led such a sheltered life that you wouldn't understand how attractive a glint of wickedness in a man's eye can be." Removing lace gloves, fanning herself, Miss Loretta came down the aisle, swaddled in the height of fashion. No one laced their corsets tighter, no woman dared to wear such a towering confectioned hat filled with vast numbers of flowers, birds, feathers, and ribbons that defied gravity. Few, if any, of the town's women would bother to wear the thickly padded bustle under a severely tailored walking suit in this heat. But Miss Loretta, ever the lady, not only did so, she tended to lecture those who didn't.

Setting her parasol on the counter with a bang, she fanned herself a moment more. "Ah declare this to be the hottest summah evah. And heah you stand, cool as lemonade."

With a face as smooth as creamed butter, which, she privately admitted to Dara, she attributed to a spoonful of Dr. Worden's Beef Iron and Wine Tonic taken every morning, she set her gloves upon the counter. Dara wondered if the alcohol wasn't the tonic's main attraction for Miss Loretta, but would never dare ask her. Admitting to forty of her almost sixty years, Miss Loretta narrowed her gaze, for she wouldn't admit to needing spectacles, took a deep breath that threatened the jet buttons of her black Kersey cloth jacket, and slowly exhaled.

Dara, accustomed to her dramatic entrances, fussy dress, and sometimes secretive manner, merely smiled and waited. Miss Loretta was a force to be reckoned with in the town. She and Elvira Dinn battled with each other to have the last word. But Miss Loretta had the advantage of being the town's oldest living resident, since her family was the first to settle here.

Button-bright eyes fixed on Dara's face as she leaned over the counter. "You haven't slept well, girl. Watch those shadows. Be a ruin to you. Might try some White Lily face wash. 'Course, at yore age, you shouldn't be needin' any. Now. Did you place yore ordahs yet?"

"No, I was about to start getting—"

"Good. Ah've got a special one for you. Ah suppose you know we're about to be invaded?"

"Invaded, Miss Loretta?"

"Land's sake! Don't be tellin' me yore hearin' is goin', too? Mah deah chile, you do not know the half of it. Now, listen. Ah want you to place an ordah for feathah ticks. Not goose down, mind you, but all chicken feathahs. An' Ah'll pay the extra charge to have them rushed heah."

Dara bit back a smile. "Miss Loretta, if you want chicken feathers, I'll tell Abner and Varina to save them for you when I go out to get fresh eggs this week. I'm sure—"

"Don't be thick as Alma Clare's honey! Ah need *ticks*. Not one, but twenty-five. Cheap ones, too."

Dara hesitated before drawing out an order form from the cubbyhole below the counter. Over the years the town had experienced the result of a few of Miss Loretta's wild schemes, but no one had really been hurt by them. She had started the land company, helped write the brochures promising Rainly as God's paradise, and lost her money in the last one. Dara couldn't help her strong feeling that this lastest scheme boded ill.

"There's no need to be starin' at me like mah birds sprung free of mah hat. Ah'll explain. It's all those empty bedrooms," she whispered. "Got two new boarders off the train yesterday. One a mighty fancy lookin' gent, too. The othah one, well, you met him yoreself. Annamae was beside herself. That gal ain't worth a lick of molasses lately. But she agreed, aftah Ah promised to blister her hide, that Ah can move all that heavy furniture Mothah insisted on bringin' down heah when Fathah objected to its unsuitability. Ah'll have more'n enough room then."

Dara's blank stare slowly became one of alarm and brought a heavy sigh of exasperation from Miss Loretta. "Think of it! Ah can fill five upstairs bedrooms with those feathah ticks. Ah did give the two front rooms to the first gentlemen to arrive. Private ones, they both wanted and paid deah for. Now," she demanded, "do you understand why Ah need mah ordah?"

"Miss Loretta, are you seriously planning on renting sleeping accommodations to the type of men that—"

"Don't look so shocked, girl. We did more'n that to survive aftah the war. But don't be doubtin' that they're comin', eithah. Mark mah words, there's money to be made, and Ah intend to have mah share. Ah might even build a hotel. Don't be frownin' so, gives you wrinkles. Ah'm well aware of the gossip Elvira stirred up when Ah first decided to rent rooms. But no one in this town forgets Ah run a respectable house, and Ah aim to keep it that way." Pointing an imperious finger, she ordered, "Now, write me up."

Dara did so, privately thinking she should find someone to get Reverend Speck to talk to Miss Loretta. She might listen to him. Then again, Miss Loretta was known to have a wide stubborn streak.

"Town's goin' to change. Rainly'll grow."

"I haven't had time to think about it," Dara answered with a spark of spirit. She was twenty-two years old, and as much as she adored Miss Loretta and Jesse, it was annoying to be thought of as a half-grown child.

"We're goin' to be news. A boomtown is what they'll be callin' us. This heah store," she stated, gesturing wildly around her, "is goin' to be a gold mine for you and yore fathah. Speakin' of him, how is he?"

Only experience helped Dara follow Miss Loretta's erratic talk. "He's feeling better since we've had no rain, but he's out at—"

"Well, Ah know he's not heah, or he'd be waitin' on me, girl," she snapped. When Dara finished writing up the order, she grabbed it. "I'll take this ovah to Luthah mahself. He read me the papers when he come for suppah last night. Luthah's of the opinion the trains'll be running full up. See 'bout gettin' yoreself help in the store. Ah've already hired Mabel and her girl to work for me."

All Dara grasped was Luther's opinion. Since he was the ticket agent, postmaster, and telegraph operator for the town, Luther usually knew what was happening. He'd been sweet on Miss Loretta for years, but she was a Parkville from Georgia and rarely allowed anyone to forget it, while Luther Marlow was merely a retired army corporal. Swallowing words of caution, Dara asked if there was anything else Miss Loretta needed.

"A loaf of sugah, three pounds of buttah crackahs, and a tin of blackstrap molasses. You have Matthew delivah that to Annamae, and you may come for suppah on Saturday with yore young man."

"We're having a fish fry at the ferry landing on Saturday, Miss Loretta. You wouldn't miss that. Besides, I don't know if Clay will be coming into town this week. He received those new seedlings from California. But I do thank you kindly for the invite."

"Girl, in mah day, we had bettah sense than to allow a man to keep us danglin'. We had ways back then of makin' a man attend us. Shame you young things don't know now. You ain't payin' attention to those reprehensible women advocatin' the vote, are you? No," she answered for Dara, "you wouldn't." Attentive to smoothing the fit of her lace gloves, she added. "Mah advice, Dara, is to watch out for men like that charmer you spoke with this mawnin'. We had names for men like him and one of 'em wasn't *gentlemen*. But Ah digress from mah point. You should be married long since and carin' for yore family—oh, don't be givin' me that buttah-wouldn't-melt-in-yore-mouth look! Ah suppose it wouldn't do me a bit of good to tell you to make Clayton jealous? Thought not," she said, shaking her head. "But that man, watch him. His kind will be fillin' the town. They talk smooth and soft, girl. Spark you down by the river one night in the moonlight and move on to the next gal before you finish tyin' your corset strings."

"Miss Loretta!"

"Don't be Miss Loretta-in' me!" She noted the blush staining Dara's cheeks with bobbing nods of satisfaction. "Yore a fine young woman, Ah prick yore temper some, but I called yore mothah mah dearest friend. God rest her, she was a woman who didn't shy away from callin' things as she saw them. And she'd be the first to tell you the same."

As Miss Loretta reached out for her parasol, Dara covered her gloved hand with her own and smiled. "Miss Loretta, how can you warn me to be careful of these men and still plan to rent out rooms to them?"

"Ah've lived through the war, girl, and with mah virtue intact. If you need more answers, take a long look in yore mirrah."

After Miss Loretta left the store, Dara didn't have a minute to reflect on her advice. She quickly came to the conclusion that the whole town was infected with the same feverish moneymaking schemes.

Mrs. Leah Tucker came in with her young daughter, Selena, in tow, purchasing every bolt of denim and bull-hide shirting in stock. To Dara she explained, "Ah decided to make up a stock of work clothes for the miners a-comin'. Mah Robert and I talked some, and don't be takin' offense, but we're plannin' to enlarge our store. I'll be orderin' direct for mah own bolts, seein' as how there'll be money enough. Ah might even think of havin' ready-mades."

And so the day passed. Before long Dara felt as if she

would scream if she heard one more plan to be rich. She had just finished cleaning the coffee grinder when Mabel Saunders arrived, all a-flutter about Miss Loretta's plans to include a laundry service and extra meals at the boardinghouse. Dara was happy for the young widow, who had struggled hard to raise her daughter alone, but Mabel shocked her with her request.

"You heah me right. Miz Loretta sez we'll be rich right soon. Ah wanna see those catalog offerin's of those Anthony Wayne washahs and one of those fancy new hotel-type wringahs. Cain't be 'spectin' me to keep up with washin's if Ah have to use mah old wood tub and board."

While Mabel labored to study the small inked drawings and Dara answered her occasional questions about the explanations below describing the special features, Dara wrote out orders to replace their depleted stock. Frowning when she realized she'd sold most of their tools, she couldn't help but recall the words of warning the man Silver had offered. But she no longer attempted to urge anyone to use caution.

"Ah believe Ah'd like this heah one," Mabel said, pushing the book forward. "An' this heah wringah."

Dara totaled the items. Dismay tinged her voice. "Mabel, they'll cost eleven dollars and fifty cents, and there'll be freight charges added."

"Ah'll keep that in mind. Now, don't ferget to ordah extra cases of bluein' an' ammonia for me. Oh, an' that Cobb's mottled German soap. You had it on special, but Ah saw it's all gone. Pit minin's right dirty work, so Ah'll need good cleanahs."

"Where did you hear it was pit mining?"

"Miz Loretta. She done tole me that's how they'll dig out this heah phosafat the papers called white gold.

Luthah, you know. He lived neah them phosafat pits in Tennessee when he was a boy."

Mabel chattered a few minutes more about everyone's plans and then left. Dara could only question people's wisdom. Jake had begun wearing his gun. He'd stopped in twice today, briefly, to check on her. Jesse and Miss Loretta expounded warnings, and so had that annoying man Silver. Wishing her father would come back early from her brother's new farm, Dara began the routine of closing the store.

She locked the front doors, pulled the shades down, covered the barrels of pickles and crackers, along with the pickled beef, then rearranged the few bolts of material left on the dry-goods table. Behind the counter she had to straighten the jars of spices, the nearly depleted tins of healing borax, powdered sulphur, petroleum oil, and bottles of witch hazel. Gathering up the scattered catalogs from where they had been tossed here and there, she placed them in their cubbyhole below the counter and pulled out her account book. The list that fell to the floor had her frowning.

She should have known her father would deliberately forget his promise to try to collect a few of the overdue bills. But then, Cyrus Owens was known far and wide as a man most generous with his less-fortunate neighbors. Dara crumpled the list in her hand. Every spare penny they had went toward buying her brother Pierce his dream of his own farm. It was one more reason why she and Clay couldn't be married. Resentment rose within her, but from long habit she stifled it. She should have taken matters into her own hands as her mother before her had done.

Polite reminders could be written and slipped along with purchases into the farm wives' worn baskets when they next came to shop. But the final decision rested with her father. Her head began to ache and she removed her spectacles, rubbing the bridge of her nose. The store suddenly seemed stifling.

Emptying the money drawer into the bank sack, Dara knew she wouldn't bother to deposit so small an amount; most of the purchases had been made on credit today. She carefully hid the sack behind the bottles of bay rum. Matt hadn't spared more than an hour or so this morning to help her, and she was tired and hungry. There was still the laundry to take in and fold, and supper to be cooked. Overwhelmed, she wanted to cry.

The scrape of boot heels in the back of the store made her look up. Despair filled her eyes before anger surged hot. The man loomed in the doorway, appearing to her like some evil specter planning her ruin. Dara didn't have the strength to cope with more of his inflammatory verbal sparring.

"We're closed," she snapped before he said a word. "Especially to your kind."

Her undisguised scorn had him stepping forward. "Someday," he intoned coolly, "you must take the time to explain that remark, but not now. I came here to get you for Matt."

"Matt?"

"Are you prone to fainting?"

"What have you done to my brother?" she demanded, hands clenched at her sides.

Chapter Three

DARA DIDN'T WAIT for an answer. She hurried down the aisle toward him. He stood blocking the doorway. "Let me by."

Sure she would panic and bolt, Eden said, "First let me talk to you."

"What did you do to him?" Dara shoved past him and he grabbed her arm.

"I've brought him home for a start." His gray eyes narrowed. Her fingers clawed at his hand and he shook her arm. "Just calm down your ruffled feathers. Do you have a strong stomach?"

"If I can survive your manhandling, I can manage anything."

"I'll keep that in mind when I decide to handle you." His grip tightened on her upper arm, eyes blazing down at her. "Matt needs you. Not your anger, or your lectures. He needs a little soft, womanly warmth and compassion, if you have any. And then . . . then he needs some doctoring."

"Where is he?" she managed to whisper, feeling she was about to shatter. She wanted to lash out at him, but where he held her arm, the heat of his hand seeped through cloth to burn her skin. There was strength in his fingers molding around her upper arm, but for some strange reason Dara had no fear of his using that strength against her. The fear came from her own reaction to his touch. A light quiver tremored her body as she felt her blood thicken warmly.

"Please, let me go . . . to him."

He couldn't deny her pleading look, which asked for more than immediate release. His hand slipped from her arm, but he gave no other indication that he was aware of what she asked. "Matt's waiting for you in the kitchen," he said, ignoring for now her accusation that he had harmed her brother.

Dara brushed passed him, running over the moss-laden river stones marking the path to the house. Running up the two wide porch steps, she nearly tripped on her skirt hem, her heels tapping against the uneven boards deeply shadowed by the twisted jasmine vines entwined with drooping pine branches.

Her hesitation was slight before she opened the glass-topped front door. Knowing he was behind her, she wanted to deny him access to her home, deny him any part of her life his coming inside would reveal, but no sane reason to stop him came to mind. The thought of Matt hurt sent her hurrying down the hall toward the kitchen.

She grabbed the doorframe for support. Her brother sat hunched over the large square oak table. Nausea rose and she spared no thought for the warm comfort of a hand on her shoulder, or the whispered assurances that Matt looked worse than he was. Her eyes had locked upon the basin filled with pink-tinged water and the cloth her brother held to one side of his face. She shrugged off Eden's hold.

"Matt?" she murmured, stepping closer. He didn't turn but slumped farther into the straight-backed chair.

Rushing to his side, she begged, "Let me see." Matt lowered the cloth as Dara gently cupped his chin, raising it toward the light of the back windows. Swallowing, she slid her hand away. Dara didn't trust herself to speak.

"There's nothing broken so far as I could tell," Eden said from where he still stood in the doorway.

Dara looked at him, unsure what part he played in her brother being beaten, but she nodded, accepting what he said.

She appeared suddenly fragile to Eden, standing as she was, leaning over Matt, hands clasped together. He gave her a moment, watched her slender throat working as she swallowed repeatedly, and found himself admiring the effort she made to regain her control.

"What can I do to help you? I didn't want to poke around in your pantry, and Matt, well, he wasn't sure where anything is."

"I'll tend him." Dara didn't consider her refusal curt. She drew strength from all the times Matt and Pierce had gotten into scrapes growing up. They always looked worse until bruises and wounds were washed clean, but this . . . Walking around Matt to the big steel range, she fitted the special handle to lift the front burner plate. Adding enough kindling from the wood box to revive the coals, she watched them flame and calmed herself. At last she replaced the lid, took the empty kettle, and turned.

"Da-ra . . . I'm be-holden to . . . Silver."

If she hadn't been at Matt's side, the mumbled words wouldn't have made sense. Giving his shoulder a reassuring pat, she didn't hide her bitterness.

"I hope you won't regret it."

Eden reached the hand pump beneath the windows before Dara. "See to him," he ordered, grabbing the kettle. "I'll get the water. And if you have any spirits, give him a glass or two. He's hurting."

With her tenuous hold on her emotions, Dara didn't want to fathom the way his concern for Matt touched her. She regretted her words of a moment before, but couldn't bring herself to look at him or to apologize.

"The pump handle tends to stick," she warned, stepping away from his overpowering presence.

Matt mumbled again and she snapped, "Don't try to talk. You're bleeding." She hadn't meant to sound so condemning, but the sight of his bruised and battered face, his torn shirt, and his obvious pain had her wishing that just once there was someone else to deal with him. Retreating into the large pantry, she held tight to one of the wooden shelves. What had Matt gotten involved in? What did this man Silver have to do with it? Questions pounded inside her head, and her brow beaded with cold sweat. She wiped it off, knowing Matt needed her first, and later, always later, she'd have time for herself.

Quickly she took down a stack of clean linen cloths, the tin of powdered sulphur, and a bottle of witch hazel, then managed to grab a jug of Abner Colly's home brew and brought it all to the table.

The basin was clean. Dara didn't notice it until she filled a glass and pushed it across the table to Matt. It was his trembling grip on the glass that made her cry out.

"What have you done to your hands? Oh, Matt . . ."

"Just don't blame . . . him," he grated from between clenched teeth, raising the glass to his lips.

"Can't your questions wait?" Eden demanded. "The water's heating, but let him get the whiskey down first."

Dara heard him sit down at the table, but she paced to the windows. Staring outside at the wooded sloped land, she wondered how Matt had met him and come to trust him so quickly. She tugged one corner of the yellow cotton curtain into place. Not a breath of air stirred, but that wasn't the only heat she felt closing in on her. She could feel that man Silver's eyes staring at her back.

"May I trouble you for another glass? I could do with a drink myself." He glanced away from her rigid spine as she moved to the far corner cabinet. The room was sun-warmed; small green herb plants filled colorful pottery on the windowsills and counter, scenting the humid air. There was a gaily woven rag rug on the highly polished wood floor, and neatly stitched samplers arrayed the pale yellow walls. Eden noted each detail. All that was missing was the aroma of fine cooking, but the room bespoke a homey welcome. It seeped into him, bone deep and peaceful, until he focused on one of the samplers. A soft chuckle escaped him. He was sure that Dara had worked it, for the words typified her. Silently he read "The Honey is Sweet, but the Bee has a Sting."

Dara heard him and almost dropped the glass. She bit back the demand to know why, angry as she was that he needed a drink. His clothing wasn't torn, it was barely soiled, and he certainly showed no visible sign of having been involved in whatever resulted in Matt being hurt. Abruptly she set the glass in front of him. Matt didn't notice her thinned lips or her quick move toward the stove, for he was staring into the dark amber depths of his whiskey. Dara watched the simmering water and felt safer with distance between them. But why did that man need to stare at her?

For stare he did. Hot as it was, she appeared as fresh and cool-looking now as she did when he first saw her this morning. The prim Miss Dara's manner seemed as fully starched as her petticoats. He smiled and poured himself a drink. Her reserve offered more enticement than another woman's blatancy. And that only reminded him of the charming sprite that had appeared in his room last night to gather up his laundry. Miss Lara Saunders might be a few years younger than Dara, but she was certainly more worldly wise. He lifted his glass and swallowed a mouthful of the liquor.

"Potent?" Matt managed to ask, taking another sip of his own.

"Firewater," he said, grinning. "Colly will make himself a fortune selling this liquor uncut." He didn't miss the defensive tightening of Dara's shoulders.

Dara didn't care if the water was fully boiled or not. She wanted this man out of her kitchen, out of her life, and knew he wouldn't leave until she had attended to her brother.

"Matt told me your folks were some of the first to settle here."

Dara banged the kettle back down on the burner. "That's right." Noting the late afternoon shadows filling the room, she took one of the long wooden matches from the china wall holder, struck it against the rough pad below, and carefully cupped the flame. Standing between the man and her brother, she leaned over the table to light the coal-oil fixture hanging over its center. She froze in the act of lighting it.

The back of Eden's hand brushed against her ribcage when he raised his glass.

"Pardon my carelessness," he said, mouth twitching with amusement.

She took a deep breath, exhaled, and adjusted her smile before toying with the idea of dropping the burning match into his glass.

He smiled benignly, as if reading her intent and warning her he would retaliate.

Dara lit the fixture.

He took a long and most satisfying pull of his drink.

Matt, bewildered by what he sensed, tried to smile.

When she set the filled basin on the table, Eden tried to draw her into conversation to relieve Matt of her intense frowning concentration.

"Did the town take its name from the Rainbow River?"

"No." Standing with her back deliberately toward him, Dara lifted Matt's chin.

"Did the name have some special significance for the ex-Confederate soldiers who settled around here?" he asked, wincing right along with Matt, even if her touch appeared to be light.

"Some say Miss Loretta's mother complained that it rained nearly every day when they first settled here and that's how Rainly got its name."

Eden refilled Matt's glass, silently urging him to keep drinking. To distract Dara, he persisted in engaging her in conversation. "Most of the people I've met in town seem excited by the discovery of phosphate and what revenue it will bring. Jesse mentioned that people had about given up hope of expanding the town after the land company failed."

Dara wrung out another clean cloth with jerky moves. "That land company," she replied curtly, "was formed to bring people who farmed and wanted to develop a good, safe town where others of their kind would also come to settle. Rainly doesn't want or need drifters." She bit her lip, hurting for Matt as she dabbed his cuts with witch hazel, wiped off the excess, and then powdered them with sulphur.

Eden set his glass down in a deliberate manner. "Not all men intend to drift, Miss Owens. For your clarification, most men think of moving from place to place as a way of searching for the perfect one that will feed a hunger inside them. And most," he stressed with an edged annoyance that she could easily ruffle his control, "would take offense for both your tone and your holier-than-thou attitude."

His rebuke stung, as she was sure he meant it to do. Yet it wasn't words of apology she spoke. "If you have taken personal offense, I'll remind you that women may not have the right to vote, but we do have freedom of speech." She had never insulted anyone the way this man seemed to incite her to do. Studying the gash over her brother's eye, she knew it would need stitches.

"Matt, I'll need to get Sophy to tend this one."

"No. You." Shakily he wiped the sweat from his brow.

"I can't sew it."

Matt insisted, his look pleading toward Silver.

"Don't ask this of me, Matt," Dara said. "I can't."

Grabbing her hands, ignoring his pain, Matt pulled her near. "Won't move. Please."

Eden hadn't intended to interfere. She would only resent him further, but he could see she was drawing upon last reserves of strength staring down at Matt's skinned knuckles. And Matt, pride aside, turned begging eyes toward him. Eden slugged down the last of his drink and pushed the glass aside.

"I'll sew it, if you'll hold Matt's head steady."

"You!" She pulled free from Matt, rounding on him.

He shoved the chair back and stood towering over her. "Me." He grinned, hoping to allay her fear. "Knowing how has come in handy a few times."

"It seems you're a man of many talents," she snapped, belatedly shocked at how easily she came to mock him.

"Dara," Matt pleaded.

"It's all right," Eden soothed. "She's been through enough." But holding her flaring dark eyes with his, he accepted her unwittingly given challenge. "Perhaps, Miss Owens, that's something else you'll find out."

Dara retreated. "I'll get a needle and thread." But as she left the room, she couldn't help thinking he was no stranger to violence, even if he was making her become a stranger to herself.

The strength of his long fingers showed surprising gentleness as he carefully sewed Matt's gash. He joked with him, keeping Matt's mind from the pain, and to Dara's contention, invoked a respect bordering on hero worship from her brother. She wasn't immune when he turned his concern toward her, softly telling her to go outside while he settled Matt into bed. Dara didn't argue. She simply didn't have the strength.

Stepping out into the twilight, the river called to her, and she walked slowly down the sloping path.

Spanish moss, dewed and dream-draped from the rising river mist, cloaked gnarled live oaks. Ancient secrets whispered to the pungent pine boughs from these majestic older sisters. In the air lingered the coy, thick perfume of vine-twisted jasmine. The soft breeze wafted the scent toward her from the star-shaped blooms. Dara breathed deeply, sighing, envying them. The night's wooing call came like a lover to tease open scented secrets. She had never known a lover's sweet coaxing, but she dreamed of the day she would. Ducking beneath the trailing silver-draped moss, she listened to the river spirits lap the thick black mud bank with its soft insistent call to join its play. Fish suspended themselves below the dark waters of the Withlacoochee River, and water plants with closed graceful heads eddied in the flow.

Dara halted before a stately pine tree, its full dripping branches offering her a hidden place all her own. Leaning against the rough-barked trunk, she felt drained. Only in her mind was there fixed a picture of stormy gray eyes, hot with promise, threatening her with a challenge she could never dare claim.

How long she stood there, she didn't know. But long before she heard a sound, her senses came alive. She didn't want to admit that she knew he would seek her out, but denying it would not make the truth go away.

"Matt's sleeping," Eden said before she could speak, pushing aside the overhanging boughs.

He made no move to come closer to her, and Dara found she was nervous, but she had to know what had happened. "Will you tell me how he was hurt?" She didn't want to look at him, but his silence, his utter stillness, seemed to force her to do just that. The shadows hid his face, but he stood merely an arm's width away from her. How did he manage to move so silently on the thick carpet of pine needles?

Choosing his words carefully, he finally answered, "Matt was with me."

"And? What happened? Where was he? What was he doing?"

He had to remember his promise to Matt and not allow her soft pleading voice to distract him. She appeared suddenly chilled, rubbing her hands over her arms, and he thought about holding her. Emotionally she was defenseless, if he judged the shaky tremor of her voice correctly. He didn't move and glanced away toward the river.

"Tell me."

"He was out at one of my claims with me, and two men jumped him thinking he was alone."

"No! No one here would hurt my brother. There was no reason for anyone to beat him up." Low and intense, she accused, "You're lying to me."

"I may be many things, Miss Owens, but a liar isn't one of them," he stated with harsh emphasis. Reaching up, he fingered the long, silky pine needles. She wasn't going to be satisfied until he told her more, and he resigned himself to that. "Matt didn't know who the men were, and I was too far away to help him at first."

Dara dragged air into her lungs, understanding what he said. "And what did you do? Order them off your claim with arrogance for your weapon while they beat up my brother? Is that what you and your kind will bring to Rainly? Men like you thrive on fear, don't you? Fear and violence! You said Matt didn't know them. Did you? Were they your kind?"

Rising hysteria punctuated every word. He released the pine branch, slowly turning to face her. "Like I told Matt, you've been through enough today."

"I have, haven't I? And whose fault is that?" His calm incited her to fury. "Is that all you have to say for yourself? Why don't you try telling me the truth? Why don't you tell me this is just the beginning? And it is, isn't it?"

"Is that where all these questions have been leading?" His laugh was as smooth as his move to close the distance between them. "It can be whatever you want," he softly assured her. "For you and for everyone else in this town. Men are already here and more are coming, and yes, I won't deny that violence will be a part of their arrival. Matt got hurt, and other men will, too, because they're dreaming of getting rich. It's most men's nature to become greedy and not count the cost. But then, you don't know much about men or their natures." His body backed hers against the tree. "Lovely Miss Dara, so good and pious. I know you'll understand my saying the strong will devour the weak. Nothing is going to stop it from happening. Be aware of that and stay frightened of it, Dara. It might protect you when no one can.

"Rainly," he continued, distracted a moment by the flash of her teeth sinking into her upper lip, "will never again be as you've known it. You can rant and rave, fight it all you want, but the town's already changing and you will, too. But not now. Now it wouldn't be fair."

Dara had heard enough. She twisted against the tree, brushing his body to turn her back toward him. His unassailable self-esteem unnerved her. Not that she needed to add that fact to the way his heated nearness affected her. She had no experience to draw upon to help her deny the strong attraction she felt toward him while at the same time he frightened her. Clay never challenged her. Clay showed his love by his respectful manner of courting her. And she forced herself to remember Clay, to reaffirm her promise to him to love, to wait, to marry. It was the only talisman she could dredge up for protection.

Dara refused to cower. She faced him. "I owe you my thanks for bringing Matt home. But that is all that I owe you. Stay away from us. Leave Matt alone. He's not your kind, and I pray he never will be."

"That's once too often you've made that slur against me. *My kind*?" His voice, though soft, held an ominous note. "And you? What *kind* of a woman are you?"

"Not for the likes of you!" Head tilted, she glared at him. "I'm promised to marry—"

"Only promised? I would think," he uttered softly, stepping to her side, leaning one shoulder against the tree to brush against her own, "that some man would have stolen the promise of you long before now."

"No! That might be your way—to steal and take—but my intended respects me." Why was she defending herself to him? Every word seemed to be dragging her into deeper involvement with him.

"So," he noted silkily, "he respects you. But tell me, little saint, has he ever made love to you?" There was a hushed delicacy to his voice, a gentleness to his fingers cupping her chin before she called upon the Lord to help her and turned her face aside.

"He won't help you now, Dara."

A shiver tremored her body. "I don't know how to make you stop saying such things to me. You have no right . . ." Eyes glazed with confusion, she looked at him. "I don't know how to fight you."

"For the sweet love of God! Do you always challenge a man with such innocent candor regardless of where it may lead you?"

Baffled by the anger shadowing his voice, Dara sensed she had inadvertently given him a weapon by telling him the truth. She wanted to recall the words and the challenge he found in them. She did nothing.

"I don't know why I should frighten you." A lock of his hair fell across his forehead as he gazed down at her. Dappled in the shadows, he sensed her continued scrutiny. His gut clenched in reaction. More than he wanted to see was revealed in her velvet dark eyes. And he spoke without thought. "It's not me you're afraid of, is it? It's you. Do I," he asked in a soft, sensual voice, "threaten your narrow, safe little world?"

"Yes!" Denials came too late. Shaking her head in disbelief of her admission, Dara pressed her body tight against the massive pine tree. He stood poised, like a night-summoned predator, dark, sleek, and far too powerful. Ignoring the stickiness and odor of pungent sap, her cheek rested against the rough-edged bark, tears filling her eyes.

"Can't you look at me now?" He was annoyed with her show of tension the moment he spoke, wanting her soft and pliant against him. Instinct warned him to give her a few minutes, and he lit a cigar, inhaling deeply, his features sharply delineated, then shadowed once again.

Dara fought off the feeling of invitation to all things forbidden in his liquid warm voice. She tried to remember everyone's warnings, even her own of not being free. But Clay never made her feel this breathless anticipation. She should be running for the safety of her home, but by his mere presence, he teased the locked doors of all her hidden dreams and longings. She couldn't run . . . not yet.

He dragged deep, filling his lungs with the smoke of rich tobacco. His eyes narrowed, becoming predatory. She had turned away from him, but didn't run. He had his answer and he'd given her time. The lit end of his cigar was visible arching out over the water. With the barest move he turned, his warm breaths feathering the damp wisps of her hair against the fragile curve of her neck.

A new awareness of male strength swamped her already overburdened senses when his body brushed against hers. Feeling trapped, she cried out for him to stop, closing her eyes as the deep evening shadows enfolded them.

"I'm not very good," he whispered huskily, listening to her muffled cry of denial that made him smile, "at obeying warnings. I told you a man's cravings could be his undoing if he doesn't try to satisfy them." He braced himself, palms flat against the tree on either side of her head. "And I admit, I've craved a taste of you."

She couldn't speak. Rage simmered inside for the liberty he dared take as if this, too, were his right. But it simmered and swelled against a tide of delicious heat threatening her. Dara wished she weren't wearing a restrictive corset. Breathing was becoming a difficulty. Her fingers kneaded the bark in reaction. Inside, she felt a fluttering sensation. And the air around them was hot and still, as if it, too, were waiting, waiting like her trapped breaths, rushing in and out of her dry lips as she felt the light ply of his soft, warm mouth trace the edge of her collar.

"Did you know," he murmured in gentle query, "that I carried the scent of you away with me yesterday? The scent of a wind-teased summer garden, blazed hot by the sun." There was absolute stillness to him as he smiled. The delicate shuddering ripple of her body stroked his own. "But now," he breathed, "now . . . you're . . ." His tongue savored the taste of her skin as he inhaled the sweetly warming feminine scent of her. "Yes . . . night-bloomed . . ." Without pressure from his body, slow unhurried tastings of the fragrant warmth of her tremored skin flooded his own easily heightened senses. Senses finely attuned to the night sounds around them.

He turned his head aside, his jaw brushing against her lemon-scented coiled braids. They tempted his hands to release them as the coiled tension inside him pooled into fierce masculine need that edged him past caution. His long lashes caught on one damp tendril. His desire was not to alarm, so he used one finger to free it, and having touched her, his calloused fingertip continued to lightly stroke the very receptive delicate center of her nape. With his eyes darkened to pewter, he lowered his lashes, gazing at her profile. The glistening sheen of her lips caused the slight pause in his stroking.

"You're very, very soft."

"No."

The word tremored forth in denial, but the unconscious move of her head to follow the path of his touch sent out familiar signals of desire. He thought she would pull away. "So warm, so soft," he murmured a moment later, hearing the thickening roil of his voice while he did no more than feather his fingertip in this gentle fashion. "I could almost imagine touching the downy breast of a duckling."

Dara felt boneless and lost under his caress. Her blood seemed to swell her body. A sigh shivered forth at the picture he called to mind. She could see those powerful hands cradling the fragile form, his voice soothing, warmly whispering, his caress easing the madly beating fright in its breast. Confusion swamped her.

And the night sounds whispered around them, both soft and predatory.

"I d-don't—" She bit back the words. The full sensual shape of his mouth tested the arched length of her neck as lightly as his breaths fanned her sensitized skin. Dara felt languid, blood heating with every tremor flowing deeper and deeper inside her. There was an enticing wickedness to his expert touch and voice, and every one of her nerves were alive to them as her breaths became labored.

"You are sweet, little saint," he murmured, watching the glide of her dainty tongue as it moistened her parted lips. "And very beguiling," he went on, turning her, angling his head to take possession of her tempting mouth, "and such a lush, intriguing bundle of contradictions."

Her shocked cry and sudden twisting move left his lips tasting the night air. "Too fast, little saint?" he asked without censure, stepping back, giving her complete freedom to run.

Dara clung to the solidarity of the tree. Her legs shook, as did her body, with every ragged breath she drew.

With a sparse move of his head, Eden turned toward the house. She hadn't heard Jake calling her. His smile was rueful. A light appeared to be moving through the downstairs rooms heading toward the kitchen.

"Go inside, innocent. It seems Jake has come to rescue you."

The mocking words barely registered as Dara glanced behind her. Now she heard Jake calling her. But when she turned back, Eden was already stepping out from under the tree's protective branches.

Begging her flowering senses to be still, Dara managed to call out, reassuring Jake she would be there in a few minutes. Had she dared to tempt exploring this man's sinful guile? Looking at him, wanting to deny these last minutes, she could feel shame overcome her. Had she dared to dream with unknown longing of a lover's coaxing?

"Go inside, little innocent," he repeated. "Go now, or I'll take your continued hesitation to mean that you don't want to leave. Jake will come out here, and if he does, you won't like what you'll hear or see."

Dara backed away from him then. Not because of what he said, but for his mocking of her innocence. With every step she took, her resolve strengthened.

"Don't worry about my innocence," she whispered softly but harshly. "It will never be yours to take."

"I don't take. Ever. But I'll see my desire mirrored in your eyes before I'm done."

She ran then, the mocking laughter following her, haunting her, and with a last look behind to see that he was gone, his parting words teased her with their challenge.

Chapter Four

THE SIGHING AND moaning of the wind from the Gulf of Mexico brought its sultry hot air heavy with storm into the last Saturday morning of August. Dara proudly kept her resolve to stay away from the man called Silver. Honesty compelled her to admit that success was achieved in part by never being alone with him in the store. She could do nothing to stop hearing the gossip about him, since his block of stores were the first to be rented, including Rainly's first saloon. But not its last, as Mrs. Elvira Dinn just informed her. Another two-story building was near completion next to the bank, directly across the street from the general store, while the large corner lots of William and Charleston streets would boast both a saloon and a gambling hall. Its owner, the town gossip said, was a woman, one Satin Mallory, if Dara believed such an outlandish name, and she had lavishly expensive tastes, if one judged by the furnishings arriving daily.

But Dara had little time to stand and gossip this morning. The store was crowded with the farm families in to do their monthly buying, and as had been the case for several weeks, men of every description were milling the aisles. Sometimes she resented the harried days that left her exhausted. There was no help for it. The steady influx of men arrived at the alarming rate of two trainloads a day, and that discounted the ones coming by wagon, horseback, and on foot. Some came with money and the knowledge of what they were about, if Dara judged by the supplies they bought, but most, she determined, were ignorant of mining not only phosphate but any mineral. Far too many were merely speculators who looked for a quick way of making money without a conscience as to how they did so.

Totaling a short column of figures, Dara absently rubbed her forehead. The dull headache was as much a part of her days as the constant sounds of hammering. Buildings seemed to spring up almost overnight. Most were ramshackle affairs that wouldn't withstand the force of a hurricane. Jesse's sawmill ran sixteen hours a day, and he mentioned only yesterday to her father that he had been approached to take in a partner and build a second mill. Jesse, like most of the townspeople who embarked on new businesses, hired skilled help in the early arriving men who found tramping through the woods or fields trying to locate a rich deposit of phosphate exhausted their funds and health long before they discovered a pit worth excavating. If they didn't work in town, they worked for the more successful mining operations numbering almost ten now, for fifty cents a day, or they worked at the new turpentine still at the north end of town in whose shanties murders were committed and remained unsolved.

Dara completed another transaction for another stranger. Her cool reserve had discouraged the most persistent of them from making any advances. Someone called for help to reach the hanging milk skimmers, and Dara stepped out from behind the counter, glad to let her father transact a lengthy order from *Señor* Suarez's men of business. She didn't like either of the nattily dressed small-statured men who, rumor held, carried secreted weapons. Their manner toward her had always been gentlemenly, so she placed the blame for her feelings on missing the days when she knew everyone who shopped in the store.

Visits were rare between neighbors now, as rare, thankfully, as the few isolated incidents of fights breaking out when the miners were in town drinking and Jake was called to restore order. The wearing of guns had become too commonplace to remark about anymore, and Rainly would soon boast its own jail on the newly developed Richmond Road.

Dara left the two farmers a selection of skimmers, knowing they would debate the merits between them before making a choice. Into the moment's silence came the thrill of a mockingbird's call, and she glanced toward the front doors as her father finished with his customers. Black-edged clouds could be seen, thick and roiling against a hazy blue sky, building their threat of a storm toward the south.

"I don't think this one will blow over, Papa." Gazing at her father's beloved craggy features worn by years of war and struggle, Dara smiled. It was rare for them to have a few minutes' break. With the exception of the gray threading his curled hair, his amber eyes and lanky frame were his legacy to Matt, while Pierce had his warm, gentle voice, even-tempered nature, and resembled, as Dara did, their deceased mother.

"I hope the rain hurries, honey. It might dampen the tempers of another storm building outside the store. The liars' bench is full. Did you notice," he asked, rubbing the swollen knuckles of his left hand, "that Clay is out there?"

"No, I didn't see him." The smile disappeared from her eyes, lips, and voice. Concern for her father took priority. "Are you in pain, Papa? I could manage in here the rest of the afternoon alone, especially if it rains."

"Don't think I don't realize you're managing too much as it is. And it's just the damp stirring my bones a bit. Trying to retire me permanently, are you?"

Dara's laugh, a silvery whisper of sound, reflected the merry twinkle in her father's eyes. "And if I did," she saucily teased, "would you be thinking to take over the caring of the household from me?"

An eruption of loud voices distracted both of them. "Maybe I should go outside and hear what they're up to," Cyrus said.

"Papa, don't. Don't get involved with them."

"What's this?" He barely hid his wince when he placed both hands on her slender shoulders. "Aren't you resigned yet to accepting Matt's decision? Or are you angry that Clay hasn't come in to see you first?"

"Neither. There are too many farmers in town today, and I just wish Clay would forget that incident with those two miners. They didn't know what they were doing."

"Dara, this is not like you. Clay had a right to be incensed after finding those men digging up his newly planted citrus trees. If I recall correctly, those specially grafted trees were ordered from California and delayed your wedding plans this spring."

Not even to her father would Dara reveal the pain his words caused.

"Will you be all right for a little while?" Cyrus continued. "Someone needs to keep an eye on hot tempers. Jake isn't in town. Seems almost daily there's trouble out at someone's claim. And I can't fault Clay or the other farmers for being riled, either. I'm just worried since there's miners aplenty in town."

Dara didn't caution him as she wanted to, but merely watched him leave as people once again crowded into the store.

Cyrus remained standing on the wooden porch, tired eyes scanning the men clustered below him. Straw hats, worn overalls, and sun-leathered faces marked them as farmers; whereas, the miners were noted for their thick mud-encrusted, calf-high storm boots, denim pants, bearded faces, and the guns they either carried or wore. He shook his head in commiseration with the farmers' plight.

The Florida lands had farmers floundering at first, forcing many of them to experiment with crops, and even now, many barely made ends meet while others, like the tall young man in the center of the group, had succeeded in taming all but the weather. He admired Clay Wescott, was proud of the man his daughter chose to marry, and owed him a debt for his unstinting help offered to Pierce as he realized his dream.

Cyrus settled himself on a nail keg, leaning against the wall, taking out his hand-carved briar pipe, a last gift from his wife. He filled the bowl and, while he tamped down the tobacco, found himself offered a light. He acknowledged his thanks with a nod toward his new neighbor.

"Haven't seen much of you in town this week, Silver."

"We're swinging into full production out at the Devil's Own," he answered, lighting a cheroot. His gaze followed Cyrus's toward the crowd of men. "I wanted to talk to you about opening a company store out at the site, but there's no hurry. I imagine you'd want to listen to them."

"You're not concerned with the farmers' growing unrest?"

"No. Should I be?"

"I'd guess not," Cyrus answered. "Your dealings have been more than fair with the farmers." Cyrus liked Silver McQuade, despite his reputation for quick brutal retaliation against any man who crossed him. "Matt's out back of the store, if you're looking for him," he added, reluctant to mention his notice of Dara's strange behavior when this man was nearby.

"I'll see you later, then."

Cyrus turned away to answer called-out greetings from several of the farmers. Worry about Clay's determination to fight the incoming tide of miners into Rainly and its surrounding lands soon captured his attention. Aware of Clay's reasons, Cyrus wanted to caution him that he was not a boy, but a man, and should realize that what he advocated would only end in violence. Cyrus had seen enough bloodshed and violence to last two lifetimes, but he sat forward, returned Clay's greeting, then listened to his impassioned speech.

"A few of us talked about forming a farm association to help any of us considering selling out to these miners. It's one solution to protect our farmlands." Clay used one large hand to brush back the disarray of silky blond hair framing his lean angular face. Expressive dark blue eyes, edged with thick sandy brows and lashes, surveyed the faces around him.

"The other problem we have is to stop the riffraff working for these mining companies from spilling into town. Most of you men are older than me," he said with a crooked grin that relieved the severe shape of his mouth. "If my father were alive, he'd be saying the same to you. He gave his life to protect our lands from the timber barons intent on destroying good farmland by logging indiscriminately. I won't stand by and see it happen again without a fight. Vogt and his partner, Teague, sold us out by hiding their find and getting wealthy before they leaked the news of the rich deposits. And we know of the other two vultures that came after them. If we don't do something to stop them now, there won't be a shred left of the town we know when they're done and move on."

"What's that you're plannin', Clay?" Hank Clare asked, shifting his bulk to a spraddle-legged stance as he waited for an answer from the man young enough to be his son.

"What we talked about, Hank." Clay stood a shade under six feet tall. His pressed cord pants and shirt set him apart from these men, but his thickly muscled body linked him to the hard physical labor that went into farming.

Encouraged, Hank began, "We've all got womenfolk to worry 'bout. There's vermin crawlin' into our town, and it'll git worse. Heah 'bout that Mex fella, Suarez? Saloon of his serves watahed whiskey, runs crooked games, and there's been shootin' out at his claims. Now he's talkin' 'bout bringin' in hired guns to pretect what's his."

"Don't be fergettin' that othah fella, Hank," someone called out.

"Ah 'spect there'll be trouble from Silvah McQuade's kind, too," Hank added above the rumble of angry voices.

"You sure you ain't riled 'cause you ain't made money yet, Hank?"

Cords stood out in Hank's thick neck as he swung his head to locate the lone dissenter. "Ah might've know it was you, Amos. We all be knowin' you favah these men 'cause you and yore boy scouted land for 'em. To mah way of thinkin', yore a skinner jus' like 'em. Jus' ask," he stated, gesturing with one ham-sized fist to include the men around him.

Clay stepped in quickly to avoid a fight. "Hank isn't the only one to express concern about his womenfolk being afraid to come into town without him or his sons. The rumors are thick that the mine owners intend to bring in gangs of convicts to work for them." He paused to give the men time to reflect on what he said. Though he was younger, too young to remember the times immediately after the Civil War, he'd heard horror stories from his parents and their friends. Most of the aged faces before him had come to manhood during those bloody years, and they were scarred with the memories.

"We need to think about what will happen here if they go ahead, Amos," Clay added, facing the thin wiry-built man.

"We all gonna jus' stan' 'round an' watch it happen ag'in?" Hank demanded in his surly voice. "We cain't," he stressed, glaring at them, "stan' aside an' still be callin' ourselves men."

"Ah ain't denyin' what yore sayin'," Amos defended. "Or you, eithah, Clay. But yore all fergettin' the money that's pourin' into town. Jus' look around. The town's buildin' up. We got a real land office, public baths, fancy restaurants and shops, and—"

"And we got gamblin' an' saloons and rooms upstairs that ain't a man jack of you would confess to visitin'." A giant of a man shouldered his way through the crowd toward Clay. Many called out greetings to Flynn Kinnel. "I don't hold with violence, but my Trevor's wife, Minna, was near raped last night out by my place. And what I want to know is what you all have in mind to stop it."

"My brother-in-law, Jake, is doing a good job, but he's only one man," Clay replied. "I propose we form a vigilance committee to help him."

Cyrus didn't want to hear any more. He saw Jesse at the edge of the crowd and moved down the porch, motioning for him to join him. Regret of what was to come filled Cyrus's eyes and heart.

Regret melded with anger in the gaze of the man Cyrus passed. Silver McQuade knew where the rumor of bringing in convicts had started. Rainly had a large population of southern men clinging to the ideals of their youth like a worn old whore refusing to see herself for what she was.

Neither Jesse nor Cyrus paid any attention to Silver, but Dara did. She couldn't stop her eyes from straying toward where he leaned against the open doorway. It reminded her of the first day he had come here, and then, as now, he boldly returned her look. Dara was the first to turn away, giving her attention to Matt, who was standing by his side. It was only for a moment. A request for spices had her turning around even as she was sure they were both still watching her.

Silver met Matt's inquiring gaze as the crowd of men moved down the street toward the livery. "Go on," he offered. "I'll wait until your sister is free to help me." He looked at Dara. No matter the heat, she managed to look cool and crisp as a Nevada stream and as rigidly starched as the linen collar she'd sold him last week. He thought of her pretended indifference to his most patient stalking, and his grin was more than satisfied. It was predatory.

Matt didn't notice. He was looking outside, edgy with excitement as the last arguing man walked away. When he did look at Silver, it was with a meld of admiration and hero worship for the calmness the man displayed.

"Didn't it bother you to hear them talk about you and the other miners?"

"No."

"But Clay's got them riled and Hank's a fighter," Matt insisted. "I know they don't like you for being a miner and opening the first saloon, even if your other stores are respectable enough."

"I didn't come to Rainly to be liked, Matt. I came to make money." Silver pushed back the brim of his hat, and his voice took on a note of gritty humor. "My father was fond of telling me that times change and men deteriorate their ideals. Nothing deteriorates a man faster than greed. It gives me an edge over those men out there. They'll talk about taking action against the miners, but when it comes to counting the money they're making, my guess is that more than a few will do nothing." Raising his hand to Matt's shoulder, he urged him to go if he wanted.

Scuffing the toe of his pebbled-leg short boot, Matt glanced toward his sister. "I can't go," he muttered. "Dara won't like it. She was upset when I left her alone in the store last Saturday."

"And most likely blamed me for encouraging you," Silver said. His shrug was careless; he was well aware of Dara's animosity toward their friendship. "You're almost a man now, and it's time for you to find your own path to walk. Your sister should come to terms with that. Your father has. Or are you afraid of her telling him?"

"Dara? Never. That's not her way. She won't yell or snitch to Pa, she just . . ." Shoving his hands into the stiff pockets of his new pants, Matt hunched his shoulders. "It's hard to explain. Dara's just got her own way of letting a person know that they did wrong."

"Could be she's just thinking of you getting hurt if you're prone to take sides, Matt. Don't blame her. I've a feeling she just means to protect you."

Matt glanced at Dara behind the counter with less resentment. "You hardly know her, but you could be right. I guess," he said with all the painful shyness of an eighteen-year-old measuring himself against a man whose reputation he envied, "knowing all about women and such is part of growing up. Pa ain't all that much for talking, and Pierce is too busy with his farm. Bet you could teach me more'n them anyways."

A brief flash of his own past brought a gleam of amusement to Silver's eyes, but he buried it quickly in view of Matt's earnest expression. Silver's grin, though, was a shade on the devilish side. "I could offer a word or two of advice, if and when you thought you'd need it. But since you've got an itch that wants scratching now, go on. And if you're worried, I'll keep your sister distracted so she won't notice you're gone."

"Sometimes I don't understand you. You defend my sister's ways, and yet you tell me to find my own path. Don't make sense, but I'm obliged."

"I respect your sister for having the courage to fight in her own way for what she believes, and then maybe," he softly intoned, "maybe it's something more."

Matt had half turned to leave. He reluctantly looked first at his sister, then up at Silver. The man stood half a head taller, was broader shouldered than Matt, but there was a hardness that made most men back away from tangling unnecessarily with him. Matt called this man friend. Silver understood the restless hunger prowling around inside him, a wild dissatisfaction so unlike his father or older brother. But Silver, he knew, wasn't a settling-down kind of man, and Dara, well, she was a marrying kind of woman. He owed this man his life, even if Silver denied the debt. Yet a strange protective urge for Dara welled inside him. Straightening, the serious turn of his thoughts reflected in the amber-eyed gaze he leveled at Silver.

"Dara's promised to marry Clay. I'll be holding on to the thought that you do respect her."

"I'm aware of that," Silver replied. "But she isn't married to him yet." His voice was calm, removing any hint of threat. "I'm afraid it's hard to get your sister to accept even respect from me."

Matt shrugged and left just as Dara stopped totaling a bill and looked up. That man had no right encouraging Matt to leave the store. She knew her anger was wrong. What challenge was there for Matt to unpack crates of button-head bucket bolts or bottles of tooth powder? There was none, and well she knew it. She had to stop hovering over Matt, she thought, and with a sigh wrapped two pint-sized bottles of bay rum for her customer. She couldn't protect Matt from Silver's influence, as her father had warned her more than once.

"Your bill comes to one dollar and fifty-five cents, Leah. And do be careful with the eggs. Neither Abner nor Varina can supply me enough, with every café and restaurant owner buying from them, too."

"They should both be thinkin' on expandin'. Are you comin' to the social tonight? Elvira and Suelle worked all day puttin' up buntin' in the church hall. Ah do hope that Ah'll see the Clare girls there. Ah want to hire both of them to help with the sewin'." She lifted her basket, then added, "Will you have Matt delivah the rest of my ordah?"

"If he comes back early enough," Dara answered, noticing that Silver was walking toward them.

"Yore brothah is jus' like mah Julian. He wants to mine. That nice . . . oh, goodness, heah Ah was jus' 'bout to tell Dara how you offahed to take on our boy, Mr. McQuade."

He tipped his hat, ignoring Dara's frosty look. "I told you it would be my pleasure, ma'am."

"Mah boy is excited to be workin' at the Devil's Own, but Ah fault you with choosin' sich a name for yore mine."

"Whatever for, Leah?" Dara interrupted with a sweet smile. "It would seem he couldn't have picked a more appropriate one."

Unruffled, Silver explained. "What Miss Owens is referring to is that the young Negro boy who worked for Mr. Vogt first found bones buried in the pit he was digging for drainage. It's one of the richest deposits assayed, but the boy thought the devil had died and left behind the huge teeth and bones. Not many folks realize fossils are protected by the chalky material some thought to be gypsum at first, but which is really high-grade phosphate."

Dara glared at him while he shared soft laughter with Mrs. Tucker.

"Oh, by the way, Dara," Leah asked, "did you know that Early and Suelle are plannin' on sellin' that lan' Early's brothah left him when he died?"

"No, I hadn't heard."

Since Dara was determined to ignore him, and Leah

was proud to be first with gossip, neither woman noticed the sudden speculative gleam in Silver's eyes.

"Suelle is heartbroken that Early is thinkin' on 'ceptin' Mistah Suarez's offah for more'n the lan' is worth."

Silver didn't listen to the rest, stepping back and away, for once glad that Dara wasn't paying him any attention. He could still hear her soft, breathy voice which stroked him when he heard it, but anger began to surface. He had scouted that land Early Yarwood owned, using his twenty-foot steel rod to bring up samples of the rock below in its special pointed slot. Having worked two years at the Smithsonian Institution in Washington, analyzing ore and mineral samples sent from all over the country, Silver was sure the land would yield far richer deposits than the claims he now owned. He'd told no one about his find, but somehow word had leaked. Lucio was as greedy now as he'd been in Mexico when they first met and later when they had partnered a silver mine in Nevada. Unconsciously Silver's left hand caressed the fancy hand-tooled leather gun holster riding low on his hip. He'd begun wearing it this past week after he had a run-in with the men he would swear Lucio had hired. So far they had managed to avoid a direct confrontation, but when Satin Mallory arrived, it might not be possible. Silver smiled, thinking of his own plans for Lucio.

Dara didn't miss his hand's caressing motion. Her mouth thinned. She wanted to keep Leah talking, but he once more joined them and interrupted them with his charming smile.

"If you're finished with Mrs. Tucker, I'd like to have a look at the new Winchester rifles before anyone else comes in, Miss Owens."

Leah excused herself, and Dara searched for the keys to the gun cases. Debating whether to light the fixtures, for the day was rapidly darkening, she called herself five variations of coward for being afraid to be alone with him. Straightening her shoulders, setting her glasses firmly in place, she marched out from behind the counter, as no soldier facing an enemy ever had, across the aisles into the far corner, where he waited. Her hand trembled slightly when she slotted the key, turned, and opened the door, holding on to its wood frame tightly when he moved right behind her.

"I promise I won't bite unless asked," he murmured in that rich, humorous voice.

Dara refused to answer. She gestured to the open case, uncomfortable with the way the shadows seemed deeper back here. "I don't know which one you wanted to see."

"The new Winchester."

"I heard you say that, but I don't know which one it is. My father or Matt usually handles the buying and selling of firearms." It was becoming a habit to have her shirtwaist collars become constricting whenever he closed the distance between them. His indrawn breath had her wondering if she'd been too liberal with the splash of lilac-rose toilet water she used to refresh herself nearly an hour ago.

He raised one hand, tempted to touch her as much as he wanted to taste, but he reached inside the case to lift out the rifle from its mounting. He bent his head to examine it, smiling ruefully. She could fidget and flutter with impatience all she wanted; he wasn't about to be rushed. He forced himself to study the fine workmanship when he would rather look at the delicate-boned features of Dara's face. A glint of humor lingered in his eyes, hidden by the thick fall of his lashes. Every agitated breath she drew only called attention to the small span of her waist and the curving fullness of her breasts. He had told her that first night down by the river that he would have thought some man had stolen the promise of her passion long ago. In the past weeks he'd learned more than he wanted to about Dara and Clay. He wouldn't call Clay Wescott a fool. If anything, the man was shrewd in all his business dealings. Dara's breathing increased, and he amended his thinking: Clay was indeed a fool.

Foot tapping impatiently, Dara asked in a prim voice if there was something wrong with the rifle.

"Has anyone ever mentioned that you sound downright insulting when you use that tone of voice?"

"No one has criticized me the way you do."

"Why do I make you nervous, Dara?"

"Miss Owens to you."

"Answer me, Dara."

"You do not."

"Ah, darlin', and here I thought you never lied. Shame on you. Whenever I come into the store, you skitter—"

"I do not skitter."

"You *skitter,*" he insisted with a grin, leaning the rifle against the case. Fully cornered, Dara breathlessly watched as his hands came to rest palm down against the wall on either side of her. Her quick little gasp made his pulse race. "I believe," he said, lifting one hand, running the back of his fingers lightly down the line of her throat, "it's too late to think of running."

There was such certainty in his voice that she looked up, eyes wide, feeling trapped. Drawing a sharp breath, she wanted to deny her awareness of the desire in his eyes and lowered her head. Words of denial perished in her tightened throat. Her eyes were level with the third button of his gray work shirt, and she slid her gaze back and forth. His chest, shoulders, and arms could not be viewed unless she moved her head from side to side. This close, his size overpowered her.

"Dara." Her name was a mere breath, rolling softly, slowly from his lips. His head angled down, whisper-soft scents of tobacco playing havoc with her senses. "Did your parents take your name from the Bible—meaning wisdom and compassion? How compassionate are you, little saint?"

With unhurried grace, he bent toward her. One of his knees flexed, and his forearms closed to cradle her head. "Will you show me, Dara?"

Heat spread inside her. She couldn't deny the strength of his physical presence, or the very gentle movement of his hand as his thumb followed the curve of her hairline, disturbing a few damp tendrils. He overwhelmed her . . . his smile, the warm fresh scent of him drifting through the fibers of his shirt, his eyes, too bright, too hot.

"Why do"—she licked her dry lips, trying again—"Why do you ask such things of me?" She could not look into his eyes. It seemed wiser to look down at his shirt tucked tight into denim pants. They were secured with a worn belt which closed with an intricately carved buckle that boasted a silver nugget as its ornament. For a single shocking moment she toyed with the idea of being brave and asking if the item had some connection with his name. But instead Dara found a yellow streak running down her back, along with a shivery sensation of warmth.

"I asked, because charity and compassion are the scope of the Lord's commands. And charity," he teased, smile at full tilt, "covers a multitude of sins. So are you very charitable, Dara?" His voice was unhurried, so even, and so much at odds with the desire inside him.

It had been a daring game to her and now ceased abruptly. She pressed against the wall, trying to escape the coaxing pressure of his thigh rubbing against her leg. There was an unexpected hardness to his body when weighed against the softness of his voice, the slow gentle moves. She didn't want to admit to the excitement that was building. It was all too unfamiliar, too warm, and desire bloomed within her.

"You didn't answer me, Dara." Breathing in the scent and sweet fragrance of her, he slowly withdrew his body. She was drawing erratic breaths, a captive once more of his arms on either side of her.

"Everything you said sounded like a preacher's words." Her eyes narrowed behind her spectacles, suspicions forming that the words, when whispered from his lips, meant nothing she learned in church.

"They are, little saint."

"You don't look or behave like any preacher I know."

"Would you feel safer with me if I said I was one?"

"Safer? Oh, no," she answered with innate honesty.

"Well, ease your mind, darlin', I'm not."

The only safety Dara found was to look down again. Well, it was a thought until she stared at his faded pants. They had certainly been scrubbed enough. Hadn't Lara bragged of the generous tips he'd given her for doing his laundry? Perhaps that wasn't all he'd tipped her for, Dara thought, and pursed her lips. But the touch of those pants would be cottony soft . . . Mentally jerking back from where her thoughts had strayed, Dara excused herself, having washed for her father and brothers enough years to know how pants wore. His narrow hips weren't a safe place to rest her gaze, either. He was most definitely graduating to a state most indecent for any lady's peace of mind. Turning her head aside, the tip of her nose brushed his forearm.

"Don't you have another name besides Silver?"

"So you can be curious, Dara? Sure, I do." His head angled a bit closer. Repeated lickings of her lips had left them glistening, and while he was tempted to close the hair'sbreadth distance, he answered her instead. "My daddy was a preacher and named each one of us from the Good Book. My name is Eden."

Mesmerized by the even rise and fall of his chest, and at the same time wanting to duck under his arm and escape Dara found she didn't have the will to move. "I have heard Reverend Speck refer to Eden as another name for paradise, and that is considered a place of delightful pleasure we all shall strive to attain. But you, sir, are being neither delightful nor a pleasure right now."

"I could make atonement for the omission, little one," he noted softly.

Dara found herself nose to nose with him. "Your father must be horrified to know how you mock his teachings!"

"Such nasty little slips of temper," he mocked, shifting one hand closer to her shoulder. "You won't attain heaven without showing some charity to those of us less fortunate than yourself, darlin'." Panic flared in her eyes, and he longed to remove those glasses to see how deep and velvet the darkness could get. "My daddy," he drawled, "knows exactly how I feel. I see him often. He was just a mite too fond of talking about the devil's temptations leading all of us astray, so I left home to find out for myself what they were."

"And did you find out?"

"Some."

"Some?" Dara couldn't help herself. She knew it was wrong to encourage him, but somehow she enjoyed this sparring with him. "Well, that wasn't much of an answer."

"I didn't think you'd want the details. 'Sides, I was just figuring, standing so close and watching you, that my daddy didn't know that much about temptation after all."

And Dara found she wasn't immune to the blistering heat of his smile. "You can't imply that I—"

"Are you afraid I might find out how right I am?"

"I am not afraid." She needed to draw one breath without the scent of him filling her. As if he sensed it, he backed off. The sight of his gun suddenly made the foolishness of the last few minutes flee. "If you are finished toying with me, make your decision about which rifle you wish to purchase. And when you do," she stressed, angry now, "bring it to the counter."

"Why the anger, Dara? I was only teasing you. And no, you won't get by without giving me an answer."

"It's that."

"That?" he repeated doubtfully. She made a vague gesture toward his left hip. "Ah, that," he said again, but softly and very coolly. "Why?" His hand slid along her slender-boned shoulder, moving up the expanse of her neck to gently cup her chin. "Tell me."

Her knees suddenly had the consistency of melted butter. Without pressure, each of his fingertips sent a message that her body, to her mortification, was willing to receive. Warnings came along with the quivering sensations his touch evoked. And when he leaned close, softly repeating his demand, she sagged against the wall, closing her eyes.

"I despise guns." Dry, throaty words conveyed a chill

that took his heat and dissolved its effect upon her. "I have," she stated, opening her eyes and looking directly into his, "no respect for men who need to use them. Guns don't solve anything. They just create trouble."

Sensing more behind her explanation, and moved by a surge of emotions he wasn't about to take the time to untangle, he softly cajoled her to tell him why.

"Ten years ago Ziba King sent his men from Fort Ogden after cattle thieves. They found them camped outside of Rainly and shot them. My . . . my mother was there," she whispered against his shirt as he drew her within the warm circle of his arms. Feeling the softness of the cloth, the hardness of his chest beneath, Dara felt eased and inhaled his male scent, clean, spice-tanged, and with it his heat. Talking about her mother weakened already battered defenses when his murmurings coaxed her to continue.

"They didn't kill her. She was shot in the back by a stray bullet on her way home from collecting eggs . . ." Her voice faltered, tears threatened, and his comfort-laden words were meaningless sounds. "She had so much pain . . . lingering for months, and no one could help her."

"Dara, listen to me. Not all men are careless when they—"

"No!" She jerked herself free. "Men who wear guns, who use them, are looking for trouble. Jake has changed. Even his wife isn't sure who he is anymore."

Eden's cool, impersonal gaze assessed her. "Some of us, like Jake, wear a gun as a necessary part of themselves to stay alive, Dara."

"It's all part and parcel of men like you coming here, tearing apart the town, raping the land, stealing from the poor farmers! I hear about people offered half of what their land is worth, and when their money is gone, you mine owners hire them for fifty cents a day while you make five hundred dollars from their sweat." Backing away from him, Dara realized where her encouragement of this man had led her. "Clay is right. You and your kind will destroy Rainly if you're not stopped."

Eden "Silver" McQuade had had enough. He went after her, lithe, hard, dangerous, stalking, and backing her down one aisle, fighting for control against the caustic words that so outraged him. Her move to turn and flee was a bare flicker in her eyes when he grabbed her upper arm and hauled her up against him.

"You," he gritted, a deadly derision simmering in the eyes he targeted upon her, "don't know a damn thing about me. I warned you once not to judge me, Dara. I've worked mining pits in North Carolina and in Tennessee. I've hacked and picked my way in ore mines from Mexico up to Nevada, and I've owned my land here, right here in Marion County, for seven years. My town land was bought two years ago. I've been mining phosphate down at Peace River for three years, and all I destroyed was a rail line that was poor at best. But I paid my workers fair wages and gave them a better railway. A railway that takes farmers' stock and produce to give them a fighting chance to be better than dirt poor."

His grip tightened even though he could feel the blood pulsing in her arm, saw her throat working, her eyes wide with fear. "And I don't," he said slowly, hard mockery lacing every word, "rape. I've never had to take anything I wanted by force . . . not land . . . and never, ever a woman."

His abrupt release stunned her almost as much as his impassioned defense did. And Dara found herself looking up at him, really looking at him for what seemed to be the first time. When had she unconsciously stored away the fact that he was always clean shaven? Why, too, was the urge so strong to reach up and touch him? It shook her, this feeling, coming as it did with the sureness that he wasn't lying, and that none of his life had been easy. Why? Why should she care? Immobile, his face was hers to scrutinize for long moments, until she reluctantly turned her head aside, but didn't, just couldn't move away from him.

"Finished?" he queried without emotion.

"Quite."

"Dare I ask the ungentlemanly question of whether or not you found anything to your liking?"

She couldn't help but unbend a little, hearing his lighter, teasing tone. "No."

"Was that an unequivocal no, I can't ask, or a no, you didn't see anything about me that you liked?" His lazy smile showed his willingness to ease the tension between them.

"A woman," Dara informed him, "wouldn't answer such a question and still consider herself a lady."

"But, darlin', I'm not questioning your being a lady. From here"—amused gray eyes lingered on her neatly pinned hair, darkening under a feathering of lashes before his caressing look stroked the length of her—"to the pointed tips of your proper little shoes, you are very much the lady. What I object to is your calling yourself a woman," he teased with indolent humor. "You're not." Satisfied to see the blush on her cheeks, he added softly, "At least, not yet."

"Don't say such improper things." Her hands cradled her flushed cheeks.

"Ah, little saint—"

"And don't call me those names, nor use my first. We are not friends!"

"Friends, huh?" He leaned against the nearest shelf, one hand cupping the back of her neck, dragging her close. "I never wanted to be friends with you, Dara. So, then," he asked, his voice suddenly sensually soft, "what should a lover call you?" He removed her glasses before she could stop him.

"A—" Dara got no further, for his lips came tasting, brushing back and forth against the soft bowed fullness of her mouth. In the sudden blood-thrumming silence, shivering fear and thrilling longing melted inside her. His mouth's feasting was gentle, but she sensed the leased tension inside him a moment before his lips firmly made a claiming demand upon her own. Her toes curled tight. Her hands clenched her skirt, and she gave herself over to the curious longing to know what his kiss would be like. The shifting move of his hand and mouth rotated her head for his pleasure. Dara leaned closer, wanting more, but as quickly as he'd begun, he stopped, and lifted his head.

"I'll respect your very delicate sensibilities if you don't continue to provoke me."

"Don't . . . you . . . dare . . . mock . . . me." Her jaw ached from suddenly clenching it. She was shaken by his kiss, and he—he seemed unmoved! "I do not provoke you. I don't want to. And you, you don't know me at all."

"Don't I? Just hush," he murmured, placing one fingertip against the parted bow of her mouth. "I'll wait and you'll run. You'll run until you're tied in knots with wanting me. But Dara, don't be afraid. I won't rush you."

He could no more resist brushing his fingertip over the lush wet satin of her bottom lip than Dara, enthralled by the hunger of his eyes, could stop herself from sliding the tip of her tongue to taste his skin.

Stunned by her action, she pulled back, staring up at him with a dazed bewilderment that begged his denial for her brazen action.

Eden McQuade denied her solace with a slow shake of his head. "You see and feel how it will be with us."

"Dear Lord! What are you trying to do to me?" Dara shook her head, realizing where they were. Anyone could have walked into the store and seen them! She was desperate to deny him, his words, and the hot promise burning in his gaze, as well as the imprint of his mouth and taste burned upon her lips. Dara spun around, needing to run from him as well as herself. She didn't want what the heat of him promised! He was wicked to tempt her like this. Clay was the one she loved—had loved all these years she had patiently waited, the years she didn't dare count, the years she set aside her dreams and longings. No! Silver was the devil's own temptation to make her think she had needs too!

Dara ran down the aisle, heard Matt call out to her, warn her. She stopped short when she saw his warning came too late.

Matt stopped, too, when he saw Silver McQuade standing with his back toward him, and beyond him Dara stood sheltered protectively in Clay's arms.

"I'm already here, Matt," Clay said, hugging Dara against him, but turning an iced blue gaze on the man in front of him. "If you hurt her . . ." he began.

"Ask her," McQuade returned, his voice unconcerned, his gaze direct.

Clay hesitated, then tipped Dara's chin upward. "Did he hurt you?"

"Answer him," McQuade demanded.

Chapter Five

DARA GLANCED FROM one to the other. She silently begged the Lord's forgiveness for her lie, but she refused to be the cause of violence between these two men. Reassuring Clay in a soft, shaken voice, she told him it was her memories of her mother's death that upset her, triggered by showing Mr. McQuade the rifle. Eden McQuade's irony mocked her attempt to smooth over the matter.

"She faced a few truths about guns and the men who use them, Wescott, and I, too, learned a few undeniable truths from Miss Owens's lips." Without turning around, he added, "Matt, put aside the rifle next to the case for me. I'll be back later to claim what's mine." To Dara, he said, "Here, put these back on. They might help you see things more clearly." Eden let her snatch the glasses from his hands, then turned to leave. He brushed by Clay, seething inside for the way Dara clung to him.

Dara's relief at his leaving without trouble was short-lived.

"This is your fault, Matt," Clay lashed out. "You're old enough to realize what kind of a man he is. Your sister is a lady and should never have been left alone here, exposed to his sort."

"Clay! You can't mean to blame my brother. I told—"

"Stop protecting me, Dara," Matt interrupted. "I don't need you to speak up for me. Don't you see it's his own guilt that makes Clay blame me or whoever else he can? Why wasn't he here with you? Why don't you marry her, Clay? Why don't you admit that it's your own fault that she—"

"Why, you little—"

"Stop this!" Dara blocked Clay's forward move toward Matt. "It's not his fault, Clay. You're wrong to blame him, more because I told you nothing happened. As for you," she scolded, turning to face her brother, "I can't believe you'd forget yourself and dare mention what is a personal matter between Clay and myself. I'm ashamed of you, Matt."

Looking at the angry tearful sheen of Dara's eyes, Matt felt his anger fade. He'd not only hurt her, but he had embarrassed her as well. Mumbling an apology to both of them, he returned to the counter.

"He isn't too big to have a strop taken to him."

"Let him be, Clay," Dara pleaded, desperate to have this incident behind them. "Don't you think there's enough tension without the two of you fighting?"

With his large hand cupping her chin, Clay urged her around to look at him. "Matt hurt you and—"

"No more, please." Her fingertips against his lips silenced his protest, but Dara couldn't meet his penetrating gaze. "Have you been to see Anne?" she asked in an effort to change the subject.

"I was on my way there and thought you'd be free to join me, but I see," he said with a quick look at the front of the store, "that you'll be busy for a while yet. I'll make it a short visit and be back in time to have supper with you." Reluctantly he eased his hand away, accepted her nod and halfhearted smile, but stood there watching her walk away. Why had she lied to him? And more, why did he have the feeling that beneath Matt's anger there had been a warning for him?

Dara hurried to tidy the kitchen after supper. The small platter of leftover fried chicken went into their new Michigan double-door icebox, the half loaf of corn bread into the stove's warming oven above the burners, relish and watermelon pickles back onto their shelf in the pantry. Setting a fresh kettle of water on the stove to heat, she glanced at the kitchen-shelf clock, impatient to get to her room and have a few minutes to herself. With her brother Pierce showing up at the last minute for supper, she hadn't had a moment for a spare thought.

A sound at the doorway made her turn. Clay stood there, the jacket to his single-breasted, square-cut, black cassimere suit pushed aside by his hands shoved deep into the pants pockets. Dara avoided his serious look by staring at the small black and gray checks on his vest. When he didn't say anything, Dara grew uncomfortable. She began chattering about her need to hurry, her disappointment that Anne would not be accompanying them to the social tonight, and finally, inanely, told him about some of the sales she had made. And he listened until her voice trailed off before he spoke.

"I had a surprise waiting for me when I went to see my sister this afternoon. McQuade was with Jake, at the house." At her startled doelike look he added, "How many times has he caught you alone in the store?"

She wished she could feign innocence of what he meant, but pretending had never come easy for her. Or so she had thought. Lately she was questioning too much. Before she could frame a reply, Clay continued.

"I don't think you told me the truth about what happened in the store today. What I can't figure out is why. If McQuade's been bothering you, I have a right to know."

"Why are you insisting that man did something to me?" She couldn't look at him, nor did she understand why Clay seemed intent on forcing her into an admission that would bring trouble. What was happening? She had never lied to Clay before this. *No?* a small voice queried. *Haven't you been lying to him right along about your feelings?* Dara couldn't answer herself and refused to think about it. She concentrated on the kettle, urging the water to hurry and boil.

"Dara, I get the feeling that you're hiding things from me." Clay moved forward, and Dara, to his shock, backed away from him. Confusion knitted his brows. "What's wrong?"

"It's late. You know that. And Papa's mad because Matt took off right after supper. Pierce will most likely be marching in here wondering what's taking me so long, since he hasn't seen Caroline all week. You're standing here, making accusations that amount to calling me a liar. And you dare ask me what's wrong?" she finished acidly, her emotions in such a tumult that she barely knew what she was saying. Why was she protecting Eden McQuade? The good Lord knew that man didn't need her protection. Or anyone's for that matter. Or was it Clay she hoped to protect? Pacing before the stove, ignoring Clay, Dara felt confusion sweep over her. Somehow she felt tricked into betraying Clay and his love for her. No! She refuted that thought. Eden McQuade's actions were his own, and she refused to feel guilt for them. She hadn't invited that man's kiss or his attentions. She most certainly wasn't attracted to him. She wasn't!

"Dara," Clay said softly, "are you sure you're not angry with me for yelling at Matt? Or is it what he said? Are you tired of the wait to marry me?"

"Stop badgering me! Oh, please, I'm sorry for snapping at you. I shouldn't . . . Clay, please, I'm just . . . just tired." But she couldn't meet his gaze. "I admit I sometimes get impatient, but we both know we have had good reasons to wait. I couldn't leave Papa to run the store and take care of the house and my brothers. You certainly can't be held responsible for losing a full season's crop to storms. And then," she continued, unaware of the bitter edge to her voice, "the following year it was replacing the leaky roof and clearing new acreage, then Anne's wedding—"

". . . along with my helping them to build their house in town," Clay finished for her. "You know I've plowed ever spare penny back into the land. And I can't expect you to live in the house until I can equal what you have here. Your family can't help us after giving everything to Pierce to buy his farm."

"I am well aware of all the *good* reasons we have waited, Clay." Dara grabbed the pot holders and took up the kettle, no longer caring if the water was hot, just wanting to escape. Her smile was intended both as a peace offering and reassurance, but it never reached her eyes as she left the room, pushing aside the angry thoughts of Clay daring to remind her why she was still single.

Stopping at the foot of the stairs, Dara glanced into the front parlor. "Papa, you haven't changed yet. Better hurry."

"I'm not coming, Dara."

Alarmed, she came to stand in the archway. Before she could question her father, Pierce spoke.

"Don't worry. He's just tired. But don't you keep us waiting hours while you primp and fuss. Clay knows what you look like, and if he hasn't changed his mind about you by now, he's never going to."

"You wouldn't by any chance be in such a hurry because of missing Caroline, would you?" she teased.

Pierce, sitting on the edge of the velvet mahogany settee between two piecrust tables, glared at her. The hand-painted matching banquet lamps lit his rugged features, showing him ill at ease in his brown worsted suit, tugging repeatedly at his starched white linen collar. Then dimples formed on either side of his generously shaped lips when he smiled at her.

Dara couldn't resist teasing him again. "If you're that anxious, you could always go on without us."

"You know Jesse won't let me see Caroline to the social alone." He rubbed at the white streak of skin across his forehead, evidence of the long hours he'd spent in the sun with his hat pulled low, then, with a nervous gesture, he smoothed back his dark pomaded hair. "Will you get yourself upstairs to change before I call Clay to take you in hand?"

"Oh, I'm going," she returned over his laughter, gathering her skirt with one hand just as Clay entered the room. He took the large wing chair opposite of where Cyrus sat reading the newspaper. "Pierce," she called out, "you really need a hair trim."

"Dara!" Cyrus admonished, peering around the paper to flash her a grin, "stop teasing him."

"That's right. I'm not the boy you had to chase around the house and bribe to hold still, Dara. Watch I don't come up those stairs and trim yours," Pierce threatened over her soft laughter.

Dara was halfway up the stairs when she impulsively looked back at the scene in the front parlor. Only Matt's absence made it seem incomplete. She listened a moment to her father's voice reading aloud about Henry Flager's completion of his hotel in St. Augustine and saw his attentiveness to Clay's comments, nodding his agreement. Dara forgot those few unpleasant minutes in the kitchen and felt once more the absolute rightness of Clay for her choice of husband. Her need for such reassurance did not escape her notice as she entered her room.

Music reached them as Clay guided his horse team to the open field beyond the church hall and one-room schoolhouse. Dara began humming along with the sounds of harmonica, concertina, and fiddle playing a lively tune. Dressed in their Sunday best, people had been arriving since early evening, for this social was an affair for the whole family to enjoy. As Clay helped her down, Dara waved to women with children in tow, grandfathers and spinster aunts, young couples arm in arm, just like Pierce and Caroline Halput behind them, all moving toward the warmth of golden lamplight and music.

With a smile firmly in place, determined that before this night was over she would have a commitment from Clay for a wedding date, Dara banished Eden McQuade to a dark corner of her mind and proudly entered the room at Clay's side.

It took mere seconds for her to realize that the gaiety within was forced. Pockets of farmers and their families stood muttering against the opposite wall, carefully separated from the townsfolk gathered around the refreshment tables. The low rumble of voices had a decided angry edge that could be heard over the lowering sound of the music.

Bewildered, Dara glanced around but could see no reason for it. Before she could question Clay, he was urging her to cross the room with him. The music faltered, then stopped altogether on a sour, jarring note.

Dara had all her questions answered in the seconds that followed. A path cleared to allow Reverend Speck to lead a contingent toward the small back door. Within its opening stood two miners with more crowded behind them. Tension lay thick in the sudden quiet. Other men converged behind the reverend, and Clay was one of the first to push himself forward after warning Dara to stay where she was. With a whispered plea, Dara prayed there wouldn't be a confrontation that ended in violence.

Eden McQuade was sitting with his back toward the wall in his small saloon, one hand cupping a glass on the already scarred table. He was about to have a confrontation of his own, and its outcome was in just as much doubt.

"We need to finish our talk," Jake Vario repeated, pulling out a chair opposite Eden without waiting for an invitation. "I've been looking all over for you. I even stopped by the church social. Never thought you were a coward."

"Did you decide that before or after you ran out and left me to handle the mess in Hamilton, Jake?"

"You know damn well why I had to leave." He refused to meet Eden's cool, steady gaze.

"Ran, Jake. You ran out on me."

"I would have killed Lucio for what he did if I had stayed. The way he had that town sewed up, they'd have strung me up quicker than a rattler strike. But I didn't come here to rehash old history." He looked up then. "Gonna share that bottle with me?"

Eden pushed it toward him, then sipped his own drink, while Jake topped off his glass and took a healthy slug. "Damn fine bourbon. No sourmash for you." He eyed the bottle devoid of a label and knew it had to come from Eden's private stock. "But then," he added, "you always were one for having the best."

"Only when I could afford it." Eden had been expecting Jake to come looking for him. After Clay had arrived to visit with his sister, they hadn't had much of a chance to talk. Neither one of them was going out of his way to confront their past, but Eden sensed Jake was on edge. He guessed it was for the same reason he was. Lucio intended to bring in convict labor to work his claims. Eden had not forgotten there were old scores to settle with Lucio, and if he brought trouble here, it would only compound the debt. But he sat there, sipping his drink, and waited, not sure how Jake would approach him, or what exactly it was that he wanted from him.

Jake didn't seem to be in any rush. He glanced around, nodded toward a few of the men standing at the bar. "Ain't fancy."

"It serves me well enough." Eden spoke the truth.

The bar was long and sturdy, roomy enough for a man to belly up and stand alone if that's what he wanted. The lighting fixtures were plain and serviceable, but threw plenty of light for a man to see his cards as well as the eyes of the men he played with. Eden made sure the games were honest ones. No tinny piano music filled the air to meld with smoke from cigars or pipes. No women cajoled a man into buying them drinks of watered-down whiskey or plain tea for triple the usual rate. The saloon was a place for a man who wanted a few drinks, a friendly game, and no trouble. Eden's place. The place he wanted for the man he had become.

Jake seemed to have reached the same conclusion. "You've changed. Didn't figure the hellraiser I knew would go in for peace and quiet." If he had hoped to goad Eden into commenting, he was disappointed. He sat across from him, watching and waiting. Jake tossed a crumpled telegram on the table. "Read it."

Eden skimmed the sparsely worded message. He already knew Satin Mallory would be arriving soon.

"Well?" Jake prodded. "Haven't you got a damn thing to say?"

"Do you expect me to believe this is some sort of a surprise, Jake? You knew Lucio would send for her." Jake wasn't looking at him, but gazing down at the tiny wet half-circles he was making with his glass. "If you think about it," Eden continued, "it's almost like the beginning, with the four of us starting out in the same place again."

"No. This time the odds are different. And nothing could be that good again." There was a bleak tone to his voice, and his eyes, when they met Eden's, reflected a bone-weary tiredness. "There's never a way to go back, like there's no way to forget some things. Not now and certainly not for me. But I've tried to make a new life here for myself and"—he stressed, sitting straight—"*nothing* is going to happen this time to destroy it."

For a moment the slight tensing of Eden's hand around his glass was the only reaction he offered to hearing the threat in Jake's voice.

"Was this the reason you came looking for me, Jake?"

"Isn't it enough?"

"No games, Jake. Spell it out so there's no mistake on

my part this time of what it is exactly that you want from me. I don't like floundering. If you're looking for revenge against Lucio for what happened in the past, count me out. He's stepping too close to my private line now, and I don't need much to start pushing him back."

"We do things legal here, McQuade. There'll be no taking of the law into your own hands."

Eden took a long pull of his drink, savoring the cask-aged flavor of smooth bourbon for a moment before swallowing. "Right. I'll keep that in mind. But you can't be in sixty places at once, and from what I've seen to date, that's what you're trying to do."

"It's my town," Jake returned with a bitter tone.

"The revenge you want is festering inside you, and that makes a man careless, Jake. We both know Lucio is greedy. He doesn't give a damn about this town or the people in it. He'll make his money, and when he's good and ready he'll sell out and move on. There doesn't have to be any trouble. You can wait him out or let me take care of him."

"That's what you intend doing? Waiting him out?"

"I had to cut my losses before, but it won't happen again. I'm not out to make a quick killing. This time I'm building something I want—"

Jake's bitter laugh cut him off. "You expect me to believe that you're thinking of settling down? And here?"

"I might be."

"That's not much of an answer."

"It's the only one you're getting." Eden's look became thoughtful. "Lucio isn't the only reason you wanted to talk to me, or you wouldn't have left that message with Miss Loretta for me to come to see you at your home. So what's holding you back from saying what's on your mind?" For a few minutes Jake glared at him, and Eden didn't think he would answer him, but then Jake grinned. It was a familiar sight, Jake's grin reflected in the bright hazel of his eyes. Eden lifted his glass in a silent toast, tossed off the last of his drink, and set the glass down. Jake refilled it.

"Eden, you're not going to like what I have to say, but that never stopped me before. My wife, Anne, is worried. She's been hearing gossip. So, take a friendly warning and stay away from Dara. Clay was upset about something that happened in the store today. He's sure that Dara lied to him to protect you. And you know she's not your kind of woman."

Eden tilted his chair back, rocking it slightly, his smile coming slow, but widening.

"It's not funny," Jake insisted. "Clay's not a man to stand aside and watch you or anyone else step into his rightful place. 'Sides, they've been promised to each other for almost five years."

"The man's a fool and deserves to lose her."

"Your opinion."

"My knowledge. My business," Eden warned, his chair coming down hard on the floor. He leaned over the table, cupping his glass with both hands, his gaze cool and steady upon Jake's face. "Stay out of it."

"I can't," he answered truthfully. "Clay's my brother-in-law, and Anne's expecting our first child. I can't have her upset. She's worried about Dara, and what's more, Clay is hotheaded. Right now he's good and steamed over the miners ruining his new grove of stock. You continue showing an interest in Dara, which gossip says is without honorable intent, and he'll use that to light a fuse whose trail he's been laying for weeks. 'Sides, this is me you're talking to. You haven't got it in you to be faithful to one woman. What's more, you've never . . . Oh, hell, Eden, she's not for you. What Dara needs—"

"You've said enough, Jake."

The noise behind them seemed to fade. Nothing Eden could have said would have pushed Jack back in time faster. He'd heard that same warning before, uttered in the exact soft tone. And he knew it was backed by the implicit knowledge that should a man be fool enough to think that Eden McQuade didn't mean it, violence would follow. Although he'd never been the target of McQuade's anger, Jake was no fool. They had once been as close as any two men who had managed to survive hell together could be, and still remain friends. It was the flicker of those memories that made Jake's decision for him. He pushed back his chair and stood up.

"Think about what I said. I won't ask more of you now. But give some thought to where you're going to stand when it comes time to choose sides. We were damn good together before we met Lucio."

Jake turned his back, and Eden, his voice barely rising to carry over the swelling din from a group of men surging to the bar, reminded him, "The blame wasn't Lucio's alone, Jake. It was Linda's, too, and you're lying to yourself to deny it."

"You're a bastard, McQuade." Jake didn't turn to face him, but his voice was raw with pain.

"Maybe so," Eden whispered to himself, watching Jake leave. "But then, it might keep you alive to believe it."

He was about to pour himself another drink when the first shots rang out. Eden didn't waste time trying to push his way clear through the miners rushing toward the front doors. He was out the back way and down the narrow alley behind the saloon before most of the men had reached the street.

The excitement was over in minutes. Jake had two inebriated miners by the collar, calling out for the crowd to break up, no one was hurt. He refused Eden's offer to help to get them over to the temporary jail.

The air was humid, the threat of promised rain still hovering as Eden turned away from the saloon entrance to continue down toward the river. If he had hesitated a moment more, he would have witnessed Dara's return to the city with Clay.

A royal duchess couldn't fault Dara's rigid posture. She ignored Clay when he slowed the wagon to speak to the milling crowd of men, and after hearing what had happened, she couldn't summon another ounce of anger. The first fat raindrops fell as Clay guided the horses into the lane running alongside the store. Clay helped her down from the jump-seat buggy, and Dara wished he would just once be impulsive enough to sweep her up into his arms. Hand in hand, they made an awkward dash for the sheltering dryness of the porch.

Before Clay could whisper good night as he was prone to do, Dara held on to his hand and led him to the wicker settee in the far shadowed corner. The thick profusion of jasmine vines twisted within the weighted boughs of the pine trees muffled the sound of the rain and created a bower scented with rich perfume. Dara sat down, ignoring the damp of her gown's hem and her shoes. She waited impatiently for Clay to reluctantly join her before she spoke.

"You had no right to force me to leave the social!"

"Dara! How can you say that? Was I supposed to stand aside and allow one of those men to dance with you?"

"Why not?" she demanded, low-voiced and angry.

"You certainly didn't have a moment to spare for me. Not to dance, or talk, or anything." She couldn't believe the anger churning inside herself. Crushing the cherry silk striped skirt of her gown with one hand, she gripped Clay's hand with the other, trying to convey the force of her emotions to him. "Clay, please understand. We hardly see each other anymore. Sometimes I believe you find it very easy to forget about me."

Rubbing his thumb against the slender length of her fingers, Clay sighed deeply. "You're being downright silly to imagine I could forget the woman I love. You saw for yourself how riled everyone is, and I just couldn't walk away from them, Dara. They needed me. You must understand that we have to take a firm stand now. If we don't, they'll run all over us. Tonight was just the start of it. First they take over our town so it's not safe for a lone woman. Next they come to our socials and try to integrate themselves. Next thing you know they will bring more trouble. The men of this town won't stand for it."

"Clay," she pleaded, "that's not what I saw tonight. I saw lonely men that wanted a chance to join in. Nothing terrible could have happened if they'd been allowed a few dances. There wasn't any liquor there, and they weren't drunk, as Reverend Speck accused them of being."

"Dara, you're a woman, and you don't understand these things."

It was the very assurance in his voice that Dara didn't know what she was saying, that she didn't mean to defend those miners, that set her teeth on edge. But then, could she blame Clay for thinking this way? After all, wasn't she always understanding? Hadn't she been patiently waiting until he deemed everything perfect before their marriage could take place? And wasn't this the way society proclaimed it should be? Men ran their world and directed a woman's in this age.

She turned her head aside, hearing the echo of Eden McQuade's voice taunting her that she wasn't a woman yet. A bitterness filled her along with the thought that if circumstances were left to Clay, she might never know what being a woman, being loved by a man, really meant.

"Honey," Clay chided, "you're not listening to me." Dara turned her head and freed her hand at the same time. "I promise you," he began, "this is the last time we'll have to wait. Once I replant the stock those fool miners ruined, I'll know whether or not my grafting methods will take. Just think of it, Dara. I'll improve not only the quality of the fruit, but the yield of my groves."

"No."

"What? What did you say?"

"You heard me, Clay. I won't wait again. I want us to set a date to be married now, tonight. You can't understand what having to wait is doing to me."

"What's happened to you? I thought you believed in me, in what I'm trying to do for us. You know—you've always known—how important this is to me." He slipped his arm around her rigid shoulders, hugging her close, his voice softening to a whisper. "Honey, I know the waiting hasn't been easy, but please, if you love me, be patient a little while longer."

Dara closed her eyes. How could he say he loved her and make her go on year after year, always waiting to experience the joy of being his wife? Did he ever once consider how old she was? Dara's thought of being like his prize citrus trees—frozen by a blight, sap and fruit and delicate blossoms dying before they had a chance to be touched by the sun—brought a shudder to her body. She couldn't stop it, couldn't control it.

"You're chilled sitting out here in the damp. Come on, let me get you inside."

Dara offered no further resistance. She stood before the front door with Clay's arm around her, frowning at the angle of the lamplight inside the parlor window. Her anger dissolved in a tide of weariness. She had tried and failed. No, not failed, she just hadn't told him how threatened she felt by the excitement Eden McQuade so effortlessly generated.

"You're disappointed in me, aren't you?" Clay asked, but continued before she could answer. "I promise you that by this time next year, we'll have our wedding. I do love you, Dara. If the waiting gets hard, please don't ever forget that. I want you to have the best, and I just can't do that now. I owe so much to the land. It's a trust my father and his family set out for me." He drew her closer within the circle of his arms. "Be patient a bit longer, and everything will be perfect the day you become Mrs. Clay Wescott."

Dara found that an ember of hope flamed bright inside her. She rubbed her cheek against the soft cloth of his jacket. "Clay," she whispered, "I know you want everything perfect for us. But that's not what I want or need." She would have felt his withdrawal even if he hadn't moved, and she had to gather her courage to make a last stand. "Let me finish," she murmured when he pulled back slightly to gaze down at her. "Do you know how hard it is for me to face people in this town, day after day, week after week, and turn aside their questions of when we'll be married? Can you try to understand how much it hurts me to see women I went to school with coming into the store, shopping for their growing families? I'm twenty-two years old, Clay. I want to be your wife and share everything with you, not wait until you achieve your idea of what will make me happy. I never wanted a better house or riches. I fell in love—"

"Are you trying to say that you don't love me still? Or are you harboring a resentment against me for wanting so much for you?"

Tears seemed to form effortlessly, but she managed to keep them controlled. Her fingertips against his lips held him silent. "Please, give me a date. I don't care how hard it will be to manage. I'm strong, Clay. I'm not afraid of hard work. If we share the building of your dream, it will only make our love stronger. I don't need a fancy new house. I need you to love me."

He stared at her upturned face, trying hard to pierce the deep shadows and see what brought the note of desperation into her voice. Drawing her hand down to his chest, he rested his lips against her temple. "What has caused all this urgency to set a wedding date? Does what happened with McQuade today have something to do with this?"

"Time's passing and you don't care," she answered in a strangled voice, hating the truth of his words, afraid to admit them even to herself, yet unable to deny them.

"Don't you think it's a strain on me to keep away from you? I want you for my wife, Dara. I've wanted that since you were old enough to notice me. Remember," he coaxed softly, rocking her gently against him. "It was spring when you first came visiting with your father, and you'd just learned how to put up your hair."

"And for a change, you didn't run off, but stayed outside with me, pushing me on the swing, talking to me and not shooing me off like a pesty child."

"And I stole a kiss from the sweetest lips."

"My very first," she whispered, willing to be lulled into the blissful state of that long-ago day.

"Your kisses are still the sweetest, Dara. I'd still steal one from you." His arms tightened around her, his head lowered, and his voice became intimately deep and husky. "You've got to know how difficult it is for a man to content himself with a small taste of the woman he loves."

"Do I?" she asked with a deep ache beginning inside her. She tilted her head for his kiss, accepting that it would be as chaste now as the very first one. Acceptance gave way to a spark of resentment. She was a woman, no matter what Eden thought, and she needed proof beyond words of Clay's loving her, wanting her. She cradled his cheeks with her hands. "Clay, if you want me to believe you, then show me . . . kiss me like a man who can't wait to make me his wife."

The tension in Clay's body gave Dara her answer before he spoke.

"I can't believe what you're saying. Why, you're acting brazen," he stated with a strong suggestion of reproach.

"Brazen!" she repeated in disbelief, pushing against his chest to be released. "Clay, let me go."

"Not until you calm down." His hands slid to her upper arms, and to Dara's shock he gave her a little shake. "We've never had a fight before, and I still want to kiss you good night."

A cold knot formed inside her. "We haven't had a fight, Clay. If you think we are, maybe you don't know me as well as you think you do."

"What do you want from me? What do you think I'm made of?" he demanded, tightening his hold on her. "I have loved and respected you. Too much to take advantage of this mood you're in now. And if you won't tell me what's causing this, I can't help you."

"You're right, Clay." The words were spoken before she could stop herself.

For a moment, a brief wild moment, Clay kissed her with a barely leashed hunger before he gently released her and whispered good night.

Coldness spread inside her along with gnawing hunger for something more as Dara stood at the edge of the porch step. She ignored the light sprinkle of rain, watching Clay urge his team down the lane and away from her without a backward glance. Angrily she brushed aside her tears. How could she love a man who showed such a callous disregard for her feelings? And why, after all these years, all this wasted time, was she just beginning to realize it?

A scraping noise demanded her attention, and she turned toward the sound, knowing without seeing who was there.

"Haven't you anything better to do than sneak around and spy on me?"

The glowing tip of a cigar showed Eden's sharply delineated face for a brief moment. Dara began tapping her foot impatiently, waiting, no thought of going inside, of running, coming to mind. There seemed to be a sudden surge within her, a reckless hot excitement of knowing he was here, and of not knowing what he would say or do. Her breaths quickened at the thought, and with eyes as old and as curious as Eve, she watched him come forward.

With one booted foot resting on the bottom step, he rested his elbow on bent knee, leaning toward her. With that rough, rich voice that seemed to stroke her soul, he said, "That was a rather touching scene I was forced to witness, Dara."

"Forced?"

"I was about to return to my office, and since this is the shortest route, I believed it prudent to remain out of sight."

"I'll just bet you did," she muttered under her breath. His lips drew her gaze, singularly beautiful, with a reckless slant to them that intensely sharpened the memory of how they felt against her own. Her skin surface seemed to heat beneath her constrictive clothes, her breaths shortening. But she was afraid of what he made her feel, almost as if she didn't know herself. Dara's good night was abrupt.

"Do you always beg him, Dara? If I had a woman like you," he whispered, stepping up closer to her, "you wouldn't need to beg me to kiss you. You wouldn't get the chance to ask. You've a mouth made for a man's kisses." He reached up to tease the soft hair at her temple, and she jerked her head back and away from his touch. Eden smiled. "I'd want you, and you'd never be in doubt about it. Maybe," he added with a hint of laughter as he stepped back, moving into the rain-swept shadows, "maybe you might find yourself wanting me, too. I wouldn't need to see the longing in your eyes, I'd be feeling the same. Think about that when you try sleeping tonight, Dara," he said over her furious sputtering. "Think about me."

She stopped herself from swaying toward him, shocked by his words, yet excited by the fission of heat those very words called to mind. But Eden McQuade talked of wanting, of needs, not of loving or commitment, and his boldness brought fear to replace the dangerous kindling of long-buried emotions. She bolted for the door without a word and Eden walked away.

Her screams tore the rain-swept dark and brought Eden running.

Chapter Six

EDEN BURST INTO the house. The sight of Dara sobbing over the prone figure of her father moved him to contain an instantaneous murderous fury. He hesitated a moment in the archway to the front parlor, taking a quick scan of the room for signs of a struggle. There were none.

"What happened?" he demanded.

She barely spared him a tear-glazed look when he knelt beside her on the floor. "I don't know. I . . . I just found him . . . like this."

Eden righted the tilted lamp and then gently pushed Dara aside to conduct his own quick examination of the unconscious man. There was swelling on the right side of Cyrus's head, but when Eden tried to straighten his left leg, Cyrus cried out. A breath he had not realized he was holding rushed out.

"I think he's broken his leg, but I'm not a doctor."

"It's a two-hour ride to—"

"I know, but he needs immediate attention. Don't fall apart on me, Dara. I could ride out to the church and get Sophy Halput for you if you don't trust me, but we could manage this between us." He turned toward her, placing his hands on her shoulders, shocked to feel the chill of her flesh beneath the thin silk of her gown. "I can set his leg, Dara," he offered, trying to impart some of his strength and warmth to her. "I just hope that nothing more than a fall knocked him out."

Dara managed to control herself under his steady gaze. She found herself agreeing with him, not wanting to question why she trusted him.

"I'll need wood to make a splint and linen strips." With a knife he drew from his pocket he split open Cyrus's pant leg. "There's no blood and the bone hasn't ripped through the skin. But get plenty of blankets first. We should get him warm."

With Eden's hand on her elbow, Dara scrambled awkwardly to her feet. The restrictive stays of her corset pressed against her ribs, but it was fear for her father that made breathing difficult. With Eden's reassurances, she recalled his help with Matt and hurried to get what he wanted. When she returned with a thick quilt and blankets, Eden was still kneeling beside Cyrus. He tried to wake him without success. Quickly he shoved both tables and the settee aside to make more room and set the two lamps on the floor.

"I don't want to lift him from here," he said without looking up at her. "Spread the quilt on the floor—I'll try to be gentle moving him."

Dara laid out the quilt and smoothed the edges, while Eden handled her father as if he were a baby, but every moan from Cyrus tore at her nerve endings.

"I couldn't find any wood to use for splints, and I don't think we have any in the store," she said, already tearing the linen sheet into strips. "I've beaten some egg whites and that should help hold his leg immobile."

Eden ignored the quiver in her voice. "Stay with him. I might have some wood strips left over from the cabinets Jesse made for me."

Cyrus drifted in and out of consciousness, crying out

when Dara gently washed around the lump on his head. There were a few deep scratches, and she wondered what had happened to him. Eden returned carrying two uneven strips of raw wood and a cut-glass decanter filled with dark amber liquid.

"Brandy," he explained at Dara's inquiring look. "I'll need more light in here and a glass."

"You need a dry shirt first," she insisted, embarrassed to see the way the wet cream-colored linen delineated the set of his shoulder and his rib cage as he brushed rain-damp hair back from his face. If Dara was embarrassed then, it was mild compared to her feelings when she returned to the parlor and found that he had stripped off his shirt. Thrusting one of her father's shirts at him, knowing it was too big, Dara turned her back toward him. Neither of her brothers was as broad across the shoulders or chest as Eden, and she wanted him covered. The few moments he took to put on the shirt and button it were agonizing ones for her. The sight of his bare torso was sketched in her mind like a bold ink drawing. If he sensed there was anything amiss in her demeanor, Dara was most thankful he had ignored it.

Four lamps made a golden circle of light on the floor as she knelt opposite him, holding her father still while Eden labored to set his leg. Cyrus roused, cried out, and then fainted. Eden's hand on her arm helped to steady her. She dipped linen strips into the large basin of beaten egg whites, then handed them to Eden so he could wrap them first around the leg and then over the short lengths of wood. His hands, she noticed, were gentle as he smoothed the sodden cloths so that they would dry into a stiff mold. Dara felt the growing tension between them, had from the first, but tonight there was an added element of intimacy and something more she couldn't explain to herself. Glancing up from wiping her father's brow, she found herself tempted to wipe the sweat beads that glistened across Eden's beneath a lock of black hair.

The tender feeling expanded inside her, and she was glad his concentration was totally on his labor. He had not boasted idly of his doctoring skills, and she was ashamed that she had derided him, but questioned the circumstances that forced him to learn it. She lost track of time, exhausted after helping him carry her father's feather tick mattress and bedding into the parlor and getting him settled to sleep there. When she voiced a protest, Eden's thoughtfulness surprised her.

"If he's down here, you won't have to run up and down the stairs to tend him."

The words lingered in her mind as she pressed a cold wet cloth against the swelling on her father's head. She knew he was resting peacefully due to the brandy Eden had managed to get him to drink. Cyrus had been awake and aware for a few minutes, just long enough to tell them that he had heard a noise and had tripped coming down the stairs to investigate it.

She took the basin into the kitchen and Eden followed her. He set the lamp and the decanter he carried on the table, refilled his glass, hesitated a moment, and then stepped forward.

Dara lingered over washing the basin and her hands, sensing his presence behind her. When she knew she had regained her composure, she turned around, her gaze fastened on the linen towel as she dried her hands.

"There's no need to worry, Dara. He'll be fine."

"I believe you. I owe you an apology, for you've more than proved your skill. I don't think Sophy or a doctor could have cared for him any better."

"Praise, Dara?"

She flung aside the towel. "Must you mock me?"

"You invite it, sweet darlin', with every lash of your tongue."

Dara didn't answer. She knew she wouldn't win any verbal sparring, and her exhaustion left her at a distinct disadvantage. He sipped from the glass he held, then frowned, staring down at the liquor.

"Is there something wrong with it?" she asked, just now realizing how late it was and that they were alone. Fear for her father had wiped out thought for anyone else, but worry crept into her mind. Neither of her brothers had returned home.

"It should be warm," he noted.

"Warm? What should—"

"The brandy," he explained. "Forgive my lack of manners. Would you care for a taste?"

Her chin lifted, her voice starched as she removed her glasses. "I do not drink spirits."

"Ah, yes. Back to being my prim miss." His grin was rueful as he noted the shadows beneath her eyes, the tiny wisps of hair escaping her neatly coiled braids, the water spots that dampened the front of her cherry and cream striped silk gown, and found himself instantly aroused.

"That was an ungentlemanly remark!"

"Remind me to teach you what the word *gentleman* means. And it's nothing your mother taught you." Her gaze locked with his, and he waited, believing it most uncivil to rush a lady one intended to seduce. Not the right time or place, but Dara, left to her own devices, would never create one. In absolute defiance of what was right, he knew he was not going to stop himself from what he was about to do. When awareness of him as a man brightened her eyes, he closed the distance between them.

Dara forced herself to lower her gaze from his and turned her head aside. Exhaustion fled as a surge of dangerous excitement filled her. He had mocked her innocence, and she had sworn he would never have the opportunity to do so again, but he tempted her with his taunts that she not only wasn't a woman, but could so easily be one with him and for him. She recalled his earlier promise on the rain-swept porch and wondered if she would see desire in his eyes and her own gaze a mirror of it. Shamed by the direction of her thoughts, she felt the need to escape him.

"I'm grateful for all—"

"Spare me the platitudes, Dara." His fingertips brushed her chin, silently urging her to face him. "Coward," he murmured. He could almost feel the tension in her body, knew her fear, but he did not offer her soft coaxing words. "Share this with me."

She stared down at the glass he held, at the way his hands cupped it between them, and watched him gently roll it back and forth. The motion mesmerized her, but only for a few moments.

"I think it's best if you leave now." Her hip brushed the counter behind her, cutting off her unconscious retreat. "My brothers will be . . ." His hand on her cheek stopped her.

"Do you think you need protection from me, darlin'?"

"Yes," she admitted with innate candor. Dara knew it was a mistake to look up at his face. Thick black lashes framed the pewter shade of his eyes, but there was a glint of mischief within them that his keen gaze did not disguise.

Eden slowly rotated the glass in his hand, then sniffed appreciatively before taking a sip. His smile was both predatory and satisfied. "It's almost the perfect temperature," he noted softly, "for you to taste."

"I don't want—"

"Where's that forthright honesty, darlin'? You do want."

"You can't know that." Her startled gaze met his. But it wasn't his look that brought forth another denial. It was his smile. Those finely molded lips of his held a sensual promise that tempted her. "No. I—"

"Hush, darlin'. There's nothing to be afraid of. Nothing to hurt you. You know that, don't you?"

Dara held tight to the edge of the counter. Her pulse raced wildly and her heart began to pound along with her blood, which seemed to rush headlong through her body. Fine tremors spread upward inside her when his gaze became thoughtful for a moment, then changed to one of understanding and something akin to pity.

"I told you how it would be between us, didn't I?" Without taking his eyes from hers, he dipped his thumb into the glass and glossed her lips with the sheen of brandy. "Now, taste it."

There was nothing seductive in his voice for all that it was soft. It was a man's demand that challenged her. Dara thought of refusing him, feeling the warmth of the liquor steal the coolness from her mouth. But the emptiness of her days and nights entreated her to give in to the wild impulse to explore the emotions he effortlessly called from her.

She closed her eyes, willing herself to use caution, and felt her blood rush down a path marked Danger that this man had beckoned her toward from the first. Parting her lips slightly, the tip of her tongue glided across her bottom lip.

"That little bit didn't hurt, did it?" he whispered, not

waiting for her to answer. "We could try again," he suggested indulgently, willing to allow her the choice.

Dara wanted to reply, what, she didn't know. His thumb rubbed brandy once again across the satin sheen of her lips, taking her silence as consent. Air eased out of her aching lungs, and she moved her head ever so slightly to retain the feel of the warm, rough texture of his thumb. Eden's reaction was immediate. His eyes brightened and hot tension ran through his body as he leaned closer.

He had carried her scent inside himself from the very first day, and now, warmed by the excitement that flared in her eyes and quickened her breaths, he inhaled the subtle fragrance of feminine arousal that heated his blood.

"Do you know," he inquired with soft, measured patience so at odds with his state of being, "that I've wanted to kiss you again for hours, little saint?"

With his body angled to one side of hers, he lowered his head, waited a moment, and then gave her no choice. His lips brushed across hers once, twice, and then returned for a leisurely sampling. With unhurried grace he licked each glistening bit of moisture he had placed on her luscious mouth. Using the barest of touches, that teased rather than sated, Eden softly nibbled, slanting his mouth first one way, then another, but never, never lost contact with the satin warmth of her lips. "Perfect," he whispered but once, his free hand spanning the boned confines of her rib cage with a languid caress.

Dara knew it was wrong to follow where he was leading her. But he wielded a dark magic so skillfully that he called her senses to life. Sensations whirled and danced away before she could identify them, leaving only his tender mouth teaching hers lessons she was more than eager to learn. When he leaned his head back for a moment, her breath rushed out and she dreamily opened her eyes.

"I didn't know," she whispered, "there were so many ways to kiss." A blush tinted her cheeks with shock for her boldness.

Eden merely smiled. "There's more." His soft laughter held a wicked note. "If you want, darlin'," he added with rich, sensual humor, nuzzling her petal-soft cheek, "I'll show you all the ways there are."

It was the temptation of forbidden pleasure in his voice that lured her. Dara swayed where she stood, locked between his body and the counter behind her. She had no fear left, not now, though there was but a hairsbreadth space between them.

His smile was at once charming but at odds with the glint of mischief in his eyes. Dara knew he was daring her, and she longed for the courage to accept.

"Say yes, Dara."

His hand on her waist tightened a fraction, taking the decision from her. He smoothly turned her, holding the glass aside. Playing hide-and-seek with her mouth, which delightfully followed his, he walked her backward toward the table. When she reached its edge, he leaned into her, ever so gently, unwilling to alarm her, and eased her onto its broad, solid surface with his hand guiding her down at the small of her back.

"I think . . ." she began, gazing up at his face.

"Don't, love," he softly ordered, setting the glass on the table beside her head.

Dara stayed absolutely still. He framed her face with his hands, leaning over her from one side. Eden lowered his head, saw her eyes wide and startled, but their velvety brown depths held the hidden passion he was rather impatient to call from her. His control was his pride, but he couldn't help but catch his breath when her lips parted in innocent invitation.

Eden wasn't about to refuse the delectable lush mouth offered so provocatively. "So very much a contradiction," he murmured, shaping her cheeks with his fingers, kissing her lightly. But teasing games belonged to the boy he once was, and within him a restless and sudden uncontrollable tide surged up, turning an indulgent kiss into a man's demand. The ache of physical hunger that sprang to life inside surprised him. He tilted her face upward, wanting a deeper mating with the mouth that had tantalized him.

There was no escape for Dara until he lifted his head a fraction. Their breaths mingled with an intimacy that forced her to admit she was afraid.

"Hush, darlin'. Just let me—"

"You'll catch what I have."

He found her chin needed kissing. His eyes caressed her delicate features, dwelling on her inviting mouth. He didn't think he would ever have enough of it.

"Oh, please, listen to me. You'll—"

"What, sweet?"

With a restless move of her head, she glared at him. "I don't quite know. It's—" Dara stared at his lips hovering over her mouth. Her senses reeled beyond caution hearing his faint groan against her hair. "Eden," she called, moving her head to realign their mouths. She lifted her head to close the tiny space between them, no thought for her bold move crossing her mind as she dared to imitate the tiny licks he generously offered her at the corner of his mouth.

His chest brushed the lush fullness of her breasts straining upward, and he felt the tremor that passed between them. "Tell me," he urged, chasing the tip of her tongue that eluded him far too quickly. "I'll promise to make it better for you."

"Can you?" She found the strength to raise her hand, noted its faint tremble, and placed it against his cheek. The beginning of his night beard chafed lightly against her palm. "Eden, I'm shaking and . . ." She couldn't finish until he stopped shaping her mouth with his fingertip rich with drops of brandy, heating it with his breaths before he once again licked away the moisture.

"The taste," he said with a husky note, his smile ever so reassuring, "improves immensely."

"It's like a fever," she whispered, closing her eyes. "And there's a deep ache inside that—"

"Oh, sweet, sweet little saint," he murmured with a note of soft laughter, "your innocent candor will be my undoing. But I promise," he added, kissing the tip of her nose, "to make it all better."

With a sigh, Dara managed to raise both her arms and drape them over his shoulders. "Then please do," she demanded in a voice quite unlike her own. She excused it, for her body did feel fever-flushed, and there was a building ache that spread inside her.

Eden pushed aside the glass, lifting her up against him, taking her mouth possessively. Her body seemed fragile, almost boneless in his arms, and she lifted her head, her mouth greedy for what he offered. With her neck arched, she pressed her breasts against his chest, her moan softly satisfied with the relief this closeness brought to sensitive skin restricted by her clothing.

He sat down with her on his lap, the chafing confines of his own clothes an irritant and a belated warning. The silk of her gown rustled with her restless move to settle her body to the contours of his. She gazed up at him with dark brown eyes glazed with passion's beginning and then shivered uncontrollably.

"Do you know," he whispered, "I believe your warning came too late, sweet."

"Too late?" she repeated, dazed by the need that urged her closer to the warmth of his body. She knew this was wrong, but the lamplight cast the most intriguing shadows on his face, and his eyes held both amusement and a glow of smoldering desire. She no longer wondered if her own gaze held the same reflection. She could feel the desire that flowered open just as she had dreamed it could.

"I think," he suggested gently, flexing his spine languidly to settle her deeper against him, "that I've already caught what you have. And darlin'," he added, gliding one finger up the row of buttons on the front of her gown, his eyes brightening to a silver sheen, feeling her fingers dig into his back, "this is only the beginning."

"We should . . . stop," she managed to say, snuggling her head against his shoulder with a sigh of pleasure. Dara felt the instantaneous tension in his taut muscular legs beneath her own and the distinct ridge of his aroused male flesh that warned her she was in danger of losing any chance to keep control. The thought was hazy, Clay was the one who demanded control, and Eden, ah, Eden, he had tempted her, and now, now she wanted to know where that temptation would take her.

Eden slipped his arm around her slender waist, his palm enticed to rub her silk-clad hip. Dara arched like a petted cat. His other hand shaped her shoulder, sliding down her arm before interlocking her fingers with his. He raised their joined hands to his lips, kissing hers before he freed it and placed it around his neck. "Better, love?" he asked as she curled with a soft moan against him. Her temple attracted a kiss, then each of her fluttering eyelids. He couldn't resist the tip of her nose and forced himself to ignore for the moment the pouty offering of her mouth lifted to his. There was softer skin that invited his lips on the undercurve of her jaw, and he lingered there.

"Do you think," she asked, shaping his ear and finding to her delight that the skin behind was downy soft, "the brandy makes me wanton?" Her fingertips caressed that one spot, and she smiled up at him to learn that her untutored touch could bring a quickening of both his breath and his heartbeat.

Her own heartbeat was erratic, but her breathing eased as he deftly opened the tiny pearl collar buttons.

"It doesn't matter, does it?" he inquired in a night-dark voice. "You do feel"—his lips nuzzled the newly exposed skin of her throat—"better now, don't you?" he finished; his long fingers, adept with a gun or cards, dealt just as effectively with the long row of restrictive buttons that hid the lush silk of delicately hued skin.

"Will you kiss me again?" she demanded, a long-denied sensuality blazing as she guided his chin upward.

The pressure of his mouth was too hard and hungry. He knew it and waited to seek out her tongue even as need became savage. Restraint was maddening, and yet the reward was incredibly rich, worth his frustration as she responded.

Her soft moan fed his urgency. He meant to ease his way into her mouth, to gently coax her tongue out of hiding, and with the beguiling skill he had learned to perfect, persuade it into a game of submit and conquer.

But Dara parted her lips for him, her desire as fierce as it was innocent, and she willingly offered him the virgin secrets of her mouth. His pleasure erupted in a groan when she set her tongue timidly against his. Eden forgot restraint, forgot her innocence, kissing her hard, deep, the way he wanted and needed to kiss her. She twisted upward, breathlessly yearning for more, and his grip tightened on her waist, his mouth fastened over hers, demanding surrender.

Alarm turned to panic and Dara felt her heart give a sudden, nervous jolt. Her attempt to push him away was feeble, and she was conscience-stricken that she had to force herself to offer this token resistance. Gathered tight to his body, she felt his strength and size, and even as she despaired of fighting the wildness surging up inside her, her fingers flexed deep into his shoulders, pulling him closer. Her head was flung back over his arm, her upper body lifting, molding itself to his, and she felt the incredible tension spread between them.

"You bastard! Get your hands off her!"

Chapter Seven

EDEN RELUCTANTLY RELEASED Dara's mouth in a gentle fashion. His hands soothed her back, his voice soft as he hushed her bewildered cry. With a glance at the doorway and the man framed within it, Eden felt his sexual tension quickly dissipate. His order to get out was issued from between his clenched teeth, his move calculated to shield her from her brother's eyes.

Dara couldn't seem to marshall her rioting senses and clung to Eden. It was the tension of his body that forced her to look up at his face. Swallowing, she followed his narrow-eyed gaze toward the door.

"Pierce!" Her shocked whisper fell between the three of them. Complete attention was focused on her brother, his features twisted with rage, and Dara sat immobile, willing time backward, unable to utter a sound. She struggled against Eden's hold, and to her mortification, the front of her gown slid open to reveal her lace-trimmed undergarments. Dara grabbed the edges together, her guilt-stricken gaze divided between both men, unaware of the control that Eden exerted to master his own passions and to protect her.

"Let me go to him," she pleaded, feelings of shame bringing hectic color to her cheeks.

"Does Clay know about him?" Pierce demanded.

"Don't. Please, Pierce, you . . . it's not what—"

"I'm not blind, Dara! Answer me. Does Clay know what a slut he planned to marry?"

Eden erupted from the chair, setting Dara on her feet in the moment it took for her to cry out a pained denial. He barely clung to the threads of sanity that stopped him from leaping at Pierce.

She grabbed his arm, trying to stop him, frightened by his sudden demeanor which told of a furious calm about to explode, but he shook free of her hold.

"Stay out of this, Dara." And to Pierce, "Apologize." His one word command was uttered softly as he closed the distance between them.

"I'm not my brother, McQuade," Pierce replied, his stance belligerent. "You don't give me orders in my house. She's my sister, even if I am ashamed of her." His eyes, filled with disgust, targeted Dara's stricken face. "How could you drag this filth home and behave like a brazen trollop?"

"You damn. . . . That's enough."

But Pierce felt a surge of confidence and wasn't about to heed Eden's soft, warning voice. He ignored Dara's cry, her plea for Eden not to hurt him lost in his own rage. Pierce needed to vent it and swung his fist only to find Eden had easily ducked his blow.

"Don't force me to hurt you, Pierce," Eden commanded, aware of what the repercussions would be. He didn't care for himself, but Dara didn't need further turmoil to divide her strong loyalties. His hands clenched into fists at his sides for he needed to shut Pierce's mouth and knew he wouldn't be able to talk him around. Not when Pierce glared at him and then ignored him.

"Does Papa know he's here? Or did you sneak him in the back door? How long has this been going on while

Clay is slaving to build a home for you? How long, Dara?" When she clutched the edge of the table for support, he demanded, "And where *is* Papa?"

Eden had had enough. He grabbed Pierce's arm, jerking him to his side. "Shut the hell up. Your father fell down the stairs tonight and broke his leg. He's asleep in the parlor, no thanks to you, and as usual your sister was here alone."

"Alone?" he scoffed. "I'm not denying what I saw for myself, and neither will Clay when I tell him."

"She's *your* sister!"

"She betrayed him and—"

Dara rushed at her brother, crying out against his accusations. Guilt swamped her, but she found that she had a temper that wanted satisfaction. She couldn't believe that Pierce was actually gloating. Her blow glanced off Pierce's shoulder, and Eden swung her into his arms, sheltering her and deliberately turning his back on her brother.

"Easy, love," he whispered. "Go see if your father is still asleep. He's in no shape to contend with hearing any of this. I'll talk to Pierce." He felt each and every tremor in her body and had a moment's regret that what had been passion was now anger and shame.

She clutched his fine linen shirt, lifting tear-filled eyes to his, a flare of resentment dying quickly. His face was slate hard. "Please, let me talk to him. He had no right—"

Pierce grabbed her shoulder and spun her around. "I've got no right!" he cried out. "You may be the eldest, Dara, but if Papa's hurt, then I'm the man of the family and I—"

"You're drunk!"

"If I was, I'm sober now. Any man would be coming

home to see what I did. I want you up in your room and him the hell out of here."

"You've never used profanity in our home, Pierce!"

"I'll use—"

"If you want to be treated like a man, Pierce, then act like one and stop abusing your sister. Whatever you want to say, direct it at me." Eden stepped to Dara's side, crowding her into the doorway. "Leave us. Now."

"Whatever you two say concerns me and—"

"*Now,* Dara," he repeated, never once taking his gaze from Pierce.

He barely waited for her to slip down the hallway before he slammed Pierce back against the wall, his arm across his throat.

"Move and I'll break your neck. Don't you ever dare to talk to her like that again," he grated from between his teeth, not trusting himself for a moment.

"You've got no call to order me. She's a—" The fury in Eden's eyes, the quicksilver tension that made his facial bones prominent, stopped him. "She's my sister," he stubbornly maintained. "Clay's my friend and has a right to know wha—" His words were cut off by the pressure Eden exerted against his throat. A strangled gasp escaped Pierce's throat, and his eyes bulged as he fought for air.

"You seem to need reminding that Dara is your sister," he noted in a cool dispassionate voice. "Clay is a fool for waiting to marry her." The strangled sounds emerging from Pierce made Eden regain a semblance of control, and he released him. While Pierce fought to recover his breath, Eden briefly explained what had happened to his father. Pierce glared at him, listening, but when he was done, the younger man offered no words of gratitude.

"We don't want or need your kind in Rainly. You miners think you got everything coming easy to you, taking over our town, our lands, and our women. But you'll find out. We've got plans for all of you. And stay away from my sister," he warned. "Clay will make sure of that when I'm done telling him what I saw."

"If Dara wants me, nothing will keep me away from her. You make sure to tell that to Clay."

"He'll kill you if you–"

"Has he ever killed a man?" Eden taunted, beyond caring how far he had let Pierce goad him. "While you're at it, don't forget what telling him will do to *your* sister," he continued softly, leaning one hand flat against the wall next to Pierce's head. "Listen to me, and if you have a lick of sense, believe this as nothing else. If you hurt Dara with that vicious mouth of yours, I'll come after you, and when I'm—"

"Dear Lord! Stop it! Both of you just stop," Dara interrupted, entering the room. "I'm not some simple minded ninny for you to fight over. And I'm not a child, Pierce, that you should tattle on to Clay or anyone else. Clay isn't married to me. He doesn't own me. I did nothing . . . nothing I'm ashamed of," she finished on a wavering note. But the scorn in her brother's eyes made her back away.

She turned blindly to Eden for comfort and went into his open arms, no longer caring what her brother saw or thought. Dara refused to give way to the tears that burned her eyes. She wouldn't give Pierce the satisfaction of seeing her cry. She needed the security Eden's arms offered almost as much as she needed his warmth.

"Mama'd turn over in her grave to see you." With a disgusted snort Pierce walked out.

Eden willed the tension to leave him, waiting until

Pierce's footsteps proved he had gone upstairs to his room before he eased Dara away from his body.

Her pale skin drew him to brush the back of his hand against her cheek, her eyes holding his, bruised with shadows and pain. He thought of all the ways he knew that would soothe her, but knew, too, from the fragile sound of her voice whispering his name, that he would use none of them.

"I didn't want the evening to end this way, Dara," he whispered with tender regret. "While I'm sorry for what your brother subjected you to, I won't apologize for anything that happened between us. No, love, let me finish." But he paused, his fingertip fanning the curve of her brow, pushing back a loose tendril of hair. Cupping her chin, he raised it, his look as hard as his words. "If Clay dares to threaten you or Pierce mentions one word about tonight, I'll handle this my way. Your brother is still able to open his mouth simply because you were here. I won't be as gentle or generous with him again."

"Eden," she said simply, unable to hold his gaze, "he's my brother. No matter his cruelty, that wasn't him talking, it was liquor. Don't hurt him."

His grip tightened on her arms for a brief moment as if he intended to pull her close, and Dara was torn between wanting him to and shame for what she had allowed to happen between them. She knew he was waiting for her to say something more, but words were suddenly beyond her.

"Dara, I . . ." He dropped his hands, spun around, and within moments his long strides had taken him to the back door, and then he was gone.

"What have I done!" she cried out in a torn whisper, the night's stillness oppressive with its silence. Racked with shivers, she slowly made her way up the stairs to her room, unwilling to light the lamp. Her fingers were clumsy trying to open the button loops she had hastily done up, and several ripped in her desperate haste to remove the gown.

A weariness unlike any she had ever experienced beset her, and her thoughts were as scattered as the clothing she removed. She couldn't begin to think back on all that had happened tonight, but resting between cool linen sheets with her pillow muffling her tears, the past hours refused to allow her peace.

There was a hurt that expanded beyond pain inside her. She knew that Clay didn't love her, not the way she wanted him to. All these years wasted, dreaming of the day they would marry, and now, now she felt cheated. The anger she felt surprised her, but remembering her brother's reaction brought a fresh wave of hurt. He was shocked at finding her in Eden's arms. She could understand that, for she had been a little shocked herself that she allowed her desire to carry her so far. But Eden had made it all seem right, as if she had a right to her needs to be held and kissed and . . .

"Dear Lord, how can I fight Pierce's anger? Why did he denounce me and then align himself with Clay as if I meant nothing to him?"

She clutched the pillow tight, unwilling to believe Pierce's cruelty, but his words lingered, echoing over and over until she wanted to scream with the pain of hearing them.

"Mama, I tried," she sobbed. "I can't be what they think I am. I want to love, Mama. If you were here, you could explain to them."

There had been other nights when Dara longed for her mother, but no answer came then, and none came now. They were all wrong about Eden. He was tender and gentle and caring. He couldn't be anything but those things after the way he had cared for Matt and her father. Eden was . . .

Her thoughts turned to his threats issued in that so-soft voice. Eden was capable of violence, and she would be a fool to deny it. But dangerous or not, he called to her passions and dreams as Clay, she fully understood now, would never be able to do. She had cried out that no one owned her, that she had rights.

But rights carried responsibilities, as she well knew.

How could she continue to let Clay believe she would ever marry him now?

Alone at the river's edge Eden silently echoed her question. He drew deeply on his cigar, glancing back at her darkened house and knew she was awake in her virginal bed, as tormented by the night's events as he was.

What had started out to be an innocent diversion had escalated into something more. He knew, but doubted Dara did, that he had no intention of stopping. Jake had accused him of being unable to settle down in one place with one woman. Once he might have said there was some truth in that.

But now . . .

A pensive frown creased his brow, and he speculated on the sanity of his own actions tonight. What devil had possessed him? He knew himself, had never questioned what he wanted, or needed, but Dara . . . such a lush, tempting bundle of contradictions . . . and what he was feeling right now for her went beyond the need for any physical gratification. How far beyond, he wasn't about to delve into.

With an angry twist of his wrist, he sent the half-smoked cigar out into the river's sluggish current, heard its dying hiss with a bitter smile, and turned toward town.

And Dara, clutching the lace curtain in her room, watched him go, envying him his freedom, her own decision made.

She could only pray the night would pass quickly and that her courage would last long enough for her to carry it out.

Chapter Eight

"DARA! DARA, CLAY'S here and Papa's awake and hungry. Dara, do you hear me? There's no hot water for me to shave with, either."

Having entered her room to dress just a little while ago, Dara cringed hearing Pierce's strident voice yelling up the stairs at her. She knew her sleepless night was evident with the shadows beneath her eyes. He called up to her again, but she didn't bother to answer him, both thankful that her father, after his restless night, was awake, and angry that everything that needed to be done seemed to fall upon her. Muttering as she hastily buttoned up her shirtwaist, she longed to yell at Pierce to heat his own hot water. But even as she hurried, pinning up her long hair in a most careless manner, she knew she was mostly reluctant to go downstairs and face Clay.

Tossing the buttonhook on her dresser, she ignored the resentment flaring in her eyes and took a deep breath to calm herself before she closed the door to her room. At the top of the stairs she heard the murmur of voices from the parlor and hurried down.

Clay was leaning over Cyrus when she paused in the doorway. She greeted him coolly when he glanced up, and she spoke before he could.

"I won't be joining you for service this morning. Papa

mustn't be left alone. But I would like you to come directly back here. We need to talk."

"Dara, I'm sorry you were alone when this happened. I was just asking your father how you managed. I wish—"

"Oh, she wasn't alone at all, Clay," Pierce said from behind Dara.

Her cry focused everyone's attention on her. And Dara, unwilling to subject her father to the scene she knew Pierce was more than ready to begin, bit her lip. "I'll get your breakfast, Papa," she murmured, blindly turning around. "And I'll heat some water for you to shave with, Pierce."

"Dara, wait, who was here?" Clay called out.

"Eden McQuade," she answered, offering no elaboration.

"McQuade?" he repeated, facing Pierce. "What is she talking about? What was he doing here after I saw her home?"

Pierce had the grace to look away, muttering, "It's best you ask Dara. Papa," he reminded him, and directed a pointed look toward his father, until Clay realized what he meant.

Cyrus stared at the two of them, his thoughts fuzzy, the pain blurring his vision. The strained silence that followed made him try to sit up against the brace of pillows, the sense of something being wrong filtering to him.

"Pierce," he called weakly, "come here, boy, and tell me what happened."

Clay glanced from one to the other. "Stay with him," he ordered Pierce, spinning around to rush down the hall.

It had been less than twenty-four hours since he had

confronted Dara about McQuade in the kitchen. The unease and tension of last night filled him once again as he skirted the table to join her by the stove. He watched her fiddle with the kettle, a calm sort of fury filling him. He shook his head as if to clear it, suddenly not sure he wanted to know what happened.

His hands lifted and hovered over her shoulders, and he was overpowered by the need to touch her, to hear her explanation that all his suspicions were wrong, and that she loved him still. But when he found his voice, its tone was one of suppliance, and he inwardly cringed that he could not control it.

"Tell me, please, Dara. You've lied to me about him, and I must know why. You've . . . well, you act so different, and I . . ." He paused, both large-boned hands on his hips, studying her slender back. "These last few weeks haven't been easy ones for either of us. I've neglected you, and for that I'm sorry. I . . . Damn you! Look at me!"

Her spine stiffened in reaction to the sudden demand, but obediently she turned around, her bleak gaze meeting his. "I want to talk to you about all of it, but not now, Clay. I've—"

"Now. Not later, but now." He loomed closer, his stance threatening, and seemed satisfied when she shied back.

"Try to believe that I don't want to hurt you, Clay," she pleaded, reaching out with one hand.

He pushed her hand aside. "Stop it. I don't want to be soothed. I want some answers. True ones. Why was he here last night after I left?" He reached out blindly and gripped the top edge of a nearby chair. "Did you invite him to meet you? Or was—"

"How could I invite him?" she taunted. "You were the

one to decide when we left the social. Or did you think—"

"Was he lurking around here, waiting to catch you alone again like the scum he is?"

"Scum? You dare to call him that when he cared for my father! Where were *you* when I needed help? Were you here with me, Clay?" she asked in a fury-laden voice, advancing on him. "Blame him, that's what you've always done. Put the blame on the weather, your crops, your needs! But you know you couldn't wait to leave me last night. After all, one kiss and ten minutes of your time was more than proper for a good-night, wasn't it? And we must always do what Clayton James Aloysius Wescott deems proper, mustn't we?"

Stopping abruptly, Dara drew a shuddering breath, grabbing out for some semblance of control and finding it gone. A bitter acid filled her, cutting down the walls of restraint that had governed her life. "You can decide for yourself why he was here, Clay. I don't think you would believe me if I told you. As for his staying and helping me, let's say he did it out of the goodness of his Christian soul and leave it be," she finished on a caustic note, turning her back toward him just as the kettle's whistling rose.

But as she reached out with the pot holder to lift it from the stove, he grabbed her hand and spun her around. "You want me to decide for myself? I will. I decide that McQuade needs a lesson he'll never forget. He won't have trouble mistaking my warning this time to stay away from you, Dara. If he survives it."

"Stop it!" Hating the unyielding look on his face, Dara lowered her gaze. This was not the talk she had planned to have with him. She knew she had handled this all wrong and was desperate to make amends. But her need for freedom warred with her need not to hurt Clay. She derided herself for this weakness and for the guilt that lingered along with the mantle of meek obedience she had worn for a lifetime. All were heavy burdens; none easy to remove. And she had to disabuse him of any notions to take his revenge against Eden McQuade.

"You mustn't blame him, Clay. I told you last night how I felt. It was your choice to ignore me just as you have always done." Gripping her hands together, she balled the pot holder between them. "Please, wait until later. Call Pierce and tell him the water is ready for his shave, and I'll get my father his breakfast."

"That's it? You think you can dismiss me like some—"

"I'm not. All I'm asking for is time, Clay. Just like you've demanded of me all these years."

With his hand thrust into his hair, he glowered at her. Dara flinched at the sound of his teeth grinding together in frustration. "And what if I want to settle this now?"

"Must I remind you that this is my home?" She gazed into his eyes, an unshakable feeling that she was right lending her the strength to stand there and bear his scrutiny. The hands he suddenly began clenching and then just as slowly unclenching drew her gaze down toward his sides. She was beset by the certainty that if she dared to provoke him further, Clay would put his hands upon her, and there would be nothing gentle in his touch. As if a veil were ripped aside, Dara saw Clay for what he was: brash, arrogant, and selfish. This was the man she had thought to marry, to love, and to . . . the disillusionment was still new and pained her. Here stood the man who had cheated her with his promises. The acceptance, no matter how bitter, gave her courage.

"I want you to leave now."

"Think you found yourself a prize, Dara? I never really knew you, did I?" he grated, loathing the sight of her. "Such a meek little thing, pretending all this time to be a decent, virtuous woman a man would be proud to marry. But you're not, are you?" he stated, stalking her around the table, his move quick to corner her at the door to the pantry. With a glittering blue malice in his eyes, he pinned her there. "You haven't the sense of a pea goose if you think I'll turn tail and run to leave you to McQuade. You're the fool if you believe he wants anything more than your innocence. When he's done with you," he stressed, leaning his face down so close his breaths were fanned back to him from her pale face, "he'll toss you aside like the harlot he'll make you." He stifled her protest with his palm across her mouth, using his other hand to press her shoulder against the door, ignoring her struggles.

"Stay put and listen. I know you lied to me about what happened with him in the store. You thought I was fool enough to believe you? I know he kissed you, and Lord knows what the hell else you allowed him to do. I loved you, Dara. I trusted you. But that's not what you wanted from me, is it? You wanted this," he claimed, pulling her shaken body against his.

Dara yanked her head back, freeing her mouth. "Is that going to salve your wounded ego? I'll never marry you now, Clay. It has nothing to do with him. You don't love me, you never did. I'm a possession to you. Get out of my—"

With a brutal jerk he grabbed her head, his fingers digging into her thick, loosely pinned hair. There was a fire lit within the blue of his eyes that told of his rage, and something more that Dara couldn't name. She whimpered, her body trembling with fear, for this was a side of Clay she had never witnessed.

"You dare go anywhere McQuade is, talk to him, smile at him, or so much as glance his way, and I'll kill him, Dara. Do you understand?" He shook her, both hands threaded into her hair, its length spilling down over his arms in wild disarray, and he was seized with a powerful passion to brand her. Need pierced him like lightning to claim her, and every one of her taunts of the night before replayed in his mind. His grip tightened, his move swift to bend her neck backward until the delicate bones of her face sprang into prominence and she was arched against his body.

"You taunted me like the innocent virgin you are, but you don't want a man's passion loosened on you," he muttered, dismissing her cry of pain. "Do you?" A dark surge of fury filled him, goading him now. His lips flattened hers, grinding down against their softness until he tasted blood.

His head jerked upward, and without a sign of remorse he stared down at her. "Is that what you wanted, Dara?"

"No," she mouthed, unable to look at him.

"Your lip—"

"Don't touch me." Her chest heaved with the effort it took to drag air into her lungs.

"You asked for it. But this doesn't change anything. McQuade can't have you. I'll kill him if he touches you again."

"Get out!" she cried, shuddering when he released her.

"Tell Pierce I'll wait outside for him. As it is, we'll be late for service."

Dara merely nodded, unable to sort out the turmoil of her feelings. She would have done anything to see him gone from her sight. Gingerly she wiped her swollen lip, sagging back against the pantry door. She listened to his departing footsteps, heard him outside rounding the house, relieved when the sound faded. Her stomach churned, and she closed her eyes until the sound of someone clearing his throat made her look up. Pierce stood in the doorway.

"If you dare to utter one sound, one word, I'll—"

"Where's Clay?"

"Waiting for you," she snapped. "I hope you're satisfied, Pierce. I'm sure you heard every word. If anything happens to Eden McQuade, it'll be on your head." Dara glanced at the stove and then back to her brother. "Get your hot water and then leave."

"Papa heard you. He wanted—"

"An explanation, his breakfast, and something for his pain. Just leave him to me as you always have. I can't see you changing what you've become."

While filling the basin and watching her cautiously, Pierce said, "Matt didn't come home last night. His bed wasn't slept in and Papa asked where he was. I didn't know what . . . Dara, I didn't mean to rile Clay. You just don't understand what men like McQuade—"

"Tell it to the Lord," she cut in. "And when you're done, come right back here so we can figure out how we'll manage the store between us."

"I'm not staying. I've got fields to plant."

"Matt and I can't run the store and take care of Papa alone! You've got to help us." The defiant look on his face was enough to loose the leash on a temper she didn't know she had. "You're as selfish as Clay. Can't? You mean you won't." Her laugh was bitter. "More the fool I am for expecting help from you. Both you and Clay are cut from the same cloth, selfish to the core. Go tend to your farm, Pierce."

Dara avoided looking at him. The sound of her name called filled her with a weary acceptance as she hastened to reassure her father that his breakfast would be ready soon.

Glancing out the back window of the kitchen, Dara noticed the stray wisps of clouds that drifted across the afternoon sky. Her father had kindly accepted her brief explanation that she was angry with Clay over what happened at the social, and yes, she agreed with him that Eden was a man to be thanked and not despised. But she had no time to linger, even if townsfolk would be horrified to learn that she was washing on a Sunday. It was simply not done. Dara found she had a decided practical streak that said she could not manage the store, the household chores usually left for Mondays, and care for her father. Rubbing the ache in her back, she wished she could leave her father alone and go look for Matt. He had never stayed away for so long. Fear that something had happened to him crossed her mind again. She tried dismissing it as she had been for countless hours, but concern nagged her.

After retrieving the fresh bar of soap she had come inside to get, she returned outside to the laundry tub and the upstanding wash-board that waited. She swished her delicate undergarments around in the water, knowing they had soaked long enough. With her back bent, she lifted each item, rubbed it carefully with soap, and then with a gentle up and down motion abraded it against the corrugated board. Dara ignored the muscle aches in her arms and across her shoulders, concentrating on her chore, willing herself to forget the morning.

The sound of a buggy entering the lane that led to the house arrested her attention. Her father called out for her, and Dara knew the flash of resentment she felt was unfair. The corset cover dropped into the tub with a splash, and she rubbed her hands on her water-splattered skirt before making sure the pins securing her hair were firmly in place.

"Company," she muttered, racing for the back door, unrolling her shirtwaist sleeves and trying to fasten at least one button on each. Visitors were the last thing she wanted or needed to contend with today, but there was no help for it. Word would have passed among those attending service this morning, taking note of both her and her father's absence, that Cyrus had broken his leg. This was going to be the first of many afternoon calls. Sunday's dinners were over, and visits to neighbors were one of the few pleasures people would not forgo, even if bored miners about town precipitated violence.

"Dara, I've got a powerful thirst," Cyrus said as she stopped a moment.

"Let me see who's come to call, Papa, and then I'll bring you a fresh glass of lemonade."

She opened the door to find Jesse and his wife, Sophy, carrying a linen-draped pie. At the instant sympathy the older woman offered, Dara ushered them into the parlor.

Jesse and Sophy stayed a little while, then took their leave when Robert and Leah Tucker arrived. Dara was kept busy running back and forth with cool drinks, serving the cakes and pies kindly neighbors had brought, and wishing the day would end. Her father was cranky with pain, but with each new visitor he insisted he was well enough to chat a bit.

She left him in the company of Early Yarwood, feeling a definite lack of excitement over Early's news of the miners' discoveries. It brought Eden to mind as she heard Early explain that fossils had been uncovered near a pit mine that proved to be giant shark remains, the jaw of a huge bear, and what Early swore they claimed was the fang from a saber-toothed tiger. "They said there was some they couldn't identify," Early stated. "Dug down nearly thirty feet and found them. Fella said . . ."

Dara excused herself, belatedly remembering her laundry outside.

Fuming over the delay to complete this chore, Dara had her hands immersed in the now cold water when she heard the jingle of harness out in front.

"Now who's come?" she muttered. Moments later she once again raced through the house, plastering a smile of welcome before opening the door.

"Oh, goodness, Miss Loretta . . . and Luther. Won't you both come in," she said, wishing she had remembered to unroll her shirtwaist sleeves.

"That you, Loretta?" Cyrus called from where he held court in the parlor. "Dara, get another pitcher of your lemonade. Early talked it dry."

Fresh glasses and more slices of cake, and nothing would do for the delicate lace cookies that Miss Loretta brought but for Dara to take down her mother's cut-glass platter. She nearly fell from the chair as she reached for it on the high pantry shelf. Miss Loretta preferred to have tea, and Dara wasn't to put herself out, for Miss Loretta would pour. Since Dara rarely used her mother's tea set, she whisked it off the dining room sideboard, hurrying to wash each of the lovely delicate porcelain pieces before she could offer it to Miss Loretta.

With gritted teeth, she listened to the kindly offered criticism. Her hair was mussed to a fright, her shirtwaist was wrinkled, and her skirt, well, Miss Loretta huffed, its condition was nothing to compare to the state of Dara's face. She bore it all silently, her patience at its end, and then made her excuses and left them.

"Cyrus," Miss Loretta remarked as Dara left the room, "you should see 'bout gettin' that girl of yore's some help. Wearin' herself to a frazzle tryin' to keep up with all that needs doin'. And you fallin' . . . in mah day . . ."

Dara stifled a laugh that she was sure had to be the first sign of madness. She could be thankful that Miss Loretta would occupy her father for hours. Leave it to the old dear to offer concern over the least of her problems. But her mood was lighter as she once again returned outside. Dwelling on what happened would only drain her.

Rubbing the poor neglected corset cover for the third time, Dara vented her frustration upon it. The sound of masculine laughter drifted upward from the riverbank. Dara looked up, sure she saw Kelsey the ferry man with his white mane of thick hair and his bear-sized frame standing off to one side. Scanning a group of several men, trying to determine if Matt was with them, Dara, without thought, lifted her hand to shield out the sun and cried out when soapy water dripped into her eyes.

She turned blindly, frantic to wipe her hands against her skirt, lifting its hem to rub her eyes.

"I hope this charming immodest display is meant to be a private one, darlin'."

Dara froze with the dark cloth obscuring her face. This was the final straw! Sputtering and swearing in a most unladylike manner under her breath, she squeezed her eyes tight, refusing to face the man who stood there, softly chuckling at her predicament. Irrationally, the thought that the events of the whole day were his fault settled instantly, and she laid them before his feet without a qualm.

Eden, having no idea of the black thoughts that his presence incurred, looked his fill. Her high-buttoned shoes were mud-splattered. Her thin cotton petticoat in itself was nothing to draw a man's attention, not when one considered that most ladies would display such charms carefully arrayed in silk and lace for his delectation. It was the lack of its usual sister layers that drew his ardent gaze as a playful breeze, taking pity on his starved senses, whipped the virginal white cotton against her knee-length drawers beneath it. His indolent inspection gathered a smile and the information that Dara Owens wore lace-trimmed garters with her serviceable black cotton stockings. Her legs, etched with painful clarity so that he was forced to shift his stance, were a vision of delicate curves, whose positioning he had spent the night pondering. Whiskey and cards had held no pleasure for him, and there wasn't a woman in Rainly whom he desired but for the one before him. The breeze, having invoked his interest, skipped away to leave a sultry stillness behind. Eden waited, patient and assured that Dara was aware of the reason he remained silent, and the sudden descent of her skirt confirmed it.

Sputtering still, venting her anger and embarrassment that he, of all people, should discover her in such a state of dishabille, Dara glared in his general direction. She could barely see. Her eyes stung and watered as she repeatedly blinked, trying to focus on his fuzzy image.

"If you had any decency, you would have kept your unwanted presence to yourself, Mr. McQuade."

Gazing at her tear-bright eyes, the delicate flush across her cheeks, and the curling wisps of hair that fell against her slender neck, he was stung with fresh insistence by the desire she raised in him. He reached out to tap her nose playfully. "If I waited," he drawled with all the heat of the August day in his voice, "for an invitation from you or your permission to call, Miss Dara Louise Owens, I'd be old and gray and too tired to play courting games."

"Let me apprise you of a few home truths, Mr. Mc—"

"Eden, darlin'. If you recall as well as memory serves me, you didn't have a bit of trouble whispering my name with decided impatience last evening."

"You are a depraved scoundrel to remind me of what is best forgotten."

Dara held the faint impression of his image in place for a moment before he was gone. She rubbed her eyes, willing the tears to flow and ease their stinging. Eden came to her side, ignored the sullen pout of her mouth, and proceeded to wipe her eyes with fresh well water and the linen towel he had snatched from the clothesline.

"Better?" he asked. Eden raised her chin with two fingers, turning her face to the right and then to the left, delivering his opinion with a connoisseur's sophistication. "Charming, love. I've imagined you with all the starch removed. You have the allure of Eve in the Garden of—"

"Don't you dare mention Eden," she cut in crossly. "I'm not going to play Eve in any garden of your making."

"I haven't invited you to do so, little saint. You shouldn't presume—"

"I'm afraid," she stated coolly, "that you have formed an erroneous opinion of me that I accept the entire blame for. I shall—"

"How noble of you."

"I shall endeavor," Dara continued, ignoring his

interruption, "to do my utmost to correct it, Mr. McQuade. I've warned you that you don't know me. My lapse—"

"*Don't tell me that I don't know you.* If I don't, who does? Clay? No, love, you wouldn't let him near you. Or," he asked with stung male pride, "was it his own rigid code of gentlemanly behavior that kept him from becoming your lover?" Eden allowed her to bat his hand away from her chin, his voice softer as he continued.

"If Clay had once tasted the lush invitation of your provocative, but alas, innocent mouth, no man could come near you." He politely disregarded her startled gasp, irrationally blaming her for his restless discontent that found its ease with this verbal retaliation.

"Clay doesn't know how to bring a secret smile to your lips that women'll envy and men would kill to see," he noted with cynical observation. "But I do, don't I, love?" His gray eyes held no pity targeting hers.

"You make that a final declaration!"

"Not final. Final words, little saint, are for the dying. I don't intend to say mine for a long time."

Summoning shredded pride, Dara muttered, "And when the time comes and you do say them, Mr. McQuade, I hope to tarnation that you choke on them."

"Such unladylike venom," he intoned, amusement alight in his eyes. Removing a cheroot from his pocket, he added, "You'll be bending knee for hours to atone for wishing me ill. I might even join you there, for I'm pleased, love, to see the veneer crack."

"Don't talk to me about my unladylike behavior." She felt a surging delight with the need to have the last word. "What does a man like you know about ladies? I can guess the sort of woman a man like you consorts with, and never, Mr. McQuade, do you hear me, never would they be called ladies. Not even if it . . . it . . . snowed down here! And you," she snapped with honeyed malice, pointing a finger in the general direction of his nose, "you will never be a gentleman."

To his credit, Eden did not laugh. An inner smile of pure mischief brightened his mouth while his eyes held a gleam of sheer deviltry. "If I wasn't a gentleman, Dara Louise," he taunted, "you would have known what being a woman meant the first time I met you." And the wild black Irish blood, too hot under a back that would never bend to another, had him step as close as he dared to her. "Last night," he stated in a constrained voice, fighting for equanimity against her goading him beyond every point of acquired civility, "I came close to taking you where you lay on the table. And if you are smart, little saint, you'll never bait me. 'Cause if you do, darlin'," he whispered as anger crested and his eyes lost their coolness, "I'll take that as an invitation to show you how *gentlemen* treat their *ladies* to points past discretion."

Dara was rigid, blinking her eyes as he blurred out of focus for a moment while she fought the desire to put her hands in violence upon him.

"Smile for me, love. I'm more than ready to do bodily harm to some unsuspecting soul."

"So, Mr. McQuade, am I." Dara didn't stop to think about what she was going to do. She walked away, gritting her teeth.

"How's your father?" Eden asked, lighting his cigar.

"As well as can be expected with half the town come to visit him."

Eden didn't look behind him, willing to give her a moment to collect herself. He had been, no, he wasn't going to excuse anything he said. "Then you won't have any objection to my going in to see him?"

"Not a one, Mr. McQuade," she announced, spinning around from the laundry tub and slapping the first garment that had come to hand across the back of his head.

Eden's exploding hiss of breath made Dara take one step back. The sodden cloth had completely wrapped around his face. He stood immobile and temptation got the better of her. She cautiously came around to view the front of him. Rivulets of water coursed down his fine black jacket, soap bubbles glistening in the late afternoon's sunlight. She squinted, saw widening damp spots on his buff cream shirt, and found herself nearing to watch the water drip down the indecent fit of his pants until it made tracks on the dust-laden boots that were . . . moving . . . toward her . . .

Eden ripped the cloth aside, spat out the smashed sodden cigar, and looked for a moment as if murder was beyond contemplation. Hunter pinned prey, and he held aloft the dripping prize in his hand.

"I . . ." she began.

"Your silence, Dara, would be melodious." And to her complete mortification, he wrung out the cloth with one hand, watching, as she did, the stream of water reduced to a few drops falling from his grip. With the seriousness one would usually reserve for items of questionable origins, Eden shook the cloth until its shape became discernible. Dangling the delicately embroidered lace-trimmed camisole from one finger by its shoulder strap, Eden frowned in silent contemplation.

Dara held her breath. That he would find some way to retaliate she didn't doubt. Regret for her impetuous act made her long to snatch the intimate apparel, which had never appeared so fragile as it did held by Eden McQuade.

"I had hoped," he blandly explained, "to gain possession of this enchanting item in a more decidedly pleasurable way. I shall, however, treasure its gift as a promise, love." His smile became indulgent as his gaze measured the distance between them, and he could feel the swell of his sex react to the lush fullness of her heaving breasts, which threatened her dress's pearl-buttoned closing.

"Soon, darlin'," he murmured. "You've nearly used up my entire store of patience."

"You can't keep it!"

But Dara had no courage to step forward as he carefully folded her camisole. Then, as if handling a priceless treasure, he tucked the damp garment into the inside pocket of his jacket.

Frissons of warmth trickled inside her, and she cast about desperately to distract herself from where his declaration led her thoughts.

"Have you seen anything of Matt?" she asked, longing to brush the sparkling water from his hair just as he was doing. "He never came home last night," she added.

"Are you worried?"

"Yes. But I need him to—" Dara stopped. He was walking away from her! "Where are you going?"

"To find him, Dara," he replied, turning to face her, but still walking backward. "I said I'd satisfy all your needs, darlin'."

Dara watched him, a grin becoming a smile that deepened until laughter bubbled forth and the day, nearing its end, no longer held the angry threats of morning. "Eden," she whispered, "a garden of delight . . ."

Chapter Nine

"THERE'S TEN MINING companies in this area alone! Can you believe that, Dara?" Cyrus asked two weeks after his accident. He sat at the kitchen table, ignoring the radiating heat from the oven that blended with the sun's setting warmth. His stout cane was propped beside him, and he shifted his broken leg, which rested on Dara's vanity bench. It was by trial and error that they discovered its height was perfect to alleviate the weight of the new cast Rainly's first doctor had applied five days ago. Dr. Richard Vance, lately of Buffalo, New York, had rented the last store that Lucio Suarez built on the newly paved Richmond Road and had hung out his shingle. His waiting room had been full ever since.

Cyrus had no use for quackery, but Eden assured him that Dr. Vance's testimonials from satisfied patients, along with the credentials attesting that he studied with the eminent Dr. R. V. Pierce of that same city, were genuine. Eden McQuade, Cyrus found out, was shrewd, knowledgeable about worldly matters, and didn't begrudge Cyrus's need to know what was happening within the town. He had enlivened the boring hours of the evenings, proved himself to be a passable chess player, and his liquor was always velvet smooth.

"It says here," Cyrus continued, ruffling his newspaper while Dara slid a tray of biscuits into the oven to bake, "that Vogt owns almost ninety thousand acres of land, and Suarez ain't far behind. Seems to be that Eden best watch himself or Suarez'll have the county sewed up along with Vogt."

"I'm sure he's well aware of what's happening, Papa."

"And thank the good Lord he is. If I had to depend on you and Matt to fill me in on what's going on in town, I'd be on the go-down sufferin' a case of the all-overs."

"Papa, that's not true. I told you that Suelle is in a snit over Jake refusing to hire another peace officer. I can't say I blame her, either. Waking up in the middle of the night to find Early poking his gun out their bedroom window when someone tried to steal one of their horses was bad enough, but when Early shot at him and missed, the man shot back and shattered Suelle's grandmother's lamp. She's heartbroken over its loss. And now, Papa, she's afraid. So are most of the women in town. But they won't talk about it to their husbands, because they're more frightened of their men carrying guns." Dara tested the oil and, when it sizzled, began frying the flour-coated strips of catfish. She refused to look up at the clock, knowing her inner senses would tell her when it was near time for Eden to arrive.

"Is is true that Tucker forbid his Selena to leave their store unless he or Julian is with her?"

"Yes. And Caroline said Jesse and his sons are carrying rifles with them if they deliver lumber out to the mines. He's been robbed once and swore it won't happen again. Sophy is forbidden to walk down Williams Street since Suarez opened another gambling hall, and they expect the arrival of that Mallory woman this week. The Gilded Lily should be in full swing by the weekend, but

Sophy's worried about the body they found near the shanties behind the sawmill. Jake threatened to burn them down, and the men clear out for a day or two, but then they just come back during the night."

"You haven't spoken to Anne, have you, Dara?"

"I've been too busy to pay social calls."

"I heard she's doing her buying at the new general store on Stuart Lane that Irish fellow opened."

"It's closer to their home, Papa. Anne needs to be careful in her condition." Dara placed the last piece of fried fish on a thick white ironstone platter and slid it into the small warming oven above the stove.

Cyrus lifted his paper to allow her to spread a linen cloth on the table, no longer surprised that she set out four plates with neatly aligned starched linen napkins held securely rolled by gleaming silver napkin rings. They were one of the few treasures Malva had salvaged from their home. Thoughts of his long-deceased wife brought forth a sigh. He longed for her to share his silent observations on the present state of affairs between Dara and Eden. The first few times Eden arrived just as they sat down to supper, Dara had been flustered, and Cyrus had done the inviting. He owed Eden a debt, but try as he would, he couldn't get a straight story from either of them about what happened the night he fell or the morning after. Pierce had not returned to town, and Cyrus excused him, because the farm work took his time. But Clay had not called, and Dara, when asked, refused to discuss him. Cyrus couldn't press her, for she had the burden of the house, the store, and his care. But he'd fiddle his britches if Eden McQuade didn't appear to be courting her.

"Seems a mite strange, don't it, that Eden rides out every morning to his mines and then returns to town each night right in time for supper. 'Course, your cooking is a draw to tempt any man, but it seems a mighty waste of time to me."

"I hadn't given it a thought, Papa." Searching the pantry shelves for a crock of pickled corn, Dara knew she spoke the truth. It just seemed . . . well, natural that Eden joined them. She certainly could not reveal to her father that she felt safer knowing he was close by each night. Matt had surprised her by taking the responsibility of sharing the burden of the store. He worked from midafternoon until closing, leaving her free to tend to chores and prepare supper. In turn, she didn't comment about his disappearing every night after supper. While her father was feeling better, Dara knew he would resent her belief that he couldn't protect them. She shuddered at the thought of how much Rainly had changed just as Eden and Jake had warned. A few months ago neighbors could sleep with their doors unlocked. Now they were arming themselves.

Setting the crock on the floor, she saw her father sat engrossed in his paper, and she reset the tortoiseshell combs securing the thick coil of hair at her nape. She smoothed the fit of her new blue and white striped serge skirt and the blousewaist of India blue muslin. Leah Tucker suggested trimming them with the new shade called Buffalo red, but she felt it too bold. Eden always noted what she wore, often complimenting her when he chastely kissed her good night. What had happened to make him change? Sitting in the kitchen, serving him supper, kept the night of her "indiscretion," as she privately termed it, fresh in her mind. Eden's behavior, while leaving her confused and vexed, had been that of a gentleman. His taunt of someday teaching her what the word really meant aroused her virginal curiosity.

"Dara! Matt's home and the biscuits are burning."

"Coming." She scooped up the crock, deciding that Eden McQuade was slick enough to have her falling for his lines like a pioneer housewife at a medicine man's show. But she was humming with excitement at the thought.

"You should have seen him," Matt whispered, leaning over his father's shoulder.

"Who?" she asked, dishing out the pickled corn.

"Eden," he replied, endowing the word with hero worship. "He sent two of the men that work for Suarez into the horse trough by Early's. I was locking up when I heard shouts and ran out front just in time to see him do it. He's . . ." Matt stopped. Eden stood at the open back door. "I was just . . . I saw . . ." Stammering, Matt blurted out, "What happened?"

"They required cooling off. I obliged them."

Dara glanced up on hearing the coiled tension in his voice. His shirtsleeve was torn, and there was a dark bruise on the undercurve of his jaw.

"Dara, the biscuits," Cyrus reminded her.

She grabbed the pot holders to remove the tray from the oven, caught by surprise at the rush of protectiveness and the compassionate need she felt to soothe Eden. She filled a basket with the nicely browned biscuits using uncommon haste and turned again to see Eden, but he stood with his back toward her at the sink with Matt. Their whispering was far too low for her to hear what they were saying, but she stole a minute to stare her fill.

He hadn't stopped at Miss Loretta's to change tonight. His boots were scarred leather, dusty from working with the phosphate. The chalky substance clung to his faded denims, reminding her of the first time she had met him. The fit of the worn, soft cloth accentuated his narrow flanked hips and muscled thighs. There were damp spots on the back of his pale blue shirt and streaks of dirt. Her breath caught as the cloth taunted across his shoulders when he leaned down, splashing water on his face. Her gaze feasted on his black hair, which needed cutting, watching, as he lifted his head and smoothed it back, the way the light gleamed on the water he left behind. There was something intimate that made her flush inwardly, seeing him repeat the masculine gesture of tucking his shirt into his pants and adjusting the set of his belt before he turned around.

Their gazes meshed across the room, and in that moment of silent communication, Dara knew there would be no chaste kiss good night. The tension she had heard in his voice appeared in the tarnished silver of his eyes, the look dangerous, and there was no relief to be found in the cynical grin on his lips. She felt he was warning her, of what, she didn't know, but her pleasure-ridden senses flowered open as the talk turned to the upcoming box lunch social after Sunday's church service.

Dara sat in the parlor after supper dishes were done, sock darner in hand, her stitches taken in a deliberate manner to alleviate the tension growing within her. Eden lounged in a chair across from where Cyrus, with obvious enjoyment, read aloud from the copy of the *New York Herald Tribune* that Eden had saved for him. She knew Eden watched her. Whenever she glanced up, his gaze was waiting to ensnare hers, but Dara couldn't shake the feeling that there was something predatory about it. She directed her attention to her father, silent for the moment while he scanned the paper for an interesting tidbit to read aloud. They had already covered the shocking Panama scandal caused by the collapse of the Panama Canal Company, and the news that Brazil was now a republic. Farm and labor groups were fighting for the curbing of industrial monopolies, and John D. Rockefeller's Standard Oil Trust controlled virtually all of the nation's oil refineries. Public protests were mounting, along with civil lawsuits against the trusts held by a few men who controlled trade by secret price-fixing.

Dara listened to Eden's surprising opinion that the strikes and overextended railroads would lead to a severe depression. He had suggested that the Withlacoochee River be cleared of stumps and snags to allow barges to make the trips to Port Inglis on Chambers Island in the Gulf of Mexico. Right now he and the other mine owners had to ship by rail to Fernandina on the northeast coast of the state, where the phosphate would then be loaded on ships bound for manufacturing centers along the upper East Coast or in Europe.

The clock ticked away. She knew it was approaching nine, at which time Eden would rise, ask her to walk him to the door, kiss her good night with melting tenderness, and leave. Gossip said that he spent little time in his saloon, and Dara knew the truth of it. Most evenings she could see his lamp burning long into the night in his mine office across the way.

"That William Kemmeler convicted of murdering Matilda Ziegler was executed today by a newfangled electric chair. Hangings always been good enough for a murderer before."

"It's called progress, Cyrus," Eden replied. "Invent something to benefit mankind, and I'll wager there are four men looking for ways to turn a profit using it to do something in a quick efficient manner."

"Killing is killing, no matter how it's done. 'Pears to me the whole country is going to hell in a basket."

"Hell was built on spite and heaven on pride, or so the Good Book says."

"Your pa teach you that?"

"He was fond of raising his children on quotes. I remember one time my brother Paradise committed a breach of manners I cannot repeat, and Daddy whupped him, claiming he was going to hell. Hell," Eden noted with a grin, "was a favorite topic in our home. Anyway, Pa said he had to mend his manners 'cause the devil was right strict on etiquette in hell, and there weren't hope for Paradise to go anywhere else. My brother earned himself bread and water for two days quoting one of Pa's favorites back to him—'The devil's snare does not catch you unless you are first caught by the devil's bait.' My brothers and I," he clarified, "figured that's what Pa was, the devil's bait."

Cyrus laughed and Dara joined in, reminded of the times Eden mentioned his own boyish indiscretions usually caused by his father first pointing out they were the devil's own temptation. He rarely mentioned his family, but she knew they were close.

"Well, I'll be horswoggled! Listen here. They found clams containing pearls in the Sugar River in Wisconsin! Don't that beat all. Some of them are valued at one hundred dollars. Just think of the swindlers heading there before those folks know what happened."

"But think, Cyrus," Eden interjected with a cynical tone, "how those *poor folks* will turn their greed around and use it against them."

"Like Rainly?"

"Greed, my friend, has become the god your towns-folk worship." He sipped his drink, then added, "Did you know there's talk of wiping out the Negro shanties? Suarez brought them here along with Georgia sharecroppers to work his mines, and now folks find their presence a blight. Clay's vigilante committee has been busy." He looked at Dara, but her head was lowered over her mending, and he had no satisfaction of seeing her reaction to hearing Clay's name. Did she regret what she had done? Beyond telling him that she had made her intent clear not to marry him, she had never mentioned Clay again.

"And was greed the reason you fought with Suarez's men?"

"No."

Cyrus knew better than to ask for an elaboration. It was the depth of privacy that Eden maintained that sometimes made Cyrus wonder what his intentions toward Dara were. His behavior couldn't be faulted, but there was something . . . He left his thought unfinished and returned to his paper.

Eden made no apology for his surly mood. He knew its cause and exactly what he could do to end it. Claws of tension raked his spine, and once again his glance strayed to where Dara sat, prim as a Charles Gibson illustration. The ornate frame of the lady's slipper chair with its dark green brocade upholstery held the same lemon-scented sheen as her mink-dark hair. He was tired, damn tired of working long hours, keeping one step ahead of Lucio, trying to talk sense into Jake, and worrying over the senseless violence that was escalating daily in Rainly. There was Dara, too, and he did not want to think of that mouth . . .

"Will you walk out with me, Dara?"

For a moment she didn't react. When she dragged her gaze up, looking at him, she felt a leashed tension intensify in herself. She gripped the wooden sock darner, uncertain of what to answer.

"Why don't you go, Dara?" Cyrus suggested, peering over his paper. "For a little while," he amended. "You haven't been able to walk down by the river for weeks, and I know you miss it."

There was doubt clouding his eyes, but he nodded toward her, and Dara set her mending down in the basket at her feet.

"I would be pleased to accompany you," she answered, rising, smoothing her skirt.

Eden tossed off the last of his drink, finding no enjoyment in his own smoked-satin bourbon. He rose, murmured good night to Cyrus, and offered his arm to Dara.

He led her down the hall toward the back door, stopping for a moment before they reached the doorway. "Before we leave, let's remove these," he ordered in a gentle voice, taking off her gilt-rimmed spectacles and leaving them on the table.

It was impossible for her to ignore the roughness in his liquid voice, or the knowledge that the tension inside her was rapidly accumulating into tiny knots as he placed his hand on the small of her back to usher her outside.

Dara lifted her skirt with one hand and felt the heated imprint of his touch through the layers of her clothing. At the head of the sloping path that led down to the riverbank, he paused for a moment to light a cigar.

His continued silence unnerved her. She tried to regain the peace of being here, listening to the cooing of doves and the buzz of the night insects, but the scent of Eden, lithe and in a dangerous mood, swamped her.

With his hand on her elbow, he guided her down the path and, once there, turned away from town. Dara stood this as long as she could, uncertain of why he asked her to accompany him, floundering to know what it was he wanted from her.

"You're not enjoying this, are you, Dara?"

"It's your . . . Eden, what's wrong? Did something happen out at the mine today? Or is the fight you had with those men to blame for your mood?"

He stopped abruptly, flinging the cigar into the water. Tilting his head back, he stared up at the widespread glitter of stars and considered the absurdity of his noble gesture to allow Dara time. And he knew that tonight he didn't want to talk, he just . . . wanted . . .

She stood before him, and he reached out to run the back of his fingers lightly down her cheek. "You still don't understand, do you?" But Dara had no chance to answer. He cupped the back of her neck, dragging her closer, lowering his head, and without a word he brushed his lips across hers, seeking the satin warmth of her mouth with a compelling need that swelled his sex into aching. With one hand he held her still; with the other he caressed her rigid back, coaxing her closer to him, a groan rising before her mouth suddenly softened and became greedy for his kiss.

Dara knew what she was doing was wrong. Modesty and virtue were not only qualities to be respected and adhered to, they were ones instilled in her. But she had no thought but to appease the need she felt in him. His mouth was hot, smoky, and tanged with liquor, and she longed for the solace of his hands caressing her back, dragging her closer, and then closer to his body. Her neck arched high, then higher still, and she pressed parted lips eagerly against his, dragging her hands through his hair, satisfying the longing she'd had all night to touch it.

The giant cypress trees sheltered them beneath their branches, but Dara wasn't aware of where they were. The night scents clung to Eden, and she absorbed them with flaring senses. Eden . . . making her feel alive, his kisses, deep, drawing her . . .

"Open your mouth, love . . . there . . . let me . . ." He drank her ardent moan, felt its spearing presence deep inside, and gathered her slender, pliant body against him, easing her upper torso into a slow, abrading dance back and forth across his chest. "Better, love," he whispered, hunger tempered by his innate gentleness.

Dara swayed, his hands guiding her hips, dizzy with the pleasure expanding, warming the tensioned knots that dissolved and reformed with frightened clarity into desire. Her mouth opened to the heavy stroke of his tongue, her fingers twisting into his silken curled hair, longing to heighten the sensations that both sated and increased need until she lost pace with her breath.

Scattering hot open kisses, his lips moved over the delicate bones of her face, his hands a murmur against her body. Dara felt her blood flow, thick and hot, his kisses burning with a caressing intensity that left her softly moaning. She trembled, aching . . .

His hands discovered the warmth of her through layers of cloth and boned guardian, rode the curve of her hip, tested the contour of her waist, and then Eden spread his fingers to sculpt the lush fullness of her breast.

Dara cried out, shocked with the feel of his palm cupping such an intimate part of her body. Desire sharpened into passion, and she knew Eden would know how to bring her to ease.

"It hurts, love, doesn't it?" he queried in a sensually drugging voice. "Here"—his palm traveled in a slow hot circle, letting the pleasurable balm of his touch bring her flowering arousal up to a peak—"that's better, isn't it?" A slow, sensuous smile took possession of his mouth, and his eyes grew sultry, tarnished silver dark and hungry.

It was too powerful for Dara. Her betraying blood rushed to meet his fingers, but he was wrong, the ache wasn't better.

Eden couldn't think of anything more than his need to bury himself within the lush femininity softly crying his name. He savored her mouth with sharp-set passion, with the abstinence he blamed her for, languidly probing her mouth with his tongue, his lean experienced fingers stroking sensitive cloth-bound flesh until the flaming response he sought began to smolder. Eden felt the infinitesimal acquiescence, and he lifted his mouth.

"Tell me you want me, love," his night-dark voice murmured.

"Eden, please . . ." Her breath rushed out, drying her lips. Dara leaned her head against his chest.

"Still too fast for you, little saint?"

Her rioting senses would not still, and Dara couldn't reply. His heartbeat thundered in her ears, her legs felt weak, her whole body heated and trembling.

Eden took her weight against him, caressed her shoulders, sighed at the feel of the heavy softness of her breasts pressing his chest, and nestled his lips against her lemon-scented hair, knowing he would not seduce her further. Why this one woman, innocent and charming as she was, should beguile him, he didn't know. But it was the sweetly given surrender of that very innocence that pricked his conscience just when he thought to overcome it.

He held her shivering body for long minutes, long for

him, since every delicate shudder of her body stroked his, and when they ceased, he urged her home.

She turned to him after he opened the back door.

"Are you angry with me?" she asked, filled with certainty that he was indeed furious since he hadn't spoken a word to her.

"Anger is not the sentiment that best expresses what I'm feeling, darlin'," he replied in a caustic tone. "Now, go inside and dream your sweet little virginal dreams—"

"Must you add the insult of patronizing me?"

"Insult, love?" he repeated, backing her against the doorjamb. "Is that what you thought I was doing, insulting you?"

Dara lowered her head, a flush stealing across her cheeks. She had no right to say anything after her wanton behavior. And it was now, when she was no longer in his arms, her senses slowly returning from the drugging ease of his sensuality, that she berated herself.

Eden lifted her chin, refusing her solace of her own condemnation. "You did enjoy every moment, didn't you, darlin'? I would know if it had been otherwise."

The sharp reminder that he was a man far too familiar with women transferred Dara's anger from herself to him.

"That was a remark I would expect from a cad."

"Didn't I tell you from the first that my intentions weren't honorable? Did you think I'd slip into the role Clay was better to play? The touching scene between you that I was forced to witness, where you begged him to kiss you like a woman he wanted, was *you*, love."

"And is that what you've been doing? Making me feel wanted?" She glared at him, furious, and he dared to smile. It took her a few moments to realize how cynical that smile was.

"Lord, darlin', you're something else when you get angry. All dark eyes and flushed cheeks, and it sure beats the devil out of the starched primness you wear most times."

"My mother tried to raise me to be a lady!"

"Oh, you're that," he agreed far too quickly, his head angled downward to whisper, "but you'd be a hell more excitin' if she raised you to be a woman, too."

"Your kind of woman? I think not. I much prefer you in the role of gentleman, but your behavior tonight indicates that was merely an act calculated to lead me down the garden—"

"I warned you that I would teach you what the word *gentleman* means, little saint. Gentle," he intoned, his voice insidiously soft, "is this." His palms framed her cheeks, and he took her mouth in a kiss of infinite tenderness. Lifting his head, he murmured, "Now, if I weren't a gentle man, then I would kiss you like this." Suffocating the cry of alarm that died in her throat, his tongue claimed her mouth with a shattering surge of passion that brought a soaring pleasure to his body.

And when he was done, he left her.

Chapter Ten

"I DON'T UNDERSTAND, Matt. Why do you need the day's receipts?"

"I need them. Can't that be enough of a reason for you?"

"No, it's not. And what would I tell Papa?"

"You don't have to tell him anything, Dara. He would never ask you where the money is, and you know it. 'Sides, I'll have it back for you tomorrow. I just need it now."

Watching Matt's restless pacing back and forth in front of the store's counter, Dara was struck by the subtle difference in him. There had been little time this past week for them to see each other or talk, but she realized she could pinpoint the exact day she began to notice that Matt was no longer a boy. Six nights ago she had walked with Eden down by the river, where he had assaulted her senses and left her. Six days ago Satin Mallory arrived in Rainly. Eden was in town each night but not to supper, and Matt hadn't been home at all.

But Dara couldn't let her thoughts dwell on Eden when her brother faced her with desperation in his eyes.

"Matt, what kind of trouble are you in? And don't put me off by saying you aren't. You just asked me to give you two hundred dollars."

"I owe it out," he answered curtly, staring down at the money spread out behind the counter. He itched to grab it, but Dara, while willing to cover many lapses on his part from their father, would never condone his just taking the money. And Dara's temper, which he honestly had never known she had, made him walk like a tomcat in thin mud around her lately.

With a guilty flush he stopped and stared down at the floor. "Dara, please. I need it now."

"It's that woman, isn't it? She's your trouble and has been from the moment she stepped off the train last Sunday."

"I don't know what you're talking about."

"You don't? I'll tell you. Last Sunday at the train station, you, Julian Tucker, and Logan Kinnel got into a fight over who was going to carry that hussy's bandbox."

"She asked me!"

"Don't you dare raise your voice to me, Matt."

He had the grace to mumble an apology. Running his large hands through his hair, Matt resumed his pacing.

"Did you tell Papa?"

"No. And neither did anyone else. I asked them not to mention it to him. But Matt, you can't be going . . . oh, no! Is that why you need the money? You've been going there and gambling!"

"And what if I have been? It ain't so terrible. I win enough hands to know how good I am."

"So good that you need to borrow money to pay debts that you shouldn't make?"

"Don't give me that holier-than-thou look, Dara. I could say a few things about what you've done that wouldn't stand the light of day." He loomed over the counter to whisper, "I saw Eden take one of your unmentionables and put it in his pocket. And you, you stood there laughing."

"Matt!" Dara gripped the edge of the counter, fury making her tremble, fear the furthest thing from her mind. How could he threaten her? How could he say such a thing to her? But when he stood back, there was panic in his eyes. It was wrong to give in to him, she knew that, but Matt . . .

"Dara, please."

"Take it." But when he reached out for the money, Dara placed her hand over his. "Promise me that you will use this to pay off whoever you owe and then no more, Matt. Promise me you won't gamble. I don't know what Papa would do if he found out."

"Papa this and Papa that. When are you going to stop living for Papa? I'm not a boy anymore, Dara. I do a man's work for a man's pay out at Eden's mine. So stop trying to treat me like a boy." He shook her hand off, pocketing the money.

"Matt," she called out as he strode down the aisle, "does Eden know about this?" He turned around and Dara was taken aback by the hard look in his eyes.

"Are you asking for me or do you really want to know if he's there every night?"

"For you, Matt," she answered after a few moments of tense silence. Not even to her brother would she admit to being curious if Eden numbered among the men that filled the Gilded Lily every night since it opened.

"I don't know. I haven't said anything to him. But maybe I should have asked him first. Eden would understand about a man's debts and honor. He sure as you're in a swivet wouldn't be asking six questions to a dollar before he did the right thing and helped me."

"Matt, you're forgetting that he's older than you. I'm sure Eden wouldn't gamble money he didn't have."

"Yeah? You don't know him very well. But if you want, go on believing that."

"Matt! Come back here. Matt . . ."

She started to run after him, knowing it wouldn't accomplish anything. Matt had what he wanted from her. If it hadn't been for the late arrival of the drummers, she wouldn't have been in the store this afternoon. They were the one thing that Matt refused to deal with. Rubbing her temples, Dara wished there were someone else she could relieve her burdens upon. Some of the goods they offered were shoddy, but it was underhanded of them to tell her how much her competition had bought. Lonn Rogan was as Irish as they came, and he had made a dent in taking on the miners' business. Dara knew she didn't care a wit, but her father did, and she couldn't tell him that the raw vitality of the miners made her uncomfortable. Eden would understand if she told him, but there had been a decided reserve between them this past week when he stopped by. *Frustrating* was the word that summed up Eden McQuade, and she had to finish tallying the accounts.

But this business with Matt wasn't something she could ignore.

"Dara! Dara girl, where are you!" Miss Loretta's imperious voice rang out.

"Back here."

"Ah declare," she stormed, coming down the aisle, "Ah don't know what's gotten into yore brothah, girl. He jest past me like chain lightnin' with a link snapped. What's got him in a snit'n basket?"

"Matt's grown now, Miss Loretta. His business is his own. I was about to close the store," she hinted gently.

"Ah can tell time. Ah ain't come to buy. Ah jest had a peek inside that hussy's place, an' Ah promised yore papa if Ah did, Ah'd come tell him 'bout it. Seein' as how yore in a cotton-spittin' mood, Ah'll take mahself off to visit with him."

With that, Miss Loretta, bustle waddling, hat swaying precariously, sailed down the aisle and out the back door. Dara admitted she was curious about the interior of the Gilded Lily—so were most women in town. Their menfolk, she learned during the week, were close-mouthed, and no amount of cajoling from wives or women kin could get one of them to describe what it looked like. Whatever little Miss Loretta viewed, she knew her father wouldn't relay the information to her. "It wouldn't be fitting for a lady to know," he would say. And Dara once again felt the restrictive chafe maintaining ladylike behavior put upon her. Sometimes she wanted to cry off the burden of being a lady just as . . .

Eden . . . Eden wouldn't be the least bit reluctant to tell her. He would likely offer to take her inside, partly for the perverse satisfaction of shocking her and partly for his simple belief that society's restraints governing what a lady could and could not do withheld her from experiencing the joy of being a woman.

Shaking her head, unwilling to stray down that endless path where he stood beckoning, Dara wished for the freedom of being a man for a few short hours. Just long enough to satisfy her curiosity.

Had she had her wish granted, Dara would have realized that young men, like Matt, his swagger cocky as he entered the white and gilded doors of Satin Mallory's pleasure palace, paid little heed to the study in ostentation of the establishment.

Once he was inside, one of Satin's silent Chinese houseboys removed his boots and replaced them with thin-soled slippers. Men balked at first, but Satin had few rules that she demanded they adhere to: no boots to mar her gold and white lush Brussels carpets; no weapons of any kind, to prevent murder done upon her premises; no limits on what a man gambled; and the word *no* was not to be uttered to one customer by the young women she employed.

Matt faced the three archways before him. He searched for Satin among the few patrons this early in the evening in the billiard room. The Gilded Lily boasted one of the new J. M. Brunswick & Balke Co. billiard tables, whose green-felted surface was supported by a small pride of ebonized and gilded lions. Gilded-lily light fixtures burned with scented oils over the cue holder and tally rack. Against the white and gold flocked wallpaper, deep cushioned baroque chairs invited spectators to lounge.

He watched for a moment as two men he didn't know placed a bet of fifty dollars on the impossibility of an upcoming shot. But Satin wasn't in the room, and Matt turned away.

Being a virgin, much to his regret, Matt made no attempt to enter the parlor on his right. Someone beyond the white velvet drapery swagged over the archway was picking out a lively tune on the piano, and he listened, with temptation thickening his blood, to the soft, intimate laughter of Miss Satin's young ladies. He called them that, with a twinge of conscience as he thought of his sister, simply because Satin referred to them as such. With a straightened spine and a lift of his chin that he no longer blushed at the sight of them, Matt stepped aside as a vision in white satin swept out of the parlor.

Her smile urged him to return it, while his Adam's apple bobbed up and down in his effort to swallow. There was a great deal to her lavishly beaded gown, but unfortunately for Matt, most of the material seemed to be concentrated below her hour-glass waist.

"You're Matt Owens, aren't you?" she asked in a breathy voice that was less affected than necessary due to her corset's tight lacing. "Satin told me who you were."

"She did?" He gulped, trying so hard not to stare at the expanse of creamy skin that swelled in provocative invitation from the low-pointed drape of satin that narrowed into stringlike proportions over her shoulders.

A cluster of pink and green ostrich feathers bobbed from her high coiffure as she nodded, lifting her hand to take his arm.

"She's inside. I'll have the pleasure of escorting you to her." Her eyelashes batted like hummingbird's wings, and Matt, with all the pent-up frustration of his virginal state, felt his blood pooled into the one body part he had no control over. With a sly glance, the shameless delight who was clutching his arm reached out and delicately stroked him. "We," she breathed, "could dispatch this cargo and play goose and duck."

His Adam's apple lodged in his throat. She was . . . She actually touched him! Matt swore to himself for every time he thought he had cleverly questioned Eden without, he believed, revealing his lack of sexual expertise. But Eden hadn't covered what to do in a situation that had him feeling as useless as stuffing a .22 cartridge in a ten-gauge shotgun! The money burned a hole in his pocket. It wasn't nearly as hot as what else was burning, but it sure enough came damn close.

"I'm Nellie." She smiled, her eyes knowing, and gently disengaged her arm from his. "I know a man like you must have a powerful thirst that needs satisfying first. But come find me later, and we'll tend to all that excess baggage."

She left behind a cloud of floral perfume, and Matt finally cleared his throat, managed to breathe, and decided right then and there he was going to have himself a high-helled time losing his virginity tonight.

He glanced up at the sound of his name and lost his breath all over again. Not five feet from him stood Satin.

"Lord, but you're the most gorgeous creature," he choked out.

Indeed, even to a jaded man's eyes, Satin Mallory was considered beautiful. Her hair was an ebony sheen coiled into a sleek chignon that allowed the perfect symmetry of her features to be viewed without distraction. Skin as white and smooth as the egret feathers curling flirtatiously over one ear to draw a man's eye to the silk of bare shoulders was draped this evening, as it had been each night, in blood-red satin that molded to the Venus-back sateen French corset. A blaze of diamonds encircled her throat. Each of her wrists were encircled by diamond cuffs over long red silk gloves. Her lips were lushly moist, a decadent sultriness lit her blue eyes, and as she raised her egret fan in a languid fashion, smiling at Matt, he was beset by the fantasy his wild imagination conjured with every inhaled breath of her spiced scent.

Beautiful, yes. But Matt was not a jaded man. He was an innocent boy enamored of an angel who treated him like the man he longed to be.

And it was now that he once again wished he could wield the skill of Eden McQuade's tongue so that Satin would offer to dislodge the cargo that had him ready to burst like a piddling puppy.

In tongue-tied awe he whispered, "I've got the money."

"Matt," she chided in a voice of melted honey, "there was no need for you to rush over to pay such a trifling debt. I know you're a man of honor, but every man has a bad run with the cards." With a graceful sweep of her train, Satin turned and with practiced ease whispered over her shoulder, "Come inside. I've saved a seat at my table just for you."

"I . . . well, I should . . ." Damn! He never did promise Dara that he wouldn't gamble. There stood Satin, a tiny frown on that smooth brow, waiting for him to accept the honor she offered him to sit at her table. He'd be a fool not to take it. Squaring his broad shoulders, he stepped to her side. "I'd be honored."

He knew he had every man's attention as they slowly progressed between the heavy gilded baroque tables and chairs. Satin smiling and nodding, her skilled fingers resting light as swan's down on his arm, made his chest expand with pride. It was a good thing he wore his Sunday-go-to-meeting suit acting as escort for Miss Satin herself. He didn't even stare at the feminine nude statuettes that lined the walls in tiny alcoves as he did the first time he came here. He'd stammered and blushed like a fool farm boy when Mr. Dinn from over at the bank asked if his pa knew he were there. Now he nodded to that very same gentleman, who waited behind an ornately carved and scrolled white satin chair, just for the honor of seating the lady.

With all the skill of a courtesan, Satin made a production of setting aside her fan, removing her diamond cuffs and sliding off, finger by finger, the red silk gloves before she broke the seal on a new deck of cards.

"Five card stud, gentlemen."

Matt, to his credit, hesitated before removing the two hundred dollars from his pocket. But Satin smiled, glanced down at the pot, and murmured, "I just know that one of you is leaving here a winner tonight." Her gaze found Matt's. "A big winner."

Two hours later Satin excused herself, and to Matt's surprise, Nellie slid into her seat. He remembered his promise to himself, looked down at the dwindling pile of money in front of him, and back at Nellie's charms. He should quit. He had won a few hands, just enough to keep him from going broke, but he still owed Satin two hundred dollars.

"Matt," Nellie said, waiting until she had his full attention, "you weren't thinking of quitting, were you? I thought we had an appointment later."

Conscience be damned! "Deal me in and yes, we do."

Satin waited by the heavy gold-tasseled portieres that led to her private quarters upstairs. Nellie's nod brought a predatory smile to Satin's lips, and she slipped past the drapery. In her rooms upstairs Lucio would be waiting, the pure white of her furnishings a perfect foil for his dark good looks and her own dramatic coloring.

Over chilled Bollinger champagne she related who was in debt, the amount, and what steps she had taken to collect.

Refilling his glass, Lucio raised it in toast to her. "Six days and you have almost paid back the cost of the land and your traveling expenses. You earn my admiration anew, Satin."

With a cool smile she acknowledged his praise. "I can't stay long."

"Ah, another of your private games this evening. And might they number among them one Silver McQuade?"

"Sorry to disappoint you, Lucio. He'll come around eventually."

"Then who has put that glitter of challenge into your eyes?"

"Why, Jake Vario has. Didn't you know our much-respected peace officer has attended me nightly?"

"Be careful, Satin," he warned, toying with the three silver nuggets on his watch chain. "Jake wants something from you."

"Yes, he does. But then, so does every man, Lucio."

"And our young friend, has he obtained what he wants?"

"Nellie will take care of Matt tonight."

"He has not been forthcoming with more information about McQuade's financial situation?"

"I've told you everything, Lucio. You know McQuade's production schedule, the yield of every claim he owns, and what he is being offered per ton. If there was anything more, you would know it. McQuade trusts Matt, and Matt, well," she drawled, "we both know how Matt feels about me. I believe McQuade cares a great deal for the boy. Unless it's all a sham to entice Matt's prim sister into his bed."

"Perhaps," Lucio conceded.

Satin tossed down the last of her champagne, finding the last dreg slightly bitter. "If Eden McQuade doesn't come on his own, I'm sure Matt's indebtedness will bring him to call."

"You have done well, Satin," Lucio said with a pleased smile.

"That's what you pay me for, doing things well."

Rainly's box lunch social was an annual affair that did more than raise money for the church. It was another family affair that encouraged the getting together of those neighbors who lived miles from town. Dara rose before dawn to fill her decorated basket. It was a change from the box she usually used, but then, Clay would be there, and she didn't want him bidding on it. She wouldn't even be going but for Miss Loretta. She had insisted to Cyrus that Annamae was perfectly capable of looking after him for the day so Dara could have a bit of socializing, and that had gained her freedom. She would be driving out with Miss Loretta and Luther, but wished that Eden had stopped by and offered to take her.

It was with Eden in mind to share her bountiful basket that Dara made smoked ham from Suelle's own Virginia recipe, hoping to please him with a food from his home state. Along with it went candied sweet potatoes, tiny quail pies, sweet corn pudding, cole slaw, bread and butter pickles, fried apple pastries whose crusts were so light and flaky that she broke two of them, and biscuits. Eden loved her biscuits. She hummed, fixing a small cloth-covered pan filled with honey butter fudge on top, knowing Eden's sweet tooth. There was barely room for plates, napkins, cutlery, and a linen cloth in the basket. Dara managed to wedge in two tin cups, but knew she couldn't fit in the jug of apple cider. With a pleased flourish, she tied the last ribbon bow on its handle and tried not to wish too hard that Eden would be there to bid on her box lunch.

The clock struck the hour, and she rushed from the kitchen up to her room, tapping on Matt's door to make sure he was awake.

"Matt. Matt, you'll be late for service if you don't hurry."

"I'm up," he groaned.

Dara stared at the closed door, hesitating. "Are you all right?"

"Go on," he called out. "I'm fine."

Breathless and flushed with excitement, Dara hid from the twinge of conscience reminding her of what she kept from her father. But the sun was shining, and the mockingbirds were singing outside her windows, and she had to hurry before Miss Loretta called.

Standing before the oak dresser's beveled mirror, she unpinned her loose braid, placing each hairpin into the flowered china receiver, then quickly unraveled her waist-length hair. Her cheeks wanted cooling, and she moved off to splash water on them from the china bowl secure in its own oak stand between the two windows. She had taken the time to sponge bathe earlier, so now she hurried to undress, eyes dancing with anticipation. A dab or two of rosewater on each wrist, a more daring application between her breasts, as she had read one supposed lady of the stage was prone to do, and Dara was ready to begin the onerous labor of getting dressed.

Back and forth she moved from dresser to bed, bed to wardrobe, laying out her clothes on the Nottingham lace spread. She blushed when she held up her cambric chemise, since it was an exact duplicate of the one Eden McQuade so boldly claimed as his. Valenciennes lace-trimmed lawn drawers, four white starched petticoats, a fresh corset cover, and cream lisle hose completed the array of undergarments in which she had to dress. Taking a deep breath, Dara began the task of putting on the lightweight sateen boned corset, thankful that her small waist made tight lacing unnecessary.

Without a breeze to cool her, she began to perspire, but stopped only long enough to whisk her long hair out of her way. Today, because she was accompanying Miss

Loretta, Dara had to put on a bustle. It was a diminished style, but it was labor to tie the many tapes to form the proper rear height. The hall clock struck the half hour, warning her to hurry, although she didn't know how she could dress faster. Each of the undergarments were fastened, tied, buttoned in record time, and she took a moment to pat her face dry. After quickly slipping into the combing mantle, she brushed her long hair and braided it into a coiled chingnon and secured it firmly.

A fine Henrietta-cloth skirt in the deep shade of old rose was settled, adjusted, and buttoned. Dara had chosen a pale pink and white striped shirtwaist of soft percale with narrow piped edges of white on the front pleats, cuffs, and collar. Kid shoes, fastened with the aid of a buttonhook, tested her patience, but finally she stood before the mirror once more to secure her mother's garnet pin and matching eardrops. She wanted to deny that most of her excitement was in anticipation of Eden's pleasure in seeing her dressed in soft pretty colors, for he often teased her that she wore sombre, prim clothes to hide behind.

A last wipe of her brow, another dab of rosewater at her temples, and she was ready just as she heard Luther drive up in his four-seater rig.

As they drove out of the lane, waving to Cyrus and Annamae, Dara curbed the impulse to ask Miss Loretta if Eden had mentioned he would be coming. The shades were pulled on the mine office windows, but that didn't tell her what she wanted to know. Sometimes he left the shades down if he was there and didn't want to be disturbed.

Stop fretting, goose. There are enough hungry men in Rainly to ensure that your basket will take a few bids. But Dara didn't want anyone else.

"Well, girl," Miss Loretta began, "Ah see you've turned yoreself out right fine. You looked a little peaked a week ago. Did yore papa share some of Dr. Vance's restorative with you?"

"Why, no, Miss Loretta, he didn't."

"Mighty fine elixir. Why, lookee there, it's Edward and Elvira. Don't she look a fright. I heard tell that Edward has been a frequent visitor to that hussy's place."

"Now, Miz Loretta," Luther put in, "don't you go an' spread gossip. We's heading for the Lord's house. It wouldn't be fitting."

"Hades, Luther. Don't be lecturin' me. Who tole me 'bout him an' a few othahs?"

Dara sat, with bated breath, clutching the bouncing buggy seat, hoping Miss Loretta would add a piece about those other names. But Luther began talking about the new train schedules and Miss Loretta about her plans to add on to her boardinghouse. Dara couldn't be forward and ask about Eden.

She hadn't been out to church since the ill-fated night of the last social. When they arrived, Dara found herself welcomed and questioned about Clay, and surprisingly, she found she could answer their questions without guilt. Her eyes scanned the crowd of buggies, wagons, and horses for Eden's Sinner. Disappointed that he wasn't here, she followed along with the crowd to where long tables had been set beneath the shade of Spanish-moss-draped oak trees. It was cooler here, encouraging people to mill about.

Squeals of delight gushed forth as each new arrival was greeted. Children darted in and out, playing tag. Dara, talking with Caroline Halput, was smiling—until she found Clay staring at her.

Her first thought was to rid herself of the telltale basket, and she pushed it at Caroline, asking her to give it to Reverend Speck for auction later. She darted through the throng, hoping to escape a confrontation with Clay, and turned to see if he was following her only to bump into a solid chest.

"Easy, Dara. What's got you in a lather?"

"Jake! I . . . oh, I'm sorry. I was . . . How are you? We all miss seeing you at the store." Dara stepped back and saw Anne. Her smile faltered at the frosty look in Anne's eyes. Dara murmured her name in greeting, and for minutes thought Anne would snub her, but her friend nodded, stepping up to take her husband's arm.

"Anne! We're not goin' to walk off as if you two are strangers."

"Don't interfere," she warned him, gazing at Dara as if she intended to do just that.

Patting his wife's hand, Jake then removed it from his arm. "Service won't start for a few minutes, and Jesse is waving me over. Why don't you two have a visit and settle what's between you."

"Jake Vario, don't you dare go off and leave me."

He adjusted the fit of his gunbelt, calling Dara's attention to it, and her gaze met his with shock.

"To service?" Dara questioned, knowing she didn't need to explain more to Jake.

"I'm not alone, Dara. Take a look around. But first, you and Anne need to remember you're best friends. Talk to each other."

Anne glared after her husband, and Dara wasn't sure what to say. Truth be told, she hadn't given much thought to what would happen here today because of her decision not to marry Clay. Thoughts and feelings for

Eden had consumed her, and suddenly she needed to talk to Anne, with whom she had shared so much.

"Please, Anne, don't let what happened with Clay come between us. Jake is right, we were—are—best friends. I've missed you."

"You hurt him terribly, Dara. Why did you do it?" she pleaded.

"Clay and I never wanted the same things, Anne. He's a fine man and will make someone else a good husband, but he refused to understand that I needed—no, *wanted* to share the work of building a home with him. Am I wrong," Dara whispered in a strained voice, "to want what you and Jake have? Your marriage is . . . Jake loves you. He shares his thoughts and feelings, his past and plans with you."

"And I suppose that Eden McQuade does all those things? You're a fool, Dara. You made my brother a laughingstock in Rainly by leaving him for that low-down woman killer!"

"Anne!" Dara was so shocked that she swayed where she stood. Shaking her head, she couldn't believe Anne had said that or that she was standing there, ready to do battle by the light in her blue eyes, if Dara dared to deny it.

Before Dara could think what to say, Anne grabbed her arm, pulling her farther from the crowd so no one could overhear them. "I'm telling you this to warn you because we are friends, Dara. How much do you know about him? Did he tell you where he came from? Or why he had to leave? Pay me some mind, Dara, his trouble with Lucio Suarez goes way back. It didn't start here over phosphate mining."

"I don't believe you. I won't stand here and listen to

you malign a man who has been kindness itself to me and my family!"

"You'd better or you'll find yourself like a pea in a hot skillet. Lucio came to town the same day I returned from Ocala—"

"I know that, Anne."

"Did you know he asked questions about Eden McQuade? Only he didn't call him that. He said his name was Silver."

"It's just a name people tagged on him because he had a knack of finding rich silver veins."

"Is that what he told you?" Anne was shaking, but pushed away Dara's hand. "You think Eden McQuade is perfect, don't you? And I suppose you fooled yourself into thinking he's in love with you, too! Well, ask him, Dara. Ask him if he was mixed up in a woman's killing in Hamilton, Nevada."

With a dawning awareness, Anne studied Dara's stricken eyes. "I know you think I said all this to hurt you, but I didn't, Dara. And if you won't believe me, ask Jake. They were friends long before either of them came here."

"You're wrong," she whispered, wiping her eyes.

"No, I wish I were, but I'm not. Jake admitted that he knew Eden when . . ." Anne bit her lip, hesitant to reveal more. "We fight a lot," she blurted out, needing to tell someone. Angry as she was with Dara for what she had done to her brother, she had carried her own fears alone too long. At Dara's coaxing, she walked a ways with her, feeling the need to talk. "Jake leaves me alone. Every night, right after supper, he dons his gun and supposedly takes a last walk through town. He doesn't come home until late."

Slipping a comforting arm around her friend's waist,

Dara struggled to reassure her. "Jake loves you and he takes his job seriously. I remember his telling me that Rainly wasn't going to be a lawless town. With all that's happened in the last few weeks, his job must take more time. He should have listened to Early and put on another officer to help him."

"It's not that. Jake goes over to see that Mallory woman!"

"Are you listening to some fool's gossip? Jake would never—"

"You don't understand! I've been tired all the time, and I'm sick every morning. I can't cook what he likes, or I get sick at night. I haven't . . . we can't . . . well, you being single and all, I can't say."

Impatience and anger warred in Dara's eyes. They stopped off to the side of the church, away from everyone.

"You can't say?" she repeated. "You accuse a man of killing a woman, tell me your husband is involved with that hussy, and you can't say!"

"We haven't made love in weeks!"

"Anne!" Dara blushed clear up to the roots of her hair. It was the pained expression on her friend's face that made Dara hug her close, murmuring soothing sounds, for she didn't know what to say. "Have you thought of asking Jake for the truth?"

"I can't. He's changed, Dara. I don't know how to explain it to you, but there's a hardness he's walled himself behind." Freeing herself from Dara's hold, Anne stepped back. "Folks are going inside for service. We'd better join them. But Dara, don't forget what I said about Eden McQuade."

Dara let her go, but stood a few moments by herself. She couldn't tell Anne that she would never believe such a lie about Eden. There was so much gentleness in him. And even if he did threaten every moral fiber of her being with his sensual assaults, she knew he would never force or hurt her. It was up to a woman to govern a man's desire, and while she knew she had allowed him liberties beyond what was proper, there wasn't a time when he hadn't, at her least show of reluctance, stopped. No, she would not believe Eden capable of murdering a woman. Anne was wrong to think her a fool. Every man had the capacity for violence—she had seen enough changes in Rainly to understand that—but Eden could no more kill a woman than she could . . . could march into the Gilded Lily!

Whoever spread such a rumor lied to Anne. With a cynical twist of mind that she didn't even realize she had, Dara wondered if Anne told her this out of revenge for Clay.

She slipped into church, standing behind those milling in the back, trying to peer over their shoulders to find a single seat. The light touch of a fingertip toying with the soft hairs at her nape made her turn around.

The blistering heat of Eden's sensual smile met her gaze. "You look surprised to see me here, darlin'."

"I hoped you would be."

"Turn around, love, or folks'll stare." Rubbing her sensitive neck, he whispered, "You'll have to tell me which box lunch is yours, 'cause no one's having the pleasure of sharing you but me."

His possessive tone was matched by his hand curving around her waist. Dara lifted startled eyes, ready to warn him against such a bold move, but he was looking over her head. Following his gaze, she tensed. Clay and her brother Pierce were staring directly at them. There was a promise of fury in Clay's look, and Dara instinctively leaned back against Eden, not out of fear for herself but to protect him. Clay's threats spun out from her memory . . ." *You dare go anywhere McQuade is, talk to him, smile at him, or so much as glance his way, and I'll kill him.*"

Dara wanted to run. If Anne told Clay what she believed about Eden, Clay would use it against him. She tried to reassure herself that no one would believe a preacher's son could commit such an act, but she didn't doubt that Clay would.

"Easy, darlin', or you'll have me out the back door. I'm just as eager as you to be alone, but you've been trying to get me here since the first day I met you. While I've no taste for repenting old pleasures, I'd solicit sin for you."

Dara believed his outrageous statement. But she didn't know that Eden would dare to do just as he pleased without regard for the consequences until his hand at the small of her back gently urged her forward down the aisle till they stopped alongside Miss Loretta's pew. Then, with that heart-stopping smile, Eden guided Dara into the empty place next to her.

"Yore a bold one, McQuade," Miss Loretta whispered.

"Why, thank you, ma'am. Let's pray the good Lord spread that enlightenment to others of this here fine congregation."

Chapter Eleven

"NOW, PIERCE, EDWARD Junior jus' bid two dollars on this here fine wooden box. You gonna let him have it?"

Caroline Halput blushed becomingly at Pierce's side. Beneath the concealing folds of her blue gown, she gripped his hand tightly.

"Two fifty," he called out, glaring at the lanky youth who thought his father's bank could buy him anything. For a moment he thought Edward Junior was going to up the price, but Caroline smiled up at him when the reverend said, "Sold."

The auction was almost over, and Dara waited tensely at Eden's side. Clay had not bid on anyone's basket. She prayed he wouldn't think to humiliate both of them by bidding against Eden. She could feel the eyes of the congregation upon them. Few couples had moved off to find shady spots to enjoy the fruits of their purchases and indulge in the ritual innocent courting under parents' watchful eyes.

Pierce, having claimed Caroline's box, returned to his place by Clay's side, his features revealing anger at whatever Caroline said. But beyond offering Dara a sympathetic smile, Caroline remained with Pierce. Dara keenly felt her brother's rejection when he failed to return her greeting.

Harmon Ansel, the soft-spoken teacher, entered into a lively round of bidding with Harley Clare over Lara Saunders's basket.

"Jest watch that girl," Miss Loretta ordered at Dara's side, the tilt of her wide hat brim indicating Lara. "She's as subtle as a train wreck, twitchin' her tail like a handful of worms in a bed of hot ashes. Don't pay her ma no min' no how. All shy smiles for pore Harmon, an' her hand's a-clutchin' Harley's till he's grinnin' like a Yankee lawyah."

"Charity, Miss Loretta," Eden chided.

"Ah'll give you charity enough to make a preachah lay his Bible down. Ah'm standin' heah, Eden McQuade, lendin' you the benefit of mah social standin'."

"Now, Miz Loretta," Luther cautioned, "don't be getting all het up. Eden here is right 'preciative."

" 'Preceiative, huh? More'n likely this heah wicked smilin' scoundral is a-figurin' on how he's gettin' rid of us aftah he buys Dara's box lunch."

"Miss Loretta, you wound me layin' such a calculated intent at my feet."

"Is that a fact? Well, boy, bettah I do than havin' the tempahs waxin' hot spill ovah."

Dara's smile at their silly exchange faded with Miss Loretta's reminder that Clay was still standing there, his eyes filled with warning. She refused to be drawn into a silent battle with him and kept her gaze on the long table where Reverend Speck stood, handing a grinning Harley change from his ten-dollar gold piece. Whispers and giggles followed Harley and Lara, more than one young man's eyes filled with envy that Harley wouldn't be eating a cold lunch under anyone's watchful eye.

Waiting with bated breath, Dara saw the reverend touch her basket and then lift one that she knew belonged to Roselee Kinnel. There wasn't a sign of Matt, and she offered the young woman a consoling smile when Julian Tucker opened the bidding with one dollar. No one was more shocked than Roselee when a thick Irish brogue from in back of the crowd upped the bid to three dollars.

Lonn Rogan elbowed his way to Roselee's side. No one had expected the big Irishman to join them. So Luther said as they all turned to watch him. Dara's gaze slipped beyond and noticed a cloud of dust south on Walnut Road leading to the church.

"Yore brothah's a fool, Dara. Lettin' that sweet gal git her hopes high an' disappointin' her. 'Pears to me Flynn is right approvin' of it, too."

And he was, slapping the big redheaded man on the back when he outbid Julian by five dollars for his daughter's basket.

Dara didn't realize that she was gripping Eden's arm until he leaned down to whisper, "I'll make this short."

Reverend Speck trailed a bit of blue ribbon in his hand. "Gentlemen, this here is the last one. From the weight of it, I can guarantee you'll be getting your money's worth. So, who's opening?"

It seemed to Dara as if the crowd turned as one and stared. Eden's voice rang clear, not overly loud, but boldly stating that he wouldn't be outbid.

"Twenty dollars."

Dara felt manipulated as she turned to Clay, others following, their looks speculative, their silence absolute.

"And a right generous offer it is. Since we have no others, this is sold to Mr. McQuade." Reverend Speck ignored the comments whispered to him by those closest. They had waited to see Clay make a stand, and he shooed them off as Eden stepped forward to claim Dara's basket. He tucked two gold pieces into the reverend's hands, disclaiming the man's thanks.

"I know you'll use it for a worthy cause, Reverend. I wanted to thank you for not making Miss Owens a target of gossip by waiting for other bids."

"He wouldn't have done it, you know. Clay's a mighty prideful man."

"Pride is the never-failing vice of fools and makes a poor diet," Eden stated, lifting Dara's basket.

When he returned to Dara's side, taking her arm to lead her away from where most families sat beneath the shade trees, he looked around for a sign of where Clay was. He didn't trust him not to cause Dara some embarrassment.

"We could, if you like, darlin', walk down the road a piece. You wouldn't—"

"Well! I nevah thought I'd see the day, Dara Owens. Your mothah would take to her bed findin' you in the company of this heah man."

Dara paled under the baleful stare of Elvira Dinn. The blue plumes bobbed on her hat as she poked her folded parasol in Dara's direction. Indignation flushed her face beet red.

Eden started forward, but Dara stopped him. "Elvira, I—"

"I can't believe we God-fearing people are forced to attend church with men of his ilk! He owns a saloon, girl. Your fathah can't know what you're up to, disgardin' a fine young man like Clay Wescott who offered marriage. We all know who's the encouragin' force behind your shockin' act. Miss Loretta—"

Dara's face burned with shame, but her fury made her shake that Mrs. Dinn would make her denunciation so loudly that people stopped talking and were once again staring. Eden's firm but warning grip on her arm both steadied and silenced the words trembling on her lips.

"I believe, Mrs. Dinn," he said with the full force of his most charming smile, "the Lord forgives all trespasses. Can you, standing upon his church's ground, not find the same spirit?"

"How dare you!" the matriarch drawled with a fulminating glance.

"He dares, Elvira," Miss Loretta interjected, drawing herself to an intimidating pose," 'cause some of us know that you've got sour grapes to press since he's taken his money ovah to Ocala."

"You jest wait until Thursday's sewin' circle, Loretta," Elvira said in parting.

"Eden, please," Dara said as soon as the woman was out of hearing, "I want to leave."

"No, you don't, miss. You stay right heah and face this down, or you'll nevah have the chance. Now, Luther's found us a right pretty spot ovah behind the church." Linking her arm through Eden's, Miss Loretta beamed her approval when he seconded her opinion.

It wasn't exactly what Eden had envisioned when he made the snap decision to come here. He knew what the speculative glances meant, and he wanted no part of the commitment they implied between him and Dara. His consolation would have been time alone with her, but he could see no way to remove themselves without bringing Miss Loretta's ire down upon them. Dara was shaken by what Elvira said, and when Matt rode up, Eden resigned himself to sharing her company.

But Miss Loretta and Luther, having thoroughly enjoyed sampling Dara's basket as well as their own, felt the two of them deserved some privacy, and with a last warning look that Miss Loretta was sure made clear to

Eden that he wasn't to move, they took themselves off to visit.

Eden smiled, licking the last bit of honey fudge from his finger, while Matt tried to get his attention with jerky nods of his head that Eden should go off with him.

Dara sat with her back against the tree, her eyes lowered to where she brushed crumbs from her lap, quiet as she had been for the past two hours.

"For Pete's sake, Matt," Eden finally said in exasperation. "Say whatever it is that has you antsy."

"I can't. Not here. I need to talk to you private like, Eden."

"Can't it wait?" Stretched out on his back, his jacket folded for a pillow, Eden's half-lidded eyes searched out the rising agitation in Matt's face. He finally had a few minutes to speak to Dara, and Matt hadn't the brains of a goose in a henhouse to take himself off somewhere else.

Dara barely murmured in acknowledgment of Eden's leaving to walk off with Matt a little ways. Elvira's attack forced her to think about what she had done. She couldn't counter it with saying that Eden, too, had offered marriage. Eden hadn't offered anything beyond opening a door to sinful pleasures. Would her mother have been horrified by what she had done? It was another useless speculation, but it kept her from thinking about what Clay would do. She knew he wouldn't have the day end with his public defeat at Eden's hands going unanswered. Restless with the waiting, Dara came to her knees and began packing her basket. At the sound of Eden's laughter, she glanced up once to where he stood with his arm companionably over Matt's shoulders and saw Early beckon them to where he and several men sat passing a jug. Eden faced her, and she smiled, glad at least that most of the townsmen accepted him.

The shadow across her quilt fell from behind her, and Dara froze. She knew it was Clay before he whispered her name.

"I don't believe we have anything more to say to each other, Clay. Please don't cause a scene."

"I warned you, didn't I? I told you what I would do to him."

Scrambling to her feet, Dara faced him. "Will killing him make me love you again? How thickheaded can you be? I don't want to marry you because you don't care a wit about my feelings and needs. Understand that, Clay. Eden McQuade has nothing to do—"

"Dara, I don't need you to defend me to him."

Once more Dara stilled. She stood there between Clay and Eden like a rabbit caught between a trap and wolf, and she didn't know which way to face.

"This is private, McQuade."

"When you threaten a man's life, I believe it becomes his business. There's no need to discuss this here, Clay. Dara will not be made another juicy bit of gossip."

"If she is, blame yourself. I respected her, but you—"

"It would give me a great deal of satisfaction to plant my knuckles where they would do the most good, but I, too, respect Dara. Subjecting a lady—"

"Lady be damned! You've made her your—"

Eden lost his patience. His fist shot out, clipping Clay's jaw, his quick side step saving him from Clay's return blow. Dara barely had time to move back. Her heels tangled in the quilt, and she fought to keep her balance until Matt's supporting hand on her elbow not only steadied her but dragged her free. He ignored her cry to stop them, refusing to take his eyes away from where the two men crouched.

In moments they were surrounded, mostly by men, and to Dara's mortification they were calling bets on the outcome of the fight. Not one answered her plea to put an end to this. She cringed with every thud of fist meeting flesh, shocked at the lustful expectancy for violence on every man's face, crying out when Eden took a blow that drove him to his knee.

"Will someone stop this! Matt, get Reverend Speck, please!" Dara couldn't do more than grab at her brother's arm, caught by the press of bodies behind her. Clay backed off a bit, watching Eden swipe at the blood on his lip, and Dara tried calling out to him, seeing the twisted fury of his face. Her voice was buried under shouts for Eden to get up, and he did, coming in fast and low to pummel Clay's belly.

"McQuade's got the makings of John L. Sullivan, hisself," Rogan called out. "Saw him fight, I did, on his road tour."

"Then put your money on him," Pierce taunted, shoving his way to the front.

Dara couldn't listen to the rest of their exchange. Tears filled her eyes. Her brothers stood on opposite sides, and there was nothing she could do to bring them together.

It was Jake, firing his gun in the air, who put a stop to it. Without regard for who was in his way, he elbowed through the crowd of men until he stood between Clay and Eden. Angry shouts drowned out whatever it was that he said, but Dara wouldn't have heard him anyway, for Anne stood at her side, berating her for what she had caused.

"Are you satisfied now?" she demanded, dragging Dara around to face her. "Do you think anyone will forget this? And it's your fault that Jake is in the middle! I hope you and that devil suffer hell's sins," she hissed, before Dara stumbled, fighting her way free. She didn't glance back when Eden called out to her, but grabbed up her skirt and petticoats, tears blinding her, desperate to escape.

Eden shrugged off Jake's restraining hand, shoving his way clear. He had no thought for anyone but Dara, didn't hear those who swore he could take Clay, would have if Jake hadn't stopped them, nor did he listen to others who taunted him for being a coward and running.

Dara's pale face, her dark eyes shocked, claimed his attention. He had to find her. She had to understand that the blame for what happened rested on his head for coming here when he knew his presence would push a confrontation with Clay. But it wasn't only about Dara that they fought.

He reached the corner of the one-room schoolhouse, coming to a stop while he searched the open field for some sign of her. The grasses were knee high, but nowhere was there a depression that would indicate Dara was hiding.

The forest surrounding the field on two sides was thick with cypress, magnolia, giant oaks, and wild cherry trees, but not a hint of pink cloth anywhere. His lip throbbed, and he wiped it with the torn edge of his sleeve, ignoring the raw scrape of his knuckles. With a determined stride, he set out across the field, running when he spied her behind a clump of fan-flared palm leaves.

"Dara." She shrank from his touch, and Eden kneeled behind her. "Don't, love, don't cry, please. He didn't hurt me."

"Hurt . . . you!" she sobbed, refusing to turn around

at his insistent coaxing. "You're too . . . thickheaded to get hurt and . . . so is Clay."

Eden withdrew his hand from her shoulder, staring at her back, not quite sure of her mood. "Dara, you're upset. I don't blame you. I . . . ." Eden found himself at a loss for words. What could he say to lessen her obvious humiliation of being a spectacle at a church social? Dara, with her strict thoughts of what constituted ladylike behavior, needed soothing, he decided. Yet once again she wrenched herself away from his touch. "Darlin', I want to comfort—"

"I don't want your comfort!" She rounded on him so suddenly that he fell back. "It was bad enough that the two of you had to use violence against each other. But that isn't why I ran. I couldn't stand watching the two of you. I hated seeing my brothers divided between you. Do you know what it did to hear Pierce goading Clay, and Matt egging you on? Do you? Don't you see?" she cried, tears running down her face, shaking with the fury and the need to make him understand. "Watching the two of you fight forced me to believe that everything you and Jake said would happen was true!" He raised his hand, and she pushed it aside. "Don't touch me! I don't want to be coddled or conned by more of your smooth-talking citified ways. I certainly do not want to be treated like a simpleminded ninny that needs protection. I hated what happened, and I feel like yelling about it, and yes," she grated, pointing her finger at his chest, "I'm upset!"

"You're also becoming hysterical, Dara. Stop it." Eden's forward move caught her by surprise, and she tumbled backward, frightened by the furious look of him looming over her. "I didn't set the rules of this game. Don't go putting the blame of it on me. Did you expect me to let Clay insult you? Did you know," he suddenly whispered, almost against her lips, "that he would have called you my harlot?"

Dara felt his lips brush her cheek as she turned her head aside. She saw his skinned knuckles, and all the fury left her. "He did hurt you," she whispered, afraid to draw a deep breath, conscious of the length of his hard body lowering to match the sprawled angle of her own.

"No, Clay didn't hurt me as much as he did you." But Clay was the last thing Eden was thinking of. He was fighting a raw primitive urge to claim the woman he had just fought over in the most basic way. Need surged through him, swamped his normal control, and he pressed his weight against the softened contours of hers, his lips trailing kisses over her ear, across her cheek. He took the heat of her tears from her dark lashes, and Dara turned her head, meeting his gaze with her own vulnerable one.

"Eden, please, I can't fight you now. But you know this is wrong." Hating the sight of the already darkening bruises on his face, she closed her eyes.

"Pleasure is never wrong, love. Let me take all the ugliness of the day away. Let me give you pleasure."

The dark sensual note of his voice was enough to arouse her, and Dara accepted the coaxing move of his mouth against her own. She wanted to lose herself in the incredible slow warming desire that Eden so effortlessly spun around her, through her, taking every thought of wrong and making it somehow right. Dara accepted the unaccustomed weight of his hard, lithe body pressing gently until an unconscious sigh of surrender passed her lips. Her mouth parted in invitation, his tongue was quick to claim hers.

The voice that whispered this was wrong faded as she engaged in the now familiar game of submit and conquer that spiked desire into sharper need. Hesitantly she accepted his tongue's lure to explore the dark whiskey-flavored interior of his mouth, moving with unconscious grace to the slow rocking dance his body taught hers. Her hands stroked his sides, pulling him closer, unwilling to question the ache he eased and tormented with every move.

It was the softened acceptance of her body, the open surrender of her mouth that brought a measure of sanity back to Eden. It would be so easy to take her now . . . so easy . . . but he gentled the depth of his kiss, slowly, so slowly easing his lips from hers.

"Love," he breathed long moments later, "I can't give you more than pleasure."

"I know," she whispered sadly, and waited, feeling the tension that held his body while desire receded from hers.

They both heard Matt calling them, and Eden moved to his side, then stood up, drawing her to stand beside him. With a decided lack of his usual humor, he muttered dark imprecations against her brother, and Dara offered him a sad smile.

"I'll get Luther to drive you back to town."

"You won't be coming with us?" she asked, knowing he wouldn't. "Your face needs to be seen to, Eden."

"There are other pressing matters that need my attention first."

Her frown quickly disappeared when her gaze dropped. When she found the courage to look up again, his own gaze was bold.

"Don't expect me to apologize for the desire I feel for you. And don't expect me to think of satisfying it with another woman."

There was an implied challenge that she couldn't refuse. "I won't."

"Getting bold and sassy, are you?" he asked, slipping his arm around her waist possessively and leading her out to the open. He waved to Matt, then slanted her a look filled with humor as he picked bits of dry grass from her hair. "Since the day was spoiled, will you drive out with me next Sunday for a picnic? I'll provide the substance and choose where."

"I would like to." Dara knew that was the closest she could come to admitting she wanted to be alone with him. But as they walked forth to meet her brother, she had to force herself to ignore the knowledge that wanting and desire were all that Eden offered.

His hand caressed her side, and he leaned down to whisper, "Must you wear this damnable corset? Lord knows, darlin', you don't need it."

"Why, Mistah McQuade," she replied, imitating Miss Loretta in an effort to dispell her own dark thoughts, "Ah declare you're wicked to refer to a lady's unmentionables. Ah feel the need for every bit of protection I can gather 'bout me when Ah'm with you, sir."

"And you believe that layers and laces along with that boned contraption will protect you from my unholy clutches?"

"If they are not enough, Ah still remember how to say no."

"Point taken, darlin'. But rememberin' how to say no and saying it might depend upon being in the right place at the right time with the right man."

Dara gasped. The teasing game had gone too far, and Matt was close, running toward them, so she couldn't form an answer.

Eden winced as he grinned, his gaze as wicked as his words. "Sunday, love?"

And Dara suddenly knew what had changed between them. She was no longer afraid of him. Oh, he threatened her moral fiber, and she longed for a commitment from this man, but she wasn't afraid to free the passionate dreams that haunted her.

"Yes. Sunday."

Chapter Twelve

BY SUNDAY MORNING Dara felt she was in a cage of the social structure in which she lived and was firmly ensnared by her growing passion for Eden McQuade. For the past three days it had rained, unusual weather at this time of year, but it had prevented Eden from his nightly return to town. The fish fry planned for last night at Kelsey's ferry landing had been canceled, and while Dara was disappointed in these happenings, she did bless the rain for a decided drop in customers in the store.

Upon her return last week her father had accepted what she told him had happened without comment, but she had caught his studied looks from time to time during the week. She knew he longed to ask her what she couldn't answer him. Other people weren't the least bit reluctant to voice their curiosity. Only the skill she had forced herself to develop in turning aside personal questions about herself and Clay allowed her to control her newly discovered temper.

She stood at her window watching the gray clouds spread the way for hints of blue and prayed the sun would brighten the day.

"Dara?"

She turned at the sound of Matt's voice at her door. "Come in."

"It seems to be clearing. I wanted to tell you that I'll stay home with Papa."

"If you want. Miss Loretta promised to come over with Luther and have supper with him." Dara hoped she hid her surprise from Matt at his offer. He had been acting rather strange all week, going out of his way to avoid giving her a chance to question him about what he was doing or when he intended to repay the money she lent him. Last week she sensed a hardness in him, and now she couldn't dismiss the noticeable maturity in his eyes. Something momentous had happened to Matt, and she was certain Eden knew about it. How much had changed from the first time she had accused him of leading her brother astray. She was more than willing to admit that Eden was good for Matt. He hadn't had a case of the green-apple nasties in weeks. Eden had been a stabilizing influence on Matt, but she couldn't say the same for his effect on herself.

"You look real pretty today."

"Why, thank you. I believe that is the first time you have ever complimented me."

"I always tell you how good your cooking is, Dara. Anyway," he added, digging the toe of his boot into the faded carpet, "a man's supposed to notice what a woman's wearing and all."

"Oh, yes, he should, Matt. And I'm glad that you decided to come up and talk to me. I wanted to ask—"

"I can't stay. Papa's sitting with a hot towel soaking his beard, and I just came up to get his razor. Anyhow, Eden will be here soon," he called out, already down the hallway.

She had no chance to muse again about Matt's avoiding her, for he called out mere minutes later that Eden was waiting.

Dara carefully placed her lace braid and lavender silk trimmed hat on her upswept hair. Uncertain of what type of a vehicle Eden intended for their use, she inserted two extra hatpins through the tiny spray of silk flowers that softened the stark line of the brim. Her blousewaist matched the lavender ribbon, and the gray cashmere shawl she carried was a shade repeated in the braided trim on her shirt.

Eden was in the kitchen with Matt and her father. Dara paused in the doorway and smiled shyly when Eden noticed her, trying to deny her apprehension. Their good-byes were brief, since Cyrus's face was lathered and Matt was intent on stropping the straight-edge razor.

"You look charming, love," Eden whispered, opening the front door. Dara stopped, taken by surprise when she saw what waited.

"Like it? I hoped it would arrive in time," Eden remarked. "It's a new-style Brewster phaeton."

"A narrow two-seater," she replied, gazing at the sleek body, leather top, and silver handrails. Dara didn't want to let hope flare that a man who invested in such an expensive carriage intended to stay and make good use of his purchase. But the hope was there in her eyes when Eden lifted her onto the plush dark velvet seat. Dara adjusted her skirt, the full bustle forcing her to sit up straight. She knew Eden's size, was familiar with his body in ways she forced herself not to remember, but when he joined her inside the carriage, Dara found they pressed shoulder to shoulder, hip to hip, thigh to thigh, and no amount of layered clothing was going to protect her from the warmth of him.

The air was redolent with the rich earthy scents from the recent rains, as well as the rawness of the new leather top, and Dara inhaled them far too greedily, willing her heart to slow its beat.

"Would you mind if we missed service this morning and rode out to the mine instead?"

"Your mine?"

"I'd like to show it to you." He slanted a glance down to her rosy cheeks and demurely lowered lashes. "Are you having second thoughts about coming with me, darlin'?"

Her startled gaze targeted his. "I . . . it's just that, Eden . . . no," she managed, unable to keep looking at him. "Is this one of Early's carriage horses?"

"Oh, Lord, love, is this what we're reduced to talk about, carriage horses?"

"Don't laugh at me."

"Never, little saint," he noted with controlled mockery alight in his eyes, taking up the reins, urging the sleek roan up the lane.

Dara stared straight ahead when they turned onto Charleston Street. She wanted to ignore the Tuckers, setting out for church, but Eden slowed, exchanged his greetings with them, forcing her to do the same.

"Are you ashamed to be seen with me, Dara?" he asked as they continued past the train depot to follow the track that closely defined the bank of the Rainbow River.

"It's not you," she murmured, gripping her gloved hands together.

"Have the town's biddies given you a hard time this past week?"

"There was nothing about their pecking that I could not handle," she replied with a lift of her chin, hoping he did not misunderstand and become offended. It was her choice.

She was lying. Eden knew there was nothing he could

do to protect her from the women's spite but offer her marriage. It was a lifetime commitment that he was not ready to make. He allowed the potholed track to claim his attention.

Gazing at the expanse of flat land, Eden thought with longing of the rolling hill country of home and said as much.

"Do your brothers live there?"

"Paradise spends his time traveling, but New York is his home now. Dev lived in Virginia until last year, when he set out as a circuit preacher somewhere out West. Dev was never one for writing much, so I haven't heard exactly where he's traveling. I'd like to show you Virginia, and New York isn't far. There's a gay and wicked city that would set your prim bonnet on end."

"You sound rather fond of it. I'm sure after being there, Rainly must appear provincial with its limited forms of entertainment."

His laugh was rich and low. "I wondered when that starched little tongue would start wagging. You had me worried for a while, darlin'. I thought I called for the wrong young lady this morning. And no, I don't miss the city or what it offers as much as Dice does."

"Dice?"

"It's a brotherly name Dev and I gave Paradise. I'll tell you the story behind it someday," he promised with a grin for the private memory it recalled.

Inside Dara, hope flared brighter. If Eden was now willing to share his family secrets with her, he must have some thought of establishing a future relationship. She was risking more than her virtue by agreeing to spend the day alone with him.

"Will you be going home to visit soon?" she gently prodded.

"Not until I have everything here settled to my satisfaction."

It was not a statement that invited her pursual, and Dara let it be. She gazed out at the land, much as Eden did, and tried to see it through his eyes. It was flat, but here, away from town, huckleberry, sparkle berry, and fetter-bush grew between palm and evergreen shrubs. In her mind she tried to compare it to the land Eden had once described of rolling hills thick with lush grasses, soft breezes, and flowering plants surrounded by hardwood forests. He claimed the soil was so rich, a seed could be dropped and would grow, while here the sandy soil needed constant replenishing of enriching fertilizers. Far off, the land rose in a terraced effect, and Dara searched for something interesting to point out to him that Virginia couldn't possibly have.

Her vigilance was rewarded as they swung into a widened place on the road. "Eden, look at the cycad. My father said the Indians used the roots to make bread during the Seminole Wars, when they couldn't remain in one place long enough to plant their corn. It's a shame you haven't seen this area in the early spring, when the flowers are blooming. It's a breathtaking sight. Blazing star and pale blue lupines, red lilies, and sometimes the unexpected find of an orchid make the land pretty."

"Don't go all defensive on me, darlin'. I wasn't comparing the two. And enjoy this, 'cause when we get near the mine, I'm afraid it will come as a shock to you."

"How did you get interested in mining phosphate? I recall you mentioned that you worked along the Peace River before coming up here."

Eden slanted her a wry glance. "Inquiring into my past, darlin'? Dare I hope this is an indication my suit finds favor with you?" Her cross look brought a chuckle.

"I was partners in a silver mine that didn't pan out, so I came home. Dice was in Washington and needed some help. The city life appealed to me, and I had an opportunity to work at the Smithsonian Institution, since I was qualified to analyze samples of ore. At a mutual friend's I met Captain LeBaron, and we spoke at length about his discovery of pebble phosphate on the Peace River. He was frustrated when he couldn't get many industrialists interested in the project and left the city for another government job. It wasn't long after that I became restless and made a trip down here to look over the possibility of mining the area. The rest you know."

"But Eden, all the newspaper stories claim that this area is where the mineral was first discovered."

"And history, love," he noted with rich humor, "will lend truth to their claim because of the value of the phosphate in this area." He guided the horse onto a smaller lane, his grip tightening by a slight degree as Dara was pressed against his side. She was all sweetly scented lavender today, starched to full capacity, and he smiled, thinking of the spot he had chosen for their picnic.

"Remember what I told you, Dara," he said as the first tall wooden drying machine came into view.

She remembered. Dara also believed that *shock* was a rather mild word to describe what she was feeling. For miles the land was pocked with excavated pits and trenches. Lengths of raw lumber haphazardly formed walkways across the outer edges. She listened as Eden described the use of the drying towers after the phosphate rock was crushed and washed, her eyes wide until the men who were working began to stop swinging their picks and turned to stare at them. Her surprise increased when Eden began greeting most of them by name and good-naturedly returned their teasing comments about his not working.

"I know it's a bit much to take in all at once," Eden began, stopping the carriage. "We'll walk about, and I'll explain the process to you."

He had already leaped down, and Dara stared in dismay at the mud.

"I guess a walk is out of the question," he said, coming around to her side. "No matter, I can explain it all from here."

"But why are the men working today? Don't you give them the day to attend service?"

"I alternate my crews. These men haven't worked since Friday. And the pit they are digging in is one that already proved to have rich deposits. When I'm about to break fresh ground, we dig several small rectangular pits and excavate them. If the deposits are rich, we enlarge the area to one this size. Then I determine the quantity and quality of the rock. Those piles you see are waste and will be removed to a site away from here."

"The wheelbarrows, Eden, what are those men doing with them?"

"They'll haul them to the conveyor belt, where others . . . here, lean out of the carriage and you'll see." Eden stood slightly in front of her so Dara could lean on his shoulder. "The men there will remove debris, stones, and other impurities from the phosphate rock. Once it's crushed, washed, and dried, it's ready for shipment."

"I never realized that it took so much work. The talk I hear in the store . . . why, I feel foolish even repeating it to you."

"Don't. I've heard enough to make me aware of how foolish men had sunk their life savings in the belief that they could just walk the land and pick up chunks of rock and be rich."

"What does Matt do here?" Dara asked, resisting the urge to touch the soft dark curling hair so close to her cheek. Eden hadn't moved, and she was content to lean with one hand resting on his shoulder and her head tilted toward his.

"Matt, it might surprise you to know, has shown a remarkable interest in developing new techniques to help us mine in more profitable ways with less accidents. He is looking into the use of steam shovels and perhaps, in a pit this rich, setting up a rail that would enable us to lower cable cars into the pit. The work would still be done by hand, but it would make it easier on a man's back."

"You really do care about your workers, don't you," she noted softly, wondering how she could ever have doubted it.

"Don't believe noble sentiment is the cause, Dara. It's simply good business practice to give a man some dignity when he labors hard for you."

With a soft laugh she leaned back and away from him. "Oh, Eden, I would never make the mistake of believing you did anything for noble reasons."

"A man of dishonorable intentions," he murmured, humor bright in his eyes. He had turned to face her, smiling to see the becoming blush tint her cheeks. "No regrets for coming with me today?"

Dara ignored the light tone, sensing there was more to his question. And when she answered, her gaze held a serious look. "No, I have no regrets. But," she added, needing to recapture the lighter mood, "if you plan to feed me sometime today, let it be soon."

"Greedy woman, of course I plan to feed you. The

basket is packed full of Annamae's goodies and stowed in the boot."

But Eden made no move to return to the carriage, and Dara found herself glancing about with dismay. "You didn't intend for us to picnic here?"

He ran a finger over the cameo pinned to her collar. "Oh, no, love. Not here. I've a private spot staked out that will leave us undisturbed to enjoy nature as it was intended."

"Private," she repeated, drawing back against the seat.

"Completely," he assured her solemnly.

"Close by, I hope."

"No. It's a ways. Worried?"

"Oh, goodness, Eden, do stop! You've behaved yourself for the most part, and there's no need to make me rethink my decision to trust you."

His finger once again drew close, but this time he touched the corner of her pouting mouth. "Foolish little saint, never trust me. But do tell," he asked, rubbing her lip, "did you wear that laced nuisance?"

"Eden! You can't expect me to answer you!"

"Ah, darlin', you disappoint me." His look was thoughtful as he stepped back and slowly shook his head. "No, I guess you won't at that. Slide your sweet bustle over, and we'll leave. I'll see to the task myself."

Dara obeyed simply because she didn't know what else to do. The man at times was impossible to take seriously! He was every bit as outrageous as the very first time she had met him. But when he teased her, she felt alive. The day was bright and her blood warmed from his nearness and the wicked threat to be on guard for the unexpected from him.

They drove off, and Eden kept the horse to a slow

pace. Once they were away from the mining site, they crossed winding streams that were overhung by trees festooned with Spanish moss that swayed with the soft breeze. Sweet bay and pine trees lightly scented the air within cool shaded hammocks.

Eden was silent and Dara made no attempt to break his pensive mood. She had never traveled this far west and was engaged in peering into the encroaching foliage when the faint sound of rushing water came to her.

Eden drew rein and remarked, "This is as far as we can go with the carriage. I'm afraid we'll have to walk." He leaped down, turning to lift Dara out, and while she stood there trying to determine where a path was, he went to the back of the carriage. With a large market basket held in one hand, a blanket tucked beneath his arm, he came to her side. "Ready?"

Gamely Dara smiled. "Lead on."

They followed the small stream, and Eden held broad-leaved palms out of her way, for there was no clearly defined path to follow. The sound of the water grew louder, and Dara wondered where they were heading. Rocks were piled to the side. The suddenness of a water fountain shooting up made her cry out, and Eden laughed.

"I should have warned you about those. But it's not much farther."

"Thank goodness," she muttered, untangling her skirt hem from the bush that snagged it.

The opening appeared ahead, and Dara ignored Eden for a moment to stare. A waterfall cascaded to the pool below, a charming untouched spot of land that entranced her.

"Eden, it's beautiful."

"I thought you would be pleased."

Dragonflies skimmed above the pool surrounded by broad ferns, and gentle geysers of crystal water bubbled up unexpectedly. Splashes of sunlight woven through the trees played over the cool shadows. Eden took her hand, leading the way to the small clearing. He spread the blanket and set the basket in one corner, smiling all the while at the enraptured look on Dara's face.

Dara knew they hadn't gone far, but the sounds of the fall were muted here. And suddenly shy, she faced away from him when he moved behind her.

With his hands resting gently on her shoulders, Eden whispered, "I've wanted to share this with you from the first time I discovered it. But there are a few alterations I must make first." He slid the hatpins free, lifted her hat off, replaced the pins in the crown, and tossed the hat toward the corner of the blanket.

"You shouldn't—"

"Today there are no *shouldn'ts,* love. And you're far too prim for such an enchanted place." He smiled, ignored another protest, and began removing her hairpins, carefully tucking them into his pocket. With a kiss he brushed her hand aside, his fingers deftly uncoiling her waist-length hair.

"Eden, it's improper—"

"And we can't," he noted softly, "have any improprieties. They are simply not allowed," he added, threading his fingers through the thick silken mass of her hair to spread it across her shoulders like a dark mink cape. "Lovely," he breathed against her ear, slowly turning her around to face him. Tipping her chin up, he gazed at her delicate features surrounded by the dark waves, and with the patience he had cultivated for this woman alone, he watched her eyes flutter closed. "Lovely," he repeated, kissing the tip of her nose, inhaling the tiny rapid breaths, and stilling the desire to feast upon the tantalizing pout of her mouth. "I seem to recall that you were greedy to eat, darlin'."

Dara's eyes flew open. He was so close, and she knew he was about to kiss her, but Eden surprised her. He set her back from him, his bow courtly.

"My lady, your feast awaits."

Tossing her hair back, Dara moved to the blanket, kneeled down, and investigated the contents of the basket.

"Eden," she said after a few moments, "there's no plates or cutlery to eat with."

"I know. Annamae fixed everything I asked her to. We won't be needing them."

"Not need them? How do you expect—"

"I'll feed you, and if you're in a charitable mood, love, perhaps you'll feel inclined to return the pleasure."

"Pleasure?" Dara repeated, beginning to hate the way she parroted him. But Eden didn't answer, for he had taken off his suit jacket, folded it, and now began to take off his tie. Dara watched in silence the progress he made with the stiff linen collar, and then, to her shock, he unbuttoned his shirt halfway before he sat down.

"I think," he began, taking gentle hold of her ankles, "that you would be more comfortable stretching out your legs so you can hold the food." He easily reached the basket and placed it close beside him so that he sat opposite her hip to hip with his own long legs stretched out before him. "If you get tired," he noted with that soft sensual voice that raked her nerve endings into awareness, "you can rest against my leg." And Dara leaned back just as he bid to find his firmly muscled calf behind her.

"Comfortable?" His gaze locked with hers.

"As if I were safe in my own parlor."

"I'm glad. It wasn't my intent to make you nervous."

"But you are going to feed me?" Dara had to clear her throat. Her voice had a rusty squeak she couldn't account for.

"So eager to begin? Ah, love, you please me more than you know." He lifted a napkin-wrapped bottle of wine and one glass from the basket, a pleased smile on the curve of his finely molded lips.

"There seems to be only one glass," Dara said.

"That's all we'll need."

Dara's *oh* squeaked past her lips.

A plate of fried quail pieces appeared, and she recognized Annamae's corn fritters on another. The assortment of crocks concealed their contents, but never once did Eden's smile waver.

"The rest can wait until later." Picking up a piece of quail, he held it up to her. "Open your mouth, love."

Dara felt a strange sensation fill her. She remembered those same words whispered when he first kissed her. Too dazed to do anything else, she opened her mouth and took the morsel between her teeth. Her eyes never left his as she slowly chewed.

"Will you offer me one now?"

She stared at him, her heartbeat increasing, and then lifted a piece to his lips. Her fingertips felt the brief warmth of his mouth, and Dara sat mesmerized as they slowly repeated the ritual with fritters, pickles, and squash biscuits. There were sips of wine between. Eden drank first, then turned the glass so that her lips came to rest where his had been. And each time he leaned forward, their bodies almost but not quite touching, Dara felt the insidious heat that flowed through her begin to thicken into want.

Watching her Eden sipped from the glass he had just refilled, then quickly set it down. He raised himself slightly and secured her hair in a gentle hold. His lips found first the tiny pulse of her throat, where he planted a kiss, and then the softest whisper touched her earlobe. Dara felt boneless and leaned back, glad of the support of his leg, for his breath was warm against her flushed skin, and she felt the elusive damp caress of his tongue tracing the outer shell of her ear. He murmured something, but it was lost in the tremors that spread outward from wherever he touched. Slowly he loosened her hair once more and returned to his original position, lifting the glass to sip again.

"Would you like another taste?" he asked, eyes the dark of tarnished silver upon hers.

Without waiting for her to answer, he leaned forward and brushed her mouth with his lips, leaving a sheen of wine upon them. Dara licked the moisture in a languid manner. "More," she whispered.

Wine, heated and tart, was once again gently offered, but when Dara attempted to lick the taste from her lips, Eden's tongue tangled with hers. He slid one hand behind her neck, dragging her head back, feasting on her mouth for long minutes until the taste of the wine was lost in the heady taste of Dara.

"You," he murmured, lifting his mouth, "impart a decided improvement on the bouquet of this vintage. I wish I could bottle your essence, love, and drink it at my every leisure."

Dara tried to muddle through what he said, finally making sense of it and agreeing that the wine's taste did indeed improve. But it was the dark tanged essence of Eden's passion that she desired more of.

He offered her no chance, leaning back and fishing

through the basket. A checked napkin rested on her lap, and he smiled, a slow knowing curve that reflected his eyes.

"Dessert, love."

"I've had quite enough, thank you," she stated in a cross little voice, piqued that he could so easily dismiss her for some sweet.

"Have you, darlin'? I didn't think so. But please, just a bite. Annamae will be hurt if I return with it untasted."

He unwrapped the napkin to reveal sugar-dipped slices of jelly roll. Breaking off a piece, he offered her a taste. Eden laughed when the sugar clung to her lips and slowly gathered it up on his fingertip and offered it to her.

"The sweetest bit for last."

His compelling voice was soft, and Dara hesitated. Then, with a shaken tremor rippling her body, she leaned forward. With the dainty tip of her tongue she slowly licked the rough grains from his finger. Her eyes were closed, and even in her innocence she knew she caused his breath to hiss sharply through his teeth. Pleased, she opened her eyes, smiling up at him as he removed the plate from her lap, his forward move bringing his lips a hairsbreadth from hers. Dara felt herself drift backward, Eden's leg no longer offering support, but just as his mouth brushed hers, the press of her bustle dug deep, and she lurched to one side.

"Good Lord, woman," he managed to say, restraint tested fully in his voice, "what was the damnable cause of that?"

"My bustle, Eden," she whispered, kneeling beside him.

He sat back, leaning his forehead against his spread

fingers. "May I inquire," he asked after several tense minutes, "why the item in question caused you no discomfort in attaining this same position last week?"

His reminder flashed a picture of her wanton sprawl beneath him, and in a prim voice she informed him, "It was a diminished one."

Eden lowered his hand. "Love, the only thing that is being diminished here is my self-esteem."

His expression was droll, and Dara relaxed, smiled, and then softly laughed.

"We can," he suggested indulgently, "solve the problem in another manner." He lifted her hand to his chest, the move tumbling her off balance as he reclined backward, and Dara found herself shifted a bit, settled upon him, and gently ensnared. "There, love, much better."

"Eden," she asked, freeing herself of the tangled waves of her hair, "do you intend to seduce me?"

His smile appeared spiced with earthly pleasures, and his eyes brightened. "Does the notion hold some appeal?"

His fingers threaded her hair, tucking it back behind her ears, and Dara, resting her chin upon her folded hands that longed to sculpt his chest, thoughtfully studied his features. His eyes drifted closed, the lashes thick, his mouth relaxed, and Dara believed him more than handsome in a uniquely masculine way, and a blend of hot yearning made her answer him.

"The notion," she whispered, "holds more than appeal, but if the option is mine, I'm afraid I must decline."

His hands caressed her back in a soothing manner, settling on her waist to lift her a bit higher. His smile deepened with male satisfaction to feel her quick little breaths spread over his lips. "Love, I don't think I can offer you the choice of options," he noted with tender regret. "You see," he added in a rich sensuous voice, "I've quite run out of patience."

Chapter Thirteen

"IS THERE NOTHING that will bring it back?" His brilliant eyes met hers. Beneath her palms Dara could feel the heat of his skin under his linen shirt, and with an unconscious kneading motion, she parted the cloth to reveal the taut muscle of his chest, the rich dark hair drawing her avid and most curious gaze. Her fingertip brushed against it, his steady heart rhythm abruptly changed tempo, and the game ceased.

"No, little saint." His hand molded her to his long body, and with a hard, flat-palmed caress, he traced the unwieldly shape of her bustle to find the softer curve of her buttocks. Sloping his hand beneath, he lifted, then settled her firmly aligned with his hips.

Dara ached with unexplored needs, feeling the hardness of him pressed against her belly. He had teased her that layers of cloth would offer no protection, and she knew he was right. There was a heat between them that spread without aid.

His lips moved gently to hers, his kiss spare, before moving to her throat, her ear, delicately feathering breaths across her flushed cheek. "Love," he murmured, seeking her mouth as it opened to him with a sigh of pleasure, "move with me." And Dara did, willing to be dragged into his kiss as his hand left its courtship of her hip, gathered up the length of her hair in a gentle fist, guiding her head back against his shoulder. With unhurried leisure he kissed her, sliding his hand between the drape fold of her blousewaist, searching out the tiny pearl buttons. His fingers deftly began to engage in his own fantasy, every slow plunging thrust of his tongue into the wine-tinted flavor of her mouth aided his patience when he realized there were more than twenty to be undone. And he had discovered, soothing the urgent little moans she gave, that she was indeed wearing the damnable corset!

"Did you believe, little saint," he asked, his enticing gaze studying the flushed cream of her skin, "that a full complement of fashion's armor would aid in your defense?"

Dara lifted her eyes to his. Withdrawing from his tongue's caress, she rubbed his lower lip with her fingertip. "I only hoped you would not deliberately seduce me, Eden. I don't know how to fight you otherwise."

"Must you think in terms of fighting, love? And while your charming admission unmans me, didn't you know what your acceptance to come today could lead to?"

Innate honestly forced her reply. "I knew."

Brushing a wayward curl from her temple," he trailed the back of his hand down her flushed cheek. "Didn't you realize, little saint, that if seduction is not deliberate, the matter becomes something else entirely?" His gaze held hers, and Eden, to his surprise, found he had a great deal of patience left. "The something else might not hold as much appeal to your delicate sensibilities." Cupping her chin, he urged it closer. "We won't go into details. Give me your mouth, love, and we'll see which you prefer."

He made no move to kiss her, but Dara, newly awakened sensuality sinking tiny claws inside her, wanted it. She lifted her mouth to his, losing herself in the dark magic of his lips, twisting her fingers into the lush thickness of his hair, her body languidly following the pagan thrust and retreat of his. Every soft press of cloth layers tantalized the need that built inside her.

Eden gently rolled her onto her side, his mouth offering her every heated pleasure he knew. The light skimming thrust of his knee, a barely noticed intrusion that spread a froth of virginal laced-edged petticoats aside, slid between her legs. Under the richly warmed caress of his hand, the soft fold of her blousewaist draped in wanton allure over the silk bareness of one shoulder, drawing his lips to taste this newly revealed treasure. And while he bathed and then sipped his fill of desire-induced mist from her skin, Dara found her innocent exploration of his nape could bring a tremble from him.

With whispered adoration for the tenderness he displayed, she asked, "Is this deliberate seduction, Eden?"

"Yes, love," he murmured, "yes."

"I don't want to know the other," she breathed through kiss-damp lips before he sought to claim them.

"I'll show you a man's passion, love." Aching hunger drove him back to the sweeter taste of her mouth, savoring its turn to an innocent sensuality that twisted her body restlessly against him. A stroke of his fingertips lowered the sleeve to her wrist, where tiny buttons snagged its decent. And while he swore at fashion's dictates, his lips skimmed the silken warmth of lavender-scented skin above her demurely cut camisole.

For Dara the tiny quivers of desire began deep down and ended with a rippling shudder. "Eden." She lifted delicately shadowed lids to stare at the rich blackness of his hair, which stroked her bared throat with every fervent kiss he bestowed. "Please . . . please give me—"

"Oh, love," he whispered, stroking her side, "I have so much I want to give you." His hand cupped the soft unfettered rise of her lushly full breast, his mouth quick to drink her startled cry, and when she answered his kiss with a wildness born of passion, he released her lips. "Watch, love, watch what I can give you." His touch was almost reverent, his thumb caressing the dark rose peak, and she closed her eyes as he finessed the crest into pouting hardness. "No, Dara, don't close them. Watch me love you." Her lashes fluttered, but she looked to see his long, lean fingers, dark against the pure sheer white cloth. The too-new eroticism had her betraying blood rush to fill sensitive skin, and she couldn't draw a spare breath. "It's choices and options, love. What will you have? More?" he inquired, his voice deep and rich with the desire that thickened it, gently rubbing the peak between his fingers. When her eyes drifted closed, and her body arched into him with erotic grace, he murmured, "I could show you another pleasure." He nestled her breast's softness within his palm, rolling his lips over the nipple, tenderly stroking it with his tongue, bathing the sheer cloth. "Shall we try it and see, just to be fair?" He coaxed the exquisite peak with his tongue, tracing a silky pattern that warmed and aroused, feeling the strain of controlling the desire to be buried deep inside her.

Dara heard her own soft moans. Pressing his shoulders, her fingers found the strength of his body all she had to anchor her dizzy ascent into Eden's pleasure-rich world of passion. Her body was not her own to govern, but his, yet no protest formed on lips eager to test the tautness of his neck. She didn't know his taste, but learned it with an eagerness that brought his body hard against her. His knee rode the quivering length of her inner thigh in tender splendor. The cloth of his pants, dark and heavy as the need that spiraled through him, rubbed against the fragile delicacy of cambric that sheathed her legs. Dara wanted the freedom to breathe. She felt full, swollen with a strange heaviness that drew her blood to the peak suckled within his mouth.

Her cry held a hint of pain, his murmurs were soft and his fingers quick to unhook the waistband of her skirt, drawing her closer. "Tell me, love, I'll make it better." She whispered in a fretful voice the shamed admission that the corset was a damnable nuisance. His laugh was rich with his own need to ease the hardened tension of his body, but he sensed a deeper distress. "Look at me, love. It's time for choices and options. We could, if you like, continue as we are, although," he noted with a decided edge to his voice, "I can't offer a guarantee for how long. I want you, love, but if you choose, we can stop now."

She looked up at him, at his eyes, the sheen of desire for her brightening them, at his lips, those finely molded lips that had taught her what sensual promise they offered and the passion that sharpened his features. She thought of the dreams that plagued her nights, of the lover who would teach her passion. The past stretched its lonely years behind her, the future, beyond this time with Eden, she could not see. A tender feeling that she knew could grow into love spread within her. He claimed no patience, he claimed his seduction was deliberate, yet he offered her the choice. A hectic color spread over his cheekbones, and she smoothed his brow with her fingertip, drifting down to touch his throat and stroke his chest. His hand caught hers, his eyes demanding an answer.

"You said I would never doubt that you wanted me. I don't." Her voice was husky, her gaze imploring. "You promised you would never need to see the longing in my eyes because you would feel it." She drew his head down with one hand, breathing the last against his lips. "Look at me. Can you really stop?"

His kiss came in answer, and the desire she had for some word of love dissolved under the demand of greedy, sharp-set passion. Twining closer, hampered by the still-fastened cuffs of her blouse, her tongue explored the dark wine-tanged essence beyond his lips. He taught her new rules to the love game they played, dueling with her tongue until she became the aggressor and his eyes darkened. He opened the bow to her lacing, rubbing his hand against the satin that hid a richer silk from his touch. With infinite care he slid the white cotton tape from each eyelet, and Dara buried the thought of his skill, refusing to be displaced from the shimmering new world he revealed. He lifted the corset free and carelessly tossed it aside. His lips teased her nipples with feather brushstrokes that left the sheer cloth clinging, and his breaths, warm, brought them to aching. There was a decided impatience in his working free the tapes that held her bustle in place, and he knew, with every hot, open kiss he scattered over her face, that he tore more than a few of them until it joined the growing array of discarded feminine apparel.

Dara dragged humid air redolent with an earthy lushness into lungs that found ease for a moment. She couldn't breathe when he encircled her waist, his fingers splayed wide, then higher, spilling the curves of her breasts over the camisole top. He gently massaged her through the thin lawn cloth, introducing her to a new shocked intimacy when he raised her to his mouth, and with a man's passion riding rein, showed her the pleasure she brought him with every love bite and tender suckling that brought heated fluids to pump and swell her body.

"Eden," she pleaded, "help me." Lifting her wrists, she offered for his inspection the cuffs that bound her, the soft drape of lavender cloth a chain between them.

"Tell me, love." His smile became a deep male promise, his gaze hidden by the fall of his lashes, and he rolled her onto her back. He leaned over her, studying the way the sunlight played over her delicately flushed features, the way the dark sheened thickness of her hair tumbled in wild abandon across one shoulder, and his lips couldn't resist pressing a kiss on the pristine white strap that appeared. He lifted the mink dark mass slowly, arranging it with a connoisseur's attention to detail above her head and gazed into her luminous eyes. "So beautiful, love." He captured her hands, raising them to his lips, and then gently nestled each one on either side of her head. Eden raised the shimmer of lavender cloth above her head, creating a veil drape against the darkness of her hair.

"I believe I found a wild orchid, all lavender, cream, and"—he paused, his breath arrhythmic, as he slowly lowered his body over hers—"the softest of velvet." He kissed her with a caressing intensity that left her molten, for she could withhold nothing of herself from him. While visions of charming games such gentle restraint suggested crossed his mind, Eden freed her of those cuffs, finding that her eager, if innocent, participation, heightened his jaded senses without aids.

Dara absorbed the weight of his body, her own body filled with a restless need that was teased by his. Her skirt was tangled about her hips, and she had a fleeting moment's regret for the deliberate use of all she could find that would yet keep her from knowing his possession.

When his kisses had brought her to another shimmering peak, he carried the weight of his body on his arms, lifting his head. "Love, I want to see all of you." With soft, sensuous anticipation he added, "Help me or I'm afraid we'll end up frolicking like puppies." Her smile came slowly, but he had eased the tension he sensed was building too quickly. He rolled to his side and stood, lifting her up beside him, taking her weight against him when she couldn't stand.

Dara was willing to surrender to his greater experience in these matters, allowing him to slide first her skirt and then one petticoat into a billowing cloud at her feet, but shyness along with virginal fear prompted her to ask, "Must you see . . . all of me?"

"Oh, love," he said, burying his face against her hair, bidding the laugh that rose to silence. "Would you care to offer a suggestion as to what I may see?"

The question shocked her. "No self respecting woman with any morals would answer that."

"Making love is not a passive experience, darlin'. I want to please you as well as myself."

She snuggled against him, blushing furiously at the frankness of his talk, and yet, curiously, his very willingness to do so eased her fear. "Goodness, Eden, I don't know." She mumbled against his shirt. "You're the expert."

"How kind of you to say so. Shall we then," he asked in a wicked tone, "play out a proper wedding night? We could, if you feel inclined, hide beneath the quilt, grope about, and see what results." His offer was indulgent as he caressed the trembling length of her back. Eden waited, the powerful desire he experienced tempered by the strength of tenderness he felt for her.

"That sounds horrid."

"I've always believed it a barbaric custom to keep a young woman ignorant of what to expect. We will go as slowly as you like." He brushed aside her hair, kissed her bared throat, and when he judged the tension eased to be replaced by the desire momentarily stilled, he added, "Don't be shy, love. Tell me. I'm very open to suggestions. We'll begin with you helping me to finish unbuttoning my shirt." Her throat pulse beat beneath his lips, and he engaged his mouth to test its rhythm for long minutes until she softened her body against him.

Dara squeezed her eyes closed. Everywhere they touched was stirred and soothed. "Eden, must I?"

"It adds," he explained, lifting her hair to place dainty kisses over her shoulder, "another pleasurable dimension . . ." Her fingers timidly stroked his chest, and his eyes drifted closed as her lips scattered kisses over his skin. Cradling the delicate bones of her rib cage, he guided her into a slow abrasive dance, rubbing her breasts against his chest, smiling to feel her tentative move to unbutton the rest of his shirt. She stopped at the barrier of his belt and Eden wisely didn't pursue the matter. "See love, we'll share . . . all there is." With a deft move the last two cotton froths drifted down, and he lifted her free of them, caressing her hips as he knelt before her.

Dara shivered and braced her hands on his broad shoulders, as Eden, with soft murmur words of praise, rid her of ankle-high button shoes and dainty lace garters. He kissed at random the pale skin of her legs, rolling down stockings, so that after minutes, she stood, barefoot and slender, swaying against the press of his lips. Expert fingers massaged her calfs, easing the tension, and she drew a soft, shuddering gasp as he grazed her thighs, all the while telling her how beautiful she was to him. No wine of any vintage was as intoxicating as the sweetly heated scent of her, and he palmed the swell of her buttocks, cupping them to bring her against his mouth. Beribboned drawers slid down her hips, caught between silky curls and the heat of his kiss.

Her cry and struggle were joined, and he looked up to see shocked dark eyes, and smothered his desire, silently swearing his belief she would drive him mad. Sensitive, experienced fingers coaxed her to fever, soothing the quiver of her thighs before molding the rise of her silky curls with the flat of his palm. Her hands closed convulsively over his thick hair, and even to her ears her cry was one of pleasure. His mouth flowed over the rise of her hip, the taut flatness of her belly, and then with one finger he lifted the fine cambric from the moistness between her thighs. With all the delicacy of a connoisseur he breathed around the kitteny soft curls, tilting her hips forward, and decided with male arrogance that his patience deserved his just desserts. Hard shivers racked her body as the last bit of modesty fell, and she knew nothing but a hot wet ecstasy that would not separate into parts. She melted from the sweet agony of sensation flooding over her, arching to meet the compelling rapture, until she was past reason and nothing was left but desire and need.

And when she couldn't stand alone but for the support of his hands, he slowly ended his feasting, sliding an arm around her waist beneath the lush fall of her hair. "Look at me, love."

Dara gripped his shoulders, her gaze reluctant until the

touch of his mouth caressing the crease of her thigh brought a pleasure sigh. He lifted his head, eyes bright with the same desire that filled hers.

A slow, sensuous smile took possession of his mouth, and a sultry flame lit his eyes. "Shall we take time for options again? We could continue or—"

Dara arched. "No more games, Eden."

"No games, love. Never that. Pleasure shared. Show me what you want," he cajoled gently, his long fingers, equally skilled with violence or seduction, caressed the dewed moistness his lips imparted, finding a pulsing beat heavy with want.

It was the redolent sensuous anticipatory pleasure of his voice that made Dara guide his sensitive hands upward, dragging the hem of her camisole with them until he cupped the heavy fullness of her breasts. She held his gaze, encouraged by his smile and the dark tarnished-silver sheen. Her head fell back, her hair brushing the bare swell of her buttocks. Dara gave herself over to the passion that intensified with the hot circled caresses he offered until she felt herself rise to a shimmering peak. He worshipped her with words, soft insidious whispers that inflamed overburdened senses, offered one erect nipple solace with his mouth. And when she drew his head closer, small kittenish moans escaping, he guided her down beside him.

Desire ran like fire inside him, and he lifted her free of that last scrape of cloth. "Help me, love," he whispered, caressing the trembling length of her leg, and gently let his fingers enter her. He barely held the control to be cautious of the intimacy he asked for. Eden found himself intoxicated yet again by the silken texture he claimed.

Her cry held the enchanting provocative invitation for

more, the arch of her hips gracefully erotic, and his mouth was hungry to take hers. Sensual languor became tiny convulsive tremors, and she clung tightly to his shoulders, pushing aside the cloth to touch his heated skin. The moves of her body became hard and restless under the skill he exerted to bring an end to fevered distress.

And when the first flush of passion burned down to an ember, she lay in a shimmering pool of languid abandon as he left her side, stripping his clothes with a fiercely leashed patience that threatened his control.

Dara opened her eyes to see his male splendor revealed in dappled sunlight, her breath caught and was lost in the moment he stilled, his gaze filled with primitive male need targeted to hers. He was lean and sleek, his powerful muscles knit beneath bronzed skin with a perfect symmetry that drew her curious gaze down to the proud rise of his manhood. He was magnificently virile, his bold eyes possessively taking her body until small shivers began inside her. Dara lowered her gaze to his slim hips, his long legs dusted with dark hair, and her eyes drifted closed, newly awakened desire fading as she clutched the quilt beneath her in fear.

"We can," he whispered, coming to lie beside her, his fingers caressing the length of her creamy pale throat, "talk about what you're afraid of"—his hand drifted down, lifting the weight of her breast to his descending mouth—"or we can simply begin again."

His nearness, the heat of his body, the intimacy of his fingers tracing delicate designs on flesh aroused to sensuality, sent her body curving toward his. With an avid greediness that surprised and delighted him, Dara flicked her tongue against his shoulder, learning the taste of his skin. His leashed restraint snapped with the eager exploration she began of his body. His mouth pillaged her tender skin with a gentle savagery, and his hands taught her body more of the delectable passion between a man and a woman. His knee made a space between her thighs, holding her slender hips still as he covered her body with his own, the incredible feel of silken skin slick with moisture inflaming him.

"Hold me, love." He didn't move, watching and waiting until her eyes opened to his entreaty. He had wondered once how dark and velvet her eyes could be and had his answer now. Her hands were shaking as they reached out and gripped his shoulders.

With a commanding delicacy he didn't know he was capable of giving, Eden used the utmost care to slowly enter her. Her plaintive whimper, the sudden tensing of her body, brought his lips to her ear. "Welcome me, love." Hot wet silk gloved the first attempt he made, and by slow degrees that cast him into fevered agony, he reached that last virginal barrier. "You're so small love, I don't want to hurt you," he whispered, and waited, poised on the rack of passion's razor edge until fear subsided and he could feel the tiny convulsive shudders begin. He knew not even the threat of hell's eternal damning would stop him from possessing her now.

Dara tentatively arched to meet his thrust, her own blazing sensuality exploded into ravenous need, and she cried out, feeling the sudden sharp sting of his bite on her earlobe, driving her lithe body upward as with melting skill he drove himself into her.

There was a hushed delicacy to the waiting shadows of the afternoon as ecstasy was taught and learned with equal delight. Eden forgot the innocence of his lover in the hours that followed. He murmured an apology when he touched the soft, distended tissue that caused Dara to cry out, not in pleasure, but in pain. When he insisted there would be no more lovemaking, Dara turned his protest to a tormented masculine groan as her dainty fingers discovered a new skill with which to arouse him.

Later, they bathed in the crystal pool's cooling enchantment. Dara, exploring her new found sensuality, teased him to teach her more. Reluctantly, Eden whispered several suggestions, at which, she exclaimed with starched primness, "Well, I wouldn't brag about what the French call it!" Eden's rich male laughter sent a covey of doves aloft before his lips found hers.

As the afternoon faded, so did passion's games. Dara grew pensive, accepting Eden's acting the lady's maid when her own strength ebbed. She managed to laugh at the tangle he made of the bustle's tapes, but there was an underlying desperation to the sound. He carried her back to the carriage, then left her to get the basket and quilt. Dara sat, hands primly folded in her lap, unaware that he had paused to observe her. Her mood disturbed him, pricking his conscience, and he found himself vulnerable to the attack it made against every defense he offered. The lingering aftermath of passion's intoxication disappeared. He knew from the abandoned response of her own sensuality that he had given her pleasure, but he had taken a far more priceless gift than her virginity, and he couldn't deny it. The roar of the falling water had not drowned out the heated whisper of her voice when he had lifted her high and impaled her with a need that knew no end. Her cry echoed in his mind . . . "Eden . . . love me . . ." It was not a plea for her body's satiation, it was an emotional demand that he fought against answering.

The breeze ruffled the trees, and he gazed up, feeling the wind and knowing its restless call. Regret filled him, and he was not a man given to it, nor would he deny her placing full responsibility squarely on his shoulders.

But Dara sat as he left her, her voice soft in answering his solicitous questions. This time the choice was his to make, and he found he could not drag her into another emotional unheaval playing recriminations and repentance.

Taking the reins in hand, he gazed down at her bent head. "Dara, we need to talk, whenever you want."

"My virginal curiosity has been answered, Eden. What else could we have to talk about?"

Good intentions be damned! Her choice of words rankled. "Let's not forget in the midst of all that misery to remember, love," he stated with a sarcastic bite, "all that passion was shared. Not taken, not forced, but most mutually enjoyed."

She raised wounded eyes to his. "I won't forget, Eden." And she waited, afraid of the emotionless set of his features, until the silence grew in agonizing length. "Please," she whispered, "take me home."

He thought about taking her mouth until it was filled with pleasure cries, not the soft bitterness he heard. But her gaze defied him, pride holding her still, and he was the one to turn away, urging the horse around.

Eden was the first to notice the rider fast approaching. He slowed the carriage and then stopped when he realized the horse was his own and Matt was riding him, hell-bent for leather. Dark mutters passed his lips, but Matt's voice, yelling when he saw them, drowned them out.

"Where the devil have you been! Jake is looking all over for you, Eden. He's got men tearing up the town." Matt ignored his sister, sawing on the reins, and Eden's dark scowl brought a mumbled apology for abusing his horse. His chest was heaving, and he obeyed Eden's curt order to take a minute before he spoke. "I was up to the mine, and they said you left hours ago."

Eden ignored the hint of a question in Matt's voice. "Never mind. Just tell me why Jake is looking for me."

"They robbed Tucker's."

"Matt," Dara cried out, forcing him to notice her. "Was anyone hurt?"

"No. But Clay was in town. He'd called a meeting of his vigilance committee, and they were there when it happened. He said—"

"Matt," she cut in, "was Pierce—"

"Will you let him finish, Dara!"

Her mouth gaped and even Matt frowned at the tone of Eden's command, but neither one argued with him, and Matt continued. "Clay got word of the robbery just as Jake heard about the meeting. They wouldn't listen to him, and about twenty of them rode out before Jake could stop them. Jesse and his boys managed to talk sense to a few men, but they couldn't stop the rest. They swore they were gonna string them up."

While Dara listened, Eden had jumped down from the carriage. He glanced at her as if he were about to say something, then abruptly turned to Matt. "Drive your sister back to town."

"I want to come with you. I can help, Eden. 'Sides," he added, dismounting, "Jake was gonna try and keep up with them. You don't know the land 'round Amos's farm, and I do." Handing Eden the reins, he leaned close to him. "Clay and the others are in a killing mood, and you'll need every man. Clay was looking for you before these three men, bold as brass, went right up to the front door and asked Tucker to open for them. You know how he won't turn down a dollar, even if it's the Lord's day, and the damn fool opened the door to them. I got your gun. It's in your saddlebag."

"That was smart, Matt. But you take your sister home." His actions were an economy of motion, wrapping the gunbelt around his waist, stripping off his tie, collar, and jacket and handing them to Matt. He swung himself up into the saddle, already turning Sinner's head when Dara's cry stopped him.

"Don't let Pierce get hurt. Please, Eden. He . . . he doesn't know what this will do to him. My brother's not a murderer." Panic choked her. She gazed up at eyes that held no pity, no emotion at all. "Promise me you'll try to keep him safe."

"Is it just for Pierce that you're pleading, Dara? Or for Clay?" Rage filled him, unlike any he had ever known. He was asking for a choice when he had offered her no promise.

For one stunned moment, she stared at him. "My brother. I'm pleading—no—begging you to keep Pierce safe."

All he could do was nod.

Sinner responded to the slight pressure of his knees, and a ground-eating stride soon separated them.

Matt joined her on the carriage seat, noted the pale sheen of her face, but while he understood that she was frightened, he couldn't help being angry.

"How could you ask that of him? Didn't you think *he* could be killed?"

"I thought of it," she whispered, refusing to look at him. Her precariously balanced emotions were pushed unmercifully to the limit. Pierce would be with Clay, and Eden rode after them. Eden who hated Clay. *What had she done?* Giving herself to Eden had placed a weapon in his clever hands that could explode an already volatile situation. If he dared even hint . . .

"Stop worrying about Eden or Jake. They're men who know how to take care of themselves."

Her temper snapped and she rounded on him. "You fool! Don't you think I know that? And what about Pierce? He's your brother. Did you think about him being dragged into this? Did you?"

Matt's sudden grip on her shoulders, the little shake he gave her, silenced Dara. "He's Clay's damn shadow, Dara. Pierce made his choice, and I made mine. We're not your little brothers anymore. We're both men. If he's riding with Clay, he'll be a party to murder if they catch those thieves." Her whimper made him ease his grip, but he didn't release her. With a taut-edged fury he added, "And if you dream that Pierce will make any attempt to stop Clay and the others, you don't know your own brother. He was riding up front, Dara. Waving a brand-new rope he took from the store. I could hear him shouting that he would stretch the first neck." He pushed her back against the seat, grabbed up the reins, and urged the horse back onto the road.

Matt was hunched over, and Dara stared at the smooth pull of his shirt across his broad back. What she saw was a man. What she thought of was his fury to be left behind. And a rush of love for the boy she helped raise made her gamble on one last desperate plea.

"Don't go after them, Matt. Promise me that. You can't let their violence taint you."

"It's too late. Didn't you know that from the first? Whoever is right or wrong, men intent on protecting or claiming what they think is theirs breed violence."

They were too much like words Eden would say, and she cried inside, knowing Matt wouldn't listen. Gathering up emotional forces scattered like the rising wind, she prayed Eden and Jake would find Pierce and Clay before they committed an act that she knew would haunt them. No matter what Matt believed, there had to be a way to stop them.

"Don't drive to town, Matt. Take me to Amos's. If we hurry—"

"Eden said to take you home, and that's where you're going. There's nothing you could say that would stop it from happening. They were waiting for an excuse to vent the fury that's been building all these weeks. Violence is all that'll satisfy them."

"Clay and Pierce were not bred for violence. They love the land and tending—"

"Every man's got it in him, Dara. You can't say the same about Jake, can you? Or Eden McQuade?"

She didn't answer. She couldn't, didn't deny that about Eden.

Chapter Fourteen

EDEN ABRUPTLY NECK-REINED Sinner into a swerve that forced the horse to rear. An abandoned oxcart blocked the twisted, rutted lane that led to Amos's farm. Eden dismounted, wary of the ominous silence that enfolded the dusk-shadowed land. His view was hampered by the curve of the lane and the thick, man-high palms and scrub pines on either side. There was no way to ride farther, and he knew he could never cut a path through the sun-browned tips of palms with any stealth. With a pat to the lathered side of his horse, he climbed over the wagon tongue, drew his gun, and proceeded with a caution forced on him by instinct. The stench of scorched earth reached him first before the bend in the lane dipped to reveal a burned field.

But it was the sight of the lone oak, a silent crowd of men surrounding it, that arrested him. He could barely make out Jake's struggling figure held by two men. Off to the side stood another three men held at bay by the rifles thrust at their chests. He was too late. Three swinging bodies were buffeted by the wind.

There was a sickness inside him, not for the murders committed, but for the power that filled those men who had taken the law into their own hands. He knew the strength of that power, knew that it would not easily be subdued. The choice was his now. He could walk away. One man was not going to make a difference.

Eden began walking forward. Someone shouted a warning shout and fired a shot. Burned rubble settled at his feet, and with a breath a killer's cool control filled him.

"Stay back, McQuade!" several men demanded.

"You're too late!" another man yelled.

Eden kept walking. Another shot hit the earth in front of him, then another. Clay's voice suddenly rose above the others. "Keep coming, McQuade. We've got one rope left."

Eden was close enough to see Clay push his way toward the front, Pierce at his side. Clay shoved the rope at Pierce and grabbed his rifle. Eden nestled the smooth handle of his gun in his palm, his gaze locked on Clay. Dara's voice came to haunt him. "Keep my brother safe." Had she lied to him? Ruthlessly he cast the thought aside. Nothing was going to stop him from settling with Clay.

He watched Clay raise the rifle, heard his snarled taunt to come closer along with the faint *click* of the hammer being pulled back.

"That's far enough, McQuade. I don't want your blood spattered on my barrel."

"What makes you so sure you'll get the chance to pull the trigger before I kill you, Clay?" Eden made his move then, raising his gun out and away from his side, his gaze never wavering from Clay's face, but his action drew a darting look from the other man. It was all the distraction Eden needed. His right forearm slammed the rifle barrel, lifting it high, and before Clay could move, he brought his gun-fisted hand upward into Clay's belly. Clay staggered back from the blow, releasing the rifle, and

Eden grabbed for it, holding the rifle and his handgun on the men surging forward.

"Hold it right where you all are," he ordered. There were grumbling mutters, but no one wanted to tangle with him. "Let Jake go," Eden called out, never once looking away from Clay, who was doubled over, clutching his belly.

"You're piling a high score, McQuade," Clay weakly called out, shaking off Pierce's offer to help him stand straight. "I'm gonna kill you."

"Those three weren't enough?" Eden asked, and before anyone could guess his intent, he tossed the rifle at Clay's feet. "Pick it up and use it."

"Eden, no!" Jake yelled, elbowing a path through the crowd to come and stand at his friend's side. He trained his own gun on the men he called neighbor and friend alike. "There'll be no more killing."

"You're gonna shoot us, Jake?" Flynn Kinnel asked.

"I'll do whatever I must to stop you men from taking the law into your own hands again. It's what you elected me to do. I know those men were guilty of robbing Tucker. They had a right to a trial with a jury deciding what was to happen to them."

"Well, we saved us some county money, Jake," Hank Clare stated, watching Eden, his own rifle held easy at his side.

"Clay, I'm still waiting for you to make your move," Eden said.

Jake moved aside, bringing Eden's back into range. "Eden, there'll be no killing."

Both men ignored him. But those facing Eden began backing away, even Pierce, the last to go.

"Pick it up, Clay. It's just you and me. I'll make it

easy." Eden reholstered his gun, his hands splayed wide and loose at his sides.

Clay forced himself to ignore the burning pain in his gut and stood tall. His gaze darted to those men who had followed his lead. There wasn't a one who would come to his aid now. He eyed the rifle at his feet, judged the time he needed to get it, and once again looked up at Eden.

He didn't find the telltale flicker of facial muscle or the blink of an eye to indicate fear. He faced a killer.

"It's a little different this way, isn't it, Clay?" Eden asked without emotion. "Hanging a man in the heat of fury with six to one odds makes a man brave. A man gets drunk on that kind of power, but one on one, no fury, just the cold thought of picking up a gun and killing a man makes you look inside yourself."

"You're goading him, Eden," Jake warned, knowing he had to stop them, unwilling to shoot either one.

"I know," came his calm reply.

"You think I'd make it that easy for you, McQuade? I figure your game. The moment I try grabbing for my rifle, you'll shoot me."

"You want mine on the ground, too?"

"Eden, he's backed off. You know that. Don't force me to use this on you."

"You do what you need to, Jake. Clay has a choice. He picks up that rifle and uses it, or he rides away."

"You calling me a coward, McQuade?"

"I'm just calling you."

Clay started to turn away, but he never completed the move. His drop to the ground and reach were stopped by the bullet that Jake fired, hitting the wooden butt of the rifle.

"Back off, Clay," Jake ordered. "Pierce, get his rifle

and get him the hell out of here. And that goes for the rest of you. Get your horses and go home."

In all the time it took for the men to obey him, Eden didn't move. When they were gone, Jake stood with Jesse and his two older sons.

"Had me helpless as a bee in buttah," Jesse muttered.

"You tried to stop them, Jesse, that's all a man can do. You and your boys want to help bury them?" Eden asked.

"Eden, you know I had to—"

"We're always making choices, Jake. He's your wife's brother. Me, I'm just a part of your past. I understand the why of it, but Clay—well, friend, just watch your back." He gazed up at the three bodies. "Figure Amos'll mind if we bury them here?"

"That weasel offahed his tree for the hangin'," Jesse answered. "Don't reckon he can object now. Eithah of you know who they are?"

"Can't tell much from what they look like now. But those boots ain't a miners," Jake said.

"He worked for Lucio. The other two worked for me."

"You bein' a preachah's son an' all must figure yore accountable. Ain't a man gonna hold you to it."

"Jesse's right," Jake added. "We tried to stop them. Clay was smart enough to hold a few men back to wait for us. They jumped us when we were forced to stop at the oxcart. I should've known better."

"It doesn't matter, does it?" Eden asked without emotion. "They're dead."

He rode back to town alone, dismounting behind his office, where privacy and an unopened bottle of bourbon waited. Stripping off Sinner's saddle, he glanced back at

Dara's house, saw the lamps lit in the parlor, and wondered if she waited. There was a bitter fury locked inside him, and he didn't trust himself to go near her. He searched above the door lintel for the spare key, and when his fingers came up empty, he filled them with his gun. Pressed flat against the wall, he leaned down to twist the doorknob. It opened easily. A shove sent the door open. The wanning moon's light didn't penetrate the dark interior. All he heard were his own steady breaths. A quick mental scan placed every piece of furniture in the room. His wide desk faced the door and the only way out. To its left, a long leather couch filled the wall. A single table and lamp stood in the back corner, behind the open door. There was no place to hide on the right wall, which was lined with shelves and cabinets. Whoever was inside was either behind the desk or the door. He braced himself for entry, crouching low, darting and rolling through the doorway, and coming up fast with his back against the right wall.

"Are you so angry that you'll shoot me, Eden?"

Dara's frightened voice cut through the dark. His harshly drawn breath was the only sound he made for a moment.

"I could have killed you." He located her curled on the couch. Belatedly realizing he still gripped his gun, he reholstered it, and then to vent his anger, he jerked the gunbelt's buckle open.

"I had to see you," she whispered, her own gaze long accustomed to the dark, following him easily, surprised he stood by the door, gunbelt in hand.

"Get out, Dara."

"Are you hurt?"

"Not the way you mean, but I don't want you here."

She knew facing him again would be the hardest thing

she had to do, but nothing had prepared her for the cold rejection in his voice. "Please, Eden, don't send me away. I was worried about you. Matt talked to some of the men, and they said you—"

"I didn't touch your brother or Clay. But don't thank me, darlin', thank Jake. He stopped it."

The ruthless cut of his voice should have warned her, but Dara was caught up in the tension of the dragging hours she had waited, anger for herself growing at the way they parted.

"Don't treat me like the china doll Clay made me out to be. Tell me what happened. I'm stronger than you think I am."

"Are you?" In a ruthless voice he told her what had happened, sparing her nothing. What Eden didn't, couldn't, tell her were his own feelings of guilt and helplessness because he was too late to stop the murders.

"Eden, please, I don't care—"

"You should, *love*. It's called self-preservation. If you haven't come to thank me, I assume your virginal curiosity wasn't satisfied. I'm afraid you've caught me at a distinct disadvantage. I'm in no mood to play indulgent lover."

"I came because I care about you! I thought you might need me." For a moment she thought he wouldn't answer her. Her fingers gripped the smooth leather arm of the couch.

"Get out. You can't give me what I need."

"And a bottle or some other woman could?" she demanded, no longer shocked that she forgot her moralistic upbringing. But then, Eden made her forget everything but him.

The door closed with a soft thud. She heard the brush of his gunbelt swing against the wood for a few seconds.

He came toward her, stripping off his shirt before tossing it aside. And the danger of his mood came with him. She uncurled her legs slowly, a shiver of fear shaking its way down her back. She moistened her lips, afraid to speak.

"You're staying. Accommodate me, love. Undress."

The words were coolly delivered, devoid of feeling, and Dara was forced to answer him. "I didn't come here for this."

He couldn't ignore the quiet desperation in her voice, but there was a savage mood cloaking his sensibilities. "This," he stated, reaching out to take hold of her arms, "is all I want from you." He lifted her up against him, his mouth closing over hers possessively, already aroused, rage for the day's happening fueling his need to lose himself in the sweetly heated scent of her. He was on fire, aching, empty, and wanting all at once. The feel of her long silky hair slipping its knot, spilling over his arms, only intensified that want. Her hands were clawing his back, and he needed to be inside her, to ride out the blackness in the silky sheath that would be soft, and wet and hot and . . . his.

"Mine," he whispered. "Tell me you're mine."

Dara didn't hear the words. She listened instead to the underlying vulnerable plea of need in his voice. His mouth was hard and hungry, and his long deep kisses made her cling to him. Feelings uncurled painfully inside her, and she was afraid to whisper them silently to herself. She desired him, yet desire was not the force that made her answer the rawness of his passion. It was the power of the whispers he breathed over her skin that made her admit to herself that she loved him.

"Hold me, love. Just hold me tight. I need you so much."

It was a plea that went beyond physical desire. The

need wasn't his alone. Whatever he wanted, she could not deny him. To do so was to deny her own love. Soft pleasure sounds emerged from low in her throat when his hand closed over her breast. The single layer of her shirtwaist offered her no protection from the heat of his touch.

"Please," she begged. "Eden . . ."

He lifted his head, his eyes savage. His blood surged hot, and he was breathing hard. "Do you want me?" The words were harsh; he had no softness left.

Dara gripped his shoulders, shivering delicately. "All I want is you."

He pressed her closer, lifting her up and into him, rubbing her over the hardened swell of his sex, and both of them shuddered. Her mouth opened under the force of his, his tongue taking her into a deep heavy rhythm that she instinctively responded to.

She felt him gathering her skirt in his hand, raising it, and she trembled with the force of almost violent arousal.

His hand was hard sliding up the length of her thigh. She knew the press of his fingers were only separated from her skin by the thin cotton drawers. He paused with his hand on her hip, then, with a wrench, the flimsy tie snapped and the garment fell. Eden lifted her free of them, kicking the cloth aside, his lips closing over one erect nipple, suckling so strongly her back arched and she cried out. There was a quickening inside her that gloried in the wildness of his mouth, the surge of his body, hot and hard, against hers. The sleek skin of his back bore the crescent nail marks she left as he turned with her, his hand between their bodies for a few moments, and then released her.

Dara opened passion-glazed eyes. He sat before her on

the couch, his trousers unbuttoned, his splendid erection blatant. Eden lifted his hand, but he made no move to draw her down beside him. "Now, love."

"Eden . . . I—"

"I'd hurt you any other way." Exaggerated courtesy was evident in his husky voice. "Come and sit on me."

Passion clamored its demand that she obey. Her heated flushed skin and sensitive nerve endings remembered every moment of the afternoon's pleasures. Without thought, her fingers moved to her throat, and not even their betraying tremble hindered Dara from slowly unbuttoning each one of the pearl fastenings. But when she began slipping it off, he stopped her.

"Leave it on and come here, love."

She came forward, stood between his spread thighs, uncertain of what to do. Eden slid one hand beneath her skirt, caressing the silken length of her leg, drawing her knee up beside his hip. He held her poised there, his passion barely controlled, reaching out to hold her hip with his other hand as she swayed toward him. Bending his head, he lowered his mouth to her breast, closing over the peaked nipple, teasing her with tiny licks, feeling the taut waiting of her body and the answering pulse that ached deep within his own. Sliding his fingers gently into her dampness, he delicately stroked the velvety soft, swollen heat of her, his lips firming their pressure on the hardened crest. Dara cried out, her hands gripping his head close, her own flung back. "Eden, please . . . I can't . . ."

He lifted his head. "You can. I'll show you, love." He slid the draped folds of her skirt high, guiding her down until she shuddered, her breath as still as his, desire radiating between them as she slowly stretched to accommodate him. And when she was hotly sheathed around him, his groan came from deep inside his throat. He lifted her with deliberate slowness, and lowered her once more, until her innate sensuality maintained his rhythm, her inner thighs brushing the cloth of his trousers, her full breasts grazing the sensuous feel of his hair-rough chest. With his hands firmly on her hips, he rose to meet her peaking ardor, and she cried out with the violently intense sensations that flooded her body.

He clamped his teeth together, a savage need washing over him, and feverishly he drove upward, plunging her over the edge. One hand twined in the length of her hair, dragging her mouth to his, crushing her lips as she melted against him, and with a last violent thrust, he joined her.

The pulsing intensity diminished slowly between them, and Dara lay against him, content, the soft caress of his hands on her bare back lulling her until Eden spoke.

"There's no going back, Dara, you know that, don't you?"

She kissed his throat, whispering, "I don't want to go back." He was still hard within her, and she languidly moved, a heated trembling spreading through her.

"Greedy, love. No more for you." But he felt himself swell inside her, his passion rekindling as if he had never had her.

"I want you." There was a provocative invitation in her voice, the slow gliding rotation of her hips enforcing her demand. She licked the pulse beating in his throat, nipped the velvety lobe of his ear, whispering over and over how much she wanted him.

"I should take you home." But his lips were already caressing the soft swell of her breast.

"Yes, Eden . . . take me . . ."

There was a wildness to the tumultuous passion that overwhelmed them, for he couldn't get enough of her, nor she of him until dawn edged its intrusion, and with it, the sounds of gunfire.

Chapter Fifteen

IT WAS EARLY Yarwood who fired the shots at two men who ran off with three of his best horses. Jake rode out after them before Eden arrived at the livery. He spared Early a few minutes to vent his anger, but his charity disappeared when Early, with a searching look, remarked, "Doan' see how you missed the excitement from yore room at Miss Loretta's."

"I wasn't in my room. Tell Jake to see me when he gets back."

"Damn! He spent the night in someone's bed, that's for sure," Early said, watching Eden walk away, his gun tucked in his pant's waistband, his shirtails hanging free.

Eden stopped off at his saloon, picked up the books along with the weekend's receipts, asked a few questions, and did the same at the barbers and the café he rented out before he returned to his office. He had learned nothing to help Jake. He was concerned over the remark his bartender dropped, that Jake was seen coming from the direction of the Gilded Lily right after the shots were fired. Eden knew he himself would stand for no one daring to question where he spent the night, not only to protect Dara, but simply because he would be accountable to no man. If anyone but Satin Mallory managed the pleasure palace for Lucio, he wouldn't worry over the implications of Jake being there.

But Jake was married and in love with his wife. He hadn't lied about what he wanted for himself or this town. Eden knew him, knew the pride of his expecting their first child, and Jake was not going to risk losing Anne, no matter what privations her condition caused.

The past came back with a vengeance. Jake had to be trying to get Satin to tell him the truth of what happened the night Linda was killed. She would never betray Lucio, and Eden knew he would never destroy Jake's belief that Linda loved him. Closing the book before him with a slam, he knew what he had to do. The scent of Dara clung to him, forcing him to acknowledge that he didn't want his past to touch her. His brother, Dice, was fond of saying that luck often rode with him. He hoped Dara didn't find out why he had to stay away.

By Tuesday afternoon Dara, bewildered that Eden hadn't been to see her, knew where he had spent Monday evening. Small town gossip spread faster than melting butter.

She bolted from the store when Matt arrived, hating the sly remarks passed within her hearing. Jesse came to play his weekly game of checkers with her father, and she couldn't wait to escape the confines of the house. For long minutes she stared at the darkened windows of Eden's office, then walked a ways down by the river trying to deny that she loved him. Tears didn't help. Nothing but Eden's presence would take the incredible pain away.

Dara shivered despite the sultry heat of the summer night. His neglect diminished their lovemaking to a sordid fall from grace. She didn't want to believe that he used her, just as Miss Loretta had warned her that long-ago morning, but used is what she felt. And with that came the one forbidden thought she tried to bury

What if she had conceived a child? Would he care? Despair filled her. Had he once thought of what she might be going through?

Eden, sipping a fine vintage champagne in the luxury of Satin's private suite, was indeed thinking of Dara. She would have been shocked to know he compared her to Satin. His body instantaneously achieved a state of arousal, bringing a purr of approval while a silk-clad body moved provocatively, skilled fingers and lips paying rapt attention to the contoured length of his rigid manhood. His breath hissed sharply, and he found himself wishing for the sweetly heated scent that was Dara's, not the spiced perfume that rose from the woman intent on seducing him. He had adroitly avoided his present position last evening by involving himself in one of Satin's private card games. He tried not to be disappointed when he learned absolutely nothing. He knew Satin was as skilled in keeping Lucio's secrets as she was in arts she had learned at every madam's side from El Paso to Denver.

Without betraying his feelings, he held out his glass. "I seem to be empty."

Satin swallowed her thought to the contrary, for the cool directness of his gaze was at odds with the blatant state she had brought him to. With a languid move she raised herself from his side and reached for the bottle nestled in its silver cooler.

"You never needed to fortify yourself with champagne before, Silver."

"Eden. I keep telling you, Silver doesn't exist, not here." He watched her every calculated gesture to entice, arouse, and inflame a man; the sly glance from beneath long black lashes, the tip of her tongue that relished the lush moistness of her lips, the deliberate provocative thrust of breasts as she returned his glass.

Eden smiled, sipped, and said, "An excellent vintage. Lucio spoils you. But the champagne is not for my fortification, Satin. I merely thought to give you time. It's unlike you to act the bitch in heat. Or were those Lucio's orders?"

"Why the hell did you come up here with me?"

"I, unlike Lucio, appreciate all your exquisite and subtle attributes. I admire your intelligence, find your mercenary tendencies make you a worthy adversary, and know that you can offer a wealth of information for—"

"The right price, Eden."

"I was going to say the right man."

With a charming tilt to her head, Satin slowly returned his smile. "Perhaps we can come to some mutual agreement."

"I'm counting on it, Satin."

"He's not here, Jake. I believe gossip holds that your friend has found the Gilded Lily more to his style."

"Dara, whatever you heard about Eden—"

"Is that Jake, Dara?" Cyrus called out. "Invite him in. I could use a bit of company."

Dara held the door aside, and Jake mumbled an apology as he walked in. He shouldn't have come here, but after walking the streets tonight, he was filled with the gut-wrenching premonition that he would use his gun before the night's end. Eden would understand, as no one else could, the fine edge instinct honed.

"Dara, don't believe everything you hear. Whatever Eden's doing, he's got his reasons."

"I am sure that he has. Would you like coffee, Jake? I was about to make some."

"Sure."

Jake left soon after, and Dara stood by the door wondering if he was going home to Anne or if he was too ensnared by the lure of that black-haired witch. Jealousy was not an emotion that she was familiar with, but Dara knew it was what she felt. Her problem wasn't the same as Anne's; she knew she had more than satisfied Eden's desire. His heated words of praise were burned in her memory, even if their explicitness could still make her blush. She closed the door, secured it, and knew there would be no sleep again tonight.

Struggling to get her father to bed, Dara was annoyed when he stopped her from leaving him.

"Is it Eden that has you upset, Dara?"

"He's a busy man, Papa."

"I suppose he is. Do you love him?"

"Papa!"

"Times like now that I miss your mother the most. She would know what to tell you. Eden's not an easy man. He's not Clay."

Dara leaned against the door, her head lowered, and wished she could talk to someone about the turmoil of feelings inside her.

"Do you want me to ask his intentions? I never had to with Clay. Knew from the first that boy was set on marrying you. I won't pry about what happened, but I'm here if you need me."

"I love you, Papa," she whispered, and slipped out the door.

By the time she reached her room, Dara found that anger had replaced every other emotion. She unpinned her hair and, with an arrogant tilt to her chin, proceeded to swear the few words she knew to her reflection.

Then she heard noises. They were muffled at first, and

she ran to the window. Shouts filtered down from the café Eden owned. Dara was about to turn away when she heard gunshots and bolted from her room.

"Dara!"

"I don't know what happened, Papa!" she yelled back, running down the stairs. "I'll find out."

"Don't go!"

But she was already across the yard, cutting behind the block of stores, dodging empty liquor bottles, slipping in the mud behind the public baths. Panting, she joined the crowd at the café's back door, trying to get someone's attention to tell her what happened.

"Mabel!" she yelled, spotting the woman off to one side with her daughter. Frantically she waved her arm to get their attention.

"It's Jake, Dara. He's been shot."

Someone elbowed her from behind, and Dara stumbled into a man's back. He shoved her away, and she nearly went down to her knees.

"He ain't dead!" someone called out.

Dara's first question had been answered, and her thoughts turned to Anne, home alone. She had to fight her way free, running again with her hair streaming wildly behind her, knowing she had to get to Anne first.

She darted across Charleston Street and up Atlanta Lane, slamming into two men who suddenly stepped from a newly framed store. Dara vented every bit of anger she harbored, finding that the hours she worked in the store gave her the strength to pull her arm free from one man's grip, tearing her sleeve. When the other man tried to grab her, she landed a solid kick with her serviceable black shoes.

Dara thought she would die when their footsteps sounded behind her. She stumbled and tripped over her skirt hem but managed to get up the steps of Anne's porch.

"Anne!" she screamed over and over, pounding on the door, sensing the two men were still there. She almost fell a few minutes later when the door opened, and she pushed Anne aside, slamming it closed behind her.

"Dara, what happened to you?" Anne raised the lamp she held high, staring in disbelief.

Trying to catch her breath, Dara knew she couldn't blurt out that Jake had been shot. Glancing up at Anne's pale features, she didn't know what to say. "Please, just . . . give me . . . a minute."

The thud of footsteps coming up the steps, the shouts and banging on the door made both young women freeze.

"Mrs. Vario . . . Anne . . . open the door! Jake's been shot."

"Jake," Anne whispered, her eyes wide and glazed before she dropped the lamp and fainted.

Dara tried to stop her fall and grab the lamp. She managed to get her arm around Anne's shoulders and ease her down, but then struggled to her feet, stamping out the spread of flame in the oil-soaked carpet. The fists continued to bang on the door, the shouts grew in volume, and Dara screamed, "Open the damn door and help me!"

"Dara! What the hell—" Eden didn't waste his breath asking her questions. Ordering Early, who followed him inside, to stamp out the tiny fire, Eden lifted Anne's limp body and followed Dara down the hall. By the time Dara returned to Anne's bedroom with a basin of water, Suelle and Mabel had managed to rouse Anne. Eden sat beside her, ignoring the women's indignant voices begging him to leave, since his presence in her bedroom while she was in a state of undress was most improper even if he was Jake's friend. Anne was moaning while he softly reassured her that Jake's wound was not life-threatening. She didn't seem to hear him. Suelle wiped the sweat from Anne's brow, Dara held her hand, and Mabel found an additional quilt to help stop her chills.

"Dara," Suelle briskly ordered, "this is no place for an unmarried woman. And take Mr. McQuade with you."

About to protest, Dara wasn't given the chance. Eden gripped her arm firmly and ushered her out into the hallway.

"What the hell are you doing out at this time of night alone?"

"What . . . was I . . . doing . . ." she sputtered, enraged after all she had been through.

His eyes narrowed. "You," he repeated, taking in the tangle of her hair. His gaze lingered on the torn sleeve of her shirtwaist and the livid finger marks bruising her skin. Eden's voice grew chillingly soft. "Who dared?"

"The type of men you and Lucio brought to this town, Mr. McQuade." She met his glittering gaze unflinchingly. "And while I may carry bruises, they didn't get close enough to leave their stench on me. You," she added, flicking a finger at his open shirt, "should have taken time to dress before running—"

"Such wifely solicitude, love? I'm not accountable to you."

Dara's face paled. "No, you're not. Forgive me for my lapse. Now, stand aside, we have nothing more to say."

He crowded her against the wall with his body, one hand gently crushing her hair. "Don't fight me, love. You won't win."

"I won't fight with you. But I don't want you touching me reeking of that harlot's perfume."

"Pot calling the kettle black?"

Her palm cracked across his face. For one eternal moment Dara held her breath, afraid of his retaliation. The sting lingered in her palm, but he didn't move.

"I suppose that was inevitable, and for what it's worth, my remark was uncalled for."

"Right now, it's not worth much. Let me go, Eden. I want to be with Anne."

"You're not staying. I'll take you home. I'm in no mood—"

"Nothing about you concerns me," she whispered, trying to slip away. "I am not accountable to you. Plain talk, Mr. McQuade. Anne needs me and you don't."

He tipped her chin up, ignoring her anger, his lips hovering over hers. "Don't I, love? I did warn you not to play games with me, Dara. It's wicked and dangerous to dare me to prove otherwise."

It was impossible to be strong any longer. She hurt too much. Dara was tired of being torn apart emotionally. She loved him, risked everything she believed in, in the hope that he could learn to love her. A few brutal words crushed that hope. But she fought back tears with the last of her pride.

Intently watching her, Eden saw the glitter of tears she blinked back, and suddenly it mattered fiercely that he had hurt her with careless words he never meant. He hesitated a moment, then cradled her close. "You're right," he murmured, "I'm not worth your pain."

For Dara, the realization that she felt safe, protected, and simply at peace when he held her added to the shock of how much she needed him. It was frightening to admit how much it mattered that he did care about her.

Her whispered plea to hold her made Eden comprehend how heavy the burdens of the last few weeks had been for her. His own guilt sharpened for adding too much, too fast, then leaving her to assume it all alone. "Let me take you home," he murmured, smoothing her hair from her face as she lifted her head from his shoulder. "And love, I wasn't *with* Satin as you implied. I told you once I'll admit to being many things, but a liar isn't one of them. If you'll recall," he added, inhaling with need the scent that belonged to her alone, "I said I wouldn't satisfy my desire for you with another woman. Look at me, love, and tell me I don't need *you.*"

"I want to believe you, but Eden," she pleaded, gazing into his eyes, "what were you doing there?"

Eden didn't get a chance to answer, for Mabel came to the bedroom doorway. "Mr. McQuade, please fetch Doc Vance. I'm afraid that Anne is losing the baby."

The hours dragged in a nightmare for Dara and the other women. They did all they could to make Anne comfortable after Eden returned without the doctor. He had just located the bullet in Jake's side and removed it. Eden didn't tell them Doc Vance was worried about staunching the flow of blood, but he did send them gallic acid to arrest Anne's hemorrhage and opium to relieve the pain. There was no more talk of Dara leaving, for Anne, screaming in agony, clung to her hand. Eden came and went, always there when Dara looked for him, but what he learned as the night passed and the long vigil was over forced him to make a decision.

Lara Saunders had come to him, refusing to say why she had been near the back of the café at that time of night, but swore to Eden that someone had called Jake's name a few times when he left Dara's house. She was across the street about to enter her own home when the first shot rang out. No, she didn't see who it was, and didn't recognize the voice, but it was a man and Jake never once asked who it was.

When Dara came to him, tears streaming down her face, Eden held her, knowing that Lucio had made his move and set Jake up. He whispered words of comfort, offering her his strength, for Jake didn't die, but his unborn child did.

Chapter Sixteen

EDEN WAS PRESENTED with his chance to settle old debts and those newly incurred by Lucio two days later.

In the past weeks he had been approached by several prominent Northern investors eager to buy land that held any promise of containing phosphate. Luther had hired two of the early arriving men, whose luck and money had run out together, to help him man the telegraph around the clock, receiving and transmitting messages that affected the transfer of thousands of dollars in capital and stock.

Eden had spent several afternoons at the Ocala House, which now resembled a stock exchange as groups milled about the lobby trading rumors, buying and selling on heresay alone. Clerks toiled all night, recording the day's money and deed transactions. Eden's trips to Tampa and Jacksonville brought him in contact with men made wealthy overnight, who were constantly seeking new opportunities to invest in. Eden's name was a respected one in mining circles, and he used his reputation to gain the information he needed. Companies formed hourly, gilt-lettered stock flooded the state, and a trade exchange was finally organized at Ocala, with seats offered at fifty dollars each. Eden owned the first, Lucio the second.

On this cool September morning, two days after Jake

had been shot and Anne had lost their baby, Eden sat in one of several "millionaire's corners" on one of the porches of the Ocala House fingering the brim of his slate-colored "governor" hat and engaged in conversation with several manufacturers from New York. He had spent the last two days studying Lucio's financial records and knew the man was desperate to find investors after overextending his land buying. He should have showed a larger profit than Eden did, since he used convict labor, but Lucio had the misfortune of being conned by two farmers who had salted their lands with phosphate-rich rock. Lucio, greedy to own more land, never had the samples analyzed. Eden smiled, thinking it most fitting that the con man had been conned.

While Eden lent his attentions to the men eager for his opinion, he carefully watched Lucio to see who he was approaching. Eden recognized a few of the men as financiers and industrialists whom he had met during his time in Washington. The telegrams he had fired off to his brother, and the answers he had received, gave Eden the advantage of knowing most of the men's monetary worth. When Lucio singled out Alfred Weeks, a fertilizer manufacturer from Massachusetts, Eden rose, buttoned his slate-gray suit jacket, and excused himself to go and join them.

Alfred's greeting was enthusiastic, his florid face beaming with a smile. "Eden, by George, I was hoping you would give me another chance to talk to you. Lucio, here, has offered me an opportunity to invest in his holdings, and since you've turned down my offer, I might take him up on it."

"I told you, Alfred, partners tend to bring added complications no matter how much money is being made." With a cool gray-eyed gaze, Eden faced Lucio. "Don't you agree?"

"Sometimes the full story is never heard."

"That could be true. But actions, ah, Lucio, you won't deny they create powerful impressions. Suspicion between partners adds an element few can survive. You know that, Lucio. You had partners."

There was a threat in his voice that Lucio chose to ignore. "*Señor* Weeks, our talk should remain private. We will—"

"Nonsense, Lucio," Alfred cut in. "Eden may have refused my offer, but I wish his opinion. After all, he does have claims near your own holdings, and the sum we spoke of is substantial. What do you know about them, Eden?"

Eden didn't answer immediately. He glanced at Lucio, satisfied to see sweat break on his brow. With a nervous gesture, Lucio smoothed back his hair, and then, with the air of confidence restored, spread his jacket and hooked his thumbs in his vest pockets. Eden smiled to see the three silver nuggets dangling from his watch chain.

"Do you still think they bring you luck, Lucio?" he asked in a silky voice.

"Always."

"Be that as it may, gentlemen, I really would like an answer, Eden."

"I believe, *Señor* Weeks, that he will not answer you," Lucio stated. "Our claims may be located in the same area, but his reasons for refusing your generous offer may be based on his reluctance to have his holdings seen. It is true that you have hired armed guards, is it not?"

"See here, Lucio, I'll not listen to an impugning of Eden's reputation."

"There's no need to defend me, Alfred. Lucio and I understand each other perfectly. However, since you insist that I render my opinion, I suggest that you send your own chemist down to inspect his holdings and analyze samples of his phosphate before the end of the month. I'll even lend your man my equipment to do the tests. If they bear out Lucio's claims, your half-million dollar investment will more than triple. You did offer him the same amount, didn't you?"

Alfred colored. "I hadn't quite got 'round to setting my offer."

Eden smiled. His eyes reflected the predatory slant of his thoughts. "Send Edward Soams, Alfred. He's one of your best. Now, excuse me," he added, glancing at his own watch, "seems it's time for my appointment with the London agent. Have a good day, gentlemen."

"Good man," Alfred remarked, sensing nothing amiss, as Eden walked away. "I'll do as he said and send Soams down before the end of the month."

"I thought we were ready to come to an agreement today," Lucio protested, watching Eden's back.

"Well, now, Lucio," he said, rocking back on his heels, "it was careless of Eden to reveal how much I offered him. But since he did, I'm prepared to offer you the same, after I have those reports."

Lucio wasn't listening, but he did agree, "*Sí*, it was most careless of him." His dark eyes narrowed. If he did not have the money he needed to remain solvent quickly he would lose everything. He had failed to remove one remnant of his past, but this time there would be no failure. If it was the last thing he did, he would destroy Eden McQuade.

* * *

Eden made one stop before he boarded the evening train. When he arrived in Rainly, he fired off another telegram to his brother, Paradise, engaged Luther's cooperation for what he planned, and decided to walk over to Jake's house, where he knew Dara would be. There was a sense of coming home as he walked down Charleston Street, shopkeepers greeting him by name, his own charming manner no longer a facade, but one of genuine caring. When did he make the conscious decision to remain here? Eden didn't know, but the restlessness inside him eased the moment he thought of Dara. He fingered the box in his jacket pocket, impatience guiding his steps when Matt hailed him from the store porch.

"Dara's still at Anne's. The doc sent Jake home this afternoon, and Sophy's there helping." Matt waited until Eden crossed over to him, admiring the hand-tailored fit of his suit. "When you get Dara, tell her not to worry 'bout supper. Miss Loretta sent Annamae over with all the fixings."

"Doc take your father's cast off today?"

"Yeah, and he's in a dither 'bout the itching. Eden, I gotta tell you something."

"What is it, Matt?" he asked with impatience.

"Before you go over there, you should know that Clay was in town. Damn angry, too. He was talking big 'bout taking over for Jake while he's mending. Said you had—"

"Will you slow down! Did he see Dara?"

"I'd guess. He went there. Don't see what—Eden, are you gonna marry her?"

"Don't you think that's between us, Matt? Why don't you tell me the rest about Clay?" he suggested, knowing that Matt asked the one question he wasn't ready to answer.

"He was mouthing off 'bout you not having the right to hire Jesse's boy Lyle to take over for Jake. Said that you needed to have yourself taken down to size, and Rainly wasn't your town. He was bragging that when he was done with you, you'd turn tail and run just like you did before. What was he talking about, Eden?"

"Nothing." He bit off the word, already striding away.

After Suelle arrived and agreed to spend the night—for Anne and Jake both needed care—Eden escorted Dara home. He listened to her account of Anne's refusal to talk to Jake and his own heartbreaking tears of blame that she couldn't stop no matter what she said. Dr. Vance had come and pronounced Anne out of danger, although he cautioned Dara to watch for fever. It wasn't the fever that worried Dara, it was the bitterness Clay's visit provoked in Anne, but she couldn't tell Eden about that.

He waited, and by the time they entered her house, Eden knew she would not tell him without his asking. Cyrus demanded to know if his trip to Ocala had been a success, and for a while their talk was of the contract he negotiated with a London agent to deliver a large shipment of phosphate by the first of the new year.

"Three thousand tons at twenty-five dollars a ton should net you seventy-five thousand dollars," Cyrus stated.

Eden smiled. "Well, I'll gross that much from the first shipment. If things work out the way I planned, I'll have this one account supplied on a quarterly basis."

"Figure yourself to get rich?"

"I might, Cyrus. I might just do that."

Dara was proud, she said as much, but avoided his direct gaze whenever she could. He bided his time and after supper asked her to walk down by the river with him.

The night scents bloomed around them as they headed away from the noise of town, Eden's memory recalling the first time he had walked here and its pervading silence. When the lights had faded into a far distance, he stopped, leaning against a tree, and without a word, he drew her against him, content to hold her. "I know you're hurting, love, share this with me. You don't need to be brave alone."

Her body softened and curved to fit the rough contours of his, and Dara absorbed his warmth and strength as the parched earth would welcome life-giving rain. She cried as he gently held her, and when done, her voice shook with the force of her feelings. "It was not knowing what to say or do to make Jake and Anne realize they still had each other. They both wanted this child so much, and she screamed her hate at him, blaming him for the loss. He cried, Eden, and all I could do was hold him when she turned away. Love shouldn't be that way."

"Sometimes, Dara, sorrow can make love strong, and there are other times, when love is divided between others, that it falls prey to destructive forces who know only hate."

She lifted her head from his shoulder and gazed up at his face. "You knew that Clay was there?"

"I knew."

"He told Anne that Jake knows who shot him. That it was his fault she lost the baby." Her palm closed over his lips, stopping the flood of swearing. "No, I don't want more of grief and fighting and hate." She cradled his cheek, one fingertip rubbing the thickened edge of his sideburn, and a warming glow spread inside her. Every breath she drew brought to her the light scent of bay rum and the heated essence that was wholly male, Eden's alone. The love she had for him flowered, and she thirsted for the blissful peace he brought to her, until the minutes passed and, with them, the bitter helplessness of her day.

"What more can I give you, love?"

He dragged his lips across her palm, and her throat grew tight, her pulse softly beginning to pound. Dara slid her fingers into the thickness of his hair, glorying in the smooth glide of his mouth down the arched expanse of her throat, the tightening of his arm around her waist, the gentle thrust of his leg between her own. Need shafted with lightning-like intensity to every nerve ending in her body. His name was a whispered plea from her lips as she scattered kisses over the bronzed skin of his face. She wanted the celebration of all that meant life with new beginnings to chase the specter of death.

Eden responded to her silent command, guiding her hips up and into him, the impelling force of his knee hard and tense between the layers of cloth that hid her trembling warmth from him. Desire spread like fire-licked brandy inside him, and his mouth claimed hers with a fevered intensity.

Shimmering peaks of ecstasy danced out of reach with his ever-deepening kisses, with the chafing abrasion of cloth that separated his skin from hers, and Dara shied away from voicing her need, showing him with every aching move of her body what she wanted.

"Tell me, love," he whispered, his own breathing ragged. "Tell me," his softly sensuous voice demanded while he stroked the lush fullness of her breast. He drank the soft moan from her lips and lifted his head, watching the play of the new moon's light on her passion-soft features. "No secrets, love," he insisted, his long fingers lightly caressing all but the already erect peak of her breast.

"Eden . . . I . . . please . . ." She clung to his shoulders, her hips pressed against him, the sear of his touch spreading and spreading . . . and it became a delicious torment to keep silent despite his coaxing voice.

"Whatever you want," he promised, lowering his head, his lips tantalizingly close. "Show me, love."

The provocative whispers curled inside her, desire kindling already heightened senses. He raised his head, brushing her lips with a delicate touch. The press of his rising knee, the slow up and down glide he maintained with a devastating expertise, built the quiver in her body, and he waited, his kisses enticing until she clung, shuddering, as white heat raced inside her. "Anything, love." He slid one bronzed hand beneath the cluster of linens and her skirt, caressing the thin-clad silkiness of her inner thigh and with one finger gently pressed the fine cambric against the already dampened heat of her.

"You," she breathlessly implored moments later. "I want you."

Her avid kiss stole his own whisper, but its echo lingered in his mind until a long while later, when, with a shuddering groan so intense that he shook, Eden found his own release and murmured, "I'm yours, love."

The light fall of rain forced him to return her home, and Eden found himself unable to let her go, but their kisses held a bittersweet flavor. He finally withdrew his mouth from the pouting fullness of hers.

"Listen to me, Dara. I said there would be no secrets between us. I want—"

Her laugh was full and sultry, that of a woman sure of her sensual power over one man. "How can you think we have any secrets after we . . ." She had to whisper the rest in his ear, her cheeks flushed, but the reward for being so bold resulted in the hard press of his body against hers.

"Tease me so wickedly, love, and I'll . . ." He didn't finish, for she tilted her head back, her arms around him, and her eyes were dark with a woman's promise. "I adore you," he murmured, stroking the tantalizing sheen of her lips. He did adore her, her delight in finding her own sensuality, the loss of shame attached to it, her shyness in demanding that her own desire for him be filled. But it was her quiet strength and the love that she offered him in every way but with words that made it hard to leave her. He admitted that Dara brought him a peace he had never known.

He had to fight the distraction she presented. "You will listen to me," he insisted, but the demand was softened by the satisfied male smile that curved his lips. "I'm going to stay out at the mine for a few weeks. I wanted to be the one to tell you so there are no misunderstandings of where I am or why."

"Eden, what's wrong?"

"It's nothing for you to worry about. I have a matter that needs my attention, and I can't work it out from here. I'll try to see you . . . oh, love, how can I stay away when you look at me like this."

"Then don't," she whispered against his lips, offering him a silent promise not to make demands, not to hold him, but aching with the need to hear a promise from him.

"I was going to wait to give you this," he said,

reaching into his inside pocket and handing her the velvet box.

Dara stared at the box he thrust into her hands, but she made no move to open it. When she finally dragged her head up, she couldn't meet his gaze. "You've made a grave mistake, Eden. I cannot accept this."

"*Cannot?* Did you think I'd bring you the more proper gifts of flowers and candy? Or a book of poetry, perhaps?" She looked at him then, her eyes snapping with anger, and he added, "You couldn't think that I'm offering this as a form of payment, could you? Open it, Dara."

She had heard that tone of voice once before when she had accused him of everything that Clay believed about him. Dara shook from the chill of it. But what else was she to think? Gentlemen did not bring ladies a gift of jewelry. She wasn't so innocent that she didn't know men often lavished such items on their mistresses.

"If I was going to pay you for services rendered, love, I'd need to buy you diamonds until you couldn't walk from the weight of them. Please," he intoned, his voice amiable in a sarcastic fashion and so, so soft, "never believe that I valued the price of your virginity so cheaply. Or could this charming display of prim reluctance be due to your seeing Clay this afternoon? Did he make you another offer? I couldn't blame him. I did promise that you would wear a smile that women would envy and men would kill to have for their own. And you wear it well, love," he snarled with barely controlled fury.

Dara bolted through the open doorway, shaking with rage. She barely managed to control it before turning around to face him. "You sanctimonious fool! If I do wear that smile, it's because I love you!" Before Eden could move, she slammed the door, turning the key with the sense of locking him out of her life. She was forced to lean against the door, knowing she could no more rid herself of him then she could stop breathing, and stared down at the box clutched in her hand.

Tension and anger drained from her the exact moment he walked away, and that's when she opened the box.

Tears blurred her vision as she traced the delicate gold links of a chain, but she had to search for her spectacles before lifting the gold heart at its end from the satin bed to read the elegant script.

"*Divide all but your love. Eden.*"

Dara ran out after him, calling his name, but he was already gone.

Chapter Seventeen

EDEN PRIDED HIMSELF on his patience but found this past month had nearly depleted his store. The wait for the chemist to arrive and begin his test of Lucio's claims, the demands of stepped-up production of his own mines, and the constant ache of missing Dara, had all taken their toll.

"Well, that's the last of the samples, Mr. McQuade. I know once Mr. Weeks has my report, he'll be most grateful for your advice. Saved him from giving *Señor* Suarez the other half—"

"You mean he already gave Lucio half the money?"

"So he said," Edward Soams replied, gathering up his papers. "If you'll be kind enough to provide me with a ride back to town, I'll send him a telegram immediately stating that the claims are worthless."

"You do that, Edward," Eden responded with a satisfied smile.

"Unlike your own," the chemist remarked, glancing at the wooden shelves lining the mine office where samples of both colorless and faintly yellow phosphate in their waxlike consistency rested. "I've never tested samples so rich."

"I know. And Edward, make sure that Mr. Weeks is informed of all *Señor* Suarez's holdings in Rainly. The land, the buildings, and the businesses he owns should go a long way toward compensating him for the loss of his cash."

"Will you be making him an offer, then?"

"I might, Mr. Soams, I just might." Eden no longer questioned his decision to destroy Lucio financially. A well-placed bullet would have ended the matter. One shot, and he would have had his revenge for past losses, for Jake being set up and wounded, and for the death of Jake's unborn child. He was aware that once Jake was well, he would go gunning for Lucio. Eden had to prevent Lucio's death from staining their lives as both he and Jake tried to forget their past and begin anew.

Greed drove Lucio to indiscriminately destroy anyone who came in contact with him. Lucio was a man who thrived on the power his wealth gave him. Eden's predatory instinct was to bait a trap from which his prey could not escape.

Alfred Weeks, for his own perverse reasons, delayed rescinding his offer to Lucio for almost ten days after he had forwarded his chemists' reports.

"This time I will kill him!"

"Stop shouting, Lucio. Surely you haven't spent the money Mr. Weeks invested?" Satin asked, her slumberous gaze watching Lucio pace back and forth in her suite.

"*Sí*. I spent it. There were pressing matters I could not ignore. And now I have incurred additional debts to have my samples independently tested to prove that this man was a fraud."

"Was he? Or did Eden manage to falsify the reports?"

"This does not matter. Not now. I must recover the money."

"Can't you just be satisfied with the reports that Regis and Chauvenet sent you from St. Louis? They are certainly respectable chemists in their own right. You shouldn't have a problem getting other investors, Lucio."

"Where do you suggest that I find them? Not in this state, now that word is given. I would need to travel to New York, and that, my dear Satin, takes money. These men would expect me to entertain them in style."

Satin rose, drawing her silken wrapper tight. "I can't see where killing Eden would solve your problems."

"If you have developed a tendre for him, you could not. He will never care for you, *querida*."

"Tell me, Lucio, did you have Jake shot?"

His black eyes snapped with anger and he stopped long enough to pin her where she stood. "Why do you ask me this?"

Satin shrugged. "Just a bit of feminine curiosity, that's all."

"Do you know why, my lovely?"

"So you did order it."

"And this upsets you? No matter. It was necessary. He was asking questions. There was some talk that he had found evidence he would present to the prison board about the convicts."

Satin turned her back to him so he couldn't see how her hand shook filling a glass with whiskey. "And Eden, what do you plan for him?"

"Since he has pitted himself against me and determined my ruin, I will retaliate."

"How, Lucio? Tell me how."

"So demanding?" he asked, coming to stand behind her. His hand brushed the fall of her black hair away from her neck. "Would you think to betray me, Satin?"

She set the glass down untasted, leaning back against him. "Do you have reason to believe I ever would, Lucio?"

"I must never," he answered, lifting her into his arms. "It is much too late for you to warn him, so I will tell you what I planned."

Eden didn't waste time wondering who had started the fire and said as much to Matt. "Just get the men organized to keep the fire away from the dredging machine. I don't care how it got started, just be thankful whoever it was was careless and used the new fence for kindling." Time and again as he worked furiously alongside his men, Eden glanced at the dredging machine that had just arrived from England and wasn't paid for. He had counted on the increased productivity the machine would supply to meet his contract demands, since it was warranted to take a ton of phosphate at a time and swing it directly into cars. Water from the nearby river was plentiful, but it was long after midnight, and the men were exhausted from their day's labor. He ordered several men to wet down the wood racked up for firing the steam engines which furnished power to operate his machinery. Eden cursed long and hard at the hour's loss to rouse the men and get them working as a single unit, passing filled water buckets down one line and sending back the empty ones down another. He had known that Lucio would find some way to retaliate after what he had done, and it was thanks to the vigilance of his guard that the fire had barely spread before the man sounded his alarm.

Eden destroyed his new fencing, toiling long into the night to help dig a shallow trench to ensure that no ember of fire could spread to the pits themselves. Phosphate dust exploded into brilliant white flames as it was ignited, but they died out quickly. Exhaustion threatened to overtake Eden and his men, but he drove himself, and them, to make the area safe. The wooden walkways would burn up like so much kindling, dried as they were from the sun. It was dawn before men found places to sit at the edge of the forest. Eden joined Matt.

"I swear to you I don't know how it got started, Eden."

"I know."

Matt wiped the soot from his face, already sweating. "What're you gonna do?"

"I'm heading into town. You stay here and let these men rest today. I'll round up as many of the second crew as I can find and send them out to you."

"It's Suarez, ain't it? He's the one behind all these accidents we're having. Come to think of it, the first one happened right after you went to Ocala last month. This have something to do with the chemist Soams?"

Eden grinned. "What do you think?"

Matt gripped his arm as Eden started to rise. "Was he behind Jake's being shot, or was it Clay?"

"I believe it was Lucio."

"And that's why you want to get even with him? For shooting Jake?"

"No, that's not all. We go back a ways, the three of us, Matt. Someone was killed and Lucio controlled the town. Jake was forced to run or they would have hanged him, and I had to cut my losses and move on."

Matt released his arm and stared up at him. "Are you gonna kill him?"

Eden looked away to where the sun rose in a splendor of gold and rose streaks across the sky.

"Eden?"

"If I have to."

But Lucio wasn't at the Gilded Lily as Eden expected. Or so Satin claimed, refusing to open the door to him. His continued search of the town came up empty. Eden's rage was controlled, for the fire was only the last in the mishaps that had plagued him these last weeks. Dynamite was discovered before they began working on a newly opened pit. Two weeks later a second charge had been set in his own sleeping quarters. The third attempt was sabotage, not the planned murder, only because he had called a halt to work due to the extreme heat of the day. His men were far from the empty barge anchored and waiting to be filled when it blew up. He had been pushing himself to the limits to be alert, and it had been four weeks since he had seen Dara. Catching sight of himself in a storefront window, Eden was convinced he had better clean up before he did see her. Lucio would surface. He always did.

Eden never glanced down by the river as he entered Miss Loretta's boardinghouse. If he had, he would have noticed Lucio walking with a satisfied smile toward the Owenses' store.

Dara was thankful that Mondays were usually slow in the store. She sat perched on her stool behind the counter, engrossed in her accounts, and didn't hear Lucio enter until he spoke.

"*Señorita*, a pleasant day to you."

Startled, Dara sat up, pushing her glasses back in place. "*Señor* Suarez."

"Your papa, he is well?"

"Yes. He's gone for a walk over to the train station. Dr. Vance suggested that he try and get about to strengthen his leg. But you didn't come in to ask about my father, did you? Was there something you wanted?"

"A few minutes of your time, that is all."

Dara slid off her stool, closing her book. "I can't imagine what we could have to talk about. Your man of business was in to pick up your account's standing on Saturday."

"The matter I wish to discuss is not of a business nature. It is personal."

"Gracious, whatever can you be talking about?" But when she tried to smile, she couldn't. The way the man glanced up and down the aisle before he leaned against the counter and removed his hat frightened her. "If there is some personal problem, I think you should see my father."

"It most directly concerns you. My varied business interests keep me from displaying as much interest as I wish in what happens in town. It is the high esteem which I hold for you and your father, *señorita*, that forces me to come to you."

"Forces you? Why?"

"You are fond of *Señor* McQuade, are you not?" he asked, his black eyes intent upon her face.

Dara merely nodded, wary of what he was leading up to. Without conscious thought she raised her hand to feel beneath her pleated shirtwaist for the outline of the golden heart she had been wearing this past month.

"And what do you know of the man, *señorita*? Has he told you of his past?"

"I don't believe it is any business of yours if he did. Now, excuse me. I must finish my work."

"Please, I do not come to upset you. I am here as a friend. Your father, he is most kind. I would not wish to see you hurt unnecessarily, that is all."

His smile did anything but reassure Dara. She knew she should discourage him, but a tiny voice nagged her to stay and listen. "Tell me."

"He is not an honorable man. There is the death of a woman between him and Jake Vario. I know the truth of this. I was there. Your *Señor* McQuade was a man to make others fear; he took what he wanted like an uncaring animal. Many times I talked, trying to stop him, but he would not listen. And the woman, she was lonely. There were many wrongs he was involved in, and I had gathered evidence to stop him. The woman, her name was Linda, she knew of this and followed him one night when she saw he would steal from me. She was foolish in her belief that he might care for her and confronted her. They struggled and your *Señor* McQuade killed her. He ran and never has he been brought to justice."

Dara was furious. She recalled the day Anne tried to tell her the same story. She refused to believe Anne, just as she refused to give credence to this man's outrageous lie.

"I'm afraid you have wasted your time, *Señor*. I don't believe you. Eden could never kill a woman. No matter what the provocation. Now, if you will—"

"A moment, *por favor*. Do not be so quick to dismiss what I tell you. I swear by all my ancestors that it is the truth."

It wasn't his words that stopped Dara from turning her back on him, it was the watch chain he lifted from his vest pocket, dangling it until the three silver nuggets spinning around caught her attention.

"You have seen one such as these on the belt he wears, have you not? The woman, she gave these to me before she died in my arms. They were in the safe when he stole money and papers belonging to me that I had painstakingly gathered for the judge when he would come. Linda grabbed the four nuggets, but he took one. To me, they hold a great deal of value, not for their being silver, but for their being the first nuggets we took from our mine. I, fool that I was, joined Señor McQuade and Jake Vario as a partner in their silver mine. I gave them *mucho dinero*. Do you still doubt me, *señorita*?"

His gloating tone was not asking her to answer, but it grated on Dara's nerves. She crushed the material over her heart pendant, feeling strength flow from the depth of the love she had for Eden.

"I wouldn't go about repeating this tale to anyone, *Señor* Suarez. Eden McQuade isn't likely to sit back and allow you to besmirch his reputation with a vile story."

Lucio always knew when to cut his losses. He replaced his hat and slipped the watch chain into his pocket, but added, "I believe you will be sorry that you did not heed my timely warning. Good day, *señorita*."

"Good riddance," she muttered under her breath, glad to see the last of him. "If he had any sense, he wouldn't dare to repeat that story to anyone."

Yet ten minutes later that is exactly what Lucio was doing, repeating his story with a slight variation for Anne. And he smiled many times in the retelling, for the pale features were lit with the flush of fury, and the blue eyes, so lifeless when he first called, reflected the bitterness of her loss and the glitter of hate.

When he finally took his leave, Anne was almost sorry to see him go. She felt alive for the first time since the night she had lost her child. There was a smug smile on her lips as she thought of how to get even with Eden. He had become the focus she pinned her fury on, for turning her husband against her brother, for costing Clay the woman he loved. Once and for all she wanted an end to Jake's dependency on him. Clay would have to be told. He would know what to do.

She paced, growing frantic at the thought of how she could escape. Early wouldn't let her have a carriage, and there was the risk of Jake trying to stop her. He had taken to leaving her alone so much, just when she needed him the most, but that, too, was Eden McQuade's fault. He had hired Jesse's boy to take Jake's job, and she knew her husband was afraid that the town would want to make the change a permanent one. Jake had nightmares about the hangings he couldn't prevent, but he was wrong to blame her brother. Clay simply did what Jake didn't have the courage to do.

Gazing out the front windows, eyes fevered with the need to get away, Anne focused on the two men across the street. They were struggling to mount a wooden sign, but all she saw was one word: livery. She studied the men, did not know either of them, and knew there was a chance they might not know her or of Jake's forbidding her to leave the house.

To the litany of hurry, she dressed, then slipped across the street to rent a horse and carriage. Soon she was whipping the spirited mare over back lanes that circled the town. She had to get to Clay. He would know how to talk to Eden. He could make that man leave town.

Eden's thoughts were of a similar nature concerning Lucio. There had to be a way to make him leave town short of killing him. He was lying back in a tub of hot water, soaking away the fatigue of the last few days, leisurely enjoying his cigar and a large glass of bourbon. He was tired of contemplating Lucio's next move once he had heard that his latest attempt to halt production had failed.

With an abrupt turn to his thoughts, Eden smiled. He would rather think about the challenge a number of varied receptions from Dara would present him. And he knew he would have to make a decision about her soon.

His eyes closed and his thoughts drifted. He would love to show Dara New York, for Dice would open the doors of the city's elite for them. His brother would find her charming, and for himself he could spoil Dara, dressing her in silks, laces, and satin that would set off her dark beauty. After installing her in a suite at the Waldorf-Astoria, there would be dinners at Delmonico's and Sherry's with their sumptuous menus, a stop at Rector's, Dice's favorite, and then the theater. He wondered what Dara would think of the likes of Diamond Jim Brady and Bet-A-Million-Bates. They were rough and brash and rich, given to excesses that shocked even New York's sophisticated crowd. In his mind Eden relished Dara's wide-eyed gaze on the new mansions springing up on Fifth Avenue. He would impose on his old friend, Ward McAllister, to invite them to one of the Astors' balls. And his sweet little saint would utter her outrage at the vulgar display of the new millionaires, never counting him among them. But he could indulge her every wish and more than a few of his own. Time was all he needed.

The water cooled and he brought an end to his fanciful thoughts rising to wrap a towel around his hips just as the door burst open. Eden had his gun in hand before Jake stepped over the doorsill. With a muffled curse, he set it down, noting Jake's frantic look.

"What's wrong," he asked, stepping out of the tub.

"I can't find Anne," Jake answered, running his large hand through his hair.

"Let me dress," was all Eden replied, struck by two thoughts. Jake didn't panic without reason, and Lucio wasn't in town. He didn't voice his thoughts to Jake, but dressed in haste, asking Jake where he had looked and whom he had spoken to. Eden merely nodded when it appeared that Jake had covered all the logical places Anne would have gone. Strapping on his gunbelt, Eden then grabbed his hat. "Do you think it possible that Clay came into town and took her out to the farm?"

"She's still in pain. Anne wouldn't have been able to withstand the ride out there. She's been withdrawn and bitter these last few weeks. Hell, you know that. But this time, Eden, I'm afraid." Jake couldn't meet his gaze, and the admission wasn't an easy one for him to make. "She doesn't want to try to forget. Anne blames me for losing the baby. Clay planted that thought in her head. I should have killed him," he stated with a gleam of hate in his eyes.

"Stop it! You wouldn't have killed him even if you knew what was going to happen. Anne is too important to you to risk losing her. And you would have if you'd hurt Clay in any way. We'll find her, Jake. And this will pass. It was the shock of all that's happened. But," he added, coming to stand beside him, "you would make things easier if you could try and remember who called your name last night."

"You think I'm lying?"

Eden studied his friend's ravaged features. "I don't know, Jake. Are you?"

"No."

"Then let's go find your wife."

Chapter Eighteen

"WHAT THE HELL do you mean that you won't help me!" Incensed, Clay faced Pierce.

"What you're planning to do is wrong, Clay. I can't destroy his mine to help you in this sick revenge. And it is sick. So much that it's eating you alive. Hasn't there been enough killing? Why go after Eden? My sister had a right to make a choice between you two. Anne was wrong to come out here and—"

"Are you saying that my sister lied to me? You know Jake's past. You know that he's friends with that scum, and you can stand there, telling me that you'll let a filthy murderer live. Or have you got a yellow streak, boy?"

With a flinty-hard look Pierce faced Clay. "I haven't been a boy for a long time. I went along with everything you planned, kept quiet when I wanted to speak up, and I wake, sickened every night, over hanging those three men. If that makes me a coward, Clay, then yes, I am one. I don't want a part in any more killing. Fight it out man to man with McQuade if you're determined to. But leave me out of plans that would kill other men—*innocent* men—who labor for him. Think about what you're planning."

"You're a fool if you can't see that my way will rid us of both McQuade and Suarez. Everyone knows they're out to destroy each other. If anything more happens at McQuade's mine, that bastard will be blamed. If McQuade gets killed, all the better. He helped ruin this town. He stole Dara from me with all his smooth city ways. If you won't help me, I'll find someone who will."

Pierce gritted his teeth. "You can't. Most of the men feel the way I do. We were wrong to hang those men. Even Hank admitted that this vigilance committee isn't right the way you want to run it."

"Then you're all yellow. I'll do it myself. And then we'll see who's right."

"Clay, they like Eden McQuade. He's been fair with—"

"I don't want to hear another damn word about that bastard!"

Pierce made his decision just as Clay turned from him. He grabbed his arm, but Clay was ready and stunned Pierce with the force of his blow. A second punch knocked him to the ground, where Pierce, dazed, looked up to see fury tinged with madness in Clay's eyes.

"I'll kill any man that tries to stop me," Clay grated from between clenched teeth, his fists curled tight at his sides.

Pierce had the sense to realize that he was no match for Clay. He sat on the ground, rubbing his jaw, watching Clay walk away.

He knew what he had to do, but it left a bitter taste in his mouth. The admission that he had placed his faith and loyalty in the wrong man hurt him. He had turned on his sister, alienated his brother, and for nothing. With the same dogged stubbornness that made him follow Clay so blindly, he got up, intent on stopping Clay. He rode out minutes later for Eden's mining site, hoping his brother would be there.

Matt, soot-grimed and exhausted, faced his brother with a cynical look. "You expect me to believe you give a damn about what happens to Eden?"

"I told you the truth, Matt. Clay intends to stop him any way he can. He's sick. It's almost like he's obsessed with a hate that's eating inside him. I came to warn you. What you do from here is up to you."

They had never been close, but Matt, with his own maturity, saw his brother in a new light. "Why did you go along with them, Pierce? You've always been a gentle man. I remember how you hated to go hunting with me and Jesse's boys. I saw you once when you lowered your site to miss a clean shot. Just couldn't understand it."

"You never said anything."

"I guess I didn't want them to make fun of you. It don't matter. Ah, hell, I don't even know why I mentioned it now. We just don't see things the same, don't think we ever did."

Pierce gazed at his younger brother, his lanky frame filled out by the hours of his labor, the ease with which he wore a gun, and Pierce found himself regretting the lost years. "I guess you're right. We've chosen different paths, and you've a right to yours. My way will leave me haunted by those men's deaths."

"You did what you thought was right at the time," Matt said, reluctantly admitting that his brother had another kind of courage to say this to him.

"Maybe. I can't go back and undo what's done. But believe this, if nothing else. Eden McQuade has been good for you. He taught you it's right to stand by your own convictions. I'm sorry that I wasn't there for you, Matt. Tell him about Clay. It's the closest I can come right now to making my own peace with him and Dara."

"You hurt her taking up for Clay."

"I know that. It's another regret to live with."

"She finally saw Clay for what he was. I don't think he could've made her happy, not like Eden. So don't be so hard on yourself, Pierce."

"Then make sure that McQuade stays alive for her."

Matt nodded, but when he turned away, Pierce stopped him.

"Be careful, little brother," he said with a grin. "I'd like to think we'll have a chance to get to know each other. And if you need me, Matt, I'll try and be there for you this time."

"Go see Dara, Pierce." Their handclasp was firm, their eyes vulnerable for a moment with remembered flashes of the past, but when Matt left him, it was with a silent promise that he could count on his brother. If his step had a swagger and his voice was sharp giving orders to double the guards, Matt didn't notice, but Pierce did with pride for the man his brother had become.

Matt left the mining site after he was assured that he had done all he could to make it secure. Eden could not afford a work stoppage for any reason if he was to meet the quota his contract with the London agent called for. He wanted Eden on site, but he hesitated before taking the road to town. Eden could have gone looking for Lucio at any one of his claims. Some instinct guided him toward Rainly.

He was furious to learn from Early that Eden had ridden out with Jake hours ago to search for Anne.

"Leave my horse saddled," Matt ordered. "I'll stop home and see if Dara knows where they went. You see either one of them, Early, you tell them to watch out for Clay."

"Sure thing, Matt. Don't reckon I'd've figured him to take things this far. Can't rightly understand it. But you'd best warn Jesse's boy, too."

Matt took his advice, cursing with every passing minute until he located Lyle Halput mooning over the new millner in her shop next to the Gilded Lily. Lyle was quick to leave off his courting, and Matt left him after Lyle promised to keep a sharp watch. Filled with indecision, Matt stood before the shop, tilting his hat back, when he heard Satin call him.

"It's been a while since you've been by, Matt. Nellie was asking for you. Why don't you come inside and have a drink with us?"

"I ain't got time. I need to find Eden," he answered curtly.

"Something happen out at his claim?" she asked with sweet concern.

"Not if I can help it."

Satin measured him with a shrewd look. "Why don't you tell me what's troubling you, Matt? Maybe I can help."

He gazed at her, then away. He had Eden's warning not to trust her after he had confessed his gambling debt to him. A raise in pay helped him keep a smooth fit to his jeans, and Dara had been repaid. But he was worried that he had been away from the claim site too long. If anything happened while he was gone after Eden especially left him in charge, he wouldn't forgive himself. Satin coaxed him again. He knew Eden stopped there occasionally. He had to gamble on every chance he could.

"Maybe you can help," he said, and then proceeded to tell her what he had learned from Pierce. "Just warn

Eden," he finished, leaving her to cross back over to the livery.

Satin watched him go. Lucio would pay dearly for this information, and she had a score of her own to settle with Eden. No man refused her pleasure after a bargain was struck. She gazed up at the gilded facade of the building. A catlike smile creased her lips. Lucio had been draining the profits from her labors. It was time to put an end to it. Innocent Matt Owens had just handed her the stakes she needed.

As Matt rode west out of town, Eden and Jake were returning from the opposite end. They were dust-laden and discouraged, having stopped at every nearby outlying farm to ask if Anne had been there. Eden slowed and then drew rein in front of Dara's store. He couldn't explain his sudden need to see her, he just felt it.

Dismounting, he wrapped the reins over the hitching post. "Check if Anne's home. I'll just be a few minutes, and then we can ride out again. You might ask Early who else was in town. She could have ridden out to the Clares' or even to the Kinnels'."

"I'll see if Sophy's back from church. Early'll give us fresh mounts. So I'll meet you here."

There was no need for him to add that he wanted Eden to hurry. Every deepened crease in his face, the bleak look in his eyes, the slump of his shoulders, all conveyed Jake's desperation to find his wife. It was the first time Eden fully understood it.

The front of the store was empty, and he followed the sound of Dara's humming back toward the storeroom. He paused in the doorway, much the way he had the first time he had seen her. She was sweeping the floor with her back toward him. The sunlight added a glint of red to her dark hair and reflected off the glasses perched there.

He drank in the sight of her, speculation no longer in his gaze, for he knew that beneath all the prim clothes was a woman who equaled his passion. Yet it wasn't desire alone that stirred him. The gentle to and fro sway of her body, the soft, lilting tone of her voice, the sense of completeness made him realize that she was all the woman he wanted.

Eden knew he had never given any woman a hold over him. Yet need pierced him to have a hold on her.

"Dara." He called her name in a whisper, holding his breath for a frozen moment before she turned.

Joy lit her dark eyes. She dropped the broom and ran into his arms, murmuring his name over and over.

"I've missed you, love."

Dara gave him no chance to say more, her kiss as hungry as his. The weeks they had been apart, the very way they had parted, were forgotten in the minutes when passion ruled their senses.

He gathered her tight to his body, wanting to take her inside himself. She was all sweet surrender, her hands greedy to hold, to touch him, just as his were for her.

She knocked his hat off, tunneling her fingers into his hair. Fevered need spread inside her and she didn't notice her glasses falling to the floor. Dara didn't think she could get close enough to the hard press of his body, desperate for the reassurance that he was here kissing her. Their lips parted and came back quickly together, whispers begun were lost in the urgency of desire.

Eden craved everything she had to give him, his mouth ruthless in possessing the tantalizing sweetness of hers. Every one of her murmurs he heard, and those of missing him, needing, and lastly, of loving him, sank deep, deep inside him. *Love*. The force of what he felt for her assaulted his senses like a blow.

Dara felt the sudden tensing of his body. She clung shamelessly to him, tears misting her eyes, feeling complete as only Eden could make her. The deep hungry strokes of his tongue ceased abruptly. His kiss eased to brief touches. Her vow not to ask him for more than he was willing to give came back to haunt her. She accepted his tender kiss in place of the words she longed to hear. When his mouth left hers, trailing feather touches across her cheek, she was afraid that he would see her need in her eyes, but he drew her head against his chest, cradling her close.

"I can't stay long, Dara," he said, filling himself with the feminine scent of her. He caressed her back, his lips resting on her hair. "I promised to ride out again with Jake. We didn't find Anne."

"I didn't know you were with him," she whispered, listening to the pounding of his heart. Rubbing her cheek against the soft cotton of his shirt, she added, "Jake was here before . . . oh, Lord!" She wrenched herself free. "Eden, Lucio was—"

He hauled her against him, his grip painful on her arms, and the words died on her lips. Dara paled to see the fury on his features. She obeyed her instinct to wait until he had controlled it, not daring to breathe.

"Tell me," he grated from between clenched teeth. Her whimper made him ease his grip on her.

She searched the feral glitter of his eyes, afraid of what he would do, unable to speak, unable to stop the tremors of her body.

Her fear cut through his fury as nothing else could. "Just tell me what he said, Dara," he ordered softly with considerable effort.

"He tried to get me to believe that you killed a

woman," she said, eyes intent on his. "I didn't believe him, Eden. I knew you couldn't do such a thing."

He released her so suddenly that she stumbled, and not understanding, stared at him. He turned his back on her. She called his name, raising her hand, hesitating before she touched the rigid set of his shoulder. "Eden? Please, don't shut me out. I already knew. Anne tried to tell me this weeks ago at the box lunch social. I knew them for the lies they were about you. But if Lucio came here, he may have gone to Anne and told her more than she knew. I was afraid at the time that she would tell her brother. Anne thinks she hates you. She would believe anything Lucio told her."

"And you don't?" he snarled, spinning around.

Dara snatched her hand back. She had to force herself not to back away from the rage in him. It took several minutes of tense silence before she realized that it was not a rage directed at her.

She had to swallow before she answered him. "No, I don't."

"But Anne hates me," he ground out.

"She blames you unfairly for influencing Jake against Clay. She believes that you got the town to agree to hire Lyle to prove that Jake couldn't do his job. Please," she pleaded, "Anne's not well. No one can hold her accountable for what she believes. I'll talk to her. I'll tell her the truth."

"The truth?" he asked with a deadly derisive tone. "And what makes you think you know what it is? You don't know me. You weren't there in Hamilton or any of the other hellholes I've lived in to know what happened. So what the hell gives you the right to stand there and proclaim your unshakable faith in my less-than-lily-white past?"

His voice was flat, emotionless. Dara stared at him balanced before her on his powerful legs, all hard, lean masculinity, his eyes coolly assessing her with a wary, almost guarded look. She had to close her eyes against it, sensing deep inside herself that he needed to shock her, but she didn't understand why. Willing herself to be strong, she offered a brief prayer and chose the only way open to her. Once again her gaze targeted his, wide dark eyes that were direct. She stepped close enough to lift his hand, feeling the ridge of calluses on his palm, and raised it first to her lips, then placed his hand against the heart she wore.

"This is what gives me the right. I've worn it since the night you gave it to me, Eden. And I'm sorry that you never stayed to hear how much I regretted my refusal. The fault is mine that you were driven to such anger. But I believed this to be a promise from the man I love. Don't," she begged, "dare to tell me that it's a lie. Don't tell me that the man who gave me this heart doesn't deserve my faith and love."

Dara trembled in the moments that he stood there, wondering if he heard her or believed her. His eyes were such a hard slate gray, his finely molded lips that had taught her passion and laughter thinned with fury. She merely waited. Once before she had risked everything she believed in for this man. Now she felt as if she had gambled her very life on his accepting what she offered him.

Chapter Nineteen

RELEASING A SHUDDERING breath, Eden ran his finger through his hair. "You don't have a single doubt in your mind, do you?"

"Of my own feelings, no."

He brought his hand back to the outline of the heart, tracing it with his fingertip. Her face was lifted to his, that proud rounded chin set firmly, her lips slightly parted, her breaths tiny catches of sound, and those eyes filled with love. He spread his hand until he could feel the increased pounding of her heart beneath it.

The complete promise of herself that she made to him almost made him whisper the words he had never given to another woman. He didn't understand why he couldn't say them to her now, but he did know he had to tell her the truth. Once again he outlined the heart she wore.

"This wasn't a lie, Dara. Nothing between us ever was."

Slowly, almost afraid to demand intimacy from him, she lowered her head to his chest. "Will you hold me?" she asked softly, closing her eyes as his arms drew her tight to his body. "I'm not a lie. I love you, Eden." And then she told him everything that Lucio had said.

He was silent for a few minutes afterward, drawing her with him as he leaned against the back wall, stroking the tension from her.

"You make me feel humble with your faith, love," he said, and heard his own underlying vulnerability he had never before revealed to a woman. "But Lucio didn't tell you all lies. We were partners in a silver mine. I had worked for him years before in Mexico. When I struck a large vein of silver in a mine that Jake and I won near Hamilton, Lucio was there, offering us the additional money we needed. I believed I could keep control on Lucio's greed, but I worked out at the mining claim most of the time and wasn't watching what he was doing in town. Jake knew, but he had met Linda by then, and he was in love with her. When he came back to the site during the week, he never mentioned the rumors that were circulating about Lucio extending credit to anyone who asked.

"I never told Jake about the times Linda came up to the site knowing he was in town looking for her. And when playing up to me didn't get her what she wanted, she went after Lucio."

"Didn't you try to tell Jake about her?"

"Did you believe Lucio about me?"

"Well, no," she snapped, pulling back.

"Stay where you are. I missed holding you. Anyway, the same held true for Jake. He wouldn't have believed me. But she was a greedy little bitch who used him. Nothing he gave her was ever enough, and Jake began gambling. He never told me that he lost his third share in our mine to Lucio. When I found out, I didn't handle it well. Jake and I had a fight, and I took off to do some independent mine surveys."

When he didn't continue, Dara prodded him. "No secrets. Isn't that what you told me, Eden? I want to hear it all, but only so that I can understand why you were furious that he told me."

"Lucio somehow got hold of the reports that I signed for a group of eastern investors that said their mines were worthless. He forged my signature to other reports that he drew up, claiming these mines had rich deposits of silver and then he salted them—"

"Salted?"

"That's what we call it when someone takes silver from one mine and places it in another. When an investor wanted to inspect the claim to verify these reports before he paid for it, there was always silver to be found. That's why Lucio wears those nuggets. They were the first ones he took from our claim and used more times than I knew to bilk men of their money."

"But you have one of them. He said you took it from Linda."

"I did," he admitted, tension once more apparent in his voice. "She knew what Lucio was doing. Being what she was, Linda wanted her share, or she swore she would tell Jake and me what he was doing. Lucio refused to be blackmailed. Jake was furious that she had lost the diamond ring he won, which Luçio has now, and so she came to me."

Dara hugged him tight, sensing he didn't want to tell her the rest. "Lucio killed her, didn't he?" When he didn't confirm it, she tilted her head to look up at him. "Eden?"

"Linda came with me the night I went to Lucio's office to rob his safe. I wanted those reports, the list of men he had swindled, and the nuggets. Linda had other ideas. When I found what I needed, she pulled a gun on me." His voice went flat. "We struggled and the gun went off just as Lucio walked in. I didn't kill her, but she had a bullet graze on her side. Linda was backing away from me, saw Lucio, and tried to tell him that she was stopping me. He shot her. Lucio accused Jake of murdering her. Jake wasn't a fool—he ran. Lucio had enough power in that town to have him hanged."

"And you? What happened to you?"

"I took off after Jake and left the evidence behind. When I couldn't find him, I went back to town, and Lucio was waiting for me. A federal marshall was coming to investigate the complaints of mining fraud. My name was on the reports, the surveys, and some phony assay letters. He gave me a choice: leave town after I signed the mine over to him, and he would destroy the papers—or face the marshall. I thought about killing him but I still had the marshall and his charges to deal with. I cut my losses and Lucio got it all."

The last was said on such a bitter note that Dara had to lean back against his arms to look up at him. "Did you think that I could love you less for telling me?" she demanded. Her hand cradled his cheek. "Look at me, Eden McQuade. Right or wrong, you and Jake made choices. Was there a chance that Lucio could have turned on you and blamed you for Linda's murder?"

"My ever practical Dara, that was a distinct possibility."

"I'm glad you decided not to stay," she murmured in an effort to lighten both their moods. But there was no answering glint of humor in his eyes, no wicked grin on his lips. "Why do you still look as if the past were something to be ashamed of?"

"For pity's sake, Dara! Leave me some pride."

"No. This has nothing to do with pride. You told me everything and I'm still here, holding you. I want an answer."

"You didn't just get bold and sassy, you've got a right testy temper, too."

"Answer me."

He closed his eyes and leaned his head back. "No man lives easy with the knowledge that he ran from this kind of a fight."

"You're not going to run this time, are you?"

"No."

Nausea churned inside her. "You'll kill Lucio?"

"I'll stop him from destroying what I've built here." If his voice was flat and hard, his eyes, opened, intent on hers, were more so. "I'll stop him any way I can," he added. Suddenly he wanted her understanding of what he was committed to do.

Dara struggled to find the right words. She couldn't condone his killing anyone. But he didn't give her time.

"Will it change your feelings for me?"

Her gaze flashed anger. "Do you think so little of me to ask that? Am I so shallow a person to you?" She shoved against his hold, but he merely tightened his arms so she couldn't get away from him. "Did you really believe that I made love with you to satisfy my 'virginal curiosity,' as you so smugly termed it?" Her breathing was erratic and she poked her finger at his chest. "I said that I loved you. To me that means loving all of you; the strength, the very gentle caring, the infuriating arrogance, and the incredible joy you bring to me every time you make love to me. I know you believe that killing isn't the only answer, but you're a man that must live by his convictions."

Her hands suddenly framed his cheeks. "I respect you for having that kind of courage. You'll do whatever you need to do, Eden. That's all I can offer you." She bit her lower lip, took a deep breath, and knew she had to say the rest.

"I've had to make some choices that weren't easy

ones. I've turned my back on all that I was taught to believe as right. I have a brother who hates me for loving you." Her fingertips silenced his move to speak. "No. Listen. Nothing matters if you care for me. I can't divide my love," she whispered, tears filling her eyes. "I can't love a part of you, without loving all that you are."

Her hands slid down from his face and came to rest between them on his chest. For a long moment he gazed down at the delicate flush of her cheeks, then lowered his head, his lips kissing away her tears.

"Don't cry for me, Dara. Don't cry at all. I never meant to bring you tears," he murmured. "I told you once that you unman me with your honesty. You do, love, you do." He stole her cry with a kiss so shattering that they both shuddered from the intensity of its promise.

When he forced himself to end it, he saw the dazed look of her wide, dark eyes, her lips, parted and damp from the hungry strokes of his tongue, and he wished for time to say what had to be said to her.

But their time together was ended a moment later when Jake called out for him. Eden brushed his thumb over her satin-wet lips as if to take her breath and her taste with him. The quick shake of his head stopped her from uttering a sound as he left her.

He met Jake midway down the aisle. "I had to come and get you," Jake said first. "Matt's in town and so is Pierce. You'd better hear what they have to say."

"Anne wasn't home."

"No."

Eden stopped him from turning around. "I think I know where she went." His fingers clenched on Jake's arm. "Lucio was here and told Dara about Linda. He might have gone to your wife, too. If he—"

"I'll kill that bastard!"

"No. Lucio is mine. But there's a chance that if he told her, Anne may have gone to tell Clay. He'd use this against both of us."

"Don't ask me to believe that my wife would betray—"

"She hates me, Jake. Not you. And Clay will twist it all to get the farmers riled up."

"No. He wants to go after you himself. Christ! I don't want to go gunning for him."

"I didn't ask you to. I'll take care of Clay. As with Lucio, it's been between us for too long." But Eden recalled a man who once swore to him that this was his town, his future, and violence would not rule it. It was this thought and Dara's words of unshakable faith that made him speak out.

"Just think about the choices you're making, Jake. If you back down over Clay now, will you ever face yourself or these people again? Do you want to have a marriage built on lies?"

He didn't wait for Jake's answer, but brushed past him and nearly collided with Matt rushing in the front door. "What the hell are you doing here?" Eden bit off. "I gave you orders to stay out at the site."

"Where the devil have you been?" Matt demanded, ignoring his question. He blocked Eden's forward move. "Just wait a minute. Pierce!" he called, and watched as Eden stepped back. "You've got to listen to him. My brother came out to the mine to tell me what Clay plans to do. Clay's alone in this, no one's going to help him. I doubled the guards before I left, but I had to find you. When I couldn't, I was going back to the mine, but Pierce had figured to look for you, too. We rode back in together." Matt glanced at his brother. "Tell him."

Eden listened, losing his skeptical look, and when

Pierce was done, he made his decision. "Matt, stay in town and keep watch for Lucio. Don't go near him. He'd kill you if he thought you were in his way. I'll ride out to the mine. It's me that Clay wants."

"I'll stay with Matt," Pierce stated, his look daring Eden to deny him that right. When Eden didn't answer him, he added, "Or if you want, I'll ride out with you and try to talk to Clay again."

"You'd do that?"

Pierce straightened, looking up at the man who stood half a head taller. "Clay was wrong to think he could solve anything by hurting you or the other miners. I guess you're all here to stay, and we need to work together. My sister won't love him again, if she ever really did, and I can't respect him." It was the only way Pierce could think of to apologize.

"Stay with your brother, Pierce. And Matt," he said, putting his hand on the younger man's shoulder, "you did the right things."

"Pierce," Jake cut in, tension gripping him. "Did he say anything about Anne coming to see him?"

"She was there. I'm sorry, Jake. Whatever she told him seemed to trigger this crazy idea that he could destroy Eden's site and get rid of both him and Lucio."

Jake glanced at Eden. "I'll help you find Clay."

The four of them left the store, intent on what they had to do. Dara stood gripping the counter, having overheard them, and was stricken with the thought that they all could be killed. Running toward the doorway, she saw Eden and Jake ride off. Matt and Pierce were halfway down the street talking to Lyle and Jesse. The joy of knowing that Pierce had forgiven her and made his peace with Eden and Matt was overshadowed by fear. Not quite sure what she could do, Dara felt the need to do something. She left the store at a run.

Once again she found herself pounding on Anne's door, calling for her to open it. Jake didn't know of the days when Anne would lock herself inside, refusing to see anyone. She could have hid herself when he came home. Clay had to be stopped, but Eden could be hurt, unless she got there first. With both her and Anne there, Clay might be reasoned with, and if Anne refused to help her, Dara knew she would make her tell what she said to her brother.

Desperate now that minutes had passed, Dara spun around, undecided what to do. She walked to the edge of the porch and was about to step down when she saw Anne driving a carriage toward the new livery. Dara lifted her skirts and ran, reaching the stable before Anne did. She barely spared a glance at Anne's disheveled state.

"What did you tell Clay?" she demanded, shaking with fury. "Do you know what he plans to do at Eden's site? Men could be killed if he gets past the guards. Clay could be killed because of what you—"

"Stop it! I know! I tried to tell him that wasn't the way. He wouldn't listen to me. He went crazy. But it's not my fault. It's yours for leaving him!"

"Move over, Anne." Dara didn't give her time to decide. She climbed into the carriage, pushing Anne aside, grabbing the reins from her hands.

"What are you intending to do, Dara?"

"Here now!" a man yelled from inside the stable. "You can't be takin' . . ."

His words were lost as Dara snapped the leather against the mare's back, turning the carriage around.

"Dara! Answer me!" Anne screamed, watching her whip the horse so hard that the carriage rocked crazily.

"I'm going to stop him."

She avoided a chance meeting with Eden and Jake by taking little-used back lanes. And her thoughts were filled with the need to stop Clay from destroying all that Eden had worked for. More, she couldn't live with the guilt if Clay destroyed himself.

Chapter Twenty

CLAY HAD TO wipe his damp palms before he lovingly picked up the sticks of dynamite. He smiled at the ease with which he had eluded the guards walking the perimeter of Eden's land. With his old felt hat pulled low, his sweat-grimed clothes dusted with flour to give him the appearance of having worked with phosphate, he was just another worker to them. No one had called out, or tried to stop him from entering the small shed where he had found what he wanted. His fingertips caressed the smooth papery finish on the sticks while he planned where he would use them. Crouching in the musty shadows, Clay thought of the layout he scouted.

The largest of the pits was directly to the left of the shed. It was almost fifteen feet deep, but access could be had to its bottom by a number of wooden ladders placed around the earthern walls. Wooden walkways criss-crossed the bottom. He wouldn't have any trouble getting down there. If he could get hold of a shovel, he could plant the dynamite, light it, and be gone before it blew.

He wasn't going to wait.

Clay tucked the sticks beneath his shirt, opening two buttons for easy access. He clutched a small match safe in his hand and darted for the door. Sweat beaded on his face as he listened to two men lingering in front of the door.

"Eden said to keep a sharp watch. He's 'round here."

"You stay. I'll head over to the drying machine."

Clay searched in the gloom for a weapon. He wasn't going to be stopped before he did what he came to do. Barrels of blasting power and cases of dynamite were all he saw. There wasn't even a stray piece of wood lying around. He turned too fast, hitting a stack of barrels, but grabbed the topmost one before it fell. The door slammed open, and he froze a second before stepping back into the shadows.

"I heard you. Ain't no sense in hidin'."

"I can't walk. I twisted my leg. You'll have to help me." Clay watched as the man lowered the rifle, swearing that he couldn't see him. "Back here," he whispered.

He willed the man forward, then lunged when he was within reach, his powerful forearm cutting off the man's strangled cry. Clay lost track of time. Minutes or seconds passed—he neither knew nor cared. At last the weight of the man's limp body signaled that Clay no longer needed to choke him.

He looked toward the open door, but no alarm came, no one passed. But now he knew his time was short. They would be watching for him. He stood in the open doorway and saw Eden at the far edge of the pit, urging men to leave their work. A powerful surge filled Clay as he watched them scurrying for the safety of the ladders. He almost laughed. Eden was too late. He struck a wooden match, lit the fuses of the sticks he held, and ran forward.

"Eden! Oh, Christ!" Jake yelled, drawing his gun. "Clay, don't do it!" Jake aimed for Clay's raised arm—he didn't want to kill him—but the shot came a second too late, and the bundled dynamite flew high, arching out over the pit before its descent. Men flattened themselves just moments before it exploded.

Eden was up and running before the dust and wooden debris settled. He didn't see Dara fighting to stop the mare from rearing in fright, sawing on the reins until she thought her arms would be pulled from her body. Anne roused herself to help Dara, but it was the man leaning from his saddle that brought the mare under control.

Shaken, Dara stared at him. And then her gaze fell on the gun he held. Her throat closed. She couldn't scream for help. The men were shouting, running to help those who had been injured in the blast. No one would hear her, but she could see Eden.

"Get down," Lucio ordered. But as Anne moved to follow Dara, he stopped her. "Not you. You have already served me this day. She is the one I want." Without dismounting, Lucio urged his horse close enough to use his free hand to grab Dara's thick braid, yanking it free. At the press of his knees the horse stilled, and he dragged Dara up against his leg.

"I swore he would not live this time."

Dara didn't answer him. She wasn't going to goad him into killing her. And she had no doubt, looking up into the near blackness of his merciless eyes, he would do it.

Still holding her braid, he took up his reins and began walking his horse forward, dragging Dara with him.

"McQuade!" he shouted, firing his gun in the air to gain his attention.

Eden was kneeling beside Clay, with Jake across from him, when they heard Lucio's shot.

Eden's head snapped up. His eyes narrowed and the blood drained from his face. He thought his heart had ceased beating in that instant he saw Dara. Fear twisted his gut. His throat convulsed, a once familiar desert dryness sucked every bit of moisture from his mouth. He couldn't breathe. Every nerve ending in his body screamed for him to move; every sense warned him to be still.

Jake shifted his body.

"Don't move!" Eden snarled, focusing on Lucio's smile as he urged his horse forward a few steps. He had to force himself to look at Dara's white face, its starkness blending with the pristine shirtwaist. A tremble began deep inside him as he noticed the taut arch of her neck and the way her eyes closed tight against the pain of Lucio's yanking her braid. He swore he would break every bone in the hand that held her chained at his side. Blood surged hot as he felt a primitive need to protect what he claimed as his, followed by a rage unlike any he had known.

Eden released the breath he held, slowly rocking back on his heels, the move taking him away from Clay's body. He waited and when Lucio continued smiling, his black eyes snapping with challenge, he carefully came to his feet, arms held away from his sides, so that Lucio could see he made no move toward his gun.

Clay moaned.

"Shut him up," Eden hissed, barely moving his lips.

"Will you sacrifice yourself for her?" Lucio asked, his voice gloating.

"Let her go." Eden didn't wait. He opened his gunbelt buckle and let it fall to the ground.

"Eden, don't be a fool. He'll kill you," Jake whispered.

"Just you and me, Lucio. No guns. No interference."

Lucio laughed. "You take me for a fool, *amigo*." He

wrapped Dara's braid around his hand and dragged her backward, nudging his horse along with her.

Dara bit her lip, tasting blood to stifle the moan that rose. She wanted to scream at Eden to stay away. Lucio couldn't use his gun and watch her at the same time. But there was no way to convey that message to Eden. He was already walking forward. His steps were slow and measured, but she sensed his fury by the set of his body.

"Man to man, *amigo,*" Eden taunted in a flat voice, desperate to get him to release Dara. He fought the urge to curl his fingers into fists, refusing to give Lucio a clue to his rage.

Dara stumbled against the horse's side, refusing to move, and forced Lucio to stop.

"The lovely *señorita* has a delicate neck, no?"

"If you break it, Lucio," Eden warned, "I'll hunt you down and tear you apart."

"But you will be dead, *hombre*. It is a just price for what you took from me."

"I'll give you the money, Lucio. I'll repay what you owe Weeks and double it. Let her go."

"See how much value he places upon you," he murmured to Dara, snapping the braid like a taut leash. The move caught her unprepared for the pain, and she cried out.

Eden lunged forward. Lucio's shot kicked up dirt to the side of him. Dara twisted, reaching up with her hands, and raked Lucio's fist that held her hair. She struggled to get herself free despite the needlelike anguish tearing her scalp. Lucio couldn't control the horse. It was dancing in place, eyes rolling, and Dara tried to watch that she didn't get caught under its hoofs. The distraction she provided for Lucio was enough to send Eden running.

He tore Lucio from the saddle just as Dara managed to tear her hair from his grasp. Her head felt as if it were on fire, but she grabbed for the free-swinging reins, afraid that Eden would be trampled. Jake was suddenly beside her, his sharp jerk on the bridle bringing the horse's head down.

"Get back," he ordered her, taking the reins and jerking the horse after him.

She obeyed him, but her eyes were locked on Eden.

He straddled Lucio's body, his fingers wrapped around Lucio's wrist. Eden repeatedly banged Lucio's hand against the ground to make him release the gun.

Lucio managed to land a solid punch to Eden's jaw. With a sharp cry and sudden twist, he rolled away from Eden. His dark eyes were frantic. The gun lay in the dirt between them. He struggled to his feet, holding his wrist.

Eden came up in a fighter's stance, bloodlust blinding him. He was deaf to Dara's pleas to stop. He had eyes for no one but Lucio, eyes that watched the other man with a promise of death.

Lucio darted to his left, but Eden was there. Lucio spun around, running along the edge of the pit, stumbling over rocks and scraps of wood. There wasn't a sound to be heard over their harsh breathing. Not one man made a move to stop them.

Halfway around the pit Eden tackled Lucio. They rolled from side to side, and Lucio managed to land several blows on Eden's face until his head snapped back with the last one. Eden began an intense battering against Lucio, no matter how he squirmed to get free.

Locking his legs around one of Eden's, Lucio struggled to throw him off balance, his outflung injured hand groping for a rock. When his search was rewarded, he fisted it in his hand, repeatedly punching Eden's lower back.

Fire spread out from his kidney, and Eden fell back with a gut-wrenching cry. He lost whatever breath he had left when Lucio kicked his body free and was up, running again. Eden barely staggered to his feet when Jake reached his side.

"Finish it." He shoved a gun at Eden.

Shaking his head to clear the pain haze enveloping him, Eden wiped the blood from his mouth. "Not . . . that way," he bit off. His eyes found Lucio on the far side of the pit.

Men crowded Lucio in a single line so that he was forced to change direction. Eden was waiting back the way he had come. Lucio looked behind him at the dredging machine, and before Eden could move, Lucio was already scrambling awkwardly up the broad platform.

Pain made Eden stumble time and again, but he wouldn't, couldn't, stop and forced himself to run. Lucio had managed to climb midway up the hoist's tower by the time Eden stood panting at the base.

"Lucio!" he shouted. "There's no place to go." But he was already gripping the supports to haul himself up. Eden swayed, sweat drenching his body from the intensity of pain. Lights danced in front of his eyes, and he shook his head to clear it. Nothing was going to stop him. His fingers slipped constantly, and his body trembled from the effort he demanded of it. The closer to the top that he climbed, the more the tower shifted from side to side. Above him he heard Lucio's curses as his foot slipped. Eden forced himself to climb another tier.

"You're out of . . . room . . . bastard." Eden stopped to watch Lucio try to grab hold of the free-swinging cable. He knew that if Lucio managed to get hold of it, he could slide down or swing himself out over the river. The swift moving current would carry him away. Eden also knew the limits of his own strength: Fighting the fire had taxed him. No sleep and the pain he was enduring almost drained him. The thought of Lucio escaping him now gave him an added burst of fury that spurred him up the short distance separating them.

Seconds later he gripped Lucio's boot, pushing with the heel of his hand against the flat sole. Sweat blinded his vision, and only instinct made him turn his head at the last moment to avoid the kick Lucio aimed at his face. Eden locked his legs around the strut and bent backward with his hands free just as Lucio made a last desperate lunge for the cable.

Eden grabbed it from below. Lucio tried to yank the thick coarse hemp rope from his grip. He kicked at Eden's chest, and the blow made Eden release his hold, but Lucio had to twist his body as the rope suddenly snapped back at his face. Eden knew Lucio's throwing up his hands to protect his face was a reflexive move, and he surged up beside him, trying to get hold of his arm. The cloth tore. Eden stared at it. Lucio fell backward, his scream echoing before his body crashed through one of the walkways and sprawled in the pi below.

Men stood stunned for a moment, then ran forward but Jake warned them back.

"He needs help, man," someone called out.

"He'll never make it down alone!" yelled another.

"Leave him be," Jake ordered, staring up. "He' make it. Just leave him be." He was distracted by Da rushing to his side. Her attention was all for Eden, an he looked away to where his wife knelt beside h brother. He knew Clay's wound wasn't serious. He hadn't shot to kill him. Anne finally looked up, meeting his hardened gaze. Slowly, then, she came awkwardly to her feet. Jake started toward her to help her, but something stopped him. He heard Clay call out for Anne to stay with him, but she continued walking until she stood before him.

"Jake . . . I . . . ." Her blue eyes were filled with tears. "I don't know if you can ever forgive me."

"You're my wife and I love you," he whispered hoarsely, holding out his arms, shuddering from the depth of his emotions when she took that last step and came against him. Feeling her tears soak his shirt, his own eyes burned and he murmured the reassurance that it was over. When her sobs subsided, Jake murmured his one regret. "I wish Lucio had told me the truth about Linda before he died."

Dara heard them. Her hand gripped the edge of the platform. She turned on them in a rage. No one's feelings mattered after what she had watched Eden go through.

"You want to know, Jake. I'll tell you." And she did, sparing him nothing. When she was finished, the rage died. She returned to her post as helpless observer, her gaze fastened on Eden, praying as he began his descent.

"Dara, please," Jake began, but Anne stopped him.

"There'll be time to talk later. She wants what I have. Dara wants Eden to hold her, the way you're holding me." She gazed at the man she loved and whispered, I've been so wrong to blame you when I lost our child. wanted to die that night. I didn't . . . ." Her sobs began gain, and she had to force herself to finish. "I didn't ant to live if anything happened to you."

"Hush, Anne. We've both got ghosts to put to rest.

Just be sure, honey. I have to arrest your brother. Thankfully, none of those men were killed, but Eden could decide to press charges."

"I trust you. I promise to always trust you to do what's right for all of us." Her gaze lifted to where Eden struggled, then lowered to where Dara tensely waited. "Will he be all right?"

Jake cradled her against the warmth of his body. "There'll be time now to make everything right, for us and for them."

Dara added that thought to her fervent prayers. Every harsh breath that Eden drew became hers. Every time he hesitated, her heart seemed to still until he managed to move again. Now he was close enough for her to see the trickle of blood from the corner of his lips.

The echo of his earlier words grew in her mind until she wanted to scream with the torment he must be feeling. He hadn't wanted to kill Lucio. Love expanded inside her as she heard her own words to him. She had declared him a man that believed in his convictions. A man that would do whatever he had to. But she hadn't understood what a price might be paid in acting on them

Her longing intensified to hold him, to cosset him with the new depth of her love. He was all she had eve dreamed of finding in a man. Every word she had state with all the passion within her took on a new, deepe meaning. Dara whispered a prayer of thanksgiving whe he finally came within her reach. Compassion darkene her eyes. His physical pain became hers, but she kne that could be healed. It was the scar this would make o his mind and soul that she feared. She raised her hand touch his leg, but lightly, so lightly that she didn't thir he had felt it. Tears burned her eyes to see his skinn hands grip the rigid bar as he lowered his feet to the ground.

His shirt was plastered to his back, and sweat ran freely down his face as he stood there swaying. She was suddenly afraid that he would turn from her after what she had witnessed.

"Eden . . . oh, love . . ." Dara reached up, her fingertips hesitant as she caressed his cheek, the cut on his lip, the line of his strong chin. She couldn't measure the effort it cost him to drag his head up and look at her.

It was the dark agony of his eyes that held her still.

"Did he . . . hurt you?" he managed to ask, his breaths ragged.

"No, love. It's you—"

"I . . . killed him."

"I still love you, Eden. More than I even knew," she whispered, desperate to be in his arms. "It's over now."

His shoulders sagged, and he caught up her hand with his, bringing it slowly to his lips. For a long moment Eden searched the dark velvet depths of her eyes, every tear that fell a knife thrust inside him. This was a pain he couldn't bear.

"I love you," he breathed against her palm, drawing her closer. "I love you," he repeated, feathering the words she had longed to hear across her mouth. "You filled needs I didn't know I had, love. You're life to me," Eden whispered, sealing those words with the promise of his kiss.

Epilogue

THERE WERE THREE weddings in Rainly that winter. Dara and Eden's came as no surprise, nor did the marriage of Caroline Halput and Pierce. But it was a bit of a shock to see blushed cheeks and a twinkle in the eyes of Miss Loretta before she said yes to Luther.

Rainly was never a peaceful community again. Saturdays were the day farmers came with their families to shop and the miners flooded the town to drink, gamble, and fight. To Jake's regret, they sometimes died.

Alfred Weeks claimed Lucio's properties and retained a shrewd Satin as his manager. Eden didn't press charges and Clay became a recluse. Matt, with Eden's blessing, went off to New York.

The year 1889 drew to a close and the Gay Nineties began.

Author's Note

RAINLY IS A fictional town, a composite of the farm communities that existed and the mining towns that sprung up during the era of phosphate discovery in the state of Florida. Most of these mining towns have disappeared, but a few have gone on and survived into thriving towns today. Phosphate is still mined in Florida.

HISTORICAL ROMANCE–

—send in the coupon below—

To get your FREE historical romance and start saving, fill out the coupon below and mail it today. As soon as we receive it we'll send you your FREE book along with your first month's selections.

Mail to: 557-73423-B

True Value Home Subscription Services, Inc.
P.O. Box 5235
120 Brighton Road
Clifton, New Jersey 07015-5235

YES! I want to start previewing the very best historical romances being published today. Send me my FREE book along with the first month's selections. I understand that I may look them over FREE for 10 days. If I'm not absolutely delighted I may return them and owe nothing. Otherwise I will pay the low price of just $3.50 each; a total of $14.00 (at least a $15.80 value) and save at least $1.80. Then each month I will receive four brand new novels to preview as soon as they are published for the same low price. I can always return a shipment and I may cancel this subscription at any time with no obligation to buy even a single book. In any event the FREE book is mine to keep regardless.

Name ____________________

Address ____________________ Apt. ______

City ____________ State ____________ Zip ______

Signature ____________________
(if under 18 parent or guardian must sign)

Terms and prices subject to change.

...te novel

DAKOTA DREAM

by
SHARON MACIVER

Their love defied two worlds . . .

Dominique, the niece of General George Custer, was a golden beauty who could not explain her fierce attraction to the shy and handsome private in her uncle's charge. Jacob, a man of dark secrets, undertook a dangerous mission on behalf of his adopted people, the Sioux—that would ensure the General's demise. Yet, his heart was forever entwined with the bold and bewitching Dominique. The Sioux warrior would risk everything for the furious heat of forbidden ecstasy.

__Dakota Dream 0-55773-445-3/$4.50
(On sale January '91)

For Visa and MasterCard orders (minimum $25) call: 1-800-631-8571

FOR MAIL ORDERS: CHECK BOOK(S). FILL OUT COUPON. SEND TO:

BERKLEY PUBLISHING GROUP
390 Murray Hill Pkwy., Dept. B
East Rutherford, NJ 07073

NAME____________________

ADDRESS____________________

CITY____________________

STATE__________ **ZIP**__________

POSTAGE AND HANDLING:
$1.00 for one book, 25¢ for each additional. Do not exceed $3.50.

BOOK TOTAL $____

POSTAGE & HANDLING $____

APPLICABLE SALES TAX $____
(CA, NJ, NY, PA)

TOTAL AMOUNT DUE $____

PAYABLE IN US FUNDS.
(No cash orders accepted.)

PLEASE ALLOW 6 WEEKS FOR DELIVERY.
PRICES ARE SUBJECT TO CHANGE WITHOUT NOTICE.

D191